CW00523440

SCALDING
WATERS

BOOKS IN THE SERIES

The Fire Within My Heart
Scalding Waters

SCALDING
WATERS

Scarlet Cherie: Vampire Series

Book Two

AYSHEN IRFAN

CONTENT WARNINGS

Scalding Waters does contain content some might find disturbing. Please see the list below:

❖ Attempted sexual assault
❖ Infrequent homophobic language
❖ Blood and gore
❖ Drug and addiction mention

All rights reserved

The characters and events portrayed in this book are fictitious. Any similarity to real persons, living or dead, is coincidental and not intended by the author.

No part of this book may be reproduced, or stored in a retrieval system, or transmitted in any form or by any means, electronic, mechanical, photocopying, recording, or otherwise, without express written permission of the publisher.

ISBN-13: 979 8 587 001 930

Cover photo by: Matt Hardy
matthardy.photo
Made on Canva

DEDICATION

To Marnie, my dearest friend, who encouraged me to pursue my dreams of English at university and has always been a rational, caring, and diplomatic person on whom I can rely.

Your friendship inspired the character of Sylvie, who I hope can help you see yourself through my eyes.

Love you.

It's raining on the road; there's a storm in my soul
I'm sick of separation, nothing ever stays whole
And it's a cold, and it's a dark, and it's a desolate
drive
Through the barren miles of leaving this cold
cutting of ties
When love tears everything apart

— IT'S RAINING ON THE ROAD,
E.J.BALLARD

Acknowledgements

First and foremost, I would like to thank Mémé, who, without, this book would not be publishable.

To my mum, who has supported my writing in every way and constantly encourages my dreams.

Marnie, who helped me redesign the cover, and brought it to life for the series. Also, Kieran, who let me bounce off ideas about necromancers and discuss magick and the arcane.

Hannah, who has supported my wild ideas and let me ramble on about characters endlessly. You were my first fan, and my first Twitter friend, one for whom I am endlessly grateful.

Reyadh Rahaman, author of *Inner Expanses*, who helped me tweak some silly little mistakes, and the first of my pals to read *Scalding Waters*. I'm so glad to have found a friend in you.

And lastly, but never least, thank you to everyone who bought a copy of *The Fire Within My Heart* and encouraged me to write more. My heart is warmed by the knowledge that some people are out there bringing my wonderful characters to life in their imagination.

I am deeply grateful for you all.

SCALDING

WATERS

CHAPTER 1

Daylight had long succumbed to dusk; I was still lying indolently in bed, eyelids fluttering like languorous butterflies against my cheeks. A couple of months ago, there would have been a body beside me when I awoke, the body of someone I could curl myself around, embrace, and against whom I could relax. But tonight, I was alone, which seemed to be the case more often than not recently. Usually, it didn't bother me too much. Seclusion wasn't new to me; I found solace in silence. Growing up without many friends meant you either adjusted to being alone or let isolation madden you.

Tonight, however, was February fourteenth. Saint Valentine's day. It felt juvenile to be hung up on such a minor occasion. I'd never celebrated Valentine's day before, so not doing anything this year shouldn't matter. Of course, I'd never been in a relationship before, and now I was. Sort of. It was undoubtedly a relationship *of sorts*, but we weren't exactly boyfriend-girlfriend. No, it was far too complicated to define. In the vampire world, the technical term would be *master* and *vassal*. Nikolaos, as my maker, was my master. Masters are meant to have a special connection with their vassals, draw off their energies, feed on their life force, and basically just get a lot more out of the deal than their vassals did. We definitely had a special connection, it just wasn't what it was supposed to be. I did strengthen Nikolaos with my power, but being a master was all about control, and he absolutely did not control me.

Nikolaos had once told me that I would be deemed too undisciplined if we were around other vampires, and he a weak master for not tightening the reins. I'd told him he was welcome to try and "tighten the reins" if he wanted, but we both knew it wasn't that simple with us. He'd said I am far too puerile for my own good, but with a smile that made it clear he didn't see it as a bad thing.

We were just too unprecedented. Even in the arcane world of vampires, Nikolaos and I would be considered abstruse, which was a part of the reason why Nikolaos was spending so much time away from Britchelstone, and I was having to readjust to being satisfied by my own company. Six months ago, Nikolaos had turned me into a vampire, not knowing I was a nymph. We suspected this was something to do with Nikolaos's lack of command as my master. As a nymph, my magick was all about life, light, and the powers of the earth. As a vampire, his power was more nefarious, born from darkness and death. His power could have smothered my connection to the magick of life, dampened it until I, too, was a creature shrouded in death, but instead, it seemed to have the opposite effect. I was sharing the warmth of life with him, empowering him from more than our blood-bond as master and vassal, but my bond to the element of fire and that connection to Mother Earth.

Four decades ago, Nikolaos had had his vampire powers ripped away from him by a demon-necromancer hybrid. That same demon-necromancer, Gwydion, known more commonly as Rune, was now my magickal mentor with whom I met up weekly. Although, recently, we'd been doing fewer lessons and more dinners with his husband, and werepanther, Kai. Sometimes, Kai and I went out hunting together. We avoided the nights of the full moon, when he was forced to shift slowly and painfully. It was like the moon cursed him, a curse he was born with, inherited, and from which he could never break free. On any other night, the process was quick and relatively painless for him. Kai favoured the forests of Nikolaos and I. He'd hunted everything in his area to near extinction; we still had lots of animals for him to munch. Even now, I hated watching him kill his prey. It was hypocritical to the point of irony, but I was too squeamish to watch him tear out the throat of a living creature. Squeamish and vampire just aren't meant to go together.

Gwydion had taken Nikolaos's powers per his request, yet Nikolaos had never fully forgiven him, nor himself. What was once a beautiful friendship bred from decadence and evil had blossomed into disdain. The evil that had bound them had gone by the name of Camille. Nikolaos had both adored and despised her with all of his undead heart. Gwydion had left her to die in a blazing fire that should have killed Nikolaos too if he hadn't saved him at the last minute. Now, Nikolaos let himself be plagued by the eternal conflict of gratitude he was free of her, and loathing that he was left alone and alive. Or as alive as a vampire could be considered. It's hard to be sure of your own grievances when you're both grateful and hateful towards the man who rescued you—a man you once loved as a brother and now hated as an enemy. When I said my relationship with Nikolaos was complicated, I didn't necessarily mean it was me who made it that way.

The first time Nikolaos and I had made love, I had accidentally shared some of my power with him, consequently bringing back some of his own. Then, in October last year, I had protected him against a great evil that sought the souls of the dead and imbued him with power again. Nikolaos was slowly growing more and more into that magick each day. This was the main reason my lover was spending so much time in the company of another. Since visiting the Empress of the United Kingdom to divulge his growing power to her, he had been called away on business an awful lot. One day a week had quickly become two; then three; four; and so on and so forth, until it had become that I was lucky to spend more than two days a week with him.

I was still surprised that the Empress hadn't wanted a personal meeting with me yet. Gwydion was just as surprised, although his erred on the side of caution. He may have been concerned—nay, suspicious—but I was happy going without that particular invitation for as long as possible.

I pulled the silk sheets off from my body, letting them slip to the floor below. Silk sheets feel great and look pretty but are not practical. I crawled over the Queen-sized mattress to stare down at the sheets pooled on the floor. I debated just leaving them there in a satiny pile but thought better of it. Just because I was feeling melancholic didn't mean I had to take it out on the bedding.

I was reaching over the side of the bed, gripping one corner of the silk, when I heard the door swing open and a familiar presence fill the room with energy. Before I even had time to turn around, Nikolaos was beside me on the bed, pulling me into his arms. He rolled me into his chest, pulling the fallen duvet with us both. I curled round to snuggle into his chest, wrapping my arm around the softness of his crimson shirt, holding him as tight to me as I could. Nikolaos always smelt of cinnamon and old, dusty flowers. It was sweet and perfumey and musky all at the same time. I took a deep breath in of that smell which meant home to me. No matter how complicated we may be, Nikolaos had become my family. Gwydion and Kai had too, but no matter how much I loved them, they didn't ignite this same warmth. A warmth that started in my chest and spread into my belly, and then down to somewhere lower. Love, lust, and comfort all in one joyous thrill. As long as Nikolaos didn't open his mouth to say something fractious, that feeling wouldn't go.

Long, slender fingers worked their way through my hair. Less than two months ago, I'd chopped close to six inches of my hair off, and it was already beginning to tickle the back of my thighs again. Something about being a vampire meant hair and nails just grew quicker than human's. Don't ask me why. It did mean I was constantly having to cut my nails or risk walking around with tiny daggers growing from my fingers. On the one hand, having hair so long was pretty cool; on the other, it was bloody inconvenient. Nikolaos's hair didn't grow at quite the same rapid speed. When we'd first met, it had only teased at the tips of his shoulders. Obsidian waves now fell like a midnight waterfall down to his armpits. His hair was a true black that so few people have without it being a dye job; darkness so rich it had blue highlights. All of that black velvet framed an ivory face carved from sharp angles and clean cuts. His face was almost feminine in its softness, whilst something about the curve of his cheekbone and squareness of his jaw kept him looking very masculine. Equally elegant as he was brawny. Anyone who thinks men can't be beautiful has never met Nikolaos.

I raised my head up enough to look into his green eyes framed by a plethora of dark lashes.

'*Joyeuse Saint-Valentin, ma chérie,*' Nikolaos whispered against my forehead, lips brushing my skin between the words in the tenderest of kisses.

Burying my head back into Nikolaos's chest, I tried to hide the blush. He slipped a finger under my chin, raising my face back to look at him. I looked up at him and burst into laughter. I couldn't seem to help myself. Nikolaos frowning made me laugh harder. This was the first time I'd ever had any man wish me a happy Valentine's Day, and, oh, the irony that it came from the lips of a vampire who had lived to see two millennia. See what I mean when I say complicated?

'I felt your melancholy when I approached, and now you laugh. Am I to be glad I can alleviate such desolation or take offence at being the target of your derision?'

I smacked his chest lightly with the palm of my hand, chastising.

'Derision? You're being particularly sensitive tonight.' I smiled up at him, adding gently, 'Happy Valentine's day to you, too, my love.'

He was momentarily taken aback. Six months in, and Nikolaos still looked affronted whenever I said something that alluded to his sensitivities as if he weren't used to people not tending to his every whim. Probably he wasn't, but he also didn't usually show this tenderness to anyone else. Haughty and churlish were his usual traits of choice. He did compassion well too, although I think it still surprised him when he let down those well-forged shields. Nikolaos had done solitude a lot longer than I. Before, when he wasn't stewing in his own company, it was to feed on women and men who threw themselves at his feet, beseeching the chill of his stoic embrace and the piercing of his fang. I did not throw myself at him; he didn't always know what to do with me because of it. Socialising is like a muscle; if you don't use it long enough, it takes a while to relearn. The skill is still there, but it's not always easy to remember how to use it. Nikolaos had not stretched this particular muscle in a very long time.

I raised my head further, stretching my neck back to take in the full glory of his handsomeness. Nikolaos took the hint, bringing his face down to brush silken lips against my own.

'Did you come all the way back here just for Valentine's day?' I breathed against his lips, such a chaste kiss able to rob me of my breath.

He simpered, looking winsome, even uncertain, for a moment. It softened him, made all that cold perfection look suddenly gentle. I didn't know Nikolaos's exact age at death, but I suspected he was younger than thirty. At that moment, he looked closer to my age.

'Perhaps,' he replied. He pulled himself together again, letting his usual austere guise conquer the uncertainty. 'Would you have preferred I did not return?'

I shook my head enthusiastically against his chest.

'You know I didn't mean it like that. I'm glad you're back. How long are you home for?'

'I have business to attend to in the city. I shall return to the Empress's side,' he said, spitting out her title sardonically, 'in two nights.'

'Business?' I asked.

'*Oui*, if you escort me upstairs, I will show you.'

CHAPTER 2

Once upon a time, the living room upstairs had been furnished and decorated in various shades of white. I use the term various very lightly, because there really isn't as much of a difference between 'porcelain' and 'daisy' as they'd have you believe. I'd finally managed to get Nikolaos to compromise on some colour. When I'd first suggested it needed brightening, Nikolaos had been disgruntled. He'd argued it was never in use and therefore didn't need to look homely. He'd used it as a masquerade for the underground lair (lovingly called the oubliette by me, much to Nikolaos's dislike) where we both slept. There was also a living room downstairs, but it was small, windowless, and the air was stale with age. He may prefer to seek refuge in the underground warren, but I coaxed him to spend more time upstairs. Besides, now I saw Kai and Gwydion so regularly, it did get a lot more attention.

Despite disagreeing with me, within two days, Nikolaos had totally transformed the front room. Whilst he had never said it out loud, I got the impression interior design was one of Nikolaos's secret hobbies. When I'd first moved in, he'd worked tirelessly to create a beautiful room for me to slumber in the daylight hours. At the time, it had seemed entirely selfless; now, I thought it wasn't just me who got some satisfaction from the deed. Nikolaos, ancient Greek vampire and my master, an interior design aficionado—who'd have thunk it?

Royal-purple and forest-green cushions sat in a sea of satiny fabric over both the sofas. Admittedly, the dining room table was still all but ignored by us, but Nikolaos had still bought a rich purple tablecloth with little gold tassels hanging down from the sides. He'd even bought a green vase to place on top, filling it with purple calla lilies. The rug between the two sofas was deep-green with gold and silver threading woven through. The coffee table had one splash of colour not designed by Nikolaos—a Wandering Jew plant gifted to me by Kai last year overflowed from the plum-coloured plant pot. Its leaves were dark purple with strokes of silver naturally occurring down the centre, shimmering brilliantly. Against all the gold in the room, the silver seemed even more striking, shining like the moon in all the sun's golden light. I'd asked Nikolaos if he had decorated the room based on the colours of my gift from Kai. He'd said if the royal-purple and green theme was complimentary to my "little gift" from Kai, then it was merely a coincidence. Although not two colours I would think to go well together, it managed to look tastefully opulent.

To get upstairs, you had to go up a flight of metal stairs opening into the larger guest bedroom's wardrobe. This bedroom led directly into the front room; the other was on the first floor. The first floor also had: an office with a computer placed on a desk older than any technology, and walls lined with bookshelves; a grand piano in striking red that I was trying to learn to use, and failing at miserably; and the only bathroom with an actual toilet in the whole building.

Four boxes rested on the usually disregarded dining table. The boxes were black with a crimson silk ribbon tied into a neat bow. Every week without fail, Nikolaos had delivered to me a bouquet of red roses. As soon as the first petals began to fall, he would either give them to me by hand or I would walk into my bedroom to find a fresh bunch awaiting me. I knew for a fact he picked them himself; several miles along from our cottage sits a rockery overflowing with verdure, including a sea of red where scarlet roses bloom. There were always exactly twenty in the bouquet, one for every year I had been alive. If he carried on adding to them every year, it might become too much. Living past one hundred is a realistic expectation to a vampire; it would make me sad to know the abundance of foliage got picked to desolation because I was immortal.

The bouquet resting atop the largest of the boxes was different. Six rich red roses, darker than the ones Nikolaos grew, rested amongst a blanket of white baby's breath and crimson asters. Black paper held them all together, red velvet ribbon wrapping around the middle. I walked towards the table, running my fingers over the shiny black box and silken ribbon. My fingers moved to the bouquet, tentatively stroking the soft petals of the roses and asters, twiddling the delicate blooms of baby's breath on their slender stems. As my fingers traced down the paper, I saw a small black envelope tucked so deep into the bouquet I almost didn't notice it. I pulled the card out. There was no name on the front. I turned to Nikolaos, cocking my head to one side, looking a question at him. He stayed where he was, leaning against the back of the sofa with an unlit cigarette between his lips, but nodded his head in encouragement. Nikolaos's only overt addiction was smoking. Very humanly, when he was nervous, he would place an unlit smoke in his mouth even with no intention to light up. The familiarity of it soothed some of his anxieties. Seeing the cigarette hanging precariously out his mouth gave me a hint he was nervous about something.

I grinned before running my finger under the sealed flap, slicing it open swiftly. Inside was a cream-coloured card folded in half. I'd never seen Nikolaos's handwriting before. Perfect copperplate letters swirled across the page with an almost dynamic grace.

The text read:

She walks in beauty, like the night
Of cloudless climes and starry skies;
And all that's best of dark and bright
Meet in her aspect and her eyes;
Thus mellowed to that tender light
Which heaven to gaudy day denies.
And on that cheek, and o'er that brow,
So soft, so calm, yet eloquent,
The smiles that win, the tints that glow,
But tell of days in goodness spent,
A mind at peace with all below,
A heart whose love is innocent!
—She Walks in Beauty, Lord Byron

God, it was heartachingly cheesy. I suddenly didn't know what to do. I stared down at the card, with its perfect text both in style and words, my back turned to Nikolaos, inert and overwhelmed. I'd never been the recipient of such fervent romance. How do you respond to something like this? I was almost scared to see what gifts awaited me in the boxes. I would have been happy just spending the evening curled up on the sofa in each other's company. Sentiment didn't have to mean such lavish gestures. Like almost everything Nikolaos did, it was superfluous and just another reminder that we could never be 'normal'. I placed the open envelope and refolded card on the table, holding my palm against it as if I could shield it from sight. I was being ungrateful, I knew that, but the panic tightening my stomach didn't ease at the thought.

Nikolaos must have sensed my hesitation. He appeared behind me, placing his own much larger hand on top of mine, where it lay pressed against the card. His other arm wrapped around my waist, pulling me harder into the tight line of our bodies.

'What is the matter?' he asked.

'I didn't get you anything,' I half-lied, voice a whisper as I choked on the oppressive overwhelm which had come over me suddenly.

I didn't need to see his face to know the smooth expanse of his forehead had formed frown lines. I spoke again, trying for honesty this time. 'I've never had anyone do something this... this romantic before.'

His chuckle tickled the top of my hair, sending a shiver down my spine. I eased further back into his embrace, letting go of some of the tension that wound my muscles tight.

'You do not favour romance?'

'I don't know. I guess I thought I would, but now I feel like...' I let the thought die off as I tried to find the right words. I settled with: 'Like I don't know how to respond. I don't know why, but it's making me panic.' I shook my head, feeling my scalp rub against his chin. He had to move his head away or risk being hit in the face by the movement. 'I'm sorry, I'm being irrational.' And I was.

Nikolaos gently pulled my hand free of the table. Using his fingers through mine, he wrapped both of our arms around my stomach, cradling me to his front using my arm to anchor me to him.

'It is unlike you to brood. What is the matter?' he asked again.

It was a good question, a fair question. One to which I did not have the answer. What was the matter? None of it, all of it, everything in between. Since Maglark's death, I hadn't quite been the same. And not just because I was a vampire, although that did play its role. Becoming the undead had given me back some of the life I had lost, but I'd lost something else as well. I still couldn't quite figure out what it was exactly, but I knew a piece of my soul had gone. A piece I would never get back. It was a missing part of me that left me harder, colder, and lost. I mourned the fragments of my innocence ripped from me the night my life had also been stolen.

I hadn't spoken to anyone about the lasting effects the events of last year had on me. Nikolaos was gone so often I didn't want to burden him when he was home. Gwydion was great as my magickal mentor, but not as a therapist. I knew if I spoke to Kai, he would comfort me, treat me with a warmth and tenderness that the other two men in my life could never muster. I could have opened up to him, and yet I hadn't. Why not? Because I knew as soon as I accepted that compassion from him, I would fall apart. For months, I had been hiding away from my feelings. Every time they reared their ugly, emotional heads, I shoved them down to a darkness I had never had inside me before. Darkness that could conceal all the horrors like the night conceals shadows.

Part of it was becoming a vampire. It was this sort of built-in defence mechanism that comes with being the undead. Evolution, magick, or something, had made it that vampires are both overly sensitive to their emotions and so much better at pushing them away. If you were to live a hundred lifetimes, feasting on the blood of humans, killing and seducing your way through the darkness, then you have to be able to withstand the lacerations on your psyche.

The other part, probably, was a hefty dose of survivor's guilt. I'd been into the mind of another of Maglark's victims, seen her battle and fight down to her last breath. I had not fought. I had laid down on the cold ground, accepted my fate, and impending death, subserviently. When we had captured the goblin, he had spat the words I had been too afraid to think at me like they were venom. Those words had stuck with me, eating me away every day that went by.

Usually, when Nikolaos was home, I worked harder to push the feelings away. I let myself enjoy his company whilst I could. Tonight, however, I was undone. Maybe it was seeing the gifts of which I didn't feel deserving. Perhaps it was the tenderness that I had become so reliant not to see from Nikolaos. Or, maybe, it was that I was supposed to be happy on this day, and that was a reminder that I wasn't. There's nothing like being expected to feel something to remind you just how much you simply don't feel.

Whatever it was, I found myself turning in Nikolaos's arms, burying my face into the soft fabric of his shirt, and weeping.

Tears streamed silently from my eyes; pearls of woe disappearing, soaking into his shirt. It was the first time I'd cried in months. I had expected to sob or wail my anger into the air, but instead, I simply stood as a few measly drops fell from my eyes. I had put so much energy into not feeling, that I'd lost the key to the prison of my emotions when I was finally prepared to unlock the door.

Nikolaos's hands stroked my head, soothing me like a wounded child. I didn't raise my face from his chest until I knew the crying had stopped. If it weren't for the few darker patches on the red of his shirt where my tears had wet the fabric, it might not have been noticeable I'd wept. Of course, part of the connection between Nikolaos and I meant that he got some of the drip back of my emotions. He was much better at shielding than I was, although I was getting better. Learning to control one power made managing the others easier. I knew enough about magick to lessen the capricious tendencies, even if I didn't fully understand how it worked. If anyone ever says they've mastered magick, they are lying. Working with Gwydion had taught me that no one really knows how it works; you just have to be confident. Feign confidence and control it, or face the consequences of it controlling you. Magick thrived off a master-servant relationship—if you don't act like master, then, well, you are the servant.

'I wish, Scarlet,' he said, using my real name one of the few times since we had met, 'that I could remedy such woe.'

'It's not your woe to remedy,' I whispered back, pulling back enough to look into his face.

'Perhaps not, but I am, at least in part, culpable.'

I frowned at him.

'I think you have enough anguish to last a lifetime without taking on the burden of this particular guilt.'

Nikolaos laughed, which I was glad for; his reactions were not always reliable. Sometimes saying something that reminded him of his past would make him shut down; others he seemed unphased. Talk about hard to read. On the other hand, I didn't really have any stone to throw about unpredictable reactions after my little display at his generosity.

'What's in the boxes?' I asked, wiping away the lonesome tear that still quivered on my cheek as if not sure it was ready to let go. I was prepared to make the decision for it.

'Gifts, for tonight.' He frowned. 'Alas, what was meant as saccharine now seems misjudged.'

I rolled my eyes, but my voice was tender when I said, 'The flowers are beautiful.'

'One rose for each month we have spent together.'

I couldn't help but smile.

'I do feel bad I didn't get you anything.'

'The gift of your accompaniment tonight contents me more than anything you could purchase.'

'Accompany you where?' I asked suspiciously.

Nikolaos smiled at me, that smile which both warmed my heart and filled me with dread. So many promises: good and evil, love and pain—all in that one upturning of lips. It was the smile he used when he was being secretive, one that told me I would have to either trust him, and all would be revealed when he was ready, or never know.

I trusted him.

CHAPTER 3

Nikolaos led me back down to my bedroom, carrying the boxes perfectly balanced on one hand. I'd have dropped them to the floor, especially going down the stairs.

Slashes of gold in the solid green of the walls caught in the firelight. The fireplace was marble with black veins creeping through it like delicate serpents. Up a small step, through an archway adorned with dark chiffon and a garland of trickling lights, was my bed. On one side, was a white vanity with a fluffy stool tucked under; on the other, stood the door to a smaller room where my clothes lived. Although, I didn't actually have enough clothes to fill the room.

When I'd first moved in, there had been several locked doors in the basement, which I'd assumed opened to something sinister. As it turned out, one of them was a whole room filled with Nikolaos's clothing. He didn't tend to stray from his usual elegant style of a well-fitted silk shirt tucked into either suit or leather trousers, so it had surprised me. I expected many things from Nikolaos, but not that he was a hoarder of clothing. He'd seemed embarrassed about it. I wouldn't have known if I hadn't stumbled upon him in there once when he'd left the door ajar. Some of the clothes were original antiques dating back to times when men still wore tunics and filtering through to more modern history—if you could call the eighteenth and nineteenth-century *modern*. It looked like a museum exhibition. Museum collectors would faint from envy if they could take a peek in the basement. Ancient tapestries, furniture, blackwork vases, and so much more were spread throughout the downstairs of our home. A portrait of Nikolaos from the sixteenth century hanging in the hallway was a particular favourite of mine. Photos are great, but they just aren't as romantic as portraits.

Nikolaos placed the boxes on the coffee table by the fireplace. I fell back onto the large, rich blue sofa beside it. Poise was, unfortunately, not a guaranteed side effect of vampirism, as I had proven consistently over the last few months. When Nikolaos collapsed onto the sofa, it was with a fluid grace; I slumped more like a treacherous waterfall hitting rocks. Cushions tumbled to the ground in a stream of musky red, blue, and green as my body pushed them off where they usually rested.

Instinctively, I placed my feet over Nikolaos's lap. Just as casually, he started stroking his hand up and down my bare legs. Masters and vassals find comfort in tactile gestures. To turn a human is no small matter. Essentially, it is committing someone to your side for as long as you both live. Few vampires have the power to break free of their master's hold. The sanctity of marriage pales comparatively.

Such a tender brush of his hands, just his fingers playing so gently up my shin and roof of my feet, made my body react. Goosebumps rippled up my skin under the trace of his touch, reacting as though I were cold when, in fact, his cool skin filled me with heat. Neither of us had fed yet; his skin was even colder than usual without stolen blood pumping through his veins. Until we fed, neither of our hearts would waste time beating more than once every few seconds as if fading. I still breathed more out of habit than necessity. Nikolaos rarely bothered. As a vampire, there's no need to breathe the way humans do. We could be totally still and breathless for a long period and then suddenly find ourselves gasping for air like a drowning man, as if the essence of life that animates us forces the body to remember it's not entirely dead. Older vampires generally have more control or understanding of when their bodies need that extra breath. I was already adjusting to so many changes becoming the undead that relearning how to breathe seemed trivial. Before feeding, our bodies precariously toe the line between alive and dead. Once we steal a human's life source, it's as if life just barely wins until sunrise; when dusk falls, the battle recommences.

'Will you tell me where we're going tonight?' I asked, already knowing the answer.

'*Non*, it will ruin the surprise.'

'It seems unfair that you've gone to all this effort, and I haven't got you anything.'

I gestured to the still unopened gifts.

'As I said, your company is gift enough, *ma chérie*.'

I crossed my arms over my chest; Nikolaos raised an eyebrow at me.

'I cannot help but feel you are procrastinating,' he observed, lips twitching.

'Maybe I'm nervous.'

'Of what?' He looked genuinely confused.

'Not knowing where you plan on taking me. For all I know, it could be to some weird sex dungeon, and those boxes are filled with leather.'

Nikolaos laughed, the sound caressing over my skin like fur, tightening intimate parts of me. I shuddered.

It was his turn to gesture. 'You will not know until you open them.'

'So, it might be some wild bondage outfit?' I teased, unable to keep the smile from my voice.

'*Non,* I know you would not be happy if I were to take you to, as you say, a "weird sex dungeon".'

I frowned again. It wasn't entirely reassuring that Nikolaos hadn't said he would not want to go to one but that *I* wouldn't. Nikolaos had been more than my first Valentine. He was also my first kiss, love, and lover. I was the first human he had chosen to turn, and that was the end of firsts on his part. A disconcerting thought that.

Nikolaos lifted my legs off his lap so he could reach over to me. He stopped with his fingers mere inches away from my cheek, just that almost-touch speeding my breath up.

'You have frowned more this one night than I have ever seen from you.'

'Sorry,' I mumbled.

'It is I who is sorry. Sorry I cannot ease whatever burden weighs upon you.'

'I'll open the presents,' I said, wanting to change the subject to anything that wouldn't bring on the waterworks again. I had been lucky earlier; if I lost my composure again, I was sure it wouldn't be so controlled. Nikolaos smiled sadly at me, relenting to my wish to let it be.

Three of the boxes were sitting on top of one another on the coffee table. The fourth, and smallest, was beside the tower of shiny black cardboard. I went to reach for the smallest one first, then drew my hand back with curled fingers. My hand hovered over it sort of awkwardly, trembling with indecision. To reach out or not to reach out, that was the question.

'Which one first?' I turned my head to look at Nikolaos, with my hand still hovering in the air.

He gave a graceful shrug.

'That one is fine,' he said.

His eyes held the faintest twinkle of humour and perplex as if he were unsure of why I was acting this way but found it amusing all the same.

I lifted the box with the lightest touch of fingertips, so carefully, as if it were the most fragile thing in the world. When the cardboard was resting in my lap, I pulled the ribbon undone. The ribbon parted in one smooth motion, falling down the side of the box to tickle my bare thigh. Inside was another square box. This one was soft and velvety and a dark crimson. The lid opened with a snap.

Gold metal caught in the dim light of the fire in the form of a delicate rope chain. A dark green gem hung from the necklace in a teardrop shape encased in gold. The glittering green gemstone was large enough to look expensive whilst simultaneously appearing delicate and tasteful. Noticeable without being gaudy. My fingers traced the soft, cold stone and then trailed along the gilded chain, the rolling bumps of the metal solid along my skin.

I cast my eyes back up to Nikolaos, still stroking along the metal.

'It's beautiful,' I said, although the words felt inadequate.

'May I?' he asked, holding his hand out to me.

I placed the red velvety box in his palm. Nikolaos placed it down on the sofa between us and got to his knees, facing me. I mirrored the action, tucking my heels under my body.

'Turn around, *ma chérie*.'

I obliged, turning on the sofa until I was kneeling with my back to him. Nikolaos wound his fingers through all my hair, moving it so it spilt down the front of my body like crimson water. I heard him fiddling with the box, and then his arms appeared in front of my neck with the gold chain in hand. The metal was cool against my skin, the gemstone heavy. My fingers automatically touched the gem where it lay against my chest, holding it in place. Nikolaos's fingers brushed the side of my neck as his hands moved to the back of my head. Such a slight, accidental touch, yet my breath caught in my throat for a moment. His fingers continued to work at the back of my neck, doing up the fiddly clasp.

I went to turn back around to face him again, but Nikolaos's hands wrapped around me from behind, holding me in place. His fingers worked their way under the black camisole I often wore to bed, pressing lightly against the tender flesh of my belly. For a moment, he stayed still, holding me to him with his fingers gently kneading into the softness of my stomach. It both tickled and felt pleasurable, but not sexual. Sensual and comforting, as if his fingers massaged more emotion than words alone could express into my skin. I knew Nikolaos loved me—not because he said it often, or bought me presents like tonight, but because the way he touched me was so tender and content. I also knew how much he struggled with feeling this way. He saw it as a hindrance, a bullet hole of softness in the armour of apathy he had spent so many centuries crafting.

Those long, slender fingers trailed across my skin to my hips. He played with the top of my silk shorts, slipping down under the elastic, tracing my bare skin between the pubic bone and thigh. The sensation made my breath heavy. A warmth spread from between my legs up my body, arching my back slightly, hips pushing into his hand. Such innocent touches could become venereal so very quickly with Nikolaos. He moved his hands back to the side of my pyjama shorts, slowly edging them downwards, so both his skin and the silk caressed my hip and thigh. A deep breath, almost a moan, escaped from between my lips.

'I suggest you remove your garments,' he whispered, cool breath tickling the back of my neck, making the hairs on my body stand to attention.

'Oh, and why's that?' I whispered back, teasing.

'Because, *ma chérie,* the second part of your gift awaits.'

CHAPTER 4

A mirror consumed the far wall of the walk-in wardrobe. I sat on the grey armchair in the centre of the room, looking at myself in the mirror, then bent down to fasten the clasps on the black Mary Jane heels, which had come in one of the three larger boxes. They were velvet with a chunky heel and front, which made them look vaguely dominatrix-y. Torn black tissue paper and cardboard boxes with their discarded lids littered the floor. With the small silver buckles done up in the tightest hole, I stood to look at myself in the mirror. The dress was a deep, forest green the same velvet as the shoes. It had a plunging—very plunging—v-neckline that accentuated my already large bust. The necklace twinkled between my exaggerated bosom, gold and green stark against the paleness of my skin. A long slit ran up the side of the tulip-hemmed dress, reaching just high enough to flash the beginning of the black lace of my thigh-highs, but not quite enough to show the suspender snap and look overly sexy. Tastefully provocative; teasing.

I turned around to look at the back of the dress, or lack thereof, in the mirror. Whilst the front hugged my figure, the back was nonexistent above the line of my lumbar. The material behind fell to mid-shin; at the front, it stopped above my knees. I'd always thought it went against some sacred rule of fashion for women as short as me to wear long dresses, but it actually looked great. The heels were high enough to make my legs appear a lot longer than they really were and chunky enough for me to be able to walk without breaking my ankle.

Draped over the armchair's arm was a faux-fur shoulder wrap that tied at the front with a black silk ribbon. At least I assumed it was faux; if it weren't, I would not be happy. Yes, I may drink the blood of humans, but it was pivotal to my survival. I'd been a vegetarian for my entire human life. Becoming close friends with a werepanther, Kai, had only helped solidify my opinion that animals are friends, not food, and certainly not clothing. I picked up the wrap. It was so soft, the black fur glittering. It didn't shine like some fake fur does, cheap and plasticky, but more the way well cared for hair catches the light. Oh god, maybe it wasn't fake.

The green looked terrific against my hair's burning red, both colours so bold and bright and eye-catching. The black heels and shoulder wrap gave a sultry elegance to the starkness of the colour combination. It was just enough colour in all that black to highlight how pale I was, without giving that washed-out look some people got when they were whiter than fresh winter snow and wearing too many dark colours. My hair hung in waves down my back like a waterfall of crimson tumbling over the green. Maybe a bold red lip or some eye shadow would have given the outfit the impact it deserved, but I'd never worn make-up as a human, and that hadn't changed since becoming the undead. So I stood there dressed for the ritz in my sumptuous clothing with an unadorned face. At least tonight, I'd actually brushed my hair; most nights, it was tied up in a plait and left alone. My hair had always been curly; however, the thickness had weighed it down into waves when it was shorter. At this length, the ends were light enough to form tight ringlets, slowly unwinding as it got closer to my head.

Just as I turned back round to face the mirror head-on, Nikolaos walked into the room. Through the mirror reflection, I watched him saunter towards me with the seductive swaying hips of a dancer. Black suit trousers, perfectly tailored to his long legs, were double-pleated and matched the jacket on top. The English-style suit looked great on him, highlighting the slenderness of his waist and line of his shoulders with stiff cashmere. What ruined the suit's conservative feel were the buttons that lined the front of the jacket and surgeon cuff: solid gold, in the shape of a lion's head, with petite diamonds embellished into the eyes. Nikolaos's shirt was silk in a dark, forest green, the exact same colour as my dress. It made his viridian eyes sparkle darker than usual. His eyes were always undeniably green, but they were usually the colour of the deep Mediterranean sea when the sun burns at midday, casting light to dance upon the top of the waters. Tonight, some of the swirling aquamarine was lost to solid, sparkling green. The shirt was stiff collared, done tightly up his throat. Spectacularly debonair, even more so than usual.

He'd showered and blowdried his hair, so it fell in a mass of black trestles past his shoulders. Nikolaos's hair was such a true black, it always enchanted me when I saw the light illuminating such bright blue highlights.

'*Tu es la femme la plus belle au monde, il n'y a pas des mots,*' he said, coming up behind me to wrap his arms around my waist.

'Maybe you should have got me a French-to-English dictionary instead,' I said, smiling.

Nikolaos bent down, not as far as he usually had to with me in heels, to press his face into the bend of my neck, his hair lost in the black fur around my shoulders.

'You are a vision to behold, *ma chérie*,' he breathed into my neck, tickling me.

I placed my hands over his arms where they held me, looking at us both in the mirror. Nikolaos, with a face made to be immortalised in marble, the strong features of his Greek heritage as pale as ivory from death. If it weren't for the green of his eyes, he would be a picture of monochrome. Me, with hair burning brighter than flame and eyes so close to red, they didn't look human. I was as pale as him, but the sprinkle of freckles over my nose and pinker hue to my lips gave me more colour. Where Nikolaos was tall and slender with subtle muscle working through his body, I was short and soft and curvy. We were opposites in every way, and yet, looking at us as one in the mirror, our differences complemented one another spectacularly.

'*We* are,' I whispered back.

My hands found their way back up to the necklace where it hung down my chest. I traced the solidity of the stone with my fingers.

'What stone is this?'

Nikolaos rolled his eyes up so he could look at our reflection. They followed my fingers circling over the green.

'Peridot, the birthstone of August.'

August is my birth month. More thought had gone into the necklace than just what looked pretty; that level of consideration made me grin goofily.

'It's truly beautiful.' I snuggled closer into his embrace. 'What month were you born?'

He paused for a moment, going very still, which usually meant I wouldn't get an answer.

Nikolaos surprised me by saying, 'I have not thought about it in such a long while,' he said, almost wistfully. 'Calendars have changed significantly over the years. You would now call it January, I believe. In all honesty, I do not remember.'

'So you don't know the date?'

'*Non,*' he said.

'Could we set one?'

He raised an eyebrow.

'Whatever for?'

'To celebrate, of course. Although I think if we were to use over two thousand candles, it might become a fire hazard.'

'*Non, ma chérie,* we did not celebrate such things in my time. I have always thought it an odd custom. Celebrating an extra year of life is a quintessential mortal tradition; when you have lived as long as I, one-year passing is an inevitable fact, and not a reminder that time runs short.'

I frowned, then shrugged. 'Guess I can't really argue with that logic.'

 CHAPTER 5

I'd never put much thought into whether or not Nikolaos could drive. For that reason, when we broke out from the forest onto the main road into town, I didn't pay much heed to the fancy car parked on the side of the road. It wasn't until Nikolaos took a few strides ahead of me to lean against the hood that I really took a moment to admire it.

With a lit cigarette gripped between his teeth, Nikolaos leant against the deep-burgundy body. Smoke poured from his mouth and nose, curling into the air like a grey phantom. Two substantial oval lights framed the thick silver grill. My attention was drawn to the hood's embellishment, a silver ornament that looked like a long, thick pin reaching almost halfway up the red bonnet, held up by a metal V encased in a metal circle. The convertible roof was down, giving me a view of the dark-purple leather seats and a flash of the silver steering wheel. It was both huge and slender, with the outer ring made of the same burgundy consistent with the interior and exterior of the car, and the inner rings polished silver.

Nikolaos flicked the half-finished cigarette onto the road. Fiery orange embers sizzled on the damp concrete, quickly fading into oblivion. He stepped back from the car enough to open the passenger side door, gesturing with a sweep of his hand for me to enter, flashing a rare, beatific smile. I grinned back at him. I could count on one hand the number of times Nikolaos had truly smiled joyously at me. This was one of those times; it warmed my heart.

The dashboard's front was taken up by what looked like a hefty, chrome air ventilator and chunky dials. Six large silver buttons bordered the ventilator, three apiece on either side. Above the ventilation, a black sign with silver lettering read, *BUICK*. I didn't know much—or anything—about cars, but I had a strong suspicion that this was an original. I had always wondered where Nikolaos got his money from. Seeing the car made me realise it was probably, in part, by him being asset rich. Nikolaos had lived long enough to hold so many antiques and originals from times long gone it must have amounted to a small fortune.

'It's a nineteen-fifty-three Skylark,' Nikolaos said, failing to hide the proud lilt to his voice. He actually sounded a little boastful.

Truthfully, I had no interest in cars, yet I could still appreciate that this one was an attractive automobile, and it made me happy to see Nikolaos chuffed. I wriggled back into the leather seat, instinctively reaching to pull the seatbelt over me. There wasn't one. In the centre of the steering wheel, a golden motif glinted in the moonlight. It didn't quite match the burgundy and silver theme of the rest of the car. I kept that opinion to myself, not wanting to rain on Nikolaos's parade. He wrapped his fingers around the steering wheel, clenching and unclenching his fist around the wheel, nestling his body back into the leather. I couldn't help but smile at the very human gesture.

This close beside me, I could smell the cigarette smoke clinging to Nikolaos. It would be unpleasant on some people; on him, it added to the floral and spiced musk that was his natural scent. When we had first met, I had thought Nikolaos wore a nice aftershave; it hadn't taken long for me to realise the trace of cinnamon and old rose was nothing that could be bottled. What had once been simply an agreeable smell was now the aroma of warmth and home to me.

Nikolaos turned the keys in the ignition, pulled down the black-headed lever behind the steering wheel, and off we went. With the roof down, my hair flew in the open-air behind me, a crimson cape cascading through the darkness. I struggled to grasp it all, clutching it in a thick bunch down my front. Just because I didn't spend much time making it look pretty didn't mean I wanted to ruin the outfit with wild, windswept hair.

Nikolaos parked off the corner of Londinium Road. It's one of the longer main roads of Britchelstone; one way took you down to the seafront, and the other stretched on for miles until you were two towns out of the city. We sat in silence, or as much silence as town on Valentine's Day would allow. Muffled music came from the pub on the left-hand corner of the side road on which we were parked. We were parked close enough for me to read the sign saying it was singles' night. The music switched to another equally cheesy ballad from the eighties. I couldn't help but bop a little bit. I'm a fan of cheesy eighties pop music, so sue me. My slight swaying made Nikolaos turn his head to look at me with ever so slight derision.

I forced myself to be still, resisting the urge to sway to *Tainted Love* by Softcell.

'Do I get to know where we're going yet?' I asked, turning in the seat to face him.

'A new bar has opened.'

I felt my eyes widen, surprised at his carelessness. 'A bar? Niko, people think I'm dead, and this is a small city. What if people I know are there?'

Nikolaos turned to me with a secretive glint in his green eyes.

'I can assure you there will be no such plight.'

'You look awfully suspicious,' I said, narrowing my eyes half in jest.

Nikolaos shrugged off the comment. He was a terse man. Admittedly, in the last few months, he had become somewhat more talkative. Or maybe I just saw him so little that I clung more dearly to every conversation we had. I hadn't realised I'd been frowning until Nikolaos raised his hand to rub his thumb over the line caused by my furrowed brow.

Britchelstone, although a small city, is known for being a hub of artistic culture. We have at least four large festivals a year dedicated to the arts, as well as many smaller ones put on almost monthly. It also has three universities, one of which is dedicated to the study of art, entertainment, and music. Subsequently, an abundance of students also means plenty of student pubs. Several are very close together on the main shopping stretch of Londinium Road.

My sister, Anna, just so happened to be one of those students. Unless she had found a girlfriend in the last six months, I doubted she would bother wasting money to go out tonight, but some of her friends might be. The people of

Britchelstone thought I was dead, and whilst not entirely inaccurate, I didn't know how I'd explain my sudden resurfacing if we bumped into anyone I knew. Of course, as a vampire, we did have the nifty little trick of alluring humans to wipe away their memory. It all just seemed like a lot of effort. I avoided mind-fucking humans as much as possible if I could help it. Feeding to keep myself alive and wiping their memories was a necessity. Going for a drink with Nikolaos to celebrate a commercialised holiday was not, in my opinion, a valid excuse to tamper with someone's brain.

I was so deep in thought over the moral dilemma, I didn't notice Nikolaos leaving the car. Only when Nikolaos opened the door on my side, his outstretched hand appearing in front of my face, did I realise I'd been mulling over it for several minutes. Clearly, Nikolaos had grown impatient waiting for me. Moral conscience was not something shared by my lover and me. He thought my care for humankind was fatuous; I thought his lack of consideration was cruel. In his defence, not many vampires make it over two thousand years by being compassionate. If I were to live so long, would I too become as ruthless? I hoped not.

I stared at Nikolaos's hand, still outstretched as an invitation for me to join him. I wanted nothing more than to feign normality. To drink and chat and dance the night away with my lover as though we were mortal—a wondrous fantasy, but not the reality. Eventually, I'd have to decide. We were already here; it was too late to turn back now. Swallowing the sudden lump in my throat, I took Nikolaos's hand and let him ease me from the car.

We walked hand-in-hand down the street, my heels making clopping sounds on the concrete. Wearing heels this high, I was closer to Adalia's height of five foot seven. It felt kind of nice to look down at the world instead of having to crane my neck constantly. Nikolaos was still five inches taller than me, but I would never be able to walk in shoes that made me six foot. Not unless I was willing to potentially break my neck. Although I'd survive the physical injury, it would be harder to recover from the wound on my pride.

CHAPTER 6

Nikolaos stopped us in front of a bar that hadn't been there when I was human. Years ago, it had been a small Korean restaurant; unfortunately, they hadn't acquired enough customers to remain open. Then it had been a hairdressers. Again, it had taken less than half a year to close down. For the last few years, the building had been derelict with a lonely *For Sale* sign collecting dust out front. Londinium road was notorious for business in that way: either you make a killing and prosper; or, despite being in such a popular area, you're invisible and attract no customers. Looking at the bar looming above us, I doubted whoever owned it would have any difficulties attracting customers.

Last time I'd seen the building, it'd had two large arched windows beside the nailed and boarded double doors. Now the entire front was done in shiny, black brick tiles, including the windows, so no one could see in or out. Slender metal bars twisted up in front of the sealed up arches where the windows had once been. Atop the window sill, faux flames roared wildly behind the bars as if they would escape if not for being imprisoned. The fire actually looked so real you'd be forgiven for thinking it was. I, as a fire nymph, knew better.

Set into the left of the building, black double doors stood proud. What should have been glass in the metal was replaced by a gold metallic sheet. Black, twisting bars, much like the ones over the windows, ran up the opulent-looking metal, with decorative lever door handles curling from it. Above the doorframe, *ATLAS* was spelt out in gold, gothic lettering with red lighting behind to illuminate the large sign. The words *deluxe* and *sultry* came to mind.

Nikolaos reached out to grip onto the handle, swinging the door open theatrically. The inside of Atlas was just as strikingly ornate as the out. Golden skirting lined the deep, blood-red walls. Aurous chandeliers hung from the ceiling with large teardrop faux rubies dripping from them, looking suspiciously like blood. I was assuming they were fake; if not, it was an obscene display of wealth. In the centre of the room stood a circular bar made of black marble with red veins. The bar encompassed a round shelving unit of the same stone brimming from floor to ceiling with alcohol and varying shaped cocktail glasses.

Dotted around the edges of the room were short marble tables, in black, of course; red chesterfield armchairs and loveseats in rich velvet choking with golden thread cushions pressed against the cold stone of the marble. Hurricane candle holders, with red stone bottoms carved in a vaguely antique design, bloomed from the tables like tulips, emitting a low, sensual glow throughout the room. Flames danced like the silhouettes of lovers over the walls, catching in the shining stone and golden cushions, getting lost in the caliginous corners. It were as if some parts of the room were untouched by light, hiding in shadows and darkness where people could retreat to whisper dark, intimate secrets.

'What do you think, *ma chérie*?'

Words eluded me. I'd never been to such a baroque establishment. I said the only thing I could think of: 'It's very... *you*.' And it was. It was as if someone had taken a peek inside the debauched and decadent corners of Nikolaos's mind and projected it into a bar. All shadows, and royal colours, and the promises of something pleasurable yet sinister to come.

'That is a shame.'

He placed his hand at the small of my back, just above the dress's lower fabric, one finger sliding back and forth over my skin. I turned puzzled eyes up to him.

'What is?'

'I was hoping you would think it is very *us*.'

Nikolaos used his hand on my back to usher me further into the room. I could feel the heat from the candles filling the space like warm water. Water in which to bathe and luxuriate. The fire began to stir something inside of me, coaxing my own internal flames to come to life. I acknowledged their presence with affection, whilst simultaneously mellowing them, subduing the stirring flames, whispering sweet nothings to lull them back to sleepy embers. My power had once been the dominant one of the two of us; now, I was getting better at working with it as one, with the power learning to obey my commands. It was working, for the most part.

As my master, Nikolaos would be able to feel the stirrings of my internal heat too. I felt his own power gently stream from his hand into the skin of my back, helping subdue the flames.

'Why?' I asked, trying to fight the shiver from his cooler power as it caressed my fire.

Nikolaos gestured grandly outwards with his free hand, saying, '*Bienvenu* to Atlas, *ma chérie.* My newest venture.'

Nikolaos sauntered over to the marble bar, pulling open a gate in the stone perfectly concealed if you didn't know to look for it. I walked over to meet him, taking the menu from his outstretched hand. Made of thick, charcoal card with '*Atlas*' embossed on the front in the same gold font as the sign out front, the menu managed to be as sumptuous as the rest of the building. Midas, Ichor, Narcissus, Tantalus, Ambrosia, and Dionysus were the only six cocktails written on the back in consistent typography.

'There's clearly a theme with the names here,' I said.

Nikolaos upturned his lips just enough to be considered a smile.

'But why Atlas?' I asked, noticing the out-of-place name.

Nikolaos went very still. In that placid state of inertia he had mastered after so long of being dead. When uncomfortable, most people will make an involuntary nervous gesture hinting at their unease. Not Nikolaos, though. He took the opposite approach, shutting down in face and body, so very still, as if he were indeed made of the marble from which he appeared carved.

'It is a name that meant something to me once,' he finally replied.

Over the months I had known Nikolaos, I could count on one hand the number of times we had touched on his past and still have fingers left over. Other than the very, very rare remark on Ancient Greece's cultures, we had never spoken of his human life. I could deduce from the Greek-themed names that Atlas was someone from his mortal life. Even if I asked about anything vampire-related, Nikolaos would only occasionally refer the answer to something from his past. I had quickly discerned that there is deep-rooted damage that comes with being alive for close to three millennia. Nikolaos didn't just breed his secrecy from a penchant for mystery; it was from years of loss built up. Alone, Nikolaos had allowed the wounds of his past to heal messily. By asking questions, it had the potential to reopen old scars and have them bleed all over him. Because of this, I let it go. For now.

'We must feed,' he said.

I nodded.

'Otherwise, our bodies won't process the human fluid.'

It was his turn to nod.

'You are learning well. Even without your master by your side.'

I grimaced at the terminology. Nikolaos's lips twitched.

'It is a truth you cannot deny,' he said.

'I still try my best to ignore it.'

'A true master would never abandon the side of their infant vassal the way I have,' he said reproachfully.

I laid my hand on top of his. 'I wouldn't want you to act like a true master, Niko.'

Tucked behind a tumbling of sheer black fabric was an archway leading into a short corridor with a sharp left corner at the end. Down the shorter aisle, which branched off, were three unisex lavatories and a staff room. There was a cloakroom set into the wall a bit before the corridor veered off. With no attendant or customers, Nikolaos, I presumed, had drawn the silk curtains across the opening in the wall. Beside the cloakroom, a gleaming metal door towered above me, locked by a numerical keypad.

It looked very out of place compared to the rest of the aesthetic and reminded me of the door at the morgue we'd had to visit last year. The thought alone was enough to send a chill down my spine. It had been one of the more traumatic events of hunting down Maglark, which was saying something as it was in the company of many horrifying incidents.

'The code,' Nikolaos said, releasing my hand to punch numbers into the keypad, 'is four-five-three.'

The door swung open to reveal a woman lying supine on a huge black leather sofa. I turned wide eyes to Nikolaos, looking a shocked question at him. With a flurry of hand, he ushered me further into the room. Damask wallpaper of black and grey covered the walls. There was a glass coffee table resting on a grey silk rug in front of the sofa. Behind the sofa, a partition crept halfway through the room. Half of a black lacquered desk stuck out from behind it. If it weren't for the unconscious women lying in front of me, I might have gone to take a closer look at the decor. She was a little distracting.

I was glad to see her chest rising and falling from sedated breathing. I knew allured when I saw it, and this woman was out for the count. Long, blonde hair curled around a round face. She wore a black v-necked jumper over black jeans and boots. Last time Nikolaos had found us a woman to feast on, she'd been blonde, too. Of course, her hair had been dyed such a bright peroxide-blonde it had been almost blinding. She'd also worn next to nothing. I'd complained about the scanty clothing.

Looking at the modesty of this one's outfit, I guess he'd taken that complaint to heart. Still, I couldn't help but wonder if Nikolaos had a thing for blondes. The vampire love of his life before me had matched the profile. Or maybe they matched hers. Was Nikolaos still chasing the woman he'd lost through the humans on whom he fed? I shook the thought away; I was just being insecure. Probably.

'Niko,' I said, turning to look at him. 'Is this a... a *feeding* room?'

'I would not have phrased it quite so tersely.'

'So, what would you call it?'

'My office,' he said blandly.

I gestured to the allured lady. Pale lashes lightly fluttered against her cheeks. Her small round mouth was set into a little 'O' as if she were about to say something.

'Right, your office. And a feeding room.'

He shrugged gracefully.

'If I were human, you would not question a kitchen.'

'But—'

'*Non*, we are not human; like it or not, we must feed on the blood of mortals. It is practical.'

'It's sinister!'

He turned cold eyes to me.

'Only if you choose to see it that way. A bar is a perfect place to find willing food, *ma chérie*. Is hunting humans in the night like beasts hunt prey any less sinister than this?'

I wanted to argue. But, in a twisted sort of way, he was right. If Nikolaos were to solicit any woman in the bar, she would go to him gladly. It was slightly less predatory.

'I s'pose not,' I replied disgruntledly.

I walked over to crouch beside the resting lady. Rolling up the sleeve of her jumper, I clasped the soft flesh of her wrist. Her vein throbbed against where my fingers lay with the ferocity brought on by fear. Never having been allured myself, I didn't know for sure how conscious the victims were, but I'd done it enough times, felt the fear of enough humans as I touched them, to know they weren't completely disconnected from reality. It was why we had to wipe their memories afterwards.

Feeling the beat of her artery against my hand made the hunger drown out my prejudice against vampire nature. Bloodlust is not like any hunger for food. It is the equivalent of walking miles through a desert and then finding a well; not eating for a month and then having someone cook the most delectable meal you can imagine; having your body starved of pleasure and then finding a lover who melds to your body as if you were made for one another. Blood fills a gap in a vampire that no human could ever experience. It offers power, strength, and the feeling of life reigniting our bodies. But, like anything that can give such a rush, too much of a good thing can quickly turn sour. Becoming a vampire means learning to tread the fine line between luxuriating in the thrill of drinking human plasma and not falling into the depths of addiction.

Nikolaos had crossed that line before. He knew the pains of addiction that I couldn't even begin to fathom. The hole in his vampire psyche could never be filled by blood alone anymore, not in the same way it once did. He walked around with a constant craving for more than just blood but flesh. Flesh from sex, from death, from torture. Nikolaos had confessed some of the sins of his past to me before, but I hadn't truly understood until he'd let the guards between us down, and I'd begun to feel the full force of the pain of his addictions. Knowing he lived with such a constant, overwhelming yearning gave me a new appreciation for his level of control.

And a fear for what we could become.

CHAPTER 7

Life filled me, coursed heat and strength through my veins. Of course, it wasn't my life, but the energy we stole through drinking from a human. The world was suddenly so much clearer, and I bounced with an energy I'd lacked earlier in the night. Some of the apathy I'd felt before gave way to the joyous high of feeding.

Nikolaos was back behind the bar. Whilst he was always alabaster pale, a slight blush of colour drowned some of the pallidity. The deep green of his eyes glistened under the golden candlelight. Thick, obsidian hair seemed lusher, bouncier than before. Something is haunting about watching the most beautiful man in the world blossom into a gift worthy of Gods before your very eyes.

The first rush after feeding is like a caffeine hit as your body adjusts to the sudden resurgence of life. All of the chains that bind the dead collapse to the ground, leaving nothing but the abundant freedom of possibility. Some of it's a lie. We still cannot walk in daylight, or reproduce, or become mortal. But for one glorious moment, our bodies are tricked into thinking we are unstoppable.

I skimmed my eyes over the menu.

'None of the drinks have any descriptions,' I observed.

'This menu is a prototype. The others are due to arrive before the launch tomorrow.'

I raised my eyebrows.

'Tomorrow? How did you manage to do all of this'—I motioned around the room—'without telling me? You've been so busy working for the Empress. Where did you find the time?'

'Amphitrite encourages her vampires to open businesses.'

'Amphitrite? Oh, you mean the Empress. You know, you've never actually told me her name before.'

Nikolaos sighed, something he did so rarely. It was a weary sigh.

'I have done my utmost to have you know nothing of her, and her of you.'

I smiled at him, my eyes flicking to where his fingers traced absentminded circles over the marble countertop.

'I appreciate that. But you've managed to build a whole business without me having even an inkling. I want you to be able to talk to me. Is Amphitrite really so dangerous I need this much protection?'

The look he gave me was eloquent; yes, she indeed *was* that dangerous, and I was naive for even questioning it. It was my turn to sigh.

'Okay, I guess you know her better than me. Ichor is the blood of the Gods in Greek mythology, right? So, is it like a bloody mary?'

Nikolaos actually looked taken aback for a moment, a moment in which I relished.

'I did not expect you to know that.'

I wriggled my eyebrows at him, tapping my finger against my nose. 'I'm full of surprises, me.'

I'd had so much spare time recently it made sense to research some of Nikolaos's history as well as my own. Adalia had suspected that part of what drew Nikolaos to tend to me after my attack was that, as a nymph, part of my magick called to his heritage. The theory was, as he was brought up as a believer, the call to him would be stronger than to someone who was a nonbeliever. As theories went, it wasn't awful, there just wasn't any way to prove it—at least not one that we currently knew.

It turned out that the Ichor was not a Bloody Mary, but actually, a sweet and spicy cocktail flavoured with ginger and hibiscus. Nikolaos poured a dark red syrup into a crystal cocktail glass and mixed it with an expensive tequila brand I'd never heard of before. No mid-tier liquor here. Ichor was garnished with a bright red hibiscus flower. I took a sip, taking in the whiff of warm clove undertone, the almost bitter hibiscus, sweet sugar, spice from the ginger, and burn of the triple shot of tequila he'd put in.

Nikolaos poured his own drink, the Midas, made from prosecco and elderflower cordial stirred with edible gold glitter served in a tall champagne float with a golden stem, and reached under the bar to switch on a stereo. Edith Piaf's *La Vie En Rose* started playing through speakers hidden somewhere around the bar. Nikolaos came through the raised hatch as the romantic instrumental started whispering throughout the room. Before the first verse had time to start, Nikolaos took the drink from my hand, placing it on the bar top.

Taking my left hand and placing it on his shoulder, Nikolaos took my right and held it bent beside our bodies. He rested his fingers lightly on the small of my back, pulling my lower body tight to him. Just as the lyrics "*Il me dit des mots d'amour*" started, Nikolaos began to gently guide our bodies around the room.

I rested my head on his shoulder, a position I'd never be able to take if it weren't for the heels, letting him move our bodies in slow unison. We swayed together without talking, only the soft melodies of the music seducing the silence. I closed my eyes, letting the feeling of Nikolaos's body holding mine consume me as we rocked.

We did not stop dancing when the song ended. For a moment, we swayed like leaves in the gentle spring breeze before Ella Fitzgerald's *Dream a Little Dream of Me* came on. Nikolaos withdrew from our original dancing position, wrapping his arms around my back and pulling me to his chest. I mirrored his hold on me, resting my head against his chest, holding his body tight to my own.

'Atlas is, was, the name of my son,' Nikolaos surprised me by saying. The words were a delicate whisper into my hair where his mouth rested against the side of my head. So very quiet, almost lost to the sound of the music.

I fought not to tense in his arms. At that moment, I knew that any movement, no matter how subtle, had the potential to make Nikolaos shut down. Since I had first met him, he had never willingly volunteered information and, even when I probed him, it was a torturous task to get him to open up.

'My wife, Kleio, died during the childbirth of our second son, Melanthios. Melanthios was scarcely two when I became a vampire. I got four years with Atlas before he was orphaned.'

'You were married?'

'*Oui,* alas, we had a mere four years together before I was fated a widower.' As my master, Nikolaos often shielded himself from me sensing his emotions, but right then, I could feel his pain like a crack down my own heart. It had nothing to do with the metaphysical relationship which bound us, and everything to do with hearing so much loss in the words of the one you love.

I didn't know what to say. I finally settled on a very unsatisfactory, 'I'm sorry.'

'Time heals old wounds, and I have had enough time for all scars to fade.'

I didn't believe him, but saying so seemed cruel.

'How did you meet?' I asked softly.

'When I returned from war, my father, Midas, had arranged the marriage. Arranged marriage was prevalent in my time, although it was often seen as a business arrangement between families. After years of battling, I did not want to return to be married, but when we met, I knew we were one soul in two bodies.'

'You went to war?' I asked, startled.

Nikolaos removed his hand from my back momentarily to tuck a stray lock of hair behind my ear.

'I have answered the rallying call countless times, marched in different colours, fought for causes both righteous and reprobate. I was sixteen the first time I spilt the blood of a foe, watched the warmth of a grown man leave his body until he was nothing more than a cadaver.'

I continued to hold his body, swaying together lightly to the gentle wind of melodies. I closed my eyes, feeling the soft material of his shirt against my cheek as we moved, drinking in the smell of old rose and cinnamon on his skin and blood and alcohol on his breath. For several painful moments, I held him, held him tight enough to know he was not alone.

'What did she look like?' I murmured, finally.

'Of all the questions to ask, why this?' He sounded genuinely perplexed as if the question had thrown him.

'Don't answer if it's too hard,' I said, nuzzling my face further into his chest.

Nikolaos squeezed his arms around my body lightly, comfortingly.

'Her hair was the gold of spring crops with eyes the softest green.'

His voice was low with memory, as if he were reciting the most delicate details of great art, concentrating on remembering all the beauty and lines and shading. So deep in reverie was he, we could have been anywhere in the world, and all Nikolaos would see was his wife still alive in dusty streets lost to history.

I'd always thought Nikolaos was searching for his long lost love of Camille in the women he feasted on, but I had been mistaken. Nikolaos hated Camille for so many legitimate reasons, but, for the first time, I knew why, at least partly, he'd fallen for her so thoroughly. Nikolaos wasn't trying to fulfil his loss of Camille; Camille was his replacement for Kleio. An immortal replica of the only woman he'd ever loved. And lost.

'Midas. That was the last name on your credit card. It's your father's name.'

I felt his hair brush against my own as he nodded.

'In my day, I would be known as Nikolaos, son of Midas. It made sense to keep the name as the times changed.' For the first time, I got a hint of his old accent, the one he had lost so many centuries ago. Nikolaos had lived on and off in France since the time it was still known as Gaul.

'What happened to your sons?'

'Melanthios died in the Battle of Sybota. He did not live to see nineteen. Atlas lived a long life as a farmer, inheriting the farms that Kleio and I left in our departure. When I heard news of his ailments, I travelled back to Corinth. He thought my presence was nothing more than the crazed hallucinations of a dying man.'

'I'm sure seeing you again brought him some peace,' I said.

'Perhaps,' he said wistfully.

I pulled back enough to look into Nikolaos's face. His eyes shimmered in the golden light with mournful nostalgia.

'Greece will always be my home, but is now a home built from walls of loss and sorrow.'

'Do you ever get homesick?'

'I pine for what Greece once meant to me as a human.'

I waited for him to elaborate. Instead, those soft, plump lips stayed pressed in a forlorn line. I stood upon the tip-toes of my heels, pulling my other hand free of his back to steady myself with a hand on his chest, and kissed him chastely on the lips.

'Thank you,' I whispered against his mouth.

'Will you accompany me tomorrow evening for Atlas's grand opening? I wish nothing more than to have you on my arm as we make our public debut.'

I smiled sadly at him.

'I wish I could, but I can't do anything public, Niko. Everyone still thinks I'm dead. And whilst they're not wrong, I'm not the type of dead they assume.

'Of course. I am a fool.'

I shook my head.

'No,' I said, grinning at him wide enough to flash fang, 'you have no idea how happy it makes me that you asked. I'm due to see Rune tomorrow anyway. Could you bring Adalia?'

'*Non,* I respect her decision to distance herself from us. I believe, of all of us, the price of catching Maglark was most costly for Adalia.'

A part of me wanted to argue that we'd all lost a great deal to catch Maglark. Gwydion had called upon some ancient, evil magick to aid in Maglark's reincarnation. If it weren't for me calling on the alive power of the earth and my nymph blood to battle the death magick, then both Gwydion and Adalia would probably be dead right now. And Nikolaos, too, for that matter. If Nikolaos had died, I might have followed him to the grave for real, so, potentially, none of us would still be here. I'd forced some of the life of my magick into Nikolaos to help chase the power back from seeking his energy of death. Part of Nikolaos's returning power was due to me accidentally sharing my own magick with him. He might not have needed to confess his newfound abilities to the Empress, Amphitrite, if I hadn't had done it. Like all magick, it can be a double-edged sword and come back to bite you on the arse. When I'd forced some of my power into Nikolaos, I hadn't expected the consequences to be the Empress taking such a special liking to him.

Adalia had given a lot to help us with the ritual. In her eyes, she had sold some of her soul to let such darkness touch her own magick. I still didn't blame her for wanting to leave us after what we had done. I'd never wanted to compromise her morals in such a way. The guilt still ate at me because, if it weren't for me asking for her help, she would never have let in the darkness.

Yes, we'd all lost a lot of ourselves to catch Maglark, but ultimately, he'd lost the most. We'd ripped his life away from him the way he had taken so many others. My only regret was that we didn't catch him before more innocent lives were lost. The only two who seemed actually to gain something from what we did were Gwydion and Nikolaos. Nikolaos had regained some of his power after so many years of being a magickal null. Gwydion had discovered that my own magick could counterbalance some of the evil. I had told him I was not going to put that to the test again. Almost losing three people I loved to sinister magick out of necessity was one thing; doing it out of some perverse curiosity was a whole other ball game. One that had no rules, and I simply refused to play.

'You have not told me how you are finding Gwydion working as your mentor,' Nikolaos said.

We'd stopped dancing and were now grabbing our drinks from the bar. Drink in hand, I walked over to one of the loveseats. Nikolaos followed behind me, taking the free half of the seat.

'I didn't think you'd want to know,' I said. Nikolaos raised an eyebrow at me. 'Well, you didn't use to like me talking about him. Besides, you're gone so often we never have time to talk.'

What was meant to sound light-hearted came out as unintentionally splenetic.

I took another sip from my drink, not meeting Nikolaos's watchful gaze. He placed a large hand just above my knee where it was crossed over the other, long fingers wrapping around the silky fabric of my thigh-highs.

'I am here tonight; I wish to know how your education with Rune is developing. I may not be fond of him, but that does not mean I am utterly apathetic towards your journey together, *ma chérie*.'

I studied Nikolaos's face from where he sat beside me. There was an earnest look in his eyes, an anticipatory set to his lips as he waited to hear what I'd been learning during all the nights he was away. So I told him how Gwydion was helping me work as one with my power, learning to control it. When we had first started working together, it was only meant to be once a week for a few hours of the night; now, I saw Kai and Gwydion closer to three nights every week. We still worked together to understand my power as well as visualisation and meditation to learn ways to control it, but now we spent more time together as friends. I wasn't sure how Nikolaos would feel about hearing my blossoming relationship with Gwydion. He surprised me with encouraging nods of the head, minute smiles, and no callous quips.

When I was done explaining, I asked, 'What about you? How's it been going with Amphitrite?'

Nikolaos and I had been talking long enough to have topped our drinks up four times. A string of bright hibiscus flowers lay forgotten on the marble table beside my glass.

Nikolaos took a sip of his own Ichor. Red syrup stained his lips the bright crimson of fresh blood before his tongue darted out and licked the staining away. I had the overwhelming urge to lap the scarlet syrup off his mouth, to taste how the sweetness of the sugar and spice of the ginger mingled with the taste of his lips.

All of the thoughtful consideration and openness Nikolaos had displayed disappeared as quickly as it had come at my question. Nikolaos's expression changed with liquid fluidity, one moment amiable and the next cold and expressionless. His eyes didn't actually move from where they looked at me, it was more as if they changed colour. Darker with his usual blank mocking.

I clumsily dug myself a deeper hole by adding, 'I'm still surprised she hasn't asked to meet me. Gwydion is, too.'

'Do you share all my business with Rune?'

'No,' I said stubbornly. 'But my involvement, or lack thereof, is *my* business. And that I do. It's not exactly like you've been around to talk to about any of it.'

'I have worked tirelessly to shield your involvement with Amphitrite.'

'See, that's what concerns me. When you say stuff like this, I feel like I should worry. There's a fine line between intriguingly mysterious and frustratingly elusive.' I reached out, resting my hand against Nikolaos's cheek. 'Is there something I need to be worried about, Niko? Would you really tell me if we weren't safe?'

Nikolaos placed his hand over mine and moved his face closer to me. His mouth hovered over my lips as he whispered, 'I would let no harm come to either of us, *ma chérie*.'

Maybe I would have argued, or not believed him, or pressed him further. But his lips pressed against mine, and the words in my throat were drowned by the sensation of his mouth dancing over my own.

CHAPTER 8

Nikolaos wrapped his arm around my back, lowering me down to lie on the loveseat, his body pressing to the front of my own. My skull rested against the armrest, propped up enough to watch Nikolaos use the back of the sofa to steady himself as his lips worked their way down my neck. His tongue darted wet and warm over the skin of my throat, running a line down the vein beating with the speed of my pulse. Frantic, enabled by the blood of the woman still lying dormant in the office.

He continued to work his way down until his lips hovered over the mound of my right breast. Nikolaos pulled his arm out from underneath me, tracing his hand down the line of my dress. Soft, satin lips moved down to my breast as his hands glided down to the top of my thigh-highs. His tongue traced the edge of the black lace of my bra, just low enough to stroke the top of my areola; my breath came out in a long sigh.

Nikolaos sat upon his knees, withdrawing both his hands from their positions to pull at the dress straps on my shoulders. He began to peel the dress down my body slowly, the velvet rubbing along my skin, teasing my body. When the dress was halfway down, I wriggled my lower body to help him pull me out of it.

With the dress discarded in a pile of green on the sable carpet, Nikolaos went back to his knees to look down at my body. The black of my bra and knickers looked so dark against the white of my flesh, the lace framing my breasts and soft flesh of my lower belly and hips. I watched the rise and fall of his chest speed as he drank in the sight of me. Nikolaos ran his hand down my thigh until his fingers caressed the side of my knee. Turning vehement eyes burning green, Nikolaos bent his face back down to my mouth. We kissed, almost chastely at first and then with growing, anticipatory fervour. His lips held all the promises of love and seduction. My hands worked their way through his hair, wrapping it around my small fists like a rope to pull him down closer towards me. I held his hair in my hands tight enough I could feel a slight strain; enough I knew it didn't hurt but would do if I moved my hand to the wrong angle. I used that leverage to hold him to me as our lips, mouths, tongues explored each other.

With my free hand, I tried to undo the buttons of his shirt. Caught up in the intoxication of passion, and a lot of tequila, my fingers fumbled too clumsily, and I could not get past even the first button done up tightly at his throat. I groaned my frustration into his mouth, trying to use the strength and speed of my vampirism to tear the shirt from his body. Buttons flew through the air, some clinking against the marble table, others tumbling silently into the carpeted ground. Nikolaos laughed into my mouth, pulling back enough to discard the shreds of cloth still attached to his body, and undo the collar of his shirt, which had somehow remained intact.

I rose to my knees to meet him, pressing my lips over the smooth definition of his chest. My mouth found his small, pale nipples. I pulled the pearl-shaped tender flesh in between my teeth, rolling my tongue over the skin. Nikolaos threw his head back, breath coming out fast and heavy. I sucked more of his nipple and chest into my mouth, letting my tongue run over the light trail of black hair surrounding it. Still exploring his right nipple, I used my hands to reach down and pull down the zip of his suit trousers. I managed the zip, but Nikolaos had to help my clumsy fingers with the button.

'Off,' I growled, pushing on his chest, so he lay on his back the way I had started.

I ripped the trousers off his legs, careful not to tear the fabric. It was my turn to take in Nikolaos lying between my legs. With the blood of a human pumping through his veins, I could see he was very ready for me. Pressed against the black satin on his boxers, he was long and hard. Nikolaos's pale flesh was framed by the loveseat's red velvet as if it were designed to accessorise the perfection of his naked body. I trailed my hand down the smoothness of his chest and abdomen, just firm enough to be considered muscled, whilst still soft enough to feel alive.

My fingers curled through the trail of hair on his lower body, playing with it, and then they found their way down the satin. I lowered my mouth to the hardness contained in his boxers, holding him through the lustrous material. I licked the long line over his erection still trapped inside the fabric. Nikolaos shuddered, breath coming out in a heavy sigh. I started working my hand up and over the hard appendage, rubbing the satin over his body, still not flesh on flesh. I crawled up his body, lowering my mouth against his, still caressing his penis.

'*Ma chérie*,' he sighed against my lips, air tickling my face.

'Yes?'

'May I remove the last of my garments?'

'Say please,' I whispered the demand, voice gone low with dominance and desire.

He cocked his head to one side as if considering what I had said.

'I thought tonight we would make love, but, *mon feu*, your eyes shine with passion darker than love.'

Nikolaos started to chuckle. I wrapped my hand tighter around his penis, squeezing with more pressure. Not to hurt him, but to remind him who was in control. Pleasured groans swallowed his laughter. Humour bled from his eyes, consumed by something salacious and carnal.

'Too much talking,' I tutted. 'Ask again and say please.'

'*Ma chérie...*'

I squeezed harder; Nikolaos turned wild eyes to me

'*S'il te plaît.*'

'Please what?'

'Please undress me, *ma chérie*, please take me.'

With that, I tore the satin from his body, letting shreds of fabric float through the air. And then I did as was asked. I took him.

CHAPTER 9

I was wet, but too tight to mount him the way I wanted to without hurting both of us. Nikolaos knew how to fix that. One moment, I was straddling his waist; the next, I was lying on my back with my hands pinned above my head by his grip on my wrists. His hand was large enough, and my wrists small enough, to only need one. With the other, he gripped my left breast, his mouth finding the right. Like I had done to him, Nikolaos sucked the delicate flesh of my nipple into his mouth. Rolling his tongue over the skin in long, deliberate circles. He used his thumb and index finger to caress my other nipple. Stroking it slowly, thoroughly, and then suddenly squeezing; every time he did, I gasped. The pain was so sharp and felt so fucking amazing.

Nikolaos moved from where he worked on my breasts, releasing his grip on my hands to place his head between my thighs. He kissed down my belly, pulling the flesh beside my belly button into his mouth, biting hard enough I cried out.

I wrapped my legs around his shoulders, resting the sharp heel against his bare back. Nikolaos sucked me into his mouth, rolling his tongue over my clitoris, dragging the flesh lightly between his teeth. His fingers found my opening, gliding into me with ease. He quickly found a rhythm, adding another finger to the mix. As his lips, mouth, and teeth worked on that little spot of pleasure, his fingers flowed inside me. With each thrust of his fingers, Nikolaos curled them inside of me, stroking deep and low. He withdrew, slowly, offering me a moment to catch my erratic breath. Or so I thought. Just as his fingers were about to exit my body, they curled upwards in a come hither gesture that hit that spot of pleasure all over again, sending my back bowing against the loveseat.

It didn't take long for the fast, fluid movements to bring me for the first time. One moment I was lying there with the pressure building up like a warm wave inside my body, and the next, I let that wave of pleasure wash over both of us. The orgasm started deep inside me, spreading down my legs, forcing the heel into his back, all the way down to my toes. It ran up my body, arching my back, pressing my opening harder against his fingers. Nikolaos took it as the invitation it was, working harder inside me whilst I rode the pleasure. My arms flew out to the side, knocking over our half-full glasses. My fingers grasped the hibiscus flowers and ice from the tipped drinks, squashing them in my fist. The coldness of the ice in my palm was shocking, making the pleasure somehow more intense as pain and sharpness so often do.

With unfocused eyes, I saw Nikolaos's face appear above mine. His lips kissed me with the taste of me still on his mouth like perfume. I licked his lips, using my hand to drag his hand up to our faces. Nikolaos moved back enough to let me draw his fingers into my mouth. I looked him deep in the eyes as my lips worked their way slowly down his two fingers, sucking off the sweet wetness he had coaxed from my body. He shuddered with my fingers still in his mouth, eyes wild and unfocused.

And then, with no pre-warning, he was inside me. Slowly working the tip of him inside my warm opening. Shallow enough, I writhed and screamed and begged him to enter me fully.

'Say please,' he growled, voice stained with his own need.

'Please, Niko, please take me,' I cried out.

And then he did as was asked. He took me.

He took me hard and thorough and furiously until my nails tore down his back, and he cried out my name. He took me until my body spasmed around his, heels bruising his flesh whilst I convulsed around him, contracting to force his body further into me. He gave until there was nothing left to give, and his own control surrendered to his pleasure.

I had enough clothing left to get dressed, although the thigh highs had been torn in multiple places. The elastic still clung to my thigh on one leg, but the fabric had been ripped free, bunching at my ankle. I tossed them in the bin. Nikolaos's clothes had not survived in quite the same way. By the time we were ready to leave, we'd filled the black bin bag behind the bar with shredded silk, broken glass, and buttons. The glass had broken in the throes of passion. Nikolaos's back was raked with red from my nails; two indents were set into his lower back where my heels had pressed into the skin too hard for too long. I'd apologised. Nikolaos had, somewhat breathlessly, told me there was no need to be sorry.

We were both dressed and ready to start the journey home. All that was left to do was make sure the woman we had fed on earlier in the night also got home safely. One of the pubs a few doors down from us had a security guard waiting outside. Nikolaos went to start the car whilst I, with the woman hanging on my side, trotted over to him. I gave my best guileless eyes as I explained to him how I'd found her too drunk on the side of the street and was worried about how she'd get home. If it had been a year ago, I would have felt awkward talking to the man. Now, I batted my eyes and smiled at him, careful not to flash fang. I didn't know what had changed to give me more confidence, it was probably an accumulation of things, but I'd learnt the incredible magic of feminine wiles. The security guard had broken what I assumed was protocol when he'd first seen me by flirting, pushing all that boyish charm he had into a grin. By the time I'd finished voicing my concerns, he'd fallen back into strict security mode. He took the blonde-haired woman from my arms with an assurance she'd get home safe. I smiled, thanked him, and turned on my heels to meet Nikolaos.

Nikolaos chose to speed home. Sunrise was still hours away; he just enjoyed the thrill of driving a hundred miles an hour down the always deserted road leading to our woods. I couldn't deny it was great fun, although my fingers were mottled from holding so hard onto the car door. I half expected us to be pulled over; half-dressed, speeding, and over the limit seemed like we were inviting trouble. Luckily, we managed to get home without a single police car passing us, and in half the time it should have taken.

Tucked into the curve of Nikolaos's body, his bare front pressing into my back, I waited for dawn with a sense of tranquillity.

CHAPTER 10

I was sitting in front of the vanity, looking at the black rose Gwydion had given me last year. It was still alive, or at least it hadn't yet wilted. Large, luxurious towels wrapped around my body and hair, the fabric soft and warm against my skin. Drying thick hair as long as mine is a bloody nightmare. I usually just left it in a towel until it was damp and then let it dry naturally. Quite lazy, really, but being imprisoned by the confines of moonlight means leaving trivial matters like haircare alone. Though Nikolaos might disagree.

I sighed, leaning my face on my elbows grumpily. I really did want to go with Nikolaos to the opening of Atlas. A small part of me wanted to throw caution to the wind and join him. We could deal with the consequences when they arose. A more significant, more sensible part of my brain knew survival as a vampire meant wrapping caution around you like a cloak and that consequences were not so easily ignored. Better to drill that lesson into me now than learn the hard way like some young vampires did. Carelessness is what got me killed as a human; carelessness and lack of fight. I still wasn't much of a fighter, however, careless I was generally not.

'When did this saturnine temperament befall you, *ma chérie*? You were not always so morose.'

Nikolaos's voice made me whip around. I hadn't even noticed him come into the room. Vampires are meant to have astute powers of observation, or so I had thought.

ook...' I struggled for the right word, finally
aking.'

gold brocade made up his Victorian-style frock
coat, with extra fabric over the shoulders like the frills on a
lizard, and buttons made of solid gold twisted into an intricate
metallic pattern. The shirt he wore was, of course, silk and
ruby-red. Fastened at his neck, the high, tight collar stood stiff,
a gold neck pin piercing the fabric with a chain hanging on
either end. His waistcoat matched the jacket all the way down
to the golden buttons and fit his slender figure perfectly.
Nikolaos had tucked leather trousers into soft leather boots,
which rode up his leg, folding at the knees, clasped into place
with golden buckles. It was very Victorian-vampire if that
vampire were in some elaborate sexual fantasy. All he was
missing was a cane and top hat. I guess he'd finally found a use
for all of those outfits he hoarded. A hat would probably ruin
the spectacular wave of his hair, blow-dried around his face like
a frame of sinuous black velvet.

He was going to be even more a treat for any straight
woman—or not so straight man—in attendance. I felt a twinge
of jealousy. It wasn't that Nikolaos and I had defined our
relationship enough to be definitively monogamous. Feeding is
such an erotic experience; it would always blur the lines of
monogamy anyway. As far as I knew, Nikolaos wasn't sleeping
with anyone else, although what he was getting up to with the
Empress was unknown to me. I tried not to think about it too
much; what could young, inexperienced me really offer a man
who had felt the embrace of many a fine lover? Besides eternity,
nothing but my virtue, which he had taken. Still, none of that

was why I was jealous. No, I was jealous because tonight he could dance and drink and laugh with any woman invited, and I couldn't share in that luxury. I would not be able to share his joy at Atlas opening.

'Are you excited about tonight?' I asked.

Nikolaos walked over to my bed, leaning his back against one of the four posters, fixing those intent eyes on me.

'I would be more so if you were to be by my side.'

'I know.' I smiled at him. 'Me, too.'

'Is it still your intention to see Gwydion this evening?'

I nodded. 'Are you going to be home tonight, or does duty call?' It came out more bitter than I'd intended.

Nikolaos frowned at me.

'Licensing laws,' he said, spitting out "laws" like it was a dirty word, 'dictate I must clinch the celebrations at one. I expect we shall be closed by two latest. I will come home once the party has ceased.'

'How long are you staying in Britchelstone for?'

He sighed. 'I must travel back tomorrow.'

'Okay,' I said, avoiding looking at him.

Nikolaos came to kneel in front of me, taking my hands in his.

'I do not like this any more than you, *ma chérie*.'

'Then, don't go.'

'If it were that elementary, I would not.'

'Okay,' I said again.

He released my hands, letting them sit limply in my lap.

'Go, Niko, you don't want to be late.' I forced myself to smile at him. I really did want him to have a good opening night. It was unfair to ruin this big event for him. 'I'm looking forward to hearing how it went.'

My next smile was genuine. He took it as satisfactory reassurance, kissing me lightly on the lips.

I got dressed in a much less elaborate fashion. Black boots, black jeans, black jean jacket with a fluffy collar, and a satin shirt tucked loosely into the jeans. The shirt was dark blue— not black, *gasp*—and looked great with the peridot necklace. I left the last few buttons undone to show off a bit of bust. I liked wearing dark colours, but the almost exclusively black wardrobe wasn't just a fashion choice. Blood tends to get everywhere. White just isn't that practical as a vampire. Or was I just messy? Maybe. I'd pulled my hair up in a ponytail on top of my head, letting it fall down my back in damp curls. Without feeding, I looked almost too pale, especially framed in a wealth of black and navy. The hairdo wasn't particularly flattering for my face shape, but it was convenient.

Locking the front door, I noticed that the Buick wasn't where Nikolaos had parked it in front of the house last night. Either he'd driven it to Atlas or stored it wherever it usually lived. We didn't have a garage at the cottage—one of the many mysteries of my vampire lover. Let's be honest, he probably took it with him. Nikolaos was going for flashy tonight, and a vintage convertible from the fifties definitely fit the desired aesthetic. I wondered if he'd intentionally coordinated his outfit to match the interior of Atlas. Probably.

I found a human to feed on before making my way to Gwydion and Kai's. I was feeling sulky, wallowing in a pit of insecurity and mild petulance. Before last night, I'd always thought that Nikolaos choosing women to feed on who looked like Camille was sort of strange, but she'd damaged him, and I'd tried to justify it. Like how some people find it too hard to leave their abusers, I'd just assumed that it was Nikolaos's own macabre way of not leaving her entirely behind. Whilst it had bothered me, I had also felt his emotions about her firsthand. However besotted he had once been with Camille, stomach-churning hatred had always dominated that twisted infatuation.

Now I knew it was because he still yearned for the love of his life from over two thousand years ago, I could admit to myself it bothered me more. Would I be less distressed if I looked like her and knew I fit that profile he searched for, or would that make me feel worse? I didn't know. I also didn't know if this was childish insecurity or if I were justified. God, were relationships always this confusing? I'd definitely been thrown in the deep end with Nikolaos. Talk about baggage.

Kai and Gwydion lived in a monolithic bungalow, if you can really call what is essentially a lonesome cave a bungalow, tucked even further into the woodland than our cottage. The building was made of stone so ancient it was crumbling in multiple places. I knew for a fact that if Kai had his way, they'd live somewhere much more homely. He needed the woodlands to hunt just as much as Gwydion did to hide in, but the cold, uninviting exterior had definitely been Gwydion's choosing. Not all the rooms had windows; the ones that did were made of glass so old it was grey and cracking like spiderwebs.

I slammed the heavy metal knocker into the wooden door and shoved my hands back into my jacket pockets. Some flecks of wood fluttered down onto the frosty ground below. Oops, hadn't meant to knock that hard. In my defence, the door, like much of the building, was so old it didn't take much to chip it further. I could feel Gwydion's power hanging in the air like something tasteable. Subtle, but hard to ignore.

It was Kai who opened the door. Seeing him, some of the frustration that had plagued me all evening instantly dissipated. Only three inches taller than me, Kai was short for a man, but what he lacked in height was made up for in width and muscle. He was totally hairless save a trail of thick, black eyebrows and short but plentiful lashes. First looking at him, you might be forgiven for thinking he was human. Until you saw those eyes. Darkness made his black pupils huge, floating in a sea of orange-amber without any white. They were leopard eyes.

Usually, Kai was shrouded in an air of languor. He was the most laid back and amiable person I'd ever met. It was a nice change compared to Gwydion and Nikolaos. Sometimes, I wondered if he really was as relaxed as I thought or if anyone seemed serene beside the other two men. No, it wasn't just my perception. Tonight, I could feel his energy humming off his body like tiny insects in the air around him. His power felt like pinpricks of heat, the energy of life that therianthropes seem to radiate if they aren't controlling it. Unless it was a full moon, Kai was better at managing it than this.

'What's wrong?' I instantly asked.

Kai looked at me with those round, kitty-cat eyes. He smiled at me, a flash of sharp white teeth seeming brighter in his dark face. There was a tension around his eyes and mouth that weren't usually there.

'Hey, darlin',' he said, American accent thick and sweet like honey. 'You meant to be seein' Rune tonight?'

It was very unlike Kai to forget anything. There was a sharp mind in all of that sleepiness.

I nodded, then frowned.

'What's wrong?' I asked again, this time reaching out to place a hand on his arm.

Kai's skin was feverishly warm. Most therianthropes, depending on the animal, ran much hotter than humans. At least, that's what I'd been told. I'd never actually met any other therians.

'Nothin', darlin', but Rune ain't here tonight.'

I frowned harder.

'Where is he?'

With my hand resting on his arm, I could feel the tension ripple through his body. Vampire senses meant I could also see the pulse in his throat speed up, and the pupil in his kitty-cat eyes widen just a touch. Still, he tried to smile at me as if nothing were wrong. If I were human, maybe I'd believe it.

'Kai, what is the matter?' Third time's a charm, right?

Wrong. Kai moved his arm away from me so we weren't touching. Therianthropes love physical contact, something about it soothes them—even Kai, whose animal form was a solitary one. I'd had to adjust to Kai's tactile nature; I wasn't a fan of people carelessly touching my body, but with Kai, it had become almost natural.

'Nothin',' he said, 'but Rune ain't here. I s'pose he must've forgotten to tell you.'

'When will he be back?'

Kai shrugged.

'Well, do you want some company tonight?'

Kai shook his head. Again, it was very unlike him. I trusted Kai to tell me if something were wrong. He wasn't secretive like the other men in our life. Nonetheless, anxiety twisted my gut, as if his tension were contagious.

'Niko's in town,' I said.

That made him genuinely smile. Kai knew how much I was struggling with his constant disappearances to carry out the ominous biddings of our Empress. It wasn't so much loneliness as it was concern. Smoke and daggers weren't fun when it was your master/lover. If I just thought he was being secretive for the sake of it, then maybe I'd have been less worried, but something about our conversation last night had left me feeling like there were things Nikolaos wasn't telling me, which I should know. Now Gwydion had gone away suddenly without telling me, and Kai was acting uncharacteristically tense. Combined, it was enough for my anxiety to skyrocket.

'Then what're ya doin' here? Go spend time with lover boy.'

I wasn't sure Nikolaos would like being referred to as "lover boy", not that he was here to complain. Besides, it wasn't an inaccurate description.

'He's... predisposed tonight.'

Kai cocked his head to one side as if he wanted to ask what I meant, then he shook his head, and said instead, 'I'm still feelin' a bit jumpy after the full moon a few days ago. I'm not gonna be much company tonight, darlin'.'

It was a very polite lie. One that said clearly he didn't want to talk anymore and wanted me to leave him. A few days before the full moon, therianthropes do get fidgety, and even sometimes one or two nights after. However, the full moon had been six days prior. I sighed and then smiled at Kai. It wasn't a happy smile.

On the way home, I passed an off-licence with one of those giant, red neon clocks where the time rolls over the screen. Letters flashed across it, drawing attention to the fact they were open twenty-four hours a day. The clock made it eleven. I had about three hours left until Nikolaos would be home. Usually, finding ways to fill that time wouldn't bother me; unfortunately, tonight I had an unyielding sense of unsettlement.

By the time two a.m rolled around, I was practically bouncing with the anticipation of hearing how the opening of Atlas had gone. Anything to distract me from the unshakable thoughts that something was wrong with Gwydion and Kai. A part of me felt like I shouldn't have left Kai alone, or at least tried to push him to explain further where Gwydion was. If something had been really, truly wrong, then he'd have told me, right? If I kept telling myself that maybe it would make me feel better. No matter how much I tried to rationalise, the knot in my stomach didn't unwind.

When it reached four a.m, according to the clock on the computer upstairs, the anxiety was overwhelming. Where was Nikolaos? He should have been home by now.

If you'd asked me a day ago if there were any downsides to winter's long hours of darkness, I would have said, no way. Tonight, pacing back and forth through the living room, feeling the press of dawn approaching, inexorably, almost painfully slowly, I felt very differently. Generally, dawn signified a vampire's impending death; vulnerability, until dusk consumed the sunlight, and we were predators once more. Now it was just another hour Nikolaos was inexplicably absent. The quicker, or in this case, slower, dawn came was just more reason to worry.

If either of us had a phone, I would have called him—even if we had a landline, I could have tried to track Atlas's number. But we did not. Overwhelmed with worry, I wasn't thinking clearly. The thought of a phone stayed niggling in the back of my head, as if there were some vital piece of information of which I just wasn't thinking. I continued to pace, trying to clear my head through the consuming sense that something was wrong. Nikolaos would not have simply not returned without telling me. Gwydion wouldn't have gone away without letting me know. Kai wouldn't be so on edge or lie to me unless there was something he wasn't telling me about Gwydion.

Back and forth; back and forth. From the dining room table at the back of the room to the front door. Waiting, waiting, waiting. And then...

Aha!

There may be no physical phone for me to pick up and dial, but there was a metaphysical one that worked almost as well—if not a little capriciously at times. I slapped myself on the forehead with the palm of my hand. I should have thought of it sooner.

Closing my eyes, I visualised a telephone sitting on the vanity in my bedroom. It was one of those desktop rotary phones popular in the twenties. I'd never actually used one in real life, but it worked in my head. I'd quickly learned that sometimes it was better not to argue with metaphysics if it worked. Sometimes masters and their vassals could communicate telepathically. Not all could do it, usually only the older ones, but Nikolaos and I could.

I envisioned rolling that numberless dial around, letting it fall on invisible numbers, calling something that didn't exist and yet did, at the same time. I waited for the ringing tone to start in my vision, clutching the receiver to my ear with both hands clenching until fingers mottled.

Nothing happened. Just an endless ringing chiming through my head until it was deafening. I pulled myself away from the vision in time to see the first touches of sunlight, whispering promises of golden life into the cold, night sky. A new panic began to fill me. The one all vampires have when dawn approaches. No matter what type of life you live as a vampire, no matter how much you pretend to be mundane or wrap yourself in decadence, when the sun approaches, we are all reminded that we are dead. Prisoners to the day. Cursed to spend an eternity shrouded in shadows.

Tiredness hit me like bricks slamming into my body. One moment, I was energised with panicked adrenaline; the next, it was almost too much effort to keep the heaviness of my eyelids open. If I stayed upstairs, I would soon collapse in a room where huge windows invited the sunlight in like a welcome guest. I would die, and then fry. Would I feel it, would fizzling in the sunlight be enough pain to fight the quietness of death? I didn't want to find out.

Using the final shreds of energy I could muster, I fled downstairs to the safety of a windowless warren.

CHAPTER 11

I rolled in the sheets, pushing them off me, so they fell like silk water onto the floor. My eyes fluttered open. I instinctively reached up to rub my eyes, the furred cuffs of my jean jacket rubbing against my face. That wasn't right. I never usually fell asleep in a jacket of all things. Sitting up suddenly, I realised I was still fully clothed, boots and all. Memories of last night came flooding back, accompanying it, the unwelcome tightness in my stomach.

Logically, there was no way for Nikolaos to have come home when I was sleeping. He'd have been as dead to the world as I was. Still, I had to check.

Nikolaos's room was larger than mine—and mine was already unnecessarily big—and done in all grand, dark brown wood from the huge four-poster bed to antique armoire. It was all very swanky, decorated with old furniture that looked straight out of a sixteenth-century palace. For all I knew, it was. Unsurprisingly, Nikolaos wasn't waiting safely tucked into the ruby red silk sheets. Nor was he in either of the downstairs bathrooms, or the clothes room bigger than both of our bedrooms.

Still wearing last night's clothing, I rushed upstairs. I would go to Atlas first and see if any of the staff there had seen Nikolaos leaving last night. My mind whirred with possibilities ranging from bad to much, much worse. Best case scenario was that he'd been called urgently back to Amphitrite's side, but that didn't explain why I'd not been able to contact him. Worst case, well, I didn't really know. There were too many worst-case scenarios. I had never been this pessimistic as a human. It probably had less to do with becoming a vampire and more because of *how* I became one. Getting murdered really does make you jaded. Who'd have thought it? Honestly, there was also the possibility that Nikolaos had just got carried away with one of the attending ladies. I just didn't think that was the case. One, it was improbable that even if he did bed one of the women (or men), that she (or he) would have any room suitably light-tight for a vampire; two, it *still* didn't explain why I hadn't been able to sense him metaphysically.

I had my hand on the front door handle when I sensed the weight of two powers coming through the forest. One of them I recognised. Necromancy calls to a vampire like a false profit calls to the weak-willed, whispering promises of life after death, light in the darkness, warmth in the cold. Promises built on lies. No matter how much you know they are false assurances, it still feels impossible to say no. I, as a nymph, had some natural resistance to Gwydion's necromancy. Through me, Nikolaos had also mustered a level of immunity he'd otherwise lacked. I had no idea how lesser vampires resisted the call.

The second power was new, one I hadn't felt before. As far as I could tell, it wasn't hostile. There was a vaguely familiar edge to it, a certain taste to the gentle pressure that was trying to get a feel for me. Magick practitioners don't seem to sweat something as mundane as a handshake, instead opting for the fancier greeting of testing power. It worked in sort of a similar way. If they were trying to be friendly, it would be just a gentle brush of power, just a small taste to get a feel for each other. Like with physical handshakes, though, some people pressed harder. Whoever this was being particularly polite.

I opened the door just before Gwydion knocked. Seeing him standing in front of me eased a part of the tension that made every muscle in my body vibrate. At least he was okay. Or that's what I thought until I saw his face. Gwydion's natural facial set of superior blankness was good enough to give even Nikolaos a run for his money. Tonight, there was something sombre about how he glided towards me, a nervousness that was very unlike him.

The woman who accompanied him was only an inch or two taller than me, all the while radiating an energy that somehow made her seem taller. It wasn't so much magickal energy as a content confidence that seemed to say she was perfectly at ease with who she was. Confidence, when it isn't arrogance, can be a very underrated feature in people. Her face was pale and triangular with high cheekbones and soft, pink cheeks. At first glance, I thought her eyes were hazel, and then I realised that didn't quite do them justice. The ring around her iris was a dark, stormy grey. Light, grey-green framed her pupil with shocking slices of golden-brown striking from the pupil like streaks of sunlight from behind a cloud.

Her hair was such a dark brown it was almost black, cut into a neat mullet, curling at the end to brush her shoulders in lighter brown ringlets. She wore a black turtleneck tucked into black, oversized jeans with white stitching up the side. A wide leather belt cinched her slender waist with a large silver buckle glinting in the moonlight. It highlighted the slenderness of her waist, voluptuous curves of her body, and ample bust. If it weren't for her body's very feminine shape, the face would have seemed more androgynous. She seemed to skate on the line of masculine handsomeness and beauty, but in the end, there was a certain softness that made her more beautiful.

The first hint I had that the unknown woman was a witch came from the pentagram hanging visibly from a silver chain around her neck. The chain matched the rings through both sides of her nostril. I realised the reason her power felt familiar was that Adalia had a similar energy, one that managed to be both forceful and amiable at the same time.

'Scarlet,' Gwydion said, drawing my attention to him. Gwydion's almost seven-foot frame looked even taller compared to how short the witch and I were. He was watching me intently with those piercing, icy turquoise eyes set too deeply into a painfully skinny face. 'This is Sylvie.'

Sylvie stuck a small hand out to me; she'd tattooed three small dots on her upper middle finger.

'Sylvie Mugridge,' she said, with a small smile. There was a faint accent to the words, one lost in the monotone of her voice.

I smiled back, taking her hand in mine. She had a good handshake. 'Scarlet Cherie.'

'Gwydion, I don't mean to be rude, but I need to go. Now.'

Gwydion raised a white eyebrow, almost lost in the alabaster of his face. He was even paler than Nikolaos and I.

'Such urgency, young nymph, whatever is the matter?' he asked, but the insolence was clear.

I glowered at him.

'Nikolaos didn't come home last night. Talking of which, where were you?' I wafted my hand in front of my face, shooing the question away. 'Actually, it doesn't matter; I need to go.'

'I do not understand your concern; this is not the first time Nikolaos has not returned to your bedside.'

'But he said he'd come home last night.'

'And our Nikolaos is a man of such honour.' The sarcasm was thick enough to taste, like something bitter.

'I'm sure he'd love to hear you call him *our* Nikolaos,' I retorted scathingly.

'Your haste is palpable, Scarlet. Is there something you are not telling me?'

'No,' I said quickly, and then wondered why I'd lied.

'Then why such a rush?'

'I just have a bad feeling, Gwydion.'

Sylvie was looking at both of us in turn, studying us as if we were doing something much more interesting than just talking.

'I'm afraid,' he said, bifurcated tongue slithering out from between dagger teeth, 'that we come bearing only bad tidings to add to your consternation.'

Sylvie added, 'May we come in?'

I opened my mouth to protest, saw the sincerity in Sylvie's twinkling eyes, closed it, and held open the door.

Gwydion and Sylvie both sat on opposite ends of the sofa facing the front door; I sat on the other with my back to it. I crossed my ankle over my knee, jiggling it up and down. It was the seventh position change in under three minutes. I just couldn't sit still.

'How much do you know about the Syndicate of Occultists?' Sylvie asked.

'Nothing, I've never heard of them before.' I remembered something, turning my face to look at where Gywdion sat. 'Wait, that's not true. You mentioned them to me last year. Although you didn't tell me who they were, just that I'd find out about them sooner or later.'

An expression I'd rarely seen from Gwydion played over his face: uncertainty.

'I may have been... misguided in my nonchalance.'

'What about the Mystics' Guild?' Sylvie enquired.

I shook my head. 'Never heard of them.'

Sylvie cast a look in the direction of Gwydion, not quite hostile but not entirely friendly either. Gwydion replied with a tepid shrug.

'It did not seem necessary.'

'Is there a point to these questions?' I asked, shuffling into yet another position. Then I added, 'Sorry, that came out ruder than I meant it to.'

'Sylvie is the dominant founder of the Mystics' Guild of Thaumaturgy,' Gwydion explained.

'The Guild is a sort of preternatural coalition. We act as a support network for those who don't have other groups in their species, offering protection or kinship. Each group has an elected spokesperson to speak on their behalf on the board, unless they have no other of their kind, in which case they automatically qualify. As long as they don't practice dark occultism, we welcome all species,' Sylvie said as if reciting. I fought not to slide my eyes in the direction of Gwydion at the last part.

'It sounds like a great idea. But what has it got to do with the Syndicate of Occultists?' I asked.

Sylvie made a gesturing motion at Gwydion, giving him the floor to speak.

'The Syndicate was established in the eighteenth century as an amalgamate of born necromancers. Unfortunately, it did not work quite with the ease of Sylvie's Guild, becoming a league of megalomaniacs. The Syndicate holds the belief that, because of their affiliation with the dead, they can become the judge, jury and, most importantly, executioner of preternatural species.' He looked disgusted.

'You said they'd wiped out most of the redcaps, or the females so they couldn't reproduce. They can't have done that with other species, too, surely? That's just too... too evil!' I exclaimed.

'We haven't got to the nasty bit yet, Scarlet,' Sylvie said. I gave her wide eyes.

'Oh, god.' I took a deep breath in. 'Okay, tell me.'

'The Guild,' Sylvie continued, 'has always been fairly small. We're a humble organisation, everything is voluntary based, and people can come and go as they please. Recently, we've had a huge influx of creatures seeking protection—people from all over the world, powerful creatures, even royalty. I mean'—she began to sound flustered—'we really aren't equipped to deal with this many people. But we can't turn our backs on them. It goes against everything we stand for.' Sylvie was tripping over her own words towards the end, not shouting or giving any inflexion to her monotone voice, but talking too fast and clumsily.

'I have heard whispers of their plots. It appears,' Rune said, 'that they have turned their attention to a power closer to home.'

'What does that mean?'

'It means, Scarlet, that they heard the call of my power last year when we reincarnated Maglark. They also felt your own magick shutting down such great evil. Such an ostentatious display of magick was sure to attract undesired attention. Unfortunately, even I did not foresee it extending to the Syndicate's scrutiny. I have declined their invitation to join the Syndicate, as they knew I would countless times before. They cannot let so much unpoliced power free.' My heart was suddenly in my throat, stomach twisting with panic so intense I froze in place. 'It is speculated they have already judged and juried us.'

'So all that's left is execution,' I whispered.

Gwydion nodded, grimly.

The megalomaniac, self-appointed police force of the preternatural world were after Gwydion and me. A force big enough to have even Gwydion spooked. And Nikolaos was missing. This night was turning out to be really, *really* bad.

CHAPTER 12

Sylvie had arranged transport for me to go to the Mystic Guild's base in Edinburgh the following night; Gwydion would travel up during the day. Sylvie and Kai would be travelling up tonight, but there were no trains that I could risk getting without hitting daylight. Gwydion was certain I'd be safe for tonight. I wished I could share that surety.

I'd taken the train ticket she'd bought for me, said goodbye to the two of them, and gone upstairs to shove the ticket in the drawer of Nikolaos's desk. I still needed to pack for tomorrow and feed tonight, but first, I needed to find Nikolaos. My urgency earlier in the night seemed tame compared to the franticness I now felt as I ran into town. Gwydion was convinced that the Syndicate wouldn't care for Nikolaos. Vampires and necromancers had a turbulent history, and many years ago, they had come to an agreement to stay out of vampire politics. Vampires have their own monarchy and police; they didn't need—or want—the Syndicate stepping in. Unsurprisingly, vampires don't like the level of control necromancers have over us. However, we dramatically outnumber them. The two groups have reached a sort of prolonged détente.

If I were a pure vampire, they probably would have left me alone, too. They didn't want me because of the part of me that was dead. No, they wanted the side of me that was very much alive. The nymph blood that still ran through my veins, igniting me with magick of the Earth and Her warmth.

Some vampires can fly. I can't. But the way I sped through the streets of Britchelstone was practically levitation. There was no time for my feet to touch the floor—just sheer desperation pushing me through the night until I reached Londinium road. I pulled my collar up around my ears. It looked like I was huddling from the icy winter air when, in reality, I was shielding myself from any passerby.

Parked outside the front of Atlas was a vintage, burgundy car. Nikolaos's Buick was sitting there abandoned in the cold night. Nikolaos was many things, but careless was never one. Leaving his car parked outside was much too sloppy.

I thought Atlas would be open by now, but the closed doors and lack of bouncers indicated otherwise. Only the flickering of the faux flames behind their metal prison gave any indication that Atlas wasn't just another one of the derelict businesses that lined Londinium road. In the shadow of darkness, Atlas looked just as tempting as it had a few nights prior. Something about the metal bars, glistening black walls, and golden embellishment screamed pleasure and sin as if through those double doors awaited your wildest dreams and darkest nightmares. Nikolaos was a master of pleasure and pain. He knew how to offer violence, make it taste like fine, sweet wine accompanying a decadent dessert; he also knew how to make pleasure something dark, twisted, so you didn't know whether to beg for more or to stop. Atlas looked fitting for that particular set of skills. Walking past, it was hard to tell what the establishment's nature was, but a part of you yearned to see what Atlas offered inside.

The light from a distant streetlamp caught on the golden metal in the right door at a peculiar angle. Stepping closer, I could see that the door was slightly ajar. Open just enough to catch the light and draw attention to itself, though not enough to see the crack unless you were looking for it. Again, very, very careless. I pulled the door open tentatively. In my head, the sound of the door creaking open pierced the night with eerie resonance. In reality, it probably wasn't that loud.

With no lights on, or windows leading outside, Atlas was cast in darkness. Only the slightest glint of red velvet and gold shone dimly in the waning crack of light from the door as it closed. The door shut behind me, locking closed with an echoing *click*. If I'd been human, then I would have been completely blind in the stretching blackness. With vampire vision, I could make out clear silhouettes of the furniture.

'Niko!' I called. 'Nikolaos, are you here?'

No answer.

The air smelt of stale alcohol and people. Perfume, aftershave, sweat, and that warm, alive smell that all humans have. One that lets you know blood is pumping through their veins, pulsating life through their bodies. So fragile. Underneath it all, I could smell something else, something that made me stop in my tracks and take in an even deeper breath. Whatever it was, it wasn't human. It was also more potent than the other faint, mingling aromas as if whatever it was were still here.

I took a step further into the room, stepping as silently as I could. The closer to the hallway at the end of the bar area I got, the stronger I could smell it. And then I could feel it, too. The slight pulsating of power, as if whoever was here was trying to null their abilities so I wouldn't sense them. This power was a flavour I had never felt before. Cold, but not like Nikolaos's vampire powers or Gwydion's icy touch with the dead. This was cool like water from a fresh spring, refreshing at first and then teeth-chattering and deadly. My fire did not like this power. Not one little bit. I could feel my fire screaming at me, *Stop, turn back, run away!* I pushed the nagging thoughts aside. Tried to soothe the anxious flames flickering somewhere inside me only magick could touch.

Much like the front door, the door to the 'feeding room' was ajar. I hesitated with my hand hovering over the solid metal. From right outside, I could feel the energy coming from the feeding room like a winter lake flowing cautiously. My fire was still begging me to turn back; it knew this magick was formidable. So powerful it dampened our own, left us fizzling out and smoking instead of roaring. I should have turned back, listened to the warning of the primal instinct in me which knew of danger beyond my conscious could ever understand.

But Nikolaos was still missing, and I had to know where he was. Did I listen to my flames, take heed to their warning and turn back? Or did I open the door and confront whatever waited for me inside. If I ran away now, I still wouldn't be any closer to finding Nikolaos. There was no guarantee that whatever awaited me would be any help, either. There was the potential that I was just stepping into further danger.

With that comforting last thought, I opened the door.

CHAPTER 13

Power flowed over me in a wash of fluid magick. Whilst it wasn't exactly hostile, it wasn't friendly either. I tried to reach down inside me to seek strength from my flames only to find they were also struggling against the force of the power. My pulse sped up. This had been a mistake; I knew it had been one before I'd opened the door. So why did I do it? I was desperate to find Nikolaos but not desperate enough to be so careless.

For a moment, the darkness and wave of magick blinded me. All I could smell was the sharp freshness of flowing streams surrounded by moss and bracken. In the distance, the sound of water lapping gently over rocks chimed through the room. I was overwhelmed and blind, only able to hear and smell a scene that I was nowhere near.

I blinked into the room. Stumbling at the sudden readjustment as I focused on the here and now. In the back of my mind, the distant sound of flowing water still rang through my head like a soothing melody, and the room had the feeling of a cold, winter wind despite being indoors in a windowless building.

Sitting on one of the leather sofas was a man, a stranger, who, although I had never met, I just knew had no place being in Nikolaos's office. He wore an expensive-looking suit in black and pinstripe, emphasising his long, slim body. The shirt underneath the done-up suit jacket was a deep cerulean with a cobalt blue tie fastened neatly around his neck. He turned a pale face up to me, a small smile playing along thin lips. I'd seen some shockingly beautiful eyes almost every day over the last six months spending time with Nikolaos, Kai, and even Gwydion, but whoever this strange man was had them all beat.

Turquoise was too mild a word. They were the cyan of Greek oceans in summer, when the sun heats the clear water and makes it something luscious in which to bathe. Teal and sapphire danced around the pupil like waves hitting the rocks of a mountain, white foam flashing through all that blue before disappearing. I mean it literally. The blues in his eyes danced and crashed and washed through his iris, mimicking the flow of an ocean.

A Van Dyke beard framed the lower half of his long, pointed face. The hair on his head, beard, and eyebrows were greying around the edges, but where the colour wasn't consumed by age, was an ocean green so light it was almost white. He'd slicked back the short hair on his head, so it was as neat and as perfectly in place as the rest of him.

'Ms Cherie, I have been expecting you,' he said, still smiling, although it didn't quite reach those strange and beautiful eyes.

'That's funny,' I replied, 'because I haven't been expecting you.'

'No, you have not, which is precisely the problem.'

I frowned.

'What does that mean?'

'Please'—he motioned to the free seat beside him on the sofa—'ensconce yourself, Ms Cherie.'

I shook my head. 'I'm okay standing.'

The man shrugged at me. It was a graceful movement, one similar to Nikolaos's.

'As you wish, Ms Cherie.' He spoke in a smooth, upper-crust accent with a vaguely Eastern European intonation. Russian, I thought, but it had faded enough that it was hard to tell for certain. His voice was as neat and controlled as his hair and clothing. 'Please allow me to introduce myself. I am Prince Vodan.'

'Prince?' And then it dawned on me. 'As in Prince to the Empress?'

Vodan's smile widened, and this time it lit up his face like the sun illuminates cold seas at dawn.

'Ah, so you have heard of us. The Empress and I were beginning to wonder if we were as surreptitious to you as you were to us.'

'Where's Nikolaos?' I asked.

Vodan's smile faltered for the first time, a flash of something close to anger darkening the blue of his eyes until they were the green and grey of deep, stormy seas.

'He is by our Empress's side.' The contempt was palpable. I tried to use our mutual disrelish to forge some sort of mutual understanding.

'You don't sound any happier about that than I am,' I said, forcing a smile, trying to appeal to him that I wasn't hostile. Confused, yes, but not malicious. Hostility was a path I never intentionally pursued.

He flashed me an inimical leer. 'I dare not question the desires of a Goddess.'

I almost went to ask if he meant Goddess literally, but something in his face made the words falter before they'd even formed. He spoke with a pensive reverence only the truly devout could muster. I'd never met Amphitrite personally, yet I was willing to bet good money that she wasn't a *real* Goddess. Or at least not the real Goddess of her namesake. Then again, Vodan's power had an apparent affinity with the ocean, and Amphitrite was the Goddess-Queen of the sea, so who was I to say it wasn't legitimately her in the flesh? As a nymph myself, I wasn't in a position to question anyone's divinity.

'Why are you here, Vodan?' I implored. My tactic of mutual understanding hadn't worked, maybe showing my genuine perplexion would help.

'I have been commanded to bring you to our Empress's side. Your master'—he sounded disgusted—'has delayed his Empress's ordinance far too long. Amphitrite is a woman of many finesses,' Vodan continued, thin lips twisting into a wistful simper, 'alas patience is a virtue even she lacks.'

Vodan stood in a swift motion as fast as any vampire could move. He was just suddenly in front of me, and I hadn't been expecting it, so the movement stunned me momentarily.

Regaining myself, I began to back away towards the door, trying to put more distance between Vodan and me. Vodan's thalassic energy pulsed through the room once again. This time it was not gentle or refreshing but wild and herculean. I couldn't breathe through the beating of power as if I were drowning in invisible waves. Waves that fought and rolled through the ocean with an unmatched fury.

Staring into those swirling blue eyes of a storm, I couldn't move. I tried to reach down to the part of me that contained all my own power. I coaxed and called my flames to come to the surface, to alight me with magick and make us burn hot and bright against the cold rage of his power. It was like trying to light a naked fire in the pouring rain. Impossible. Vodan tutted at me.

'Nikolaos ought to have obliged his Empress's decree sooner.' He sighed, taking a further step towards me. 'Now it is too late.'

Before I had time to ask what was too late, the power, which had been receding like the drawing back of a wave before it devours the rocks below, crashed over me. I was choking on invisible water, the burning sensation of salt and cold ocean waves drowning me. I could feel the sea flowing up my nose, down my throat, until I was spluttering and gurgling on the sensation. His magick doused me in the tears of the sea; all I could see was blackness, my eyes burning and stinging as if I were blinking in salt. I could smell the crisp brininess of sulfide and seaweed and water touched by the hands of countless aquatic creatures. I fell to my knees, blindly choking onto the carpet, trying to cough up a sensation. But you can't force your body to purge what is not real.

Darkness flooded me in a tempestuous swell like the final waves that consume the drowning man, sealing his doomed fate. Some part of my consciousness let me know I had fallen onto the ground below. Carpet scraped at my skin as I writhed and fought against the unbeatable. Swells of the ocean crashing and lapping over itself and me, the desperate pleas of sea birds, and the violent melodies of stormy winds whistling tunes of seduction to sailors echoed through the room, deafening me. The sounds grew increasingly louder until it all married to one, crazed noise of thundering chaos. My body ached, from the pains of my throat as it convulsed against the force of ghostly seas to the roaring sounds that made my head quake.

With burning lungs, frozen bones, and sensory subjugation, I felt the sensation of the carpet below my writhing body beginning to slip into nothing. A boundless murk consumed me; I felt the world go still, stranding me to wallow in the sudden dark silence until there was nothing.

CHAPTER 14

Melody; soft and sweet, causing goosebumps to ripple up my flesh. Édith Piaf's voice floated through the darkness like the clouds tumbling through crisp spring skies. I was dancing in a golden-lit room, consumed by the sensation of Nikolaos's body holding me as we swayed the way blades of grass dance in the breeze. So beautiful; so tender. The smell of cinnamon, and smoke, and flowers that had dried almost to dust but never lost their perfume floated through the air. I took in a deep breath, drawing in the scent of my lover, and moved my arms to hold him closer to me.

There was no familiar musk to breathe in further. Only the painfully brisk stench of old stone worn down by stale water and glacial air. My hands met something cold, something solid, as chains rattled at the persistence of my movement.

Burning. My wrists burned. Such a soaring, intense heat that started where the chains bit into my wrists' flesh and shot up my arms as if following the route of my veins.

Rationalise, Scarlet, try and rationalise.

I can't get burnt, so why was my arm alight with pain? The only things I knew that could burn vampires this way were either silver or holy objects. As a deity, I was immune to holy objects, but we'd never tested silver on me. The chains would indicate that that was the most likely culprit to the heart-stopping affliction.

I still could not open my eyes, but now I had noticed the pain, it was all that I could feel. The sensation of burning pokers shoved into my bloodstream pulsed through my upper body. What was meant to be a scream came out as a strangled keen. I lamented, body rigid with pain, tension sending a shudder from toes to spine that made me buck backwards. My back hit violently against the stone wall behind me, causing my hands to further fight against my restraints.

Each time my flesh rattled against the chains, another pain-induced buck sent my body battling against the suspension. I was trapped in a vicious cycle of pain and movement, and helplessness. Biting my lip hard enough to send a spill of copper fluid into my mouth, I forced my body to be still. My limbs were stiff with agony, muscles so tight that that in itself was painful, but at least I was still. My hands were curled in a fist; even if I had wanted to risk opening them, I didn't think I had enough movement to be able to.

A sound somewhere between a sob and wail escaped my lips, cutting through the sound of music that just days before had been sweet and beautiful, an abstract souvenir of tenderness shared. Now the lyrics sounded grating and sinister; an eldritch melody.

Finally, I forced myself to open my eyes and face the daunting reality which awaited me. As a child, I'd always believed that closing my eyes tightly shut, or hiding under the comfort of the duvet, would protect me from the phantasmal monsters which lurked in the darkness. Now, I knew that whatever monsters prowled would not be stopped by my own denial and that they were not confined to skulk only in shadow.

Tonight, there was no warmth or comfort in which I could seek refuge, no duvet or blanket to shield me from such a dire fate, only the keen wind blowing distantly against stone walls, the sound of water dripping onto the ground below, and the pain that radiated through my body as I burned.

Now that my eyes were open and focused on something other than excruciating pain, manic terror sliced its way through me. I tried to concentrate on my surroundings as the song started replaying, the music reverberating through the room, a haunting echo. As I had suspected, the room was built of stone turned black with age. Green, diaphanous fabric cascaded from hooks on the ceiling, tumbling chaotically to the ground below, with black consuming some of the green like a growing shadow where it had fallen into puddles. Behind the wall beside me was a window; the cold, winter breeze flowed through the room, each blow of air sending the fabric floating outwards, and then pulling it back, sucking it against the half-open glass, as if it were suffocating. Only the wall opposite me was covered in opaque cloth, hindering my view of what lurked behind.

I was bound to wooden beams in an X-Cross shape, black metal framed a hole in the wood where silver chains threaded through, encasing my wrists. I whimpered at the sight of sizzling flesh; silver excoriated the skin of my wrists, red and raw indents running like a macabre bracelet, marring me. Seeing it made the pain more real, and I fought the overwhelming urge to pull and tug until I was free of the shackles. I forced my head to turn away, looking anywhere except the odious wounds.

I looked down my body to see my feet were not bound by silver but old metal shackles which encased my ankles. My clothes from before had been replaced by an outfit which made my throat tight with fear and disgust. Satin drowned my body in the form of a turquoise chemise hanging past my knees. Two wide slits went up the side, revealing the curve of my arse where my underwear had been stolen from my body. Fashioned from tulle, a cyan net bloomed around the satin from under my bust like a fishnet floats in the water before damning its catch. The netting pooled down to the ground in a wash of blue, catching around the shackles which imprisoned me.

I heard the creak of metal at the same time a rush of air curled through the room, just strong enough to send the fabric blemishing my body swirling around the chains and me. Footsteps echoed on the stone, the sound of feet sloshing against puddles in the cracks of the ground. Movement disrupted the flow of air, sending the opaque fabric wall dancing through the air as if weak hands beat against the jade cloth. I felt my heartbeat speed up, as much as any living deads' heart could. Whoever approached was closer now; I could hear the heaviness of their feet slamming as they approached. The sound was... wrong. Neither shoe nor flesh could imitate that wet, slapping sound. I thought of fish flapping against the deck of a boat, their gills catching in the final light of day as they fought against their dying moments, gasping to be back in the water they called home, the home from which they had been torn. The thought consumed me, the sound of gulls squawking and ocean tides lapping against the wooden vessel as the sea breeze sent the sail shuddering. Wind whipped against my face, bringing with it the stench of aquatic life and salt. I squeezed my eyes shut, forcing away the flashing images of sails in the wind and vast, untouched oceans which I had never seen, images of someone else's life from long, long ago.

Somewhere in the chaos of sunlit seas, I had lost my sense of the here and now. Someone had been approaching, someone who had chained me up and stolen my clothing along with my dignity. Now was not the time to lose focus. I reached down inside myself to where my power lay. In my mind, I saw it as starting in my sternum, as if the fire grew around my heart wild and free, spreading warmth into my belly and expanding through my entire body. It wasn't so much reaching with a hand, albeit a metaphysical one, as it was with an intention. The way some people reach with a gaze to plead or ask or show love. Some people, like Adalia, would say it was a gaze of sorts. I was looking into myself with my third eye, an eye which had taken me twenty years to open, and now I had, it never really closed. With my two eyes closed, I used that third ocular to find my power.

Since gaining control of my magick, reaching out to the energy that empowered me had become like second-nature. All it took was a moment of concentration, and then my fire would awaken like an inferno lion unwinding from its catnap, ready to prowl the Savannah. Tonight, it did not happen. I could feel my flames, but they were neither beastly nor roaring. No, tonight, they were damp and weak; fire caught in the rainfall. This aggressive magick, whatever it was, was not only fighting against me but also my power.

I could have screamed my frustration into the darkness, let my anguish drown out the howls of angry oceans and crazed birds. But that was no longer me. I screamed for no one; my wails would not be heard by anyone else who wished me ill, not after the events of last year. With that thought, I did all I could think of: I tried to reach out to Nikolaos again. As my master, his touch could make me stronger, the same way I could aid his power levels.

I pictured that familiar rotary dial landline, which had become so familiar to me it almost felt tangible, despite me never using one outside the corners of my psyche. It was harder to visualise the phone than usual; every time I tried to concentrate on picturing my desk at home, the sounds of squawking birds would overpower my senses, or the warm shadowy corners of my room would blast into blue like the spring skies when the sun casts too-bright light down onto the earth. I'd been learning to meditate with Gwydion and Kai; I used all those months of training to focus my mind on the scene I wanted. The phantom sounds began to disappear until I was left with an almost echoing silence, but it was silence nonetheless. I could see the phone sitting on the vanity, waiting for me the way it always did when I needed to contact Nikolaos. I, as a silhouette figure in my head, picked up the receiver, turned the numberless dial, and waited for the ringing to start.

Silence.

'Come on, Niko, please, please, pick up. Respond!' I begged silently, at the same time as someone grabbed onto my wrist, curling fingers that were too long and too slimy to be human around me, slamming my hand into the silver shackles.

My vision began to shift from the shadowy comfort of my bedroom to a stone room where water dripped behind shimmering fabric, and something sinister waited impatiently. Music had started playing again; maybe it had never really stopped, that same fucking song going over and over again.

CHAPTER 15

My eyes flared open, eyelids batting wildly as I tried to blink away the distortion in my vision. I could make out the shape of a tall, slender man beside me, leaning one elbow on the wood of my mount, using his other hand to stroke down the rough texture absentmindedly. Noticing me come around, the man straightened his body, clasping both hands behind his back as he took a step backwards away from where I was suspended. With my vision cleared, I could see him clearly. I recognised him as Vodan, Amphitrite's Prince, and my kidnapper.

Cerulean still framed Vodan's upper body, except he'd now lost the suit jacket somewhere, and the tie was looser around his throat. His Van Dyke beard's moustache was curled upwards with his smile, giving the illusion of couth. I knew better. Couth people did not kidnap you and chain you to sinister wooden beams, nor did they use their magick to break you down to nothing, no matter how friendly they pretended to be.

'Ms Cherie,' he said, green-white bristles moving as he spoke and swirling blue eyes shining with an inappropriate glee. 'You are awake.'

'I think we're past pleasantries, Vodan. You can drop the *Ms*,' I said in a surprisingly calm voice, especially after the pitiful wails that had escaped me mere minutes before.

Vodan shrugged, long arms still clasped behind his back.

'As you wish, Ms—Scarlet.' His lips tugged upwards at my name, his eyes bashfully averting my gaze.

'What I wish is for you to let me go,' and this time, I sounded much less sure of myself.

That disgustingly ill-fitting smile grew into something rapturous.

'We all wish for that which we cannot have. Your Nikolaos has proven that by denying our Empress. He must face the consequences of such transgressions.'

'What is it that the Empress wants, Vodan. What has he denied her that warrants such a response?' I pleaded, tears beginning to burn behind my eyes. Fear and helplessness were starting to take over that previous bravado I had managed to muster, a weakness I had never experienced until last year when Maglark murdered me. And now I was in the throes of it again. What had Nikolaos done; how could he be so reckless to put us both in such danger? He had looked me in the eyes and sworn to me that we were safe. He had lied to me. Anger bubbled up within the sense of paralysing forlorn. Fight or flight battled within me, the arrogant instinct of the predator which I had become fighting to overcome this powerlessness. That anger burnt through me, the first stirrings of my magick flaring to life like a match igniting in the darkness. I felt a spurt of relief that my flames were back when Vodan tutted at me, and that swarm of power washed over me again, damping my own.

'I forewarned Amphitrite that it is not Nikolaos who holds the power, despite his title as your master.'

'I'll go with you, Vodan. I didn't know that Amphitrite wanted to meet me until tonight,' I pleaded. 'We can go tonight, now, just unchain me, and I'll come with you. I'll talk to her with Nikolaos.'

Vodan smiled bitterly. 'I now see it is no longer the power she truly desires.'

Fearing I already knew the answer, I whispered, 'What is it she desires?'

Vodan looked down at the ground. 'The touch of a beautiful man, alas he continues to deny her. Such insolence in the face of perfection.'

'I don't understand…'

'Decades I have loved our Queen-Goddess, swearing loyalty to her and her alone, offering devotion in the face of all her evils. Natheless, she could never accept me, Ms Cherie, not in my true form. Not as I am meant to be.'

The smile had gone, replaced by a sickly bitterness that darkened the rich blue of his eyes into grey and swirling charcoal.

'Amphitrite didn't send you to get me, did she?' I whispered.

Just as the music began to replay, that same soft harmony thundering off the stone and fabric as if it were a melodic bullet ricocheting through the room, he fixed his gaze from the floor solidly back onto me.

'No, Scarlet Cherie, she did not.'

CHAPTER 16

Vodan lifted what had once been his human hand from behind his back, bearing scaled, misshapen hands to the dim light. Thin webbing grew from between his fingers, shining a blue-tinted grey. Where the tips of his long fingers had once been slender and well-manicured were now swollen and globose with thick, black, talon-like claws curling from his nailbed. That scaly amphibian hand crept closer and closer towards my face until Vodan's fingers stroked down my cheek. I violently turned my face away from him, pressing it into the wood and sending my hair flying down my front like a scarlet cape to hide behind. As I moved, the silver bit into my wrists, and once again, my body bucked in pain to the sound of shaking chains and sizzling flesh.

I bit my lip, trying to hold back the whimper, but nothing could stop the tears from flowing down my cheeks. Vodan used those inhuman fingers to trail one of the curls of my hair, letting it slip through his fingers gently. With my eyes squeezed shut, I felt the prick of his talons, threatening the skin on my upper chest as he dragged a nail down to the top of the chemise above my breasts. My stomach churned at the sensation of bulbous, clawed fingertips digging into the side of my right breast, thumb trailing over my nipple.

Only one other man had ever touched me this way. The man whom I loved, the one to whom I had promised eternity and given my body, heart, and soul willingly. Now a stranger dared trail his fingers down my body the same way Nikolaos did, the same way I had learnt to caress and pleasure myself. I wanted to be angry; I wanted to rage and scream and kick my fury into Vodan. God, I was angry, so desperately angry.

Blanketed over all that adrenaline and hatred was the still nothing of fear when you know you are helpless. My heart did not beat faster; in fact, it did not beat at all. I could not breathe, nor did I hyperventilate; my breath was frozen in my lifeless lungs. I was stiller than the dead, lying in wait for whatever horror awaited me, whilst Vodan's fingers squeezed tighter around my breast, and his breath escaped him in a slow, shuddering release of air.

'Oh, Ms Cherie,' Vodan breathed out, a convulsion running up his body, making his fingers squeeze harder against me. 'You do not know how long I have waited to feel the flesh of a woman under these hands.'

Through the veil of red behind which I cowered, I could see Vodan take a step back. He began to undo the buttons of his shirt, letting the fabric collapse onto the damp floor. His belt buckle chimed through the room, clanging where it fell beside the discarded shirt. Last to go were the trousers, sliding from his body, taking the socks with them as he pulled each leg off slowly, deliberately, but with jagged movements thrumming with urgency. Vodan stood there naked in front of me, the cold breeze throughout the stone prison not deterring the long, ready length of him. I wanted to close my eyes and look away, but I couldn't. I could not let myself be a coward again. I had died in the throes of timidity, had my heartbeat stolen to the music of silent lament, never screaming for rescue. I would not fall victim to my own silence again. During those last agonising moments of my mortality, I had been craven. As the undead, I had sworn never to fall prey to the hands of another again. I was not fragile, but a predator. I was vampire.

I turned my face towards Vodan, letting the hair which I hid behind tumble down my front, cascading over the same areas of skin Vodan had violated. My pulse sped, mouth drying, tongue rough and bitter between my teeth.

I locked eyes with my capturer; his chest rose and fell heavily, eyes darkened to chaotic grey with a salacious glint. Vodan's bare chest glinting drew my gaze down his body. Where hair would grow on most men was covered by a layer of powder-blue and green scales tipped with obsidian. Vodan looked at his chest; following my line of sight, he raised his deformed, mutant hand to his chest and ran his fingers along the patch of scales, eyes fluttering closed as he did so.

When Vodan opened his eyes, all of the dynamic colours had gone, drowned by a deep, solid red swimming around his too-wide pupils. We locked eyes, just as a low, sinister gurgling rippled from between beard-framed lips.

Vodan's breathing continued to speed up, coming out in fast, shallow breaths until I thought he might hyperventilate. His scaley chest rose and fell maniacally, each breath a loud, ragged gurgling as if he were drowning, choking on some invisible liquid.

The black-edged scales on his chest were spreading like a contagious skin disease, drowning out the smoothness of his skin in iridescent slime. Wet popping sounds rang through the stone chamber, Vodan's muscles cracking and elongating before my eyes. I'd seen Kai shapeshift before, but that had been different from what was happening with Vodan. Kai had once told me that he felt being a therianthrope was like being cursed by the moon. When he shifted on any night other than the full moon, the process was relatively quick and painless. With him, it was as if his beast tried to break free from his human prison, an animal dominating his humanity. Vodan seemed to be being swallowed up by whatever the fuck he was, his body contorting and folding in on itself, scales spreading over his skin. I watched in horror as his arms cracked and crunched, the broken bone pushing against his arm until I thought it might tear through, and then reknit itself into one, long limb covered in scales, swollen hands brushing down to the floor.

Vodan's slender torso arched backwards, long arms flailing through the air as he contorted. The flesh on his stomach seemed to stretch and swell as if air pumped through his body, rapidly distending him. Another gurgling roar echoed through the room; his body expanded like a balloon, bloating and lengthening until the pristine, attractive older man I had first met earlier morphed into a repulsive beast.

Vodan's final form was barely humanoid, only the face having some resemblance to what he had once been. His triangular face had stretched abnormally long and thin, covered in a layer of scale. The Van Dyke beard was greener, like moss over rocks, frizzing around swollen, green-tinted lips. Where his once sharp, angled nose had been was now unrisen with two black nostrils like coal pits in his face as if his nose had been cut clean off. Vodan's hair had grown, too, flowing to become wakame down his round body, slithering over his skin and getting caught in patches of rougher scales. His torso had rounded to something huge and looked close to bursting, the black and green-blue scales on his belly turning white where they strained over his stomach. Vodan's legs were bent and warped, the joint in the knee too large and knobbly. If it weren't for his gigantic, round torso, his arms and legs would look normal-human sized, but the sheer size of his gut made the rest of him look too long and gangly. Patches of blacker iridescent scales poked out from underneath moss and algae that clung to his body, growing from him the way it grows on abandoned rocks in riverbeds.

Vodan looked at me with lidless red eyes almost hidden by wiry eyebrows sticking up at all angles. He began to stalk towards me, webbed toes slapping against the stone as he took clumsy, shuddering strides on bent legs. With each jagged movement, something between his legs swayed with the movement revealing that he was still partially erect in this new form. I forced myself to stare into his beady, clay-red eyes and not show the fear that knotted my stomach, leaving a metallic taste on the roof of my dry mouth. Pants came out from his black-hole nostrils, bringing with them sprays of water. He was now close enough for the droplets to land on me, warm over my neck.

I raised my face to look up at him, so distracted by this new form that the burning on my wrists had almost ceased to background noise. I knew that there was still so much of the preternatural world that I had never seen, never even began to dream of, but this creature who stood before me now was like something out of a twisted fantasy, a distant nightmare—how could he be real? Even as a vampire, I questioned the plausibility of what stood staring down at me, with the look in his eyes of a cat staring at a mouse caught in a trap. Like that mouse, there was nowhere for me to go. I was trapped, left to the mercy of Vodan in his true form.

Vodan smiled at me, baring brown teeth. He brought his face down closer towards me, casting an extraordinarily long tongue out of his mouth, whipping against my cheek. I cringed, eyes squeezing shut at the sensation of it sticky and dry down my face.

'You taste of fear,' he gurgled, sprays of salty spit hitting my face, 'the way she tastes of disgust.'

'Please, Vodan, please let me go,' I whispered, horrified, my throat burning with the scent of fishy, stagnant water.

'Tonight, Ms Cherie, I ask you to call me by my true name. I want to hear you whisper *Vodyanoy* with the tenderness she has refused me for all these years.'

Even now, with me chained and pleading for my life and virtue, Vodan purred with detached politeness as if I were a willing lover and he bashful.

Vodan lowered his face to my neck, taking in a deep breath just above my skin, letting that breath out again in a slow exhalation. He sighed deeply, the way a connoisseur sighs after a sip of fine wine or a smoker after that first morning hit. Vodan pressed his lips against my collar bone, kissing me almost nervously, his amphibian hands wrapping around my waist. My stomach churned, and I bucked again, trying to get away from the caress of his lips. I tugged my wrists down in an attempt to get free, forcing the silver to bite into my flesh.

Shrill and piteous, I screamed. Metal tore through my flesh, burning me, sticking to me where the skin was red and raw. I forced my legs out in an attempt to push Vodan away from me. The chains broke, clanging to the floor, and just like that, my legs were free. I was in such immense pain it was an adrenaline rush, spiking until the inevitable crash hit, and I would be weakened. I bit my lower lip, preparing myself for the next soaring crash of pain that was about to come.

For a moment, I let my toes brush the ground so that not all my weight was on my wrists. I knew what I had to do next, but I was dreading it. I kept one foot on the floor and brought the other one up, resting on the wood, ready to push off and give me momentum. I was just short enough for my knee to reach Vodan's mid-thigh without his bulging form getting too much in the way. I had two choices but potentially only one chance. Aim for the knee, or the stomach. His knee was lower and at a bad angle, but if I hit it right, I might just cripple him enough to put more space between us. I didn't think I could do as much damage to his stomach. I had to decide; fast. The sound of my shackles breaking had caught him off guard; all I had was now.

It had to be now.

I bounced on the tip of my toes, preparing myself, gaining momentum, and then I used the weight on my tiptoes to push off from the beam with my other leg, extending it outwards, aiming for the right knee. I hadn't made a clear decision for which body part to aim; I had to trust myself to think fast in the moment. The ball of my barefoot made contact with Vodan's kneecap with a wet crack as it dislodged from the socket. He went down with a cry, falling to the ground in a heap. As he collapsed, he grabbed the leg that had hit him, pulling me down until all my weight tugged against my wrists and the metal sliced through my flesh. I howled, feeling like the silver would force its way through my wrist and pull my hand free from the bone. Blood began to pour in rivers down my body from the wound, coating me in red.

'You cunt!' he screeched, gurgling on his pain.

I tried to pull my foot free of his grip, but still Vodan held on relentlessly. He used my leg to pull himself up, climbing up my body to pull himself to a standing position again.

Now standing, Vodan rested all his weight on the left leg, using his right hand to hold my knee to his side. He reached for my other leg, gripping onto it and forcing it behind his body at a sharp angle. I whimpered.

We were pressed skin to skin, me staring into his face from inches away, my blood spilling over both of our bodies. His globe-like stomach pushed against my upper abdomen and breasts. I could feel another part of his body forcing itself against me, most of his erection lost to the agony.

Vodan gripped both my legs behind his body with one hand, using the other to grab under my arse and angle me enough for the right point of entry. My whole body burned with fear, but this fire was not one that could help me. Helpless fury filled me, turning me weak against his inhumanity. He'd pushed the dress upwards, exposing the most intimate part of my body. No, I would not let this happen. But I was fucking helpless. The slits on my wrists were draining my blood, my life-source, taking with it my power as a vampire. Soon I would have no strength left to fight. It was now or never. And never as a vampire is a very long time.

I forced all my incandescent helplessness into the invisible part of my spirit where my flames lived and let loose all the barriers between my magick and me. I roared for my flames to come to me, a call to arms for us to fight against Vodan's physical form and his power. Like a door shattering open, I felt all the walls that shielded me from the world crumble. The magick—or whatever it was that kept me moving, thinking, feeling—charged those relenting embers to soar and energise me. With all the barriers down, I called for Nikolaos one last time, pleading with the blank space in my third-eye to see him and for him to see me.

Nikolaos's head looked up with a start, eyes wide and startled. He lounged on a sofa, stroking the auburn hair of a man whose blood was currently filling our veins—his veins. I knew that the man's hair felt silken, and his blood tasted sweet.

I wanted to ask where he was, whose head lay in his lap like a content cat whilst I had got in this mess searching for him, worried for his safety. All the while, he had been consorting with humans, drinking in their blood. I was furious, but there was no time to rebuke him. I got a breath of power, letting me see the room more clearly; I could suddenly see the golden hues in the man's hair and the slight flush to his skin where he lay panting in pleasure, and I somehow just knew that Nikolaos was with the Empress.

I let Nikolaos see through my blood-covered eyes the gargantuan figure about to force himself on me. Nikolaos flew up from the sofa, his seething wrath jolting through me like an electric shock. I drew on that energy the way I feasted on blood, tearing his rage from him and using it to fuel my own power. My flames burnt like the sun in the centre of my being, arming themselves to fight against the man who had tried to quench them. We would not let him prevail.

Nikolaos's cool touch of power danced with the fervent heat of my fire, both of them combining to send an invigorating surge of energy through me. Like a wolf howling to the moon, I bellowed a roar to the room and clenched my fists, using that strength to tear the chains from the wood. I brought both fists down full force behind Vodan, whipping his back with the silver. He fell backwards with a grunt, trying to free himself of me. I kept my legs wrapped and fell with him. My knees crunched into the stone floor under his weight. I did not care as long as I was on top; no pain could distract me from the ultimate goal of triumph. Vodan's hands flailed behind me, trying to grip onto my back and tug me off of his body. He managed to latch his arms around my back in an attempt to pull me off him to no avail. I was not powerless. I was Scarlet Cherie, vassal to an ancient vampire, and deity of fire. The Prince of a false-idol would not take me down.

I raised one of my shackled hands to the air and brought it down with ferocity, beating the silver chain into his face. Blood spattered over us both; for a moment, I was unsure if it was my own wound reopening or a fresh one on him. Raising my wrist, I saw the bloody mess over one half of Vodan's face. One of his nostrils had split to show the bone under the green-black scales, taking with it a slice of his lip, which left him suspended in a gruesome snarl. Blood flowed from the wound, dousing us in a veil of liquid red. Vodan dug his talons into my back, tearing through the fabric into the soft flesh above my sacrum bone. I cried out, bringing the chain back down.

The next blow barely struck the other side of Vodan's face, this one clumsier in my state of pain. Vodan took this opportunity to push me off of him, using his claws as a handle. We rolled over the blood-covered floor. He stared down at me with bone glistening in half of his face. Vodan pinned me down with his stomach, using one of his forearms to press against my throat. I spat and choked against the crushing of my windpipe. In retaliation, I brought one of my arms up, grabbing him around the neck. The silver trailed down his front, pressing into my collar bone, burning one of the few untouched parts of me. I gripped onto the end of the chain with my left hand and quickly wound it around his neck once more, gripping the metal into my palm so tightly it sliced through my skin like a hot knife through butter. Whimpering, and with my throat being crushed, I used my burning hand to pull the chain tight around his neck. I tugged until his eyes began to bulge from their sockets, and each strained breath became a fruitless gasp spraying blood over my face. I pulled and strained against the searing pain until Vodan's gasp on my throat weakened, and he collapsed in a heap on top of me.

CHAPTER 17

I'd found the stereo playing the song on repeat and smashed it.

The phone connected to it via Bluetooth was also lying in pieces. It was 7 p.m of the following night; I still had three hours until my train to Edinburgh left. Shattered glass and plastic lay scattered around me, some drowning in pools of blood seeping through the stone's cracks. Vodan's unmoving corpse lay sprawled beside me. The green scales had faded to colourless grey, dim and unshining. His eyes were still open, the red of them cloudy and distant, staring off into a realm I no longer could see, one where he would remain for eternity. Vodan was dead. I had killed him with my bare hands. I'd never killed anyone before, never watched the life drain from their eyes as they stared helplessly at me. At the time, it had seemed the only solution; I'd done what I needed to do to survive. That didn't feel like enough anymore. He'd been a person, someone's son, Amphitrite's Prince and companion for decades. Now he lay a cadaver beside me.

Tears streamed down my cheeks, slicing through the blood drying to a cracking, tacky substance over my face. The dress I had woken up in was torn and shredded, half the netted material hanging unattached to the chamise. I ripped what was left of the fishnet off, leaving it to soak up the blood on the floor. I looked down at my wrists. Vampires struggle to heal silver at the best of times; with the amount of blood I'd lost, it would be even more strenuous. I could see the tendons in my wrist carved out of the blackened wound. I waited for it to hurt, but the pain never came. Nothing came besides the numbness. The horrors committed by my own hands had obtunded more than just my body, but my mind. The silence I sat in was thunderous; I looked out at the world with a fresh perspective, one that was blurry and static and distant. The silence was too loud; the noises of the silver chains clanking from my wrist to the floor too quiet. A part of me knew that I was still crying, although the tears didn't feel like my own.

Shards of glass and debris bit into the balls of my feet with each step towards the exit, towards freedom. I parted the bloodstained fabric in the direction from which Vodan had appeared. I'd expected a solid door between the outside world and me; however, that was not what greeted me. Black paint chipped off a metal gate door; the lock appeared to have been busted many years ago. Patches of copper rust stood out dull and sharp in contrast. Without a lock to keep it shut, someone had threaded a modern metal chain through the gate's bars and the frame that attached it into the stone.

The handle was neither cold nor warm under my hand; like everything else, it felt like nothing, surreal and non-existent. This was all that stood between me and freedom. I should have been celebrating. There felt like little reason to rejoice.

The world around me remained vague and staticky. My heart ached, a deep, throbbing pain, felt somewhere distant. It was my heart, my pain, only because my ribs incarcerated it. My eyes only let me see because of the cage of my skull. Tendons and muscle bound my body together, but beyond that, they were not mine. You cannot feel that which does not exist. And I did not exist. You can never escape reality. So what do you do when the burden of the ineludible crushes you? You fade away and leave reality to exist without you.

CHAPTER 18

Britchelstone had once been a small, depraved fishing village that had bloomed into a, albeit still small, quirky city rivalling much larger cities in its rising. Much of the old architecture, from a time when criminals and prostitutes sauntered the streets, remain, especially on the coastline—one of the more significant attractions of Britchelstone. Under the promenade has mostly evolved into clubs, bars, pubs, and restaurants, stretching out onto the pebbles. The old archways that had never been redeveloped are filled with concrete, leaving the wanton history of their remains a secret. Or so I had always thought.

Vodan's nefarious lair led out directly under the pier to another locked gate, this one barely big enough for an adult to squeeze through. I wrapped my fingers around the bars, looking through them at freedom.

Lights flashed through the night like blue and red neon lightning, the slits in the pier's floor above me blazing with colour. Music blared, playing a contrast of genres until it all merged to one chaotic rhythm. Even over the music, I could hear the pre-recorded voice of a man announcing a change in the pace of one of the more adrenalising rides. When I was a little girl, my dad and I used to go to the arcade on the pier and play the penny machines. It was our thing, something precious shared between a father and daughter. If only he could see his little girl now, bloodied and broken under the arcade. His little girl, the vampire; the murderer.

Breaking through the chain was no more onerous than snapping a twig; it wasn't made of silver. I squeezed through the tiny space sideways, bending the metal just a touch, sucking my breath in to make it through. How Vodan had managed to get me through it whilst unconscious was beyond me. I turned my back to the beach, using my strength as the undead to pull the metal chain apart and then re-loop it. No one would be getting through there without some incredibly strong bolt cutters, and it was such a small space anyway that I didn't think anyone would bother. I looked up to the right, noticing a tiny window that was too high for anyone to peek through. Twenty years I had lived in Britchelstone, and never had I noticed it before tonight. Of all the places Vodan could have taken me, he'd chosen one of the busiest yet most hidden. I was enraged. Vodan had selected a place where, at any moment, anyone could have heard my screams. All it would take was for the music to stop and the joyous howls of people having fun to cease. He'd been so confident that the busyness of everyday life would not stop for anything, arrogant that he could violate me, maybe even kill me, and no one would ever know. How many others had been killed so openly, waiting for the bubble of normality, which everyone lived in, to burst enough to be rescued, for them to hear the cries and screams for mercy? Vodan had no breath left to cry for help. Vodan would rot.

If I'd been human, then I would never have been able to make it home from the beach within three hours, let alone to the station as well. I'd also have had to walk through the city wearing bloodied rags and with wrists that looked as if I'd tried to do something very final to myself. I'd made it home to pack my bag. Neither Gwydion nor Sylvie had told me how long we would be up in Edinburgh, only that a powerful group of necromancers was hunting us. I'd thrown enough underwear and clothes into a leather duffel bag to last me at least a week. I'd pack the shampoo and conditioner after my shower.

The downstairs shower was modelled on an old Greek bathhouse, with carvings running up three of the stone walls, the fourth taken up by a mirror with lights built behind it emitting an orange glow. It was more decorative than practical, with nowhere to store toiletries, so Nikolaos and I had to bring them in with us each time we showered. Nor was there a sink or toilet, just a lonely shower head protruding from the ceiling and a vent in the ground to drain the water. Nikolaos had suspended vine-filled wicker baskets from the ceiling, some with dark-green vines almost long enough to touch the brownstone floor.

When I'd first moved in, a black vase on a marble column had been at the back of the room, framed by two of the more luxuriant baskets. When Nikolaos had told me that the pottery was from his human hometown, Corinth, and travelled with him throughout the millennia, I'd asked him to move it somewhere safer. I was clumsy at the best of times; adding water into the mix seemed like tempting danger. Now, it was in the downstairs hallway, below a portrait of Nikolaos from a time when cameras were inconceivable, and people would sit for hours for a great artist to capture the glint in their eye. It wasn't the only painting in the hallway, but it was my favourite by far.

I turned the handle beside the door almost as far as it would go. Water beat down onto the stone, a humming chaos echoing. Soon the room was filled with steam, fogging up the mirror. Only then did I discard my robe, abandoning it on the floor. I didn't want to see my body; some of my wounds would have healed by now, but blood still clung to my flesh like tacky hands refusing to let go of me. My body was a sea of red, some of the blood mine, some of it Vodan's. It had all merged into one, painting me into a gruesome picture, one that was damaged and dull. The sanguine strokes did not care which pot they'd come from; it dried as one work of art, united over my flesh.

I watched the steam dance and curl through the room and could not bring myself to take a step towards the pounding water.

Come on, Scarlet, it's just a shower, I thought to myself.

I could rationalise it in the front of my brain; my dry mouth and weak, fluttering heartbeat were not so convinced, nor were my arms and legs, which refused to move. The heat from the steam was already beginning to turn my hair frizzy; if I were human, I would have been sweating out by now from the heat. Even Nikolaos couldn't shower with me when I had it this hot. I found it comforting. Nikolaos wasn't here to tell me to turn the temperature down. He had left me to return to Amphitrite's side, closing down the connection between us, so I didn't know where he was. Had Gwydion made contact with Nikolaos? Did he know that the Syndicate were after us? I'd have to wait until I was in Edinburgh to find out, which could only happen if I pulled myself together and washed the remnants of blood off my body.

I reached my arm out to the falling water, toes in a puddle, spats of liquid hitting against my shins. The scalding water's caress whipped against the raw wound on my wrist, still not healing from the silver. For the first time, I properly paid heed to the marring of my flesh where the silver had seared into me, revealing enough layers of it that, if I'd been human, it would have killed me.

My knees buckled beneath me. I collapsed onto all fours under the water, feeling it pound against my back. Droplets sliced down my body into the holes Vodan's claws had made over my spine. I cried out in pain, the water flushing out the wound I had forgotten about, arrogantly assuming it would heal like all the others. But vampires don't heal inflictions made by other powerful creatures, and there was no doubt that Vodan had been powerful. My fists curled over the stone, burning where the shower reopened the abrasion in my palm.

Whimpering, I balled my face up, squeezing my eyes closed. I found no solace in being blind. With closed eyes, I was no longer safe at Nikolaos and my home but back in the stone chamber, haunted by vintage music, each drop of water feeling like Vodan's threatening touch along my body. I could see his scaled face and red eyes watching me like a man dying of famine, starved of food, of touch, of love, and then offered salvation at no cost.

My stomach turned, and I fell onto my front, body freeing itself of what little it had left in it. I curled up into a ball, hugging my knees tight to my chest, coughing up an empty stomach. I spat bile onto the floor, thick saliva trailing down my face. All the while, my eyes stayed open, staring at the fogged-up mirror. Salvation came from staring mindlessly at anything in the room I was in; as long as I was here, at home, Vodan could not hurt me. He was dead; I had survived. So, why did it feel like the price of my survival was more final than the true death?

I scrubbed my hair and skin until they were raw, squeezing the empty bottle of shower gel into my hand as it rasped its exhaustion. It had been full when I'd come into the bathroom. Yet still, I did not feel clean. The blood had been aggressively scoured from my body, taking with it layers of skin, but I could still feel it clinging to my skin, phantom touches haunting me, defiling me.

Collecting myself up from the floor, I looked down at my feet to see water running red swirling around my toes, thicker than it should be. Despite the shower's scorching temperature, I was shivering uncontrollably, cold in places unable to be comforted or warmed.

I didn't have the luxury of time to continue scrubbing my body until I was nothing more than a skeleton. Besides, the wounds on my back, wrist, and chest were beginning to hurt more from being reopened and irritated by the sweet-smelling chemicals I had furiously lathered into them.

Bloodied rags discarded on my bedroom floor taunted me from where I sat on the edge of my bed, still shuddering in the clean robe. I'd collected the train tickets from Nikolaos's desk upstairs, checking the time on the computer at the same time. I had forty-five minutes until boarding. The orange-tipped paper tickets peaked out from the side pocket in my bag, a reminder that I was running out of time. If I missed the train, I would be a sitting duck waiting for the Syndicate to come and have me at their mercy. The duel with Vodan would be in vain if I surrendered myself so weakly. Not that I felt particularly strong.

I cursed myself for not having a more covert wardrobe, then in the same breath, cursed Nikolaos for having a much more elaborate style than I. Most girlfriends could steal their partners' hoodies, almost as if marking their territory or solidifying their relationship. Nikolaos wasn't a hoodie sort of man. What did I have to mark my territory, to project to the world that he was mine and I his? A psychic connection and eternal bond by blood and aura. Right then, I would have rather taken the comforting garment.

Clothing did make me feel slightly better. The jeans and jacket were not strong armour, but they took away an element of the vulnerability I was feeling.

Whilst I didn't think Britchelstone Station would be busy at this time of night, I was still meant to be dead, and CCTV littered our streets. It's easy to forget being continuously monitored until you're hiding in plain sight. On the streets, it felt safer, but the station was more of a risk.

Walking past the vanity to collect my bag forced me to confront my reflection. I looked paler than usual, sickly in all the black I wore. The freckles along my nose were too dark, eyes too wide and hollow. I looked scared and haggard as if the night had aged me. I realised I had yet to feed. Soon, the train would be leaving; there would be no time to stop off. I'd have to wait until I was on the train to find a donor.

A meal on wheels.

CHAPTER 19

Britchelstone Station's architecture is an oxymoron of modern-Victorian design. The navy-blue, criss-cross metal beams that make up the ceiling still look untouched from when it had opened in the nineteenth century. Glass turned black from the night shielded me from the rain, but the station seemed to be perpetually cold. Suspended from the ceiling is an antique clock painted black with gold hands. I don't think it has worked for close to a century, not that it mattered, as the seven billboards with their square, orange lettering display the time as well as the train and bus timetables.

The only lights came in the form of the blue-painted street lamps sticking out from the tiled ground, shining dull and lifeless. The twenty-four-hour coffee stand was the only shop still open this late; the Marks and Spencers, card shop, Bagel Man, and WHSmith closed for the evening. An electronic billboard stood high above the ground, flashing commercials for perfumes and fast food.

Right in the centre of the station, over a long crack in the floor stretching out almost halfway through, was an old piano made from light-wood, keys so worn they had faded from years of love. Britchelstone would be bustling with people at peak times, packed so compactly into the station that it would be hard to move—like sardines in a tin. That was the great thing about Britchelstone: even when the suits and business mongrels were running to and from the exit with their expensive briefcases, in the middle of the capitalist chaos, there'd almost always be someone filling the space with music. It was what I loved about the city; no matter how much we grew and evolved, there was an immortal quirkiness to it.

Tonight, the station was silent. Above the barriers, the electronic timetable shone neon-orange lights alerting me that my train was due to leave in ten minutes. Almost empty, the few people who did remain huddled into their seats on the benches, sipping takeaway cups of caffeine, whispering in hushed tones. I kept my head down, collar pulled up as high as it would go, doing my best to be inconspicuous. I shuffled to the barriers between me and the train to safety. The weakness that came from not eating for two days was beginning to become unbearable; whatever adrenaline that had been carrying me through the evening had drained along with my repose.

I pulled the ticket from my bag and shoved it into the mouth of the barrier. The barrier beeped at me and spat the ticket right back out. I tried again, only to face mechanical rejection once more. After the third attempt, I was very close to kicking the thing clean off its hinges and storming through. I needed to feed, and soon, this anger was unlike me. Feeling the presence of someone looming over me, I looked up to see one of the station workers smiling down at the pitiful sight of me with my disobedient ticket. He was pushing retirement age with dark skin and eyes such a deep brown they were almost black. The neat stubble on his chin and neck was beginning to look entirely white. I followed the line of his stubble down to that succulent, throbbing vein in his throat. It called to me, begging me to taste it, to pierce the skin and release the blood from its fleshy cave.

My tongue darted over my suddenly dry lips, moistening them. He, the worker, smelt so sweet, like summer fruits at the time of harvest in that precarious sweet spot of ripeness where one day more and they'd begin to rot and one day less they'd not have that perfect succulence.

'... Miss?'

I forced myself to look at his dark-pink lips set into a slight frown to go along with the concerned eyes.

'Sorry.' I shook my head. 'What did you say?'

'Can I check your ticket, please?'

Just as I went to hand him my ticket, a man in a suit knocked me with his laptop bag hard enough I stumbled. Both he and I turned to look at the hurried man, who spared a glower in my direction, hazel eyes narrowed and hostile. His ticket spat back out at him. With a frustrated huff, he turned to the two of us.

'Here's my ticket'—he shoved his hand past me towards the station worker—'now let me through.'

'I'm just helping this lady, and then I will be with you, sir.'

The nice older man smiled at the rude interrupter. I felt a pang of guilt that just moments before I'd been thinking of him as food. The interference gave me time to look at his name tag, the little green badge read, *Stephen* in white letters with the station logo above. The rude guy let out an exasperated sigh, checking his watch dramatically. Stephen's smile didn't waver, but I saw the increase in his pulse and the way he swallowed just that bit too hard. I had to admire his dedication to customer service.

'My train leaves in five minutes.'

'I will be right with you, sir.' Stephen turned back to me, looking at the ticket still in my hand. 'This way, miss.' Stephen ushered me over to the large gate for people in wheelchairs, and those with buggies and large luggage, or for when the ticket barriers weren't working—which happened more often than not. Stephen pressed the fob attached to the keys on his belt to the reader and let me through the gate. I passed him with a sympathetic smile whilst still trying to be covert. Luckily, I was the only of Maglark's victims not to have a picture included in the news article about them, which did take some of the pressure away from hiding. Was I just being paranoid? Honestly, this was the first time I had stepped this far out into town since becoming a vampire other than for a quick feeding, or on Valentine's Day with Nikolaos. So, yes, I probably was being overly anxious. After the night I'd had, I felt justified in my trepidation.

I made my way to platform six, the final platform at the station and the one dedicated to longer journeys. Halfway down the walkway, I heard the clips of expensive leather brogues clicking against concrete. Rude Guy from before was rushing in the direction of platform six, his unfastened overcoat flying out behind him as he half-jogged towards me. He wasted another glare, but I just shrugged it off. Someone was a sour puss.

I made it on the train with a minute to spare. Trains destined this far up North had reserved seats. I checked the carriage number on the ticket. It was at the very front in first class—I'd never travelled first class before. Fancy. Really I could have chosen anywhere to sit, seeing as there was no one else on the train except for Rude Guy and me. I wasn't about to pass up on first class.

Just as the train began to drive out of the station, I made my way down the long carriages. A male's voice, thick with a Scottish accent, announced what train we were on and how long the journey would be: just over six hours. Thankfully it was winter; otherwise, there'd be no way of me making it to Edinburgh in time to miss sunrise. Flying would have cut the journey by more than a third, which would have been preferable, but also much more of a risk. I definitely wasn't in a risk-taking mood.

Truthfully, and at risk of sounding ungrateful, first class was quite disappointing. All of the carriages had been long with comfy seats, plug sockets, and an alright amount of legroom. Admittedly, the first-class carriage was spaced out more, so there was more privacy, and the seats did look plusher, but other than that, I didn't see much difference. What was really disappointing was that, when I went through the *swooshing* doors, I was greeted by an unfortunately familiar face.

I took my seat at the front of the carriage, to the right of the doors leading to, what I assumed was, the driver's carriage. Rude Guy sat to my left. I lay the book from my bag onto the table. Considering neither Nikolaos nor I had phones, the plugs were wasted on me. He wasn't big on technology other than the computer in the office, which I had seen him use once in the past six months. I'd always enjoyed reading as a human; without any other distractions as the undead, reading had become my main pass time. Nikolaos's literary collection was nearly as vast as his wardrobe, so I was never out of options. Admittedly, some of them were in languages so ancient, they were not spoken any longer, or in French, which did mean I couldn't read a solid portion of them. Maybe one day I'd learn. It wasn't exactly as if I were short on time.

I reached up to put the bag on the shelf above my seat and could feel eyes boring into me as if trying to inflict actual harm with just his eyes. I looked over my shoulder to glare back at the culprit. I had more time to really look at him now. He'd cut brown hair with the first threatening of grey into a short, neat style, which didn't quite suit the extra chin that was beginning to form, as if he were refusing to let go of a style that had complimented him in his younger years. Everything about him was stern and tense, from the too-straight posture to the deep-set wrinkles and perfected lower.

'It's rude to stare, you know,' I said, lowering my arms from above my head to turn and look at him. He scoffed in retaliation.

'Don't think just because we're the only ones on the train they won't be checking your ticket.'

I leant my back against the table, genuinely confused. 'What—'

'They'll kick you out of first-class once they come to check your ticket. I'll make sure of it. I paid for peace and quiet.'

My mouth gaped open at his audacity. 'Excuse me?'

His eyes flicked down my body as if to say, *See, you don't belong here*. I'd borrowed one of Nikolaos's rarely-worn trenchcoats to cover the gory wounds on my wrist, which was far too big on me, brushing against the floor. The only jumper I could find big enough to cover me, the way I felt I needed, was one I wore to sleep in sometimes when Nikolaos was away, leaving me the house to myself. It was cosy, crinkled, and hung almost to my knees with the sleeves devouring my hands. My boots were muddy from running through the forest at vampire speed to get to the station in time; some of the mud had splattered over the tights on my shins, weighing down the end of the previously pristine jacket.

My focus wandered away from his face down to his meaty neck. I told myself I'd be the bigger person, to leave it alone. Maybe he'd had a terrible day; maybe he was usually a kind and polite man. No, men who have perfected that particular look of disdain and ugly combination of contempt and repulsion in their tone were not novices of hostility. No one humble could serve arrogance with such a honed deliverance. Still, I didn't have to rise to it, right?

On the other hand, I was so very hungry, and that strained vein in his throat throbbing angrily up and down was bewitching in its torment of my famine. A part of me still felt guilty about feeding on humans; a more significant part, the predator side, understood that survival was key. By becoming a vampire, humans had developed from the familiar to food. I also had adapted a reverence for them as a species. Although they were weaker, they also sustained me, and I could not be what I was without them. It was the circle of life, the ecosystem that kept us all thriving. The cow feeds on and fertilises the grass. The insects eat the grass, and the chicken eats them and the greenery. The fox eats the chicken. Their bones go into the earth and help it grow... and so on and so forth. Once upon a time, it all made sense, and everything had its place. Humans would farm and forage the land and the animals whilst also giving back to nature. Then they became arrogant, enthroned themselves as kings of the food chain through sheer ruthlessness and needless destruction. The ecosystem that had worked between all of Earth's children, from the animals to the trees to the ocean, was disturbed, breaking down to something disorderly.

Like most modern-day humans, I'd spent my life thinking that we were where it ended. Humans were the ultimate marauders, who had climbed up the ladder to a throne of blood. What happens when you reach the top? You fall. Mother Earth's creatures, beings of light and life, could only fall into the laps of the raptorial shadows. Shadows like vampires, who took the form of their human counterparts but who had evolved into something formidable.

Those who knew of the supernatural world understood that the circle of life we are taught, as humans, to see is just an atom within something so much larger. A system where humans and animals are not always mutually exclusive, and where being human means being food or cannon fodder for creatures discarded as mythology.

It had been a lot to take in at first, and then, like with everything, the novelty began to wear off, and the weird and wonderful had become quotidian. Whilst I didn't find my new life as the undead boring, nor did it still have that unique sense of overwhelming wonder. I'd been establishing normality in the wayward, adjusting to a new routine in a way I felt comfortable. Until everything went tits up.

Still captivated by the man's pulse, I didn't feel any shred of guilt for looking at him like food. I walked over to his table, slipping into the seat opposite him. He fixed me with a gaze trying to be scathing, but I'd spent enough time around Nikolaos and Gwydion to build an immunity to scorn, and, honestly, his attempt paled in comparison. I made unemotional eye contact back, looking at him not just with my eyes but with that part of me that saw a human and thought, *weak*. I couldn't tell you what exactly it was that made a vampire able to allure a human other than the simple explanation Gwydion gave: magick.

I felt the moment my gaze captivated him like a candle being struck and illuminating the darkness, the sudden blazing heat of two consciences being shared. All of his contemptuous personality bled into blankness, face going slack, eyes dropping into relaxation. This was the part I didn't like. Yes, the power rush of capturing a human's mind was thrilling, but taking away someone's free will still felt morally ambiguous. I justified it by telling myself that, without my gaze, he would feel pain and fear. Nikolaos had once warned me that becoming a vampire meant having to sacrifice part of your moral compass to the darkness. I'd sworn never to be that way, sure that I would be the exception to the rule. Then I'd realised that giving yourself over to iniquity was not so much a choice as it was necessary to survival. Either you gave up shards of your morality willingly, or the bloodlust clawed it from you. Like all magick, it was a double-edged sword, and this particular blade was balanced on the shreds of my remaining humanity.

'What's your name?' I asked, voice low with the thrill of power, tender despite his prior behaviour.

'N-Noah,' Noah stammered back, some of that earlier hubris lost to a lazy drone.

All humans seemed to react differently to being allured. Like Noah, some gave themselves over to my power with ease, falling into an instant state of tranquillity as if I were the salvation to finally accepting peace. Others resisted until they simply could not fight it any longer. I didn't battle those people too hard; it felt more of a violation to force my way so aggressively into their minds.

One of the most upheld laws in the vampire world states, we cannot alert a human of our existence unless there is a good enough reason, which meant I really did have to allure a human and then rid them of the memory when feeding or risk the wrath of Amphitrite. Some laws just earnt you a slap on the wrist from the local Magnate, but mindlessly sharing our secrets to those not deemed worthy was a statute punishable by the Empress herself, usually resulting in death. Exceptions had been made, for example, in the cases of human and vampire relations. Though, even then, the human would have to be brought before the local council and swear their loyalty. The idea was that the human would vow to take the secrets of vampires to the grave with the unsubtle hint being that, if they breathed a word to any other mortal, that grave would be dug early and with no plea hearing.

I stood, holding my hand out to Noah. 'Come with me.'

Noah stood up from the seat, using one hand on the table to push himself up. He half fell out from the chair, stumbling over his feet. I caught hold of Noah's arm, my small hands barely wrapping around half of his surprisingly solid bicep. Usually, his weight would be nothing for me to hold, but I hadn't fed in closer to forty-eight hours, and the combination of his body weight and the movement of the train slammed me back against the table. I landed at an angle, back twisting and table hitting into the claw wound on my back. I cried out as the pain hit me, the tender flesh protesting my carelessness.

I felt my hold on Noah's mind slip like a rope through my fingers. One moment he was mine, and the next, the option for his free will came flooding back. All it would have taken was Noah to push against me that little bit harder. I waited for Noah to be free of me. It did not come. He didn't want to let go of his guilt-free chance of momentary peace. I was the excuse his psyche needed to release the tension winding him so tight without the effort of having to do it himself.

Don't ever think feeding on humans is a one-way transaction. Humans crave freedom from their mundanity, from the coils in which they are so wound up, almost as much as we crave blood. Hell, sometimes even more.

CHAPTER 20

Noah had tasted as bitter as his glower, his sweat reeking of desperation to be released from the confines of his life. I could not offer the redemption Noah sought, but I could feed on him and give him some solace. I'd lead him back from the train bathroom to his seat in first class, sat beside him, and offered him all that I could under the circumstances. Through my connection to his mind, I had shared with him the surety of finding happiness without penitence. I had planted the seed of knowledge that striving for comfort did not make him a bad person. Then I had collected my bag and moved carriages to one far away from first class.

The world passed me by in a blur of bright city lights in the darkness. Rain pelleted against the window, turning the glass cold against my cheek. We were over halfway through the journey, with only a couple of hours left until reaching Edinburgh. *The Great Gatsby*, the book I had brought to start on the train, was not sinking in no matter how many times I reread the same sentence. Little black print, faded in the well-thumbed novel, didn't look like words to me anymore, just blobs of ink on paper in a code I could not understand. My mind was elsewhere, thoughts fleeting through my brain faster than the train through these Northern cities.

I didn't want to be alone with my thoughts. Darkness and bloodshed flooded my mind until it was too uncomfortable to be inside my own head. I watched the lights fly past me, getting lost in their golden illumination streaming through the night like mechanical stars, and did anything I could to not think too hard about anything. My wrists and back ached, a constant, painful reminder of what I had done tonight.

Whether Nikolaos knew of the Syndicate's machinations was still unknown to me. With a start, I realised that no one but me could contact him, so he had no way of knowing unless I could get a hold of him again. I was so off my game tonight, barely knowing which way was up. Noah's blood had strengthened me enough that contacting Nikolaos should be easy. I closed my eyes and visualised the phone, with the receiver pressed solidly against my ear as if it were a tangible item and not just a figment of my imagination. The strangely real phone rang in my mind's ear, soft and distant. My connection to Nikolaos as my master, the part of him that gave me that magick I needed to live on as the undead, opened up. I felt it like a sense of relief in my body, a locked part of my being opening up to be made whole by my other half. Ring, ring, ring, ring.... Nothing.

Once again, my deceitful lover was unreachable. When I'd thought he was missing, I'd been a high-strung ball of concern; now I knew he'd disappeared to serve by Amphrite's side, I was angry. I knew he had an obligation to serve our Empress and that he was trying to keep me away from the potential perils she could bring our way if she so wished, but Vodan's actions earlier had proved his methods were misguided. Vodan had confessed that he had gone rogue. The question was: could I believe him? I had to trust that Nikolaos really was doing what was necessary to keep us both safe and that neither he nor Amphitrite knew of Vodan's plans. Besides, for as long as he was with the Empress, he was safe from the Syndicate. No way would a group of necromancers be able to penetrate the base of the European vampire Empress. At least that thought was comforting, enough so that I snuggled into the back of my seat and picked up *The Great Gatsby* again.

Edinburgh's Station is a lot more modern than Britchelstone's. Everything about it felt more high-tech whilst managing to keep a particular charm. Walking towards the ticket barriers, I passed Noah. I half expected him to glare at me again. Instead, he gave me a smile that softened the deep lines in his face and motioned for me to go through the only open ticket barrier first. I obliged with a nod and smile in return.

I saw a familiar face waiting for me beside a silver 2007 Toyota Yaris. Kai leant against the back passenger door with his arms crossed over his chest, the forest-green t-shirt he wore straining over the muscles in his upper body. In all the time I'd known Kai, I don't think I'd ever seen him wear a jacket. Even in the Scottish winter temperature dropping close to minus degrees. Waverley Station's car park's fluorescent lights were blinding after growing so adjusted to the night, especially towards the end of the journey where it had been almost entirely unlit countryside. My night vision was so good as a vampire that sometimes actual light was too intense.

I ran the rest of the way towards Kai, dropping my bags to the ground by his feet to fall into his chest. Kai wrapped his heavily muscled arms around me, holding me close to his extra-warm body. The tears started before I could stop them. Kai's familiarity, the sudden safety of being held by someone I loved and knew loved me, was so overwhelming that once they started, they didn't stop.

My knees buckled below me, and Kai had to lower us both to the ground slowly. He cradled me in his lap, my face pressed against his shoulder, hands balling into fists in his t-shirt so tight I heard the rip of fabric at the seams. My screams were silent. I felt the brush of my fangs against his skin as my mouth gaped in a noiseless wail. There were no sounds pitiful or enraged enough to release the pain ripping through my body. My heart ached with the agony of a thousand fists as if someone were pulling me apart from the inside.

'Darlin'...' Kai began, letting the words trail off.

Kai held me in his arms, letting me shred the remaining fabric off his back until it lay in tatters around us, the rest of it caught in my squeezed fists. When I finally pulled back from him, the dark skin of his chest was soaked in my tears, glistening under the unnatural white light. Well-manicured fingers stroked my hair, pushing it back from my tear-stained face.

'Let's get you in the car, darlin',' Kai whispered, scooting me in his lap, so we were face to face. He brought both thumbs towards me to wipe away the remaining tears on my cheeks. 'There, all better.' He smiled at me with such genuine care that, if I hadn't cried all of my energy out, it might have set me off again.

Kai put my bag in Sylvie's boot before sliding in beside me in the back. The front passenger seat was taken up by a woman I hadn't met before. She turned in her seat to look at me impassively, brows furrowing together above the pale blue of her eyes just enough for me to notice. She'd cut her hair into a shorter and choppier mullet than Sylvie's, dyed a blue-tinted black with actual navy highlights running underneath her fringe. It looked great. Dark blue eyeshadow was expertly applied around her hooded eyes with a slender flick of silver eyeliner meeting the end of the design. I waited for her to introduce herself. After several more moments of staring, she still didn't. Sylvie looked at me in the rearview mirror, her beautiful hazel eyes bloodshot from lack of sleep.

'Scarlet, this is Angelika,' she said, putting the car into reverse out of her parking space.

Sylvie knocked Angelika's leg lightly with the back of her hand as she moved the gear stick. Sylvie's touch seemed to drill some sense back into the other woman, who stopped gaping at me enough to glower. She turned around to face the front, leather-clad arms folding over her small chest. Even sitting down, I could tell Angelika was small, not in the short way I was, but small-boned.

Kai wrapped one of his arms around my shoulders, pulling me into his naked upper body. 'She ain't met a vampire before,' he whispered low enough no one else would hear it.

'We are a novelty, I suppose,' I breathed back, getting my arm squeezed tenderly in response. On any other day, I would have made conversation or introduced myself further. Tonight, I was drained, with the sensation of dried tears making my face feel dirty. Really I'd not stopped feeling dirty since Vodan first touched me as if each of his caresses had left a layer of invisible grime on me which no amount of scrubbing could cleanse.

There was an undefinable tension in the car that went further than Angelika's surprise. I could see the rigidity in

Sylvie's motions as she put the parking ticket in the machine that let us out, whilst the pulse in Angelika's neck beat too hard. Kai was not immune to it, either. The way he held me to his body was unduly taut for my usually languorous friend; I could taste the unease in his aura the way I had tasted the bitterness in Noah's blood earlier on.

'You smell of blood, Lettie,' Kai said in the same hushed tone. Without thinking about it, I pulled the sleeve of my jumper further down my wrist, moving my wounded back away from the seat.

'You smell of apprehension, Kai.'

'It's been a... an intense few days,' he said loud enough for the others to hear this time. Angelika snorted crudely.

'Intense. That's certainly wan word for it.' Angelika's Scottish accent was thicker than Sylvie's, her voice surprisingly deep for such a small frame.

'What's happened since the last time I saw Sylvie and Gwydion?' I asked, sitting upright in my seat with the thrill of adrenaline. Kai shifted his arm from behind me, avoiding eye contact.

'Oh, I don't know, how aboot oor flat being stuffed to the brim with shapeshifters, who are openly homophobic. Us gays are disgustin', apparently, but not disgustin' enough to refuse oor offer of shelter,' Angelika spat.

I gaped at Kai. 'Did they actually call you disgusting?'

He shook his head. 'Not really, no.'

'What do you mean, "not really"?'

Kai sighed. 'They said I was a *muerdealmohadas*. A pillow biter.' He shrugged. 'I've been called worse.'

'And they called us *marimachas*. I've seen the way they look at us, the way they stop whispering when we enter a room. In oor own fucking hoose.'

I wanted to ask what she meant by *marimachas,* but Kai spoke before I had time to open my mouth.

'Panthers are a secretive group. We ain't used to sharin' our ways with humans.'

'We aren't just humans,' Angelika huffed, and she sounded indignant. 'And of course, *you* wid stick up for them.' She pronounced 'you' like 'yee', all of her 'r's rolling over her tongue.

'Well, we ain't *shapeshifters*. But they're my people.'

'They arnae mine!'

Sylvie drove us over a bridge, turning on the windscreen wipers just in time for the rain pour to turn from light to drowning. 'The Guild is about coming together as one whilst also retaining individuality and cultural traditions. They may not be your people in the literal sense, Angie, but we are united as one cause, and that makes us a unit,' Sylvie said, sparing a glance at the other woman.

'They canny have their cake and eat it. Either we arnae worthy of them, and they can leave, or they can show us some goddamn respect under oor roof.'

I felt Kai tense and had the suspicion that this wasn't the first time he'd heard this particular rant.

'The Reina has already sent off most of her men that were making you uncomfortable, Angie. She didn't have to do that. We are all adjusting to a new situation.'

'Oh, how good of her,' Angelika replied with seething sarcasm.

'It ain't a sexuality thang. They're fine with me, and trust me, the guards ain't goin' to have half a problem with human lesbians as they will with a queer of their own kind,' Kai said, sounding as bitter as I'd ever heard him. The conversation was going too fast for me to keep up with and had some much-needed context missing.

As if sensing my confusion, Sylvie said, 'We've run into some complications. The Guild's base isn't equipped for this many people. Kai's Reina has brought all of her people to the base to seek protection and offer military aid. We've had to transport all of our members to Angie's family home in the countryside; only those willing to be in the front line are at our flat.'

'Reina?'

'God, some vampire ye're!' Angelika turned in her seat, focusing all of her frustration on me. Underneath her indignance, I could smell the fear on her like sweet perfume on the tip of my tongue.

'The Queen of the panthers, my Queen. You'll meet her back at Sylvie's,' Kai replied, voice tired.

'It's a lot to wrap your head around, especially this close to dawn,' Sylvie added.

'What help is she gonny be'—Angelika jabbed her thumb in my direction—'if she doesney even know about the therian hierarchy. This is preternatural 101.' I think I preferred it when Angelika was gaping mindlessly at me.

'We don't take in people based on how much help they'll be, Angelika. We offer protection to everyone. As my partner, I would prefer you to uphold the ethics of our Guild.' Despite sounding calm, Sylvie's foot pressing down on the pedal, making the car go just over the speed limit, was indication enough to her frustrations. Her ring-clad fingers wrapped tightly over the gear stick, mottling her knuckles.

'Once things have settled, we'll need to look into getting a bigger base. Angelika is valid in feeling like our space is being imposed upon, but it's for the greater good right now.'

'You're pretty damn optimistic we're gonny survive this, Sylvie.'

Sylvie had stopped driving, parking up beside a three-story house converted into flats. Angelika's protests had stolen my opportunity to see the views of Edinburgh. Kai and I were both sunk into the backseats, trying to avoid the direction of her bitterness. Maybe Angelika was blind to it, but I noticed the way Kai's shoulders were rolled and stiff in a way I had never seen him before. I wonder if she knew just how much she had pissed him off for him to show it this way.

Angelika opened her door and stormed from the car, slamming it behind her so hard it made the whole car shudder, leaving the three of us in the sudden silence of near-dawn Edinburgh. Sylvie sighed, resting her forehead against the wheel.

'Sorry 'bout that,' she said.

I shrugged. 'We all have bad days.'

'This is more like a bad week.'

'A lot's going on; I understand that,' I said, still too drained to put any emotion into the words. Sylvie raised her head from the wheel to look at me.

'Yes, Scarlet, I think you understand it more than most.' With that, she chucked the car keys to Kai and departed the vehicle.

And then there were two.

CHAPTER 21

Still shirtless, Kai entered into the freezing night without a complaint. The sky had lightened to a deep, navy blue, dark enough it seemed black to the untrained eye, though us nocturnal folk knew better. Dawn threatened the horizon, preparing to engulf the stars and wash the world in golden light. The pressure of dawn weighed down on me, depleting what little energy I had left.

Kai led me through the unadorned stone hallway, up the winding staircase with its thin metal bannister, to the third floor. Sylvie had left the door on the latch for us; Kai pushed it open with his back and ushered me inside. I went to take a foot into the house and was hit with such a force, it sent me backwards onto the floor.

'Oh, damn, I forgot,' Kai muttered, shaking his head.

Still stunned, I turned wide, surprised eyes up to him.

'Sylvie, can you come 'ere!' he called out.

I picked myself up from the ground before Kai had a chance to offer me help up. My hand tried to go through the threshold with no luck. An invisible force pushed against me, one thrumming with the soft caress of power, energy that was blessed as a warning against magick of darkness. Sylvie appeared from behind a corner with a steaming coffee cup in hand.

'What's wrong?' she asked, looking at both of us in turn.

Kai nodded his head in my direction. 'You need to invite Lettie in.'

She looked confused, and then her eyes widened in understanding. 'Oh, of course. Scarlet, I invite you into my home.' I felt the invisible forcefield give way; just like that, I could enter. Before, I'd not noticed anything unique or different about the doorframe, it had been ordinary, but now, I could see something had changed. It was peculiar, as if nothing had happened, but at the same time, a slight shimmer in the air had depleted to nothing. I was almost sure I imagined it; then again, the sensation had been so tangible. It might just have been my mind tricking me into making the magick physical. My fingers reached out towards the empty air, tracing through nothing, though that same thrum of energy had not fully rewound into itself. I walked through, stroking my fingers down the wood beside me as if it were something wonderful. It wasn't. Had I just imagined that shimmer of magick?

I'd known that vampires needed permission from the owners of blessed houses to enter; however, that didn't take away the peculiarity of experiencing it firsthand. I felt strangely rejected by it as if it were proof that I was a creature of evil. When we'd first discovered my immunity to holy items, I think I had taken it as misguided confirmation that I wasn't an actual being of darkness. Tonight proved I had been wrong. Gwydion had explained to me last year that vampires were only repelled by the magick of particular intentions. Holy items blessed by a prayer that sought to evoke the power of benevolence and light would repel a creature of darkness, such as vampires, but it also worked both ways—though Gwydion was the only person I knew personally who toyed with the line of light and darkness, life and death, so readily.

Power washed over me like a wave of heat, propelling against my body, stealing my breath. So much warmth, so much life. The energy of powerful shapeshifters. Not only could I smell the rich musk of dark fur touched by the sunlight, but I could feel it winding over my body, the palpable power prowling around me in the circle, rubbing itself over my skin, causing goosebumps to ripple up my body. Such intense warmth, so much primal energy, feral and overflowing with life to the point my heart fluttered in my chest, answering the call of their animal power. Underneath all of the dark fur and feline musk was a scent that stood out from it all. One energy burned bright and golden in the sea of ebon coats, standing taller and broader than the rest with fur that glowed with the colour of burnt sunrises and with a power to match.

I knew the owner of that power before he emerged from the same corner from which Sylvie had appeared. He, whoever he was, came in the form of an unassuming man, standing only a few inches taller than Kai, though far less broad through the shoulders. His slicked-back hair was flaxen like sand that's warm under bare toes. Dark, rich umber and ochre highlights ran through the sandy blonde, some of the strands closer to black than brown towards the tips of his short cut. Eyes a soft, light brown, the colour of molten citrine, watched me intensely as I instinctively took a step closer towards him, responding to the pull of his power. I admired the flairs of vibrant honey shooting off from where his large pupils watched me. My eyes wandered down his face, tanned a light brown, a colour some may call olive. Adalia was olive-skinned; he was more pale brass. His lips were full, with dimples at the edges of his mouth softening the triangle of his face into a picture of winsome attractiveness.

His hands ran down the front of his beige cashmere jumper, smoothing the edges of it over his trousers in a gesture I recognised as nerves, the light trail of hair on his fingers catching in the hallway light. Realising he was fidgeting, he straightened himself back up and slid his fingers into his taupe, slim-fit chinos. Sylvie and Kai were both watching us, Sylvie looking unreadable and Kai vaguely amused. Kai let my bags rest on the floor, walking over to slap the other man lightly on the back in a very masculine display of affection.

'Lettie, this is Doctor Quillan. Quillan, this here's Scarlet Cherie,' Kai said with a teasing smile.

Doctor Quillan furrowed his brow at Kai before turning to me with a bashful grin, highlighting the deep dimples in his cheeks. He pulled both hands from his pockets, stretching one out to me and using the other to sweep back his already immaculate hair.

'Laith, my name's Laith.'

Our fingers entwined, sending a jolt of energy through him into me. I snatched my right hand back from his grip, clutching it to my chest. The wound on my wrist throbbed.

'Sorry, that's never happened before!'

'It's fine,' I replied, still nursing my injured wrist. 'Nice to meet you, Laith.'

Laith ran his hands back down the cable knit of his jumper, fingers twiddling with the collar of his faded green shirt peeking over the round neck collar.

'Laith's a doctor,' Kai reaffirmed; it was my turn to frown at him.

'You mentioned that.'

'You're injured.'

'I'm not,' I protested.

'I can smell the blood on you.'

Kai came up and sniffed me, the heat from his face radiating off him. He was so comfortable showing skin it was easy to forget that he was half-naked.

'I'm a vampire, Kai, that's hardly unexpected,' I whispered.

He gave me the look my comment deserved. Louder, I said, 'Besides, I feel like I need to greet the Queen before doing anything else. I've never met royalty before. And I want to talk to Gwydion before sunrise.'

Kai and Sylvie exchanged a look that I didn't like.

'Under any other circumstance, I'd agree with you,' Laith reasoned, drawing my attention to him, 'but I've met Reina Onca, and she is not here as a monarch but as an equal.'

'But—'

'Please, darlin',' Kai pleaded, earnest eyes imploring my relent.

Sylvie and Laith—or *Doctor* Quillan—showed me to the bedroom where I would be staying. The windows were large and square, looking out over the shared garden at the back of the house. A white desk complete with laptop and black lamp sat beside the door, folders left open, and papers sprawled all over the surface and plug-in keyboard. The bed was nondescript with a black faux-leather headboard and grey bedding messily made.

A vanity with lights all around the mirror had been pushed to one side of the room, along with the abundance of professional make-up bags accompanying it to make space for the coffin taking up a good portion of the floor space. I'd never seen a coffin until last year when Gwydion, Nikolaos, Adalia, and I had raised a slew of zombies to catch Maglark.

'This used to be our workspace,' Sylvie explained, looking wistfully at the blue tac left on the wall as if she could still see what had once been there.

'You're good for taking us all in, Sylv.'

'Angie doesn't agree.'

'She focuses too much on the now. You've always been big picture,' Laith soothed.

Sylvie nodded like that validated some hidden self-doubt. I was still fixated on the macabre wooden elephant in the room.

'It's all I could get this short notice; I hope it's okay,' she said, following my gaze to the pale oak box with silver handles. I didn't know what to say, nodding my head wordlessly. 'The Guild has never worked with vampires before; neither the main base nor this flat is light-tight.'

I regained enough control of my facial expressions to smile at Sylvie.

'This is... perfect. I really appreciate your hospitality.'

Sylvie gave a curt nod, pulling off one of the silver rings on her small fingers and replacing it repeatedly. She retreated from the bedroom, leaving Laith and me alone in the quickly ceasing darkness.

Pre-dawn exhaustion struck me, smiting me into submission of the growing daylight. Laith instructed me to sit on the bed; I obliged, but I wasn't happy about it. No way would I have time to see Gwydion before sunrise, nor meet Reina Onca, Kai's Queen. I did not want to see the state of my butchered wrists nor the puncture in my back. I'd been doing an excellent job of pretending I was not injured, playing blissful ignorance to the sight of my defiled body.

I sat on the edge of the bed, fingers finding their way over the soft, warm fabric. Oh, how I had missed cotton sheets. The mattress was comforting under my body, heated as though it had retained the therians' high temperature. Laith fished the keyring from the front of his leather satchel, using the little key on it to unlock the flap on his matching doctor's bag, which was almost the same size as the one I'd brought with me. He knelt in front of me with the half-open bag, ready to pull out whatever was needed. I caught glimpses of a stethoscope, alcohol wipes and gel, a box of rubber gloves, a thermometer, and other medical trinkets. He pulled on a set of the blue medical-grade latex gloves, fitting them expertly over his hands.

'Right,' he said, smiling up at me from where he knelt. 'Where are you hurt?'

'I'm not,' I argued, avoiding his too-amiable gaze at the risk his kind eyes would set off the tears again—if I even had any left to shed.

My face turned away from him, which brought me staring at my reflection in the light-up vanity. I was pale, not the pale of the dead but that dewy, shocked pale that comes after you've seen something so horrendous it chills your blood too much to give you life. Dilated pupils smothered the red-amber of my too-wide eyes, giving me an intense, distant stare. Tears had dried down my cheeks in a faint pink trail of woe, leaving my under eyes dark and vaguely reddish. When I'd first become a vampire, my tears had been as translucent as any humans. Now the sanguine-tinged tears were just more indication of my departure from mortality.

I turned to look over my shoulder at the coffin Sylvie had brought in for me. She'd gone out of her way to make me comfortable, but the thought of stepping into the wooden cage made me suddenly woozy. There was a bitter-sweet irony to it; whilst Vodan lay dead and discarded in his stone tomb, I was the one being sentenced to flee the day in a coffin. He may be dead, but I was damned. I could feel the panic bubbling up in my stomach just thinking about stepping foot in the coffin. My unnecessary breath came out in ragged pants, increasing in their desperation as I could almost feel the sensation of wood trapping me in. The more I fought to catch my breath, the more shallow they came until I was caught in a vicious cycle working myself into a further panic.

'Hey, hey, it's okay. Look over here, at me,' Laith soothed, wrapping his hand over the top of my fingertips peeking through the jumper sleeve.

Another jolt of electricity shot from his hands into mine, this time stirring the fire within me. My sleepy fire shivered, breathing in the sensation of Laith's energy, and then roared to life through me. It worked to calm me down, to really look at the small wooden box and see that it wasn't actually that small. I may have to face eternal damnation, but that was a hell of a lot less final than death.

I turned to look down at Laith, knowing that, whilst my pupils were still too wide, they were no longer the eyes of a scared child but a powerful stalker of the night. His energy responded; the touch of his vast golden shadow of a beast answering the call of my flames. Underneath the nondescript smell of his cologne was the aroma of sun-touched fur and dry dirt, stone burnt by the sun sitting underneath the branches of olive trees, and the aromatic resin of mastic trees.

My fingers found the soft waves of his hair brushed back from his clean-shaven face, somehow both silken and coarse at the same time. Unlike Kai, Laith didn't have permanent kitty-cat eyes, with the whites still shining around his iris, but somehow I just knew what he was; I could see it so clearly. Underneath the cordial look in his golden-brown eyes was the potential for danger. The black and brown streaks through his sandy hair echoed the image of a king's crown, one not forged of gold nor silver, but a crown worn from birth as king of the jungle. It was all so obvious now; how could he be anything but a beast, a lion.

'Lion,' I breathed out, the blood-tainted heat from my breath blowing onto Laith. He shuddered, body settling like a bird rusting its feathers.

He nodded. 'Lion.'

Laith tentatively reached up to remove my hand from where it rested on his head, accidentally wrapping his fingers around my wrist. I whimpered in response to the shooting pain.

'So, this is where you're hurt?' he asked, but was already turning my palm upwards.

I panicked, snatching my hand away from him. Laith let me steal my hand back without protest. 'Why won't you let me examine where you're hurt, Scarlet?'

'It's not you that I'm hiding it from. *I* don't want to see.'

He nodded like that made perfect sense.

'Lots of people don't like to see blood.'

I snorted. 'That's *really* not my problem here.'

'Not afraid of blood, eh?' He grinned at me. 'Then c'mon and show me, I promise to be gentle.' I sighed, but the glint in Laith's eye as he grinned at me was contagious, and I returned the smile despite myself.

'You do know I'm a vampire, right?'

He shrugged, cocking his head to the side. 'The coffin gave it away.'

'If you insist, Doctor Quillan.' I shrugged the jacket off my shoulders.

Laith rolled up my left sleeve with his gloved hands, bearing my arm's abrasions to the light. The deep inside of the wounds were mostly a thin layer of black and red tissue leaking out a yellow fluid. Around the edges had turned white, the skin peeling off in blisters, with charred areas scabbing over.

Laith let out a long whistle. 'Y'know, I wasn't expecting this. If I were to hazard a guess, I'd say these were third-degree burns.'

'Did you get your medical license through guesswork?' I quipped, sounding fractious even to me.

Laith peered at me from behind where he held my left hand up with its raggedy bandages from home. He started to unwind the fabric, the air cold against the deep wound over my palm.

'Nope, through a lot of studying and pressure from my senior doctor mother. I'm a GP, not a burn specialist.' He picked up my right hand. 'When did these occur?'

'Tonight.'

Laith's brown eyes widened.

'You're healing exceptionally well; even therians would take longer than this. The right is basically healed.' He was right; my right wrist was mostly large yellow blisters with very little damage past the epidermis. 'Still, if you were human, I'd be driving you to hospital right now.'

'Lucky I'm not then.'

'I can dress the wound for your own comfort and cleanliness, but, as a vampire, you run no risk of infection. Painkillers won't work, either. Honestly, at the rate you're healing, I'd say dressing these wounds could do more harm than good. I know some therians heal around bandages and we have to cut them out. Nasty stuff.'

'Vampires actually don't heal during daylight, so that wouldn't happen.'

Laith put my hand back in my lap, tapping my hand lightly with his in a gesture intended to be comforting.

'That's good to know. You're the first vampire I've met.'

'You're my first lion.'

'That you know of.' He winked at me. 'Are you hurt anywhere else?'

I debated telling him about the claw mark in my back, or the burns over my collar bone, then thought better of it. I hadn't wanted him to look me over in the first place, and it had all seemed like a colossal waste of time anyway. Besides, I sensed the pressing of dawn nearing rapidly, sending that spike of panic it always did. Sunrise brought upon the reaction of fight or flight, but this was no battle to be won by a vampire; flight was the only option. Seek refuge in the shadows until darkness defeated light once again, and we were free to roam the night.

'I … uh, no,' I said unconvincingly.

Laith didn't look like he believed me as he stood up, pulling off the gloves and packing up the unused bits of medical paraphilia placed on the floor by my feet. He knelt down by the desk near the door, discarding the blue gloves in a bin and placing the bag back in its place against the wall.

Without turning around, he spoke: 'Do you want to talk about what happened, Scarlet? Those aren't wounds that don't have a story.'

'This isn't a story you'd want to hear.'

'Try me.'

I sighed. 'Nor is it one I'm ready to tell.'

He turned to look at me, fixing me with the full intensity of his earnest gaze.

'That's okay, Scarlet, but if, or when, you feel ready to tell your story, know that there are people willing to listen without judgement.' His eyes flicked to the window where sunrise trembled on the edge of the navy sky, ready to burst at any moment. Laith stood, clothes rustling with the movement. 'I'll leave you to sleep.'

The coffin waiting for me to give myself over to it seemed to be leering at me. I bit my trembling lower lip hard enough to draw blood, turning my head down to look at my now healed knees.

'Do you want me to stay with you until sunrise?' he asked from in front of me.

I hadn't heard him move.

I nodded, not trusting myself to speak without breaking. I accepted the offer of his outstretched hand, letting him pull me to my feet. This time there was no spark between us, just the strangely familiar comfort of his hand in mine.

The coffin was surprisingly comfortable, if not cramped. If I were any bigger, it might have been more of an issue, but sometimes being on the shorter side has its perks. Admittedly, I'd never expected fitting comfortably in a coffin to be one of them. After the night I'd had, I would take any small blessing.

I tucked myself under the baby-pink blanket Laith had fetched for me. Laith lay on his side on the floor, propped up on his elbow, mirroring my position.

'I'm going to need to close the top soon,' he whispered, voice low and intimate in the dimly lit room, the only light coming from his back, casting the room in a soft orange glow.

'A few moments more,' I murmured back, resting my head on the pillow. 'Tell me about yourself, Doctor Quillan. How did you get to be medic of the Guild?'

He flashed me that brilliant coy smile again, bowing his head down, sending gilted hair flopping over his face.

'There's not much to tell, really. My mother—'

'The big-shot doctor.'

He chuckled. 'That's the one. She heard about the Guild and strongly suggested I offer my services up, which I did. I think she thought I'd find a nice female werelion to settle down with.'

'Any luck with that?' I asked, eyes beginning to grow heavy.

'Nope, but I haven't really been looking. Between Kas and work, I've got a pretty chocka schedule as it is right now.'

'Kas?'

'Kasar, my son.'

'Oh.'

Although the sun hadn't yet fully broken through the night, the weight of dawn tugged me into slumber. I wanted nothing more than to sleep, to find solace in nothingness and forget all about Vodan, about Nikolaos, about the Syndicate. Laith had distracted me from the wooden cocoon I had no choice but to sleep in, offering some comfort for which I was grateful. For the next twelve or so hours, I could give my mind over to nihility. Sometimes, I felt loss at slipping into the prison of daytime of which all vampires were hostages; other times, like tonight, I fell into the void willingly, embracing nothingness with open arms.

'Now, what about you, Scarlet Cherie. I feel your story is far more interesting than mine…'

The first touches of light blue cracked through the purple sky, and sleep embraced me, but not before I felt Laith pull the blanket more firmly over my body and close the casket lid.

CHAPTER 22

Even perfect night vision cannot prepare you for true darkness, the nothingness of awakening in a wooden box with not even a splinter to let in the hints of light. My arms shot out to the side, only to be met with solid oak. The small space was closing in on me. I'd had more space last night. My shoulders had not been so restricted then. I punched upwards without thinking about it, responding to the sudden panic of being trapped for the second time in two days. The full force of my strength sent the coffin lid flying up, crashing against the wall hard enough I was worried I had damaged it.

'Bloody hell!' a male voice exclaimed at the same time someone else groaned.

I shot upright, looking to whom the voices belonged. A man with sleep-tousled red hair sat up in bed staring at me, the one eye he wasn't rubbing free of sleep wide and surprised. Beside him lay a woman, her thick black hair spread over his lap where she rested her head. From what I could see, both of them were naked, only the thin bedsheet saved me from seeing far more of these two strangers than I cared to. A third body lay beside the woman, too covered by the sheet for me to make out who it was. Only the deep, heavy breathing hinted that they were still asleep. From the deep purr with each breath, I was assuming a man.

'Sorry, I, uh, I didn't know other people would be in here.'

'Bed space is limited,' the woman muttered, curling around to snuggle up to the third stranger.

'You must be the vampire,' said the red-haired man.

'What gave it away?' I retorted with a smile which he returned sleepily.

'You've caused quite a fuss here these last few days.'

'I only arrived this morning.'

He shrugged. 'That may be, but some of the panthers thought bringing you here with their Queen was dangerous. What with the Syndicate being after you and all. Sylvie has really argued your case.'

'She didn't mention it to me.'

'They're a they, just so you know. And nah, they wouldn't. Not after pointing out the hypocrisy of it all. Everyone here is in the same boat, or almost everyone.'

'So, what are the Syndicate after you for then?'

'Me, personally? Nothing. I'm here as a representative for my Reynard and Vixen.' He answered the question without me having to ask, adding, 'The foxes. This many new therians in a territory without prior permission from the ruling group is unprecedented, but desperate times 'n' all that.'

'Shut up and go back to sleep, Ethan,' the woman protested, awkwardly reaching behind her to whack his chest. Ethan the werefox nestled down into the sheets, throwing his arm over the other two bodies.

'I'm coming, Tanya,' he muttered under his breath to the woman. To me, he said, 'I'm going to get some shut-eye. One of the panthers, that real burly bloke, was waiting up for you, last I heard.'

Armed with the knowledge that the majority of Kai's people were not happy about me being here, I went to find him and face the dissonant music. I was looking forward to seeing Gwydion. He was always good at spinning even the most troublesome of situations into one working to his advantage. Arrogance is a deeply frustrating trait in people, but when it's earnt, can you really hold it against them? With Gwydion, I'd learnt the answer to that was *no.*

I made sure to be quiet when stepping out of the coffin so as not to disturb the three sleeping people—again. Ethan's snoring drowned out the murmuring breaths of the third man as well as the woman's soft, sleepy exhalations.

I crept past Ethan's sleeping body towards the door. My fingers were wrapped around the handle when a voice from the bed whispered, 'Scarlet.'

Laith was sitting up in bed with the sheet spooling around his lap, showing his naked upper body with its trail of golden hair over his chest and lower abdomen, leading further down. The blanket covered just enough of his lower body to hold some element of modesty whilst also showing me that his just-woken-up state had had the effect it does on most men. His neat hair from last night was now sleep-tousled and wild around his face like a mane. If my veins had blood to spare, it'd all have been sent to my cheeks.

He stretched his arms up towards the ceiling, throwing his head back, upper body straining with the huge stretch. Then he shook his body lightly and turned a contented face to me.

'Sorry, did I wake you as well?' I whispered, body still awkwardly half turned towards the door.

'Don't be; it was about time I got up anyway.'

'I think Kai wants to talk to me.'

'Yeah, I don't think he's slept. Was pacing up and down last I saw him'—Laith looked at his watch—'which was only a few hours ago.'

'Really, Kai was?'

That was very out of character. Kai was the relaxed yin to Gwydion's more tightly wound yang. I'd never once seen him pace, but had seen him fall asleep accidentally on more than one occasion. No, he was not a pacer, was our Kai. 'Is Gwydion with him, too?'

Laith's face dropped to an attempted blankness far from perfect, reminding me of the shared look between Kai and Sylvie last night when I'd asked to see Gwydion.

'Maybe you should go talk to him,' he suggested. 'I'll get dressed and join you.'

I didn't need telling twice, pulling the door open with far less consideration for the two other sleeping people in bed with Laith.

Kai was so close to the bedroom door that I almost ran straight into him and the fresh cup of coffee in his hand—so white it was more milk than coffee and with three sugars, the way he always took it. Back at home, Kai used half cream instead of milk, although I didn't know anyone else who did that. I think it was an American thing.

His sudden presence made me yelp, grinding to a halt just fast enough to avoid crashing into him.

'Kai!' I exclaimed.

Kai looked down at me, startled, the large, dark bags under the glowing amber of his inhuman eyes ageing him. For the first time, his beautiful panther eyes seemed out of place, wrong in the tired set of his human face. Had those lines around his eyes always been there?

My hand found his arm instinctively, fingers curling around all that muscle, so thick that I could barely encircle half of it. Tension ran through his body, his muscles reacting to the clenching and unclenching of his fist.

'Kai,' I said again, less shrill this time. 'Where's Gwydion? I need to talk to him.'

I didn't want to tell anyone about what had happened with Vodan—I was having a hard enough time admitting it to myself—but of all the people I had to confide in, Gwydion was the one who would comfort me by offering logical solutions. He may never hug me or tell me everything will be okay, but he would always know what to do next, and if he didn't, then we'd think it through until there was a solid plan in place. I'd left Vodan's body to decay, and although I was confident that no one would find him, a well-thought-out plan sounded good right about now. Nikolaos would know what to do, if only I could contact him. There was almost certainly to be repercussions for killing Amphitrite's Prince. Had Nikolaos told her what I'd done? If so, I wasn't just hiding out from the Syndicate. I had to have faith that Nikolaos would know how best to handle the situation without throwing me totally under the bus and endangering us both. So far, I wasn't reassured. Once we'd dealt with the problem at hand, I'd focus on Nikolaos and the Empress. For now, he was safe with her, and I could only balance the weight of so many catastrophes at one time without them crushing me.

If I told Kai what had happened between Vodan and me, he would try his best to comfort me in a way I did not need right now. The thought of anyone's hands on my body, whether as a friend, as a lover, or as a caregiver, made my stomach churn and sent a chill through my body. What made their touch different from his? All hands, even human and not amphibian ones, had the potential to finish what he had started. It felt like everyone was a ticking time bomb just waiting to explode and rain terror down over me. No, I did not want anyone to touch me. I wanted answers to the many mounting questions.

'Scarlet...'

'Where is he, Kai?'

'I...' He hung his head. 'I don't know. We went to pick him up yesterday; the train arrived, but he never did.'

I squeezed his upper arm, tracing my thumb up and down the corded muscles in his bicep. Kai's love language was tactile, like a lot of therians, or so I had been told. We may never be lovers, but the intimacy we shared as two friends was a love unto itself.

'We were gonna tell ya when you arrived 'n' then ya seemed so fragile. I wanted Laith to look over you 'n' make sure all was well before breakin' the news.' That was Kai, always holding the sky up for others when the world came crumbling down around him. Gwydion may have a certain ruthless practicality, but Kai would kill you with kindness.

I stared at him, face gone slack with processing. Everything inside me had gone still, my brain working so hard to understand what Kai had just said that it was a barrage of thoughts with which I couldn't keep up. Kai's words had gone in, but I wasn't comprehending them. Gwydion couldn't be missing; he couldn't. We needed him; Kai needed him. I needed him. It was like my whole body had frozen, time slowing to nothing until the horrible reality of what had just been said passed. Nikolaos had gone this still several times, but I'd never understood until now the need just to freeze, to become a statue that could disappear.

'Scarlet?' Kai said, frowning at me.

Vampires have this built-in defence mechanism, which makes us both shut down and go on high alert. We are the masters of compartmentalising. It kicked in like any human response, suddenly bringing me back into the moment so the world was in sharp focus and every thought in my mind ceased to be. I looked at him with my wide, overly-focused eyes, and couldn't think past the nothing. All the colours in the room were sharper, though all the edges had become blurred and soft. There was always a price to pay for such a perfected reserve—a hefty one. But it would come later, and at this rate, there was so much potential horror awaiting us, that the costly value of my sanity seemed worthless.

I removed my hand from Kai's arm, clenching a fist at my side, unclenching it, feeling every line in my palm.

'Did you hear what I said?'

I nodded past the lump still in my throat, licking dry, cracking lips.

'Yes. I want to ask if you're okay, but it seems redundant.'

His lips quirked into a side smile, though there was nothing happy about it.

'You can ask.'

'Are you okay?'

'No. Are you?'

I shook my head. 'No.' But even as I said it, it didn't feel authentic. I was impenetrable, as numb to the world as I was dead.

Laith chose that moment to come through the bedroom door, clothed in all soft tan and dark brown. He squeezed past me from behind, placing a hand on my shoulder to move me out of the way. I flinched, recoiling from the touch.

Laith held his hands up in front of his body. 'Sorry, Scarlet. Didn't mean to make you jump.'

I pulled the arm of my jumper further down my left hand, scrunching it over the slash in my palm, waiting for pain that never came. Kai observed us with those vibrant eyes which saw everything. Kai may not comment, but he missed very little.

'Where's Sylv?' Laith asked.

'With the Reina, talkin' battle plans.'

'Let's go join them,' I said, my voice distant and soft.

Both men looked at me, Laith arching a golden eyebrow, Kai's thoughts running across his face like a theatre show of emotion.

'Are you sure you're ready?' asked Kai.

'We have no time to lose.'

Neither men could argue with me on that.

The Reina had positioned two guards outside the front room, which Sylvie had turned into the joint forces' meeting room, a place of sanctuary for those offering up their bodies to battle. Or at least that was the intention. Those who sought safety without being willing to shed blood for the cause were carefully hidden away in the middle of Bumfuck Nowhere, Scotland. Angelika's family ran a bed and breakfast farther north, which they were staying in, paid for by the Reina. I didn't remember signing myself up to be in the frontline, but I guess Gwydion and Kai had volunteered me.

I would have spotted the two guards for what they were from a mile off. Both men had their wrists locked in front of their bodies like any good security guards would do, and they both screamed of intimidation. The man on the left was over six foot, standing a whole foot taller than me. He was broad enough to make Kai look slim-built with shoulders comically wide and the muscles to match. His arms were close to the size of my thighs, and my thighs ain't small. The black t-shirt he wore strained over the muscles in his arms, the seams visibly struggling to contain all that hard-won strength. His hair was as dark as the rest of his outfit, shaved close to his scalp. Really the buzzcut did nothing to complement the brutish build of his pockmarked face, but I didn't think he was going for complementary. No, definitely scary.

At first, I thought the other man was just as dark-skinned and bald as Kai, until I realised it was not skin but sable fur catching the light. Round, brown eyes stared out of a shapely face covered in a fine layer of glistening, black fur. Where the other man was all height, muscle, and perfect posture, this one was closer to my height and more slender through the shoulders than I. His relaxed, slightly slumped posture added to the illusion of delicacy, but the air he radiated was pure danger. His power thrummed through the air with ferocity; I sensed it curling around me, scenting me. I shuddered at the sensation of his energy brushing against me.

He took a step away from the door, turning his nose up to sniff the air in front of me.

'She smells like vampire,' the taller guard spat, his South American accent thick.

'Yes, and something else. Something alive,' he, the furred man, snarled at me, voice so deep it sounded more animal than human.

'Our Reina is expecting us, Dario,' Kai addressed the taller man, coming to step closer towards the sniffing guard and me.

Dario, as the only one still by the door, wrapped his big fist around the door handle but didn't make a move to open it. Someone from inside the room pulled the door to, almost sending Dario stumbling. He shot around, ready to be angry, but was stopped in his tracks by whoever was in the doorway. Dario stood up even straighter, not that his posture needed any work.

'My Prince,' Dario said, bowing his head.

'What is the holdup, Dario, Luís ?' a thickly-accented, well-spoken voice said from behind Dario's looming frame.

'Nothing, *mi príncipe*, my apologies,' Luís growled, taking a step back from me.

Dario stepped aside wordlessly, letting their Prince enter into the corridor. The Prince in question stood a few inches short of six feet. Through the perfectly tailored salmon shirt he wore, I could make out the definition of his washboard abs. The prince had tucked his shirt into suit trousers which, from Nikolaos's penchant for fashion, I knew were expensive and had been tailored to the long line of his leg. Short black hair was slicked back to show off the cut of his perfectly square jaw and wide-bridged nose, with a neat trail of hair framing his full lips. Thick, shaped eyebrows set into an arrogant arch framed eyes such a pale, glassy green they were closer to white. Muted yellow made up the ring around his iris, just dark enough compared to the green that it managed to look stark.

'*Encantado*,' the prince said to me, holding his hand out to me with the palm down. Gold rings decorated his fingers, one in the shape of a jaguar head with emeralds for eyes.

I had a moment of panic, unsure of what to do. I'd never met royalty before; I'd never even met anyone rich enough to display such an extravagant display of wealth on his fingers alone. The jaguar-ringed finger was raised slightly higher than the others, all of which were held close to my face. I stared at his fingers offering themselves to me for a moment too long and then gripped the tips of his fingers with mine and gave them a little shake, eyes locked on the prince's.

My tiny grasp on the tips of his fingers shook up and down, each shake stealing more of my dignity. I wanted to curl into a ball and shrink into myself. Laith didn't help the matter by turning his upper body away from me, hand going to his mouth as his shoulders visibly shook with the resistance to laugh. I turned pleading eyes to Kai beside me, with my fingers still awkwardly holding the prince's. He tried his best to give me blank face, but I saw the strain in his face, sucking in the corner of his lower lip and eyes glistening with unshone laughter.

I dared to turn my pale face up to the prince, who watched me with a combination of bemusement and offence.

Kai regained enough control of himself to say, 'Scarlet, may I introduce to you Prince Otorongo the Second, son of Reina Onca and Rei Otorongo. My prince, this is Scarlet Cherie.'

Otorongo II took his hand away from my grasp, fingers slipping through my own in what felt like slow motion. Why couldn't I be a poised, elegant vampire like we were *supposed* to be? Nikolaos would have known to kiss his ring, he might not have actually done it, but he'd have held his rejection to the crown with an air of grace. Becoming the undead hadn't made me any less clumsy; I was now just an immortal clutz. Great.

'My mother wishes to meet you, Miss Cherie. Kai and Sylvie have sung your praises, much to the dismay of many of our advisors.' He fixed me with his gaze, and some of that arrogance slipped to show an astuteness I'd missed before. 'I hope they are right, for we have taken their word over the contentment of our people.'

I hoped they were right, too.

CHAPTER 23

The power from the room hit me first, and then came the smell. Therians always smelt like wet animals to me, a sort of bitter, furry musk that was overpowering to my sensitive sense of smell. Come to think of it, Laith's scent hadn't been quite the same deterrent. He smelt more of sun-brushed fur that was dry and warm. Maybe it was just a leopard thing.

Reina Onca needed no introduction to spot her. She rested on a throne with her people curled by feet; a combination of human and kitty-cat eyes in human faces watched us approach with a mixture of hostility and caution. Onca didn't sit on an actual throne but Sylvie's sofa, though she could have been sitting on a chair of detritus, and the debris would yield to her regality.

Initially, I thought Onca was tall until I realised her stature had nothing to do with height. Onca sat on the sofa with her head resting on her hand, legs tucked neatly in where she luxuriated. Like Kai, there was a definite feline energy to her, a presence of languour and elegance. She was all curves and swells of flesh, with a full, voluptuous figure contained within a vibrant blue silk shirt complimenting her skin's dark tones. Much the same as her son, her fingers were adorned with golden rings, one of which matched the jaguar jewellery he had worn. A sapphire hung down her front on a delicate golden chain, matching a bracelet and one of the rings on her short fingers. The belt buckle holding up her black jeans matched the theme. I doubted that was real gold, though it did have the same glinting sheen to it—who wore a belt buckle made of real gold? Royalty, that's who, I suppose.

Otorongo II did not look much like his mother, save the glassy green and yellow of his eyes, though, like Kai's eyes, Onca had no white around the iris, only pupil and colour. Onca's facial expression did not betray her sorrow; it was the swollen, red hue to her eyes, cheeks, and nose, the trail of dried tears down her cheeks which she had desperately tried to wipe away, and the dark bags under her eyes which gave her secret away.

Two guards, a man and a woman wearing the guards' attire, stood behind the sofa upon which Onca sat, both of them glaring at me in particular. Kai moved towards his Queen, the collection of people on the floor parting like the Red Sea for him to approach. There was so much agility in each of their movements, so even just them crawling or scooting away to clear the space had a fluid, dance-like grace to it. Laith remained by my side, standing just a bit behind me, but I could feel his energy like a blazing heat in the wash of black fur, as if each panther were smoke and he a fire. His power was reacting to being a lone lion amongst the shadow—the pack name for panthers—and the burning of his energy was drawing on my own fire.

Kai knelt in front of his Queen, bowing his head in subservience. Onca ran her manicured fingers over his head, stroking the smooth baldness. On his knees, Kai made a sound I'd never heard him make before, a sort of purring snort of air through his nose. Onca looked down at him, offering a slow, deliberate blink in return. I could recognise that these actions held significance without understanding what they were. I wanted to ask what it all meant, but to show my ignorance in the presence of their Queen seemed uncouth. In my defence, I hadn't known that I would be meeting royalty, nor that it would come with particular feline customs—and Kai hadn't forewarned me. Did I, as a vampire, have to genuflect to Onca as a sign of respect? Nikolaos would probably say no. Laith hadn't, and he was the only other non-panther in the room as far as I could tell, so it seemed a safe assumption to hang back and not approach Onca until she summoned me.

I had assumed wrong. One moment my feet were planted firmly on the ground, and the next, I was dangling by the scruff of my neck. Hands bunched into the collar of my jumper pulled me off the floor, tight enough that the fabric cut into my throat, choking me. The hand which held me was warm against the scruff of my neck, that fever-heat at which all therians naturally run.

Panic struck me. I waved my arms wildly behind me, trying to swipe at whoever was throttling me. Everything became like double exposure in my vision; distantly, I knew that I was being choked in a room of panthers, but all I could see were stone walls thinly veiled by blue fabric. Music that had not been playing before hummed through my head like a ghostly scream echoing through a cave. Surely the others heard it too; it was so loud. So very, very loud.

The hands which held me felt wrong against my neck, scaly and cool instead of warm and human. I stopped struggling to tense up, my body recoiling at the sensation of a stranger's hands on my body. My vision went blurry as the first tears tried to fall, but until I fed for the night, I wouldn't be able to cry. That didn't stop my eyes from cracking, the thick red-hue liquid trying to force its way out.

My entire body felt wrong, as though fingers were crawling over my skin, defiling every inch of flesh. I could feel things that I knew weren't really there, but that didn't make it any less real, any less terrifying. Every colour in the room was too intense, overwhelming as if all the colours surrounding us would overpower me. Every eye watching me seemed malicious; every one of them mocking me for being weak. I could hear each of their heartbeats, all of their inhalations and exhalations of breath pounding through my head like a drum beating too loud and too fast. I was breathless with no breath to catch; my heart was still when what it wanted to do was pound its way through my chest. I saw everything too fast, hearing all the noises too loudly; the feeling of his—I assumed it was a he—hands on my skin like they were crushing me. Everything became a blur of overwhelming sensation.

I closed my eyes, trying to drown out some of the senses. Two snarls echoed through the space, one a deeper breath of air from beside me and the other farther into the room. Whoever held me responded with a spit of air back, sprays from the exhalation blowing onto my neck as he tightened his grip on me, yanking me up higher. I opened my eyes to see Laith half-crouched beside me in a combative stance, human teeth exposed in a snarl that should have been fanged. From where he sat beside Onca, Kai was on all fours with his face contorted into an antagonistic grimace.

'Enough of this. Release her, Dario,' a woman's voice commanded, her tone leaving little room for argument. Her accent was thick and sweet like honey, tongue rolling over the *r* in Dario the way it's supposed to be pronounced.

Every face in the room turned to look at Onca.

'She did not greet you, *mi Reina*,' Dario huffed from behind me, his breath uncomfortable along the top of my head. Human and cat eyes found their way in our direction, blinking up at the man who dared question his Queen.

Onca raised herself from the sofa in a flash of liquid movement. One moment she was sitting, and the next, she was walking towards us. She placed each leg dramatically in front of the other, a cat stalking its prey, each motion intentional and calculated.

She stopped halfway between us and the sofa, the sea of people at her feet crawling around her, some rubbing up on her legs like cats scent marking.

'It was not a question, Dario, but a command from your Queen.'

The tension in the room grew with each of her words, her voice still as sweet as honey garnished with the edge of threat. Sugar and spice and everything nice is all well and good until it kills you.

'But—'

'Release her!' she spat, and a brush of power flew through the room, her energy a phantom of furred heat. Her yellow-green eyes burned with a feral fierceness as her power washed through the space like scalding water, burning each person it touched. My own power responded to the heat, my unfed flames igniting inside of me to the call of her energy. It felt like heat, but it did not smell of fire and calcine the way mine did; her power brought with it the scent of arid air through deciduous forestry. The combination of her earth energy and my fire ran a shudder up my spine, twisting me in Dario's grasp. I felt it touch the familiarity of Kai, and soothe in his presence, but stronger than that, I felt it unite with another power behind me. Lion, Laith, Doctor Laith Quillan. For one glorious moment, I drank in the thrill of a therian with her level of power and the heat she generated combining with the golden glow of Laith's lion. And then that high began to push just this side of painful, where the rush becomes too intense, and you regret every moment leading up to such a sudden thrill.

All therians run hot, but Onca's power burnt, a heat either to warm you at night or sear you to your core. Tonight, she offered no comforting warmth with her ability. I felt it brush over every therian with their eagerly watching faces, though I knew where it was aimed.

Dario fell to his knees with me still in his grasp. We collapsed onto the carpet, me on my stomach and him on all fours above me, panting and wheezing with the force of her power. Arms pulled me out from underneath Dario's shuddering body. Laith collected me in his arms, wrapping his arm around my waist to steady me. I pushed away from his grasp, hard enough that he stumbled, and I almost fell a second time. I did not want anyone else touching me. I had a moment to feel a twinge of guilt at denying his help when a loud bray ricocheted through the room, drawing my attention back to Dario. His howl was echoed with the cry of some of the other people, each of them responding to his distressed call. Some of them rolled onto their backs, hands wafting through the air playfully, whilst others collapsed onto all fours, turning their necks up to make sounds no human throat should be capable of making.

I recognised the sound of bones snapping to mean shifting before Dario's hunched shoulders began to pop from their sockets visibly. I'd seen Kai shift enough times to know it often looked painful, though he reassured me it never hurt as much as it may seem, unless there was a full moon. When a full moon hit the sky at its highest point for the night, Kai was forced to shift, and it was neither painless nor smooth. Like the guiding light of the silver moon, Reina Onca was bringing Dario's beast, forcing him to shift.

Kai, recovered from his bout of anger, understood the consequences of what was about to happen more so than anyone else in the room—or he just cared more. Either way, he stepped through the crowd of arching bodies to stand abreast with his Queen.

'Reina,' he began, reaching out his hand and then thinking better of touching her, 'I ain't questionin' your ways, but Sylvie has invited us into their home, and forcin' Dario to shift will mess up this 'ere carpet.'

It felt like such a mundane point in the midst of such an extraordinary display of power, but it got her attention.

Onca turned to look at Kai, who I now realised was a good few inches taller than Onca, which made her closer to my height.

He continued, 'An arbitrary show of power against our own ain't gonna help us fight the enemy.'

Onca took in a deep breath, nodding her head, and as quickly as the scorching power had filled the room, it depleted like water running through a hole in the ground. Dario fell onto his stomach, panting furiously. Luís appeared by the larger man's side in a flash of black, but he made no attempt to help him without permission from his Queen.

Onca's voice rang clear and assertive as she announced, 'May this be a reminder to *mi gente*, we have come as allies to all here not of our kind'—she gestured around the room—'to fight united against one cause. Only those who have sworn fealty to me as their Reina will treat me as such, but in this battle, we are equal. Whilst in this house, we work as a front against those who have wronged us, have hurt us, have stolen from us. You have volunteered yourselves as *guerreras,* though at any time, you may leave the ranks to seek safety with the rest of our *Sombra.* We were invited into Sylvie's home as refugees and made to feel like guests, and they and their people will be treated with the respect deserved.'

Such a rush of power on an empty stomach had depleted me of much-needed energy, and I found myself stumbling once again. Laith managed to catch me by my arm just in time before I fell to the floor, but the bolt of energy between us was too much so soon.

'Are you well, Scarlet?' Onca glared at the man on the floor, and I never wanted to be the target for such a piercing look. 'Though I see no wound, I fear he has hurt you.'

I tried to swallow the dry lump in my throat; even then, I still wasn't sure I could speak.

Kai stepped up again, saying, 'She needs to feed.'

Onca cocked her head to one side, considering the information offered to her.

'Whilst I wish to make amends for Dario's imprudence, I cannot offer my people to you as food. We are predators, not prey.'

'Everyone invited here is free to choose to be a donor, but I don't expect it from anyone I have offered protection to here at the Guild,' Sylvie said from where they leant against the doorframe. Ethan and Angelika stood to their left, Ethan leaning casually against the doorframe. To their right stood the woman from earlier, the one who had laid naked by Laith's side. I hadn't noticed any of them come in. I wondered if they'd all been witness to tonight's ordeals.

'I am food for no one,' the woman, of whom I still didn't know the name, said, raising her hands up in the air as if to say, *I'm out.*

'Me, neither. Sorry, love,' Ethan agreed, though he softened his deliverance with a smile.

Angelika was the only one who didn't speak up. She was clutching Slyvie's hand so tight her knuckles had gone white. I could see the pulse in her throat bouncing up and down like a mad thing. Her fear smelt good, sweet and sugary, but plain. A silver pentagram hung from her neck, matching the pair hanging from her earlobes, but I knew, despite her protestations last night, Angelika was human.

'I'll do it,' Laith said, shrugging lightly.

'Honestly, Laith, you don't have to do that. I can find a human; I didn't come here expecting anyone to offer themselves to me.'

'It'll be an experience.'

I frowned at his nonchalance. 'No, I don't think you understand. I won't be able to allure you, as you're a therian. It will hurt. A lot.'

He shrugged. 'I'm sure some of my needle-phobic patients would think it is poetic justice.'

'Are you sure?' Kai and I asked at the same time.

He grinned at us both in turn with that smile that lit up his whole face and echoed a youthful glow from his younger days, not that he was particularly old now.

'I'm sure.'

Ethan let out a long whistle from by the door, his sleep-tousled red hair wild around his face. 'You're a braver man than me, mate,' he said as Laith and I began to walk towards the hallway. Sylvie gave Laith a considering look as if they were seeing their friend in a whole new light for the first time. Angelika just glowered at us from where she shielded herself behind her smaller partner.

'I could've told you that anyway,' Laith said as we passed through the threshold, making Ethan chuckle to himself.

Laith opened the bedroom door, nodding his head in the direction of the unlit room.

'After you.'

I walked in wordlessly. I wasn't sure that Laith really understood what he was offering or how much it would hurt without the power of allure to numb the pain. Surely it was my responsibility to warn him. I turned around to do just that, but I could see the element of anxiety flickering over the warm brown of his eyes, mingling with the sincerity he'd displayed from the moment we had first met. Laith knew exactly what he was getting himself into; he was entrusting me not only to make this the least unpleasant as possible but also with his life. No one should trust a stranger with such a colossus gamble so soon after meeting. And yet, he did, and I found myself finding it endearing instead of foolish. Though, really, foolish it was.

CHAPTER 24

Laith sat on the edge of the bed, back straight, fingers twiddling with a loose thread coming out of the mahogany jumper he wore, only a few shades darker than his brown trousers. My eyes kept wandering to the side of the bed he had been sleeping in only an hour earlier, naked and pressed against a woman's body.

'You seem distracted. Is everything okay?'

I looked over at the patiently waiting lion with his nervous fidgeting. My own hands were rubbing up and down the lid of the coffin on which I sat, the wood smooth under my fingers.

'I don't want to hurt you.'

'I trust you to make it as painless as you're able.'

'Why?'

He shrugged. 'Because that's what I'd do.'

'When I woke up, I spoke to Ethan.'

Laith looked down at his dynamic hands. 'Oh, yeah, what did you talk about?'

'He said my presence here has caused a bit of a rift. Why is it that all the therians seem to have a problem with vampires? Or is it just me in particular?'

'I don't have a problem with you being a vampire, nor with you, for that matter. If I did, I wouldn't be offering up a vein,' he reassured.

'You and Kai are the exceptions, I suppose. But the others...'

185

'Scarlet, do you know how many times therians and other species have worked together?'

I shook my head. 'No.'

'None. When Sylvie brought the Guild together, it was with the intention of offering a safe haven and support network for species who were lonesome. Obviously, anyone is welcome to join, but the supernatural community generally keep to themselves. By the Reina coming here and asking for protection from the Guild, it is the start of something unprecedented.'

'I didn't realise.'

'There seems to be a sort of unspoken divide between the community. There are vampires, therians, necromancers, deities, and others. And whilst each group may mingle with the others, they do not work together. Especially not therians and vampires.'

'Or vampires and necromancers.'

'Yep.'

'Why is that?'

'Most people would say it's because of the Wulf Crusade of 1118.'

'Never heard of it.'

'It was the catalyst to the vampire monarchy becoming what it is today, as well as the end of the werewolves reign of terror over vampires in England and Europe. The Wulf Cyning Brothers, Ethelwulf and Beorhtwulf, or Emperors Osker and Erik as they're known today, saw that the werewolves were the dominant species across Europe and decided to fight back. Most of the wolves were Vikings, many of whom had settled in Normandy, so after the Battle of Hastings, the two men single-handedly turned humans into armies of vampires, setting up battle stations for their warriors to protect lesser vamps from the wolves. There was a third companion of the brothers, said to be a lover of Erik, and whose allure could enchant even the most powerful of wolves, but I think people have just added to the story over time. Otherwise, there'd be three original kings.'

Laith moved position, so he was lying on his back, hands clasped under his head, face turned to me as he continued to explain the history of my species about which I knew nothing.

'Vampires get stronger with each vampire they make. If they were turning armies worth, then they must be super powerful,' I said.

'Yeah, they are. Which is part of the reason that, although the monarchy says there is an equal balance of power, everyone knows it's not true. They're the two true kings, and the monarchy is theirs, the way the Guild is Sylvie's.'

'Sylvie told me they have set it up so there's no one leader on the Guild's board.'

'Mm, they have, but the Guild is Sylvie's baby, and they're definitely the parent of it.'

I nodded. 'Yes, I can see that.'

'Anyway, to cut a long story short, after years of battling smaller groups of werewolves with their vampire army, the lycanthrope king, Wulfrick, entered the battlefield. A hoard of Viking werewolves entered into combat with a swarm of vampire warriors. The wolves played dirty, though, and brought necromancers to fight their corner, but the vampires fought back by alluring humans armed with silver to act as cannon fodder. The vampires won, eventually, by getting to Wulfrick and killing him. Alpha wolves are still called Wulfrick in his honour.

'Now vampires think they're the top dog of the supernatural world. For years, lycanthropes were killed on sight by any vampire, but now I think Osker and Eric let them live in their respective territories if the alpha pays them the Wulf Tax.'

'It's a mortal sin in the vampire world to share your blood with a necromancer, you know. Knowing the history of it now makes it make more sense,' I said.

'Actually, your friend Gywdion helped ease some of the tension between necromancers and vampires when he formed the Syndicate. He instigated a meeting between the Wolf Cyning Brothers, agreeing that they would stay out of vampire politics if the vampires agreed to do the same. It helped ease some of the animosity whilst also creating a further divide between the communities.'

'How do you even know all of this?'

Laith sat up and grinned at me. 'I'm a big history nerd, but less so when it comes to human history.'

'What's the other theory? You said the crusade was only one.'

'Oh, right, so the battle is the very palpable theory of separation. It's clear cut, bloody, and logical. But this is the world o' magick, so logic doesn't usually come into consideration. People say that the moon enslaves both therians and vampires, but vampires represent death, and we are life.'

'You don't agree?'

'I'm not magickally inclined, and I don't waste my time trying to make sense of the illogical. Battle and war make sense to me; theories of symbolism just don't in the same way. I can't deny that there is a certain... energy given off by vampires that, as a therian, I find kind of peculiar, but I don't know if there's that much depth to it.'

'By vampires, you mean me.'

'Yes,' he said, voice as soft as I'd ever heard from him, 'but peculiar doesn't mean bad, Scarlet. Life'd be boring without the weird and wonderful.'

'Oh, great, so now I'm weird, too!' I teased, rolling my eyes theatrically.

'And wonderful,' he replied, flashing me that bashful smile once again.

'We really need to find out what's happened to Gwydion, and the others will be wondering where we are. Are you sure you don't mind doing this, Laith? You won't be able to heal a vampire wound as quickly as a normal one.'

'I don't mind being your meal, though can I request you bite me in a place easily hidden for work if it won't heal?'

I felt my cheeks try and fail to turn red as I avoided his sincere eye contact.

'The only place you'll be able to hide is your thigh,' I mumbled, hands rubbing the coffin lid with more urgency.

Laith let out an uproarious laugh so unexpected it made me jump.

'I'm sure the brachial artery will work just fine.'

Laith pulled the jumper over his head, messing up the waves of his hair. I don't know what he'd done to style it last night, but the straight, neat silk of his hair looked wavier after sleeping as though, if it were longer, it would be curly. His cotton shirt underneath was a browny-red, with the buttons loose around his neck. He unbuttoned the wrist, rolling it up his forearm, but it didn't go up far enough to reveal the brachial artery clean enough for me to get a good bite.

'I'm going to need to remove my shirt. Is that okay with you?'

Until that moment, all I'd been thinking of was the pain element for Laith without taking into consideration the intimacy of feeding. After last night with Vodan, pleasure had been far from my mind. I couldn't imagine the touch of anyone feeling right again; sensual had become sordid.

Laith kept his fingers on the first done-up button around his chest, still and waiting for my approval. I nodded but turned my head away to not watch as he undid his shirt. Illogical, I know, as there was no way for me to avoid seeing him shirtless. Soon, I would be locking my lips around the bend in his arm, pressed up against his bare torso. But there was something amatory about watching someone undress, the vulnerability of someone showing themselves unadorned by garment.

'I'm ready,' he whispered, voice gone to a soft, deep whisper too intimate in the low light.

I turned to face him, letting myself watch how the dim orange light from the bedside lamp danced across the tan of his chest. He was more muscular than his slender frame would lead you to believe, with a trail of golden hair dancing between small, dark-pink nipples.

Laith's eyes gleamed, the honey colour darkening to rich whiskey. I forced myself to look at his face and not get distracted by the hair like spun gold over his torso. His hair flowed around his face in soft, multi-toned waves catching the light. It was too dark in here; we needed more light. I walked silently to the light switch by the bedroom door, flicking it on. The room felt warm, and not in the way I liked; it was stifling. I rubbed my palms against my tights as if my hands were sweaty, though I knew they weren't. The fabric rubbed over the still-healing wound on my palm, some of the pain centring me again.

The bed creaked underneath where I sat on the edge, as far away from Laith as I could without falling off.

'This will hurt,' I warned again, avoiding looking anywhere but where my hands rested in my lap.

'I know.'

'Okay.'

His body was half turned towards me, bunching his stomach slightly. I was so intrigued by that line in his body, the way it dented the smoothness of his belly. Laith held his arm out to me, offering me up his blood, his flesh, his pain. My fingers wrapped around his arm, and once again, that electricity that had been between us since we'd first met last night sparked between us. This time neither of us pulled away, letting the current of energy flow from between our two bodies into each other. He let out a deep breath of air, arm tensing in my grip with the shudder which ran through him. My fire stirred lightly, but we were both tired and needed sustenance.

Laith placed his hand over mine, guiding my hand up to the brachial artery pulsing just above the bend in his arm. His fingers rested on mine a moment too long, fingertips so light against my own it was a phantom touch, all the while I could feel his pulse speeding up.

I lowered my mouth down to where my fingers rested, lips brushing fleetingly over his soft skin. My head raised upwards, fangs exposed to the light, ready to strike.

Laith made a rookie mistake, though who could really blame him in his conscious state, and tensed up, but it was too late. I brought my mouth down into the vein by my thumb, fangs sinking in fast and deep. He cried out, whole body flinching from the pain.

That first oh, so sweet drop slid into my mouth like it was made to be there and... and oh, my fucking god!

Such glorious decadence, the richness of truffle chocolates that crumble and melt in your mouth, and the sweetness of sugar syrup on the tip of my tongue. I sucked on the wound, bringing a moan from deep in Laith's throat.

'Fuck,' he breathed out, the growled words trickling from his lips. 'It burns.'

I began to pull away, but Laith's fingers wrapped through my hair and pushed me harder against his arm.

'It feels amazing.'

I didn't need telling twice.

I sucked harder and faster, taking each droplet of his blood into my mouth. My tongue lapped it up, spreading the thick liquid throughout my mouth, savouring the flavour as if it were the most precious thing on earth. It was so warm down my throat, far warmer than a human's. The heat entering me brought my fire with a passion, sending my flames blazing through me in a wash of intense tranquillity. I felt my fire flow through me and meet Laith's energy, his lion's energy, which burned like golden light in front of me.

Our two energies flowed out our bodies, through each of us, and into the air. Laith's lion brushed up against me, inside me, sandy fur rubbing along parts of me that only magick could touch. I shuddered with the sensation of his huge beast caressing over my body, scent-marking me and my power. My magick bled into him the way he was bleeding into me. I felt it rush through his veins, each inch it pulsed through, encouraging his beast to work deeper inside my aura.

Blood always sustained me, gave me that little spark of life that I needed to survive the cold hours of darkness, but this was such an extraordinary rush. His blood did not just feed me, but nourished me, satisfying parts of me I didn't know were crying out to be held. Laith's power filled me, and I filled him, until, for a moment, I could feel my lips locked around his arm whilst also feeling the sensation of having someone suck on a fresh wound. He was right, it did burn, but it felt so good.

Laith collapsed backwards, his arms wrapping around my back to bring me with him. I had to unlock my jaw or risk ripping his arm open. I ended up straddling his waist, his arms still locked behind my back. I dug my nails into his chest, head thrown back, letting the rush of his blood fill me with bountiful waves of peace and heat and life. Such life! My breath came out in a long sigh, a breath taken deep from within my lungs in a place I had not breathed since becoming a vampire.

My ties to Nikolaos burst open before he had a chance to shut them down. He saw me straddling my lion's waist, legs tensing around his torso to grind myself further into his body.

'*Ma chérie,* what have you done...' Nikolaos whispered through my mind, his voice like the silk to Laith's fur, so the sensation of both men's power made me cry out.

And then he was gone with the next jolt of energy that ripped through me, sending my spine shooting upwards and eyes flaring open. My nails ripped down Laith's naked chest, tearing tracks through his skin just deep enough to bleed him.

The room was cast in a glow of golden light and heat as if we'd brought the sun down to earth, and it shared its energy with us, lighting up the night outside. I looked down at Laith to see his eyes had bled from human brown to full lion, the whites consumed by umber. His wide pupils were mirrors, reflecting me with blood over my mouth like a lover's smeared lipstick. My own eyes were entirely black, the pupils black fire in the golden chaos.

The palpable energy we had summoned was a red nimbus around me, but around Laith it glowed neon yellow in the shape of a colossal feline. The lion's face looked out at me over Laith's, both their eyes shared as one. His hands dug into my back, fingers exploring under my shirt, and with the pressure, the press of phantom claws wanting to draw blood from me. I felt my knees sinking into the bed below me, both him and I being consumed by the mattress the way the cherubs sink into clouds. We were both so light, weightless as we floated on the high of the power we'd called. His body and mine were one; our energies shared to become one sylphlike entity so light the air carried us away, all the while so heavy our bodies sunk into ataraxy. I perceived the earth rotating in space, the moon's decline in the sky above, and the earth below us crumbling to give way to new life.

I'd never understood that therians shared a similar bloodlust to vampires, but at that moment, I knew a part of Laith wanted to rip me open just as much as I did him. And that was just more of a thrill.

The sensation of his claws resting over the wound Vodan's talons had inflicted made the breath catch in my throat, though this time it was from the thrust of fear that spiked through my chest.

Niko's words came back to me.

My darling, what have you done?

What had I done? The rush of power no longer felt thrilling but degenerate, the difference between taking pure cocaine and rat poison. For a moment, it all feels the same, and then you realise you've poisoned your body, and no high is worth the detriment. My body rode a stranger, his energy touching me in places that only Nikolaos had before, that I thought were special between just us, unable to be sullied by any other. Nikolaos and I not being monogamous didn't make it feel like any less of a sordid affair, for Laith had not just touched my body but my soul. The heat around us blazed into a burning red, suffocating the room, and then collapsed in on itself to darkness.

All of those tears I had been unable to shed, lost to the void of apathy, burst from my eyes, raining down my face in streaks of red, globs of lava.

Laith let out a growl, releasing the grip he had on me.

The bedroom door burst open, letting the light of the hallway slash through the sudden darkness in which we had found ourselves. Both of us turned to see Kai, Ethan, and Sylvie standing in the doorway.

'Jesus Christ,' Ethan exclaimed.

With Laith's blood pumping through my veins like heroin, my senses had spiked. I could see the bristled texture of Ethan's orange-brown hair where it was spiked up, each strand unique, down to the shadow of facial hair on his face I hadn't noticed before, and each long, red eyelash. His eyes were a light brown, with a darker ring around the misshapen pupil. Every vein running under his pale skin glowed with the flow of his blood, giving him the life I lacked. Out of those frowning brown eyes, I saw a look of horror. I followed his gaze to the man below me, his arm cast to the side, leaking blood all over Sylvie's fresh sheets. Laith had gone very still underneath me, neck limp and face slack. I knew he wasn't dead; I'd seen dead before—last year, when we'd gone to the morgue to see Sophie, Maglark's final victim—and death did not look as peaceful as this. Laith was still riding the tranquil high from which I'd broken, gouching on the rush of my heat through his veins.

I could also hear the slow and steady beat of his heart as if it were my own. No, I didn't just hear it; I felt it distantly in my own chest.

'What the hell were you two doing?' Ethan asked, rubbing his hands up and down his arms. The hairs on all of their arms stood on end, goosebumps trailing their bodies.

My heart pounded in my chest, each beat trying to tear itself out of my body. All I could hear was the thumping drumbeat of my heart echoing throughout my body. Everything felt distant and distorted, a layer of confusion between the world and me, when in that moment, all I was was a vessel for my terrified heart and breathless lungs. I tried to take in a breath but no air was enough. Trembling like the tears on the edge of my eyes, the world was shaking. I gulped down more air but to no avail. Each failed breath filled me with panic; adrenaline surged through my body, and, in a flash, I was standing up. I had to move, I couldn't be still with this much fear racing through my body. I felt like I was dying, but I was already dead.

I needed to be out of this room with its closing-in walls, free of the disdainful gazes of my friends and acquaintances. My clothes were suffocating me. They were getting smaller with each passing second; I wanted to gag on the sensation of cloth around my throat. I ran out the door into the hallway with its too-bright light glaring overhead. Each breath I took was too shallow and cool, the air ice trying to freeze me from the inside. I was choking on my own breathing, and for the first time in half a year, I could feel the touch of air hitting parts of my lungs turned black with death.

I ran into the bathroom, the door shuddering as I slammed it closed behind me. My body was moving too fast with my thoughts unable to catch up. We were in full panic mode, my body and I; all we knew was that we needed to be doing something, anything, to calm down.

Without thinking, I tore my strangling clothes from my body and left them shredded on the floor, turning on the shower. Even though I only turned on the hot tap, the water took a while to heat, freezing droplets beating against my skin.

The water drew me to my knees, bowing my body down to the cold acrylic tub, my tears lost in the flow of the shower turning red.

Someone knocked against the door. 'Scarlet,' Kai's voice called through the wood.

I heard whispering, the hushed tones of Sylvie's voice speaking too low for me to hear even with my vampire senses at the highest they'd ever been. Kai swore under his breath, and the next knock that came rattled the door hard enough I jumped.

'Scarlet, darlin', you can't get in the shower. This house is blessed. It's holy water!' Kai said with increasing urgency but his voice was lost to the monotonous drone of water splashing over my body and the vague static in my head.

I wanted to contact Nikolaos and explain what had happened. I needed him to understand what he'd seen, even if I didn't understand it myself. There was no phone in my head this time, I wasn't thinking clearly enough to envision that, just the pure need for him to respond to my call. My power reached outwards towards my lover, searching for him at the Empress's side, only to touch the golden fur of a dazed lion. Laith responded to my distress call; he felt my pure yearning for someone to make it all better. To make me safe. Nikolaos did not respond. There was a wall between him and me, a wall I could not penetrate that hadn't been there before. When I'd imagined the phone in my head it had seemed like a dead line;

now, with my power released freely, I could feel the barrier between us. It wasn't him that had put it up; someone or something was blurring our connection. I collapsed onto my side, too helpless to fight whatever was working against us. The water streamed crimson with my tears; all I could do was sob and hope the water washed away my woes.

CHAPTER 25

Wood shattered as the door crashed open, splintering onto the linoleum. Distantly I'd known that the pounding on the door had not stopped, the strength of the knock increasing with the worried pleas of Kai and Laith. To answer to them would have required a voice; Vodan had stolen my words from me.

I didn't turn to look at who had smashed the door to smithereens; my focus was entirely stolen by one small spot on the acrylic, staring into it and seeing nothing. Even when someone turned the running water off and wrapped my body in a towel, I didn't stop staring into the blank space. Only Kai's familiar scent let me know that it was he who had picked me up from my pitiful position in the water.

Kai carried me like a baby wrapped in a blanket towards the bedroom, my damp hair soaking his shirt. He lay me down on the stripped duvet as gently as he'd picked me up, careful not to expose any of my body as he did so. I curled up on the duvet, the old fabric rough, my face resting on his lap as a pillow. Someone else placed a blanket over my body as Kai's hands stroked down my hair, smoothing the damp tangles of it back from my face. I knew it was Laith who was with us without seeing him.

'You gave me quite the fright there, darlin',' he whispered.

I reached down to pull the blanket further up my body. Kai stopped stroking my hair to grab my wrists in his hands.

The wounds had healed to a dark pink trace all the way around, so it looked like I wore a bracelet of my trauma.

'Lettie, please talk to me. What happened to you before you came here?'

He let my wrist go without a fight; I hugged my arms to my chest using the blanket to cocoon myself in, so only my face was visible. Kai's voice held such sorrow that I looked up in time to see the first tear break free of his yellow eyes.

'I can't talk about it,' I whispered, my voice sounding like a stranger's.

'You can,' he argued, voice cracking.

I reached up to wipe the tears away from his cheeks.

'I don't know how.'

'We're here for you, Scarlet. Whatever it is you've gone through, you aren't alone,' Laith said from behind me.

I sat up, drawing my knees to my chest and resting my head on Kai's shoulder. Both men had their entire focus on me, and there was no judgement on their faces. Laith was still shirtless, the white bandage on his arm stark against his tan.

Laith reached his hand out to me; I laced my fingers through his, letting my palm rest limply in his grasp. He squeezed me encouragingly, and I let the feeling of his hand in mine be real with no ill intent.

And then, with a deep breath, I chose to face the demon that had been haunting me and tell the two of them all about Vodan. Tears were shed, more so from Kai than me, as I had no more energy left to cry, no more anger left to give. I spared them some of the details, the parts which still were hazy in my mind from lack of processing. Neither of them interrupted me whilst

I spoke. Even when my voice betrayed my pain, and my words were choked and broken, they were patient with me. There'd been some parts of myself I wasn't ready to unveil to the world yet, and that was okay, because I had shared some of the crushing burden that was making the air feel unbreathable and life unlivable. Just that slight relief of pressure was cathartic.

When I was done, I curled back into a ball, letting Kai's body heat warm me from behind, Laith's hand in mine still solid and comforting. With Kai's body spooning me, I closed my eyes, letting myself be in that moment.

Together, we let the silence fill the room, the echo of my words lost to the darkness.

CHAPTER 26

Kai's breath was warm against my neck; each inhalation heavy with sleep. I opened my eyes to the sensation of Laith's fingers stroking back and forth over my hand. I didn't know how long we'd been in the bedroom. It wasn't possible for me to have slept at night, yet I felt groggy and unfocused.

Laith held a finger up to his lips, nodding his head in the direction of Kai.

'This is the first time he's slept in days,' he whispered.

'What time is it?' I asked.

Laith looked at the watch on his wrist.

'Almost three; you've been asleep for a few hours.'

I startled, making Kai grumble in his sleep. His arm flung over my front, pulling me closer into his body.

'Vampires don't nap.'

Laith shrugged. 'It looked like you were asleep.'

'Have you been here the whole time?'

'Yeah.'

'Why?'

'In case you needed me when you woke up.'

I realised that the towel I had been wearing had slipped down with the cover revealing a lot of my bust. I pulled the blanket up, careful this time not to disturb my sleeping friend. I felt embarrassed about my breakdown earlier; there was no way that a bunch of therians hadn't heard the whole ordeal. I also owed Sylvie an apology about the door. It had never occurred to me that running water in a house that had been blessed would be considered holy water, though I guess it made sense. Kai knew I was immune to crosses, but we'd never tested my resistance to other blessed items. I hadn't meant to worry anyone.

'Will you pass me my bag by the door so I can get dressed?'

Laith let go of my hand to pick himself up from the floor. When he was back by my side, he raised the bag up and down, weighting it.

'It's nice,' he said.

'Thanks.'

'I'll leave you to get dressed now.'

Kai barely stirred when I shimmied out from under his arm; he'd always been a deep sleeper. I knelt on the floor, holding the towel up around me with one arm whilst using the other to rummage through the contents of the duffel.

I collected my clothes in one arm, going to stand behind Kai's sleeping form so that I wouldn't flash him if he opened his eyes. Black knickers, the least frilly ones I owned, went on underneath black jeans. The shirt was navy and sheer with ruffles around the top which required something either under or over it not to expose myself. I opted for under, throwing on a silky vest.

Laith was nowhere to be found in the hallway. I thought it was empty until I heard a rustling from by the front door, which was hidden around the corner from me. I peaked around to see the woman who had shared a bed with Laith and Ethan pulling on her leather jacket, a cigarette bobbing between her lips.

She turned around, saw me, and jumped.

'Woah! You snuck up on me.'

'Sorry.'

'No worries, my senses aren't as good as the others' yet.'

'Can I join you?'

'Yeah, sure.'

She fished the tobacco, papers, and filters from her pocket and handed them to me. I stared down at them, unsure of what to do.

'You don't know how to roll?' I shook my head. 'Here, have this one, I'll roll another.' She plucked the cigarette from between her half-smiling lips and handed it to me in exchange for the paraphernalia.

The winter wind was biting, even colder than we got back home at Britchelstone, not that it bothered me that much as a vampire. Wind rustled the leaves in the trees across the road from us, whispering their wind-swept secrets to one another. In the distance, cars filled the air with their pollution of light, fumes, and noise. The chatter of big cities, where nature, humans, and urban development work as one to form a new, neo-dialect. It was late, dawn a near promise on the edge of the darkness, so the busyness of human life was more a creeping hum where the night-owls and early-birds unite as one for a short moment. I always loved this time of night, just as the sleepy silence begins to give way to a new day with new potentials and opportunities.

'You're Scarlet, right?' my companion asked, drawing me from my daze.

'Mmm, yeah.' I turned to her. 'I'm sorry, I didn't catch your name.'

'I'm Tanya,' Tanya said, rubbing her hands together and blowing into them.

She huddled into her leather jacket, pulling the collar up around her neck. Tanya pulled the tobacco from her pocket, lining it up in the rizla with the filter and then rolling and licking it in one fast, efficient motion. She offered the spark wheel lighter to me first. I breathed in the dose of nicotine, feeling the smoke enter my lungs, burning them in the way I'd come to enjoy. The smoke slithered down my throat like a carcinogenic serpent. Tanya was having more trouble lighting hers in the blowing wind, her thumb working tirelessly over the spark.

'Here, let me help,' I said, taking the lighter from her shaking hands. I didn't need to spark it; just a small pulse of my power was enough for the gas to catch light and bloom to life.

'Thanks. That was impressive.'

Tanya took a seat on the top step, taking a deep drag, turning her head up to the sky to blow out the smoke. I watched it dance through the night and disappear off into oblivion until the next exhale came. Tanya's shoulder-length hair spiked out from underneath her grey woollen beanie, brown eyes almost as dark as her hair.

'Can I ask you something?' I asked.

Tanya turned her black-brown eyes to me, cocking her head to one side.

'You can ask, don't know if I'll answer, though.'

'What did you mean by, "My senses aren't as good as the others' yet"?'

'Do you know much about therianthropes?'

'Not as much as I thought I did, it seems.'

Her full lips tugged at the sides, almost smiling. 'Yeah, neither did I until a couple of weeks ago.'

'What do you mean?'

'This time last month, I was on holiday in America. Me and my boyfriend were meant to go, but we broke up, so I thought, fuck it, I'll go by myself. I met this guy in a bar, and we went back to his, but I started to get this weird feeling, y'know, like something was a bit dodgy. Anyway, turns out we were only a few days away from a full moon, and this guy'd been drinking.' I think I knew where this was going, but still, I let her tell her story. 'The dude fucking shifted whilst we were... Well, you can guess what we were doing. Sliced me up real good.'

'Oh, my god.'

'Yeah, it wasn't pretty. He took me back to his pack, or Skulk—I don't know, I'm still making sense of the terms. I was taken in by the doctor there and dosed up on painkillers. A few days later, when the moon hit full, well, I shifted.

'So, now, here I am. Couldn't have picked a better time, really, with us being on the cusp of a supernatural war and all.' She laughed loud and sudden, the sound strident 'God, I can't believe those words just left my mouth.'

'I didn't even know that you could become a therianthrope that way.'

'Yeah, they call me a shapeshifter instead as I don't have beast blood or something. The American Skulk put me in contact with Sylvie, who contacted the Reynard here to arrange a meeting with him. Ethan already had plans to come here, so they made him my Companion.'

'Companion?'

'I don't know if all the groups do it, but the foxes set up a Companion scheme, so first-time shifters have someone with experience with them. Usually, it's with children with younger foxes who have gone through the change recently themselves as turning a human into a fox down here is illegal, but it works the same way with me. He's been a lifesaver. Him and Laith both, to be fair.'

Tanya tossed her cigarette onto the ground, reaching a long leg outwards to stamp it out with her boot.

'Laith isn't a fox.'

'No, but he's a doctor, and I was cut up pretty bad even after shifting for the first time. They thought that sharing energy at night might help me heal quicker, and it's been working.'

'That's why you were in bed with them,' I murmured.

Tanya frowned at me over the other cigarette she was rolling.

'Ethan said that new shifters could sometimes shift in their sleep close to a full moon.' She handed me the rolled cigarette. 'Laith suggested sharing energy and heat, but we couldn't wear clothes just in case I shifted. To be honest, I thought I'd find it really weird. But since shifting for the first time, wearing clothes feels weird, or something, I don't really know how to explain it.'

'That actually makes sense. Kai has said something similar to me before. I think if he had his way, we'd all be naturists, but he still respects my boundaries. There's not anything sexual about it, which is kind of nice.'

Tanya nodded her head, handing me the lighter again. I lit both of our cigarettes.

'Your friend Kai seems really nice. Cute, too.'

'He's lovely, but married. Oh, and gay.'

Tanya flicked her barely-smoked cigarette onto the ground, leaving it to glow long and orange against the concrete.

'Best ones always are,' she said, using the railing to pull herself up.

Tanya held her finger down on the buzzer until a flustered voice I recognised as Angelika's snapped, 'What?'

'It's Tanya. Let us in.' Tanya turned to look at me over her shoulder. 'She's always so moody.' While a part of me agreed that with Tanya, in defence of Angelika, I'd probably be pissed off too if someone had held the buzzer down.

Angelika buzzed us in, but it was Laith who answered the door.

'You leading Scarlet astray, Tanya?' Laith teased as Tanya hung her jacket on the coat rack. To me, he said, 'Smoking kills, you know.'

Looking him directly into the eyes, I replied, 'I'm already dead.'

He chuckled nervously, slicking back the hair that was falling into his face. 'Ah, yeah, sorry, force of habit. Being a doctor and all.'

Tanya's incessant buzzing hadn't woken Kai, but Laith told me that Reina Onca had requested our presence, including Kai's. Tanya and I had wasted close to an hour outside and the night was beginning to slip away without any of us achieving anything. We crept through the corridor, trying not to wake up the sleeping Sylvie and Angelika again. Humans really can't go that long without sleeping, and they were the most human of all of us. At least Kai seemed a little perkier after his catnap, if not still a muted shadow of his usual jovial self. Tanya had left us to go to bed before sunrise, plodding off to join Ethan. She'd said that watching the sunrise always made her feel ill. Too many nights of partying when she was younger had left the residue of a comedown on the breaking of dawn. To me, it just meant that I was running out of time before 'dying' for the day.

I'd asked Kai about panther protocol before entering the room with the waiting Reina and her people, information that I wished I'd been privy to earlier on in the evening. He'd told me that, to show my respect and allegiance to the Reina, I would usually be expected to touch my nose to the snout on her ring, which was their equivalent of a crown. Most panthers would also prusten to display affiliation, though as a non-therian, that was not expected of me. Although Reina Onca had not come here expecting anyone to show obeisance under such extenuating circumstances, I wanted to honour and observe their cultural practices. Kai'd shown me the correct way to do this, so I was going in prepared.

Onca still lounged upon her throne. Some of her human cats were curled up on the floor, their breath heavy with sleep; others were barely staying awake where they sat at the dining table. As we walked in, a man's face slipped from between his hands, face almost planting onto the tablecloth. Luís and a female guard had taken up position behind the sofa, with the other guards paired up on both the windows.

A silver armchair was positioned beside the black sofa, a seat reserved for their prince, I presumed, though he was nowhere to be seen. All of the furniture in the front room was a clash of colours and mismatch of designs. An ornate silver frame housed an A3 zebra print poster in bright pink and black. Under the coffee table, a solid silver item with curling feet and a glass top, lay a misshaped zebra-print rug—this one in traditional black and white. Rose-shaped fairy lights hung down the sides of the hot-pink curtains. Zebra and tiger print cushions lined the sofa behind Onca with a long, fluffy baby pink one long enough to hang over the edge. A lone black cushion with diamantes reading *slut* was pushed far into the corner of the sofa, stuffed half down the back, so the lettering was squeezed and distorted.

There was a three-tier bookshelf with the top having been turned into an altar. I knew enough from Gwydion and Adalia to recognise the four points of the altar: a small succulent in a purple pot with amethyst surrounding it made up earth; white, half-burnt candles had to be fire; a little jar of water was, well, water; and a white feather which I could only presume was air. A silver pentagram was in the centre of the elemental circle, and a plain silver chalice was to the far left with an equally unadorned silver athame to the right. Even though Adalia wasn't an active part of our lives at the moment, I had asked Gwydion to teach me some more about witchcraft so I could understand her craft. I remembered him saying how some witches will have altars representing the male and feminine energy, with yonic objects, such as chalices, on one side and phallic, such as athames, on the other. The centre point was where those two energies met as one, if one so chose to go down that altar path, which it looked as though either Sylvie or Angelika had decided to do.

Someone had put a white chest of drawers beside the window with three busts lined up along the top, one of which was a phrenology head with tattoo-like drawings over it, and the other two as plain and emotionless as the dead, with wigs giving them some semblance of life. A gag and ball had been placed over the barely carved lips on the head with an unkempt red wig, the ball matching the hair, whilst a PCV cap rested over the blonde-haired head.

Dario knelt on the floor in front of Onca, his huge back perfectly straight, wide palms planted on his thighs. He didn't quite manage to mask his distaste at my sight, but I saw him trying, and that had to count for something.

'Scarlet, thank you for joining us,' Onca said. 'Please, all of you, come to me.'

She held her perfectly-manicured hand out towards us. Kai was the first to take a step towards his Queen, with Laith and I dragging behind.

'Miss Cherie,' Dario said when we were in front of him, turning his lump of a head to look at me. He gave good eye contact in an intimidating, I-could-crush-your-skull-between-my-palm-and-I-know-it kind of way. 'Please forgive my previous impertinence.'

He looked up at me expectantly, and I didn't know what he wanted me to do. I looked behind me to Kai, who motioned for me to hold my hand out and nodded his head in the direction of Dario. I did as he suggested, holding my hand down to the man who knelt by my feet. He stared at it; I saw the wealth of emotions flying over his face as he battled with his pride. With a scathing look from his impatient Queen, Dario's pride lost the battle, and he took my much, much smaller hand in his own. He was surprisingly gentle with me, his hands cupping my own with such a feather-light touch. Dario lay his lips against my knuckles in a gesture I thought would be a kiss. I was about to pull away when he gripped tighter onto my hands and expelled a jet of air through his nose against them with a sound not dissimilar from a horse snorting. It both tickled and was so unexpected that I pulled my hands away from him suddenly; this time, he let them go.

'Thank you, Dario, I appreciate your apology,' I managed to say through the surprise. Dario accepted the statement with a slight nod of head and grumble.

I turned to Reina Onca, armed with a newfound confidence in the correct way to approach her as both Queen and ally. I knelt in front of the feline Queen, eyes rolling upwards to look at her dark-skinned face and striking green eyes squinted into a slight frown. Onca, knowing what I was doing, though seemingly unsure why, responded how any Queen should when being shown subservience. She reached her hand out to me and let me take it between my own. The jaguar ring on her finger glinted under the light of the front room, emerald eyes staring out through the gold with a fierceness caught in stone. I looked at Kai for reassurance, who nodded his head at me. I lowered my face down to the ring and, in a similar fashion to Dario, rubbed my cheek over her fingers. If I were trying to show affiliation whilst also making a stand that I thought I was on the same hierarchical level as her, I would rub my face against her cheek instead. Kai had told me that I did technically have the ground to observe the practice in that way, but I didn't know how Onca would react to me displaying my status as her compeer.

Her ring was surprisingly warm under my cheek, the intricate carvings and points of the metal unforgiving along my flesh, smooth in some areas and grating in others. She was so warm against my skin, even warmer than Kai or Laith, as if she ran at a temperature almost too hot for any human body to contain. My flames reacted to her heat; they felt the power within all that warmth buzzing under the surface, flaring to life.

Onca pulled her hand back suddenly, the edge of the metal slicing along my cheek, making me gasp. I felt the first trickle of blood make its way down my skin. It was that sharp, sudden pain which paused for a moment before returning with a vengeance, the pain that lets you know the wound is deep as if your whole body freezes for a second as it prepares itself to bleed.

'You smell of life,' she breathed against the top of my head.

Onca placed a hand under my chin, turning my face up to hers. Onca's eyes were wide and fluttering, pupils like saucepans in all the green. I knelt on my knees with my face so close to Onca's that we were almost kissing; her breath was warm against my lips, bringing with each one the scent of rain on thick forests lost deep in the Peruvian jungle. She regained control over herself with a shudder, settling back into normality like a bird ruffling its feathers.

Unexpectedly to me, and I think everyone else in the room, Onca brought her cheek beside mine and rubbed it up and down with that very inhuman prusten noise the cat therians could make but shouldn't be able to in their human throats. Blood smeared between our faces, wet and warm, as she rubbed it further into my cheek. Kai had briefed me enough to understand the significance of what was happening. If I had wanted to show Onca we were on an equal level, I would have rubbed against her cheek, but she would not respond, nor would she have made any active move to return the gesture. By doing this, Onca was saying that she saw me as an equal. My eyes flicked to Kai from where he stood to the side behind her. He watched us with a furrowed brow and smile playing over his lips; shocked, but happy.

Onca drew back with a shuddering breath, her lips fighting to quirk into a smile and shaking with the rush. She ran her finger down my cheek, coming back with a drop of blood quivering on her fingertip. Still fixing me with her unfocused gaze, Onca placed the bloody finger between her lips just as the drop of blood broke free and trailed down her skin.

Long, dark eyelashes fluttered against Onca's cheek whilst she struggled to regain control of her slack face. She looked like the proverbial cat with the cream, except this kitty cat was the Queen of panthers and drinking my blood.

Onca pushed her finger farther into her mouth, plump lips locking over the base, then oh, so, slowly pulling back up. At the tip, her tongue circled around her nail as if she just couldn't let any of the flavour go. Watching her suck my blood so deliberately, with such fever and content, sent a jolt of something through me, tensing my lower body and legs, that was not magick yet still powerful. I couldn't help but notice the way the faintest brush of red graced her lips, turning the soft pink of them into a dark blush. It was so subtle, no one else might have noticed, but I was a vampire, and if there is one thing that we can see above all else, it is blood.

The unfocused attention of that languorous gaze shifted to Laith still standing behind me. Laith seemed to know what was expected of him without Onca needing to say anything. He took a step towards us, his body heat pressing against my back. Onca extended the previously-gory hand to Laith. He reached for her at the same as his other hand wrapped around my shoulder, and the electric bolt of energy we sometimes shared shot through him into me and subsequently Onca. Whether it was on purpose or not, Onca's own power responded to Laith and me. I was the wire between two sources of intense electricity, feeding them to one another. Caught between two very different animals, the burning heat of the Savannah sun on dry, dusty ground behind me fought with the stagnant, damp warmth of forests and rain that makes you sweat until your clothes are soaked through. Air touched by endless woodland and rain stroked over me, a cooling touch against the unmoving breath of deserts.

We were caught in each other's power, my fire stirring between them both like a blaze of burning red amongst green and gold. Laith was not powerful, or at least not in the same way as Onca, but I could see him behind me with a vision that needed no eyes, a shadow in a nimbus of golden light at my back.

Onca's true gift retaliated against our fire, such power, that had granted her the crown. Her touch shot through me and into Laith, her call to bring his beast. Laith's fingers dug into my shoulder blade, hard enough that if I were human, the bone might have cracked. His touch burned me through my top, so much body heat coming off the man, enough to make me sweat. But vampires do not sweat, so why was I? I opened my eyes, which I did not realise I had closed, for all this time, I had been seeing the panther Queen and my lion in a crystalline picture. Onca's head was tilted backwards, her eyelids fluttering wildly as she tried to open her eyes against the intensity of our trio. I don't think she had meant to send her call through me into Laith, but we were all trapped in the unexpected storm of power which we had brewed.

Laith's knees buckled below him, collapsing him to the floor behind me, his hand never breaking from its position on my shoulder blade. I felt his spine bow backwards with the absolute need for his lion to be free of this puny, weak human form. No lion should be trapped in such a defective form. Why would anyone walk on two legs when they could fly through the lands on four? Why smell with this nose when you could sniff out prey on the wind from miles away? Nothing made sense to the part of our brain that was beast. Money, clothing, politics, words, all so convoluted and none of them logical in a world where all that mattered was prey and pride. Therians walked and talked like humans, but now I was experiencing the constant battle between being the humans they were expected to be and letting the beast take over, giving in to a simpler way of life.

We, my lion and I, threw our heads back in the fight against the shift. We didn't want to turn now, not in front of all of these people in Sylvie's home, not with the Syndicate after us, and so much to do. The lion in us didn't understand these concepts; he just wanted to be free.

Our lion. My lion.

A growl came from behind, rumbling through Laith's body with a ferocity that reverberated through me. We shared the thrill of the brewing roar fighting its way up our throat, wanting to tear through the too-human windpipe we had. The shared sensations were quickly becoming overwhelming; I needed to try and ground myself against our internal battle.

Laith was trying so hard not to give in to Onca's whim, the wiles of her power like a warm hand in the coldest of nights. Her magick was not one of force or dominance, it did not rip the beast from his skin the way it could do, but it whispered promises of a simpler life where he could be released from the stresses and strains of humanity, and that was more powerful than sheer force. It felt very similar to the necromancer's call to a vampire. I didn't know much about therians, but I did have some experience with similar power.

Until now, I'd been ignoring the connection Laith and I had formed together when I'd fed from him and the instant attraction we'd had for one another. It had felt like just another problem with which we had to deal. Now, I knew how to help him.

Using my knowledge of vampire powers, I reached down to the metaphysical cord that bound us in a similar way I did when connecting with Nikolaos. The vehemence of magick can so rarely be soothed by anything vocal; one must respond to passion with emotion. When I'd first met Gwydion, he'd tried to use some of his necromancy on me as a sort of test; I'd drawn on Nikolaos's power as my master to help me fight off his call to the undead. Instead of drawing on Laith for strength, I offered him my resistance to Onca's power over his beast. I let go of the part of him I was holding onto, which made his lion feel like my own, to instead share with him the part of me that had no animal for her to control.

Therianthropes burn with so much life. Their energy is thick with humans' earnest nature and the primal, simpler ways of their beast. Looking at it logically, though magick so rarely is, if a necromancer calls to the death of a vampire, Onca was whispering her sweet nothings to that fervent force of life within Laith.

Laith was empowering the parts of me that were all fire and nature and earth, the fragments of myself that I had never understood as a human and now were feeding me back shreds of life in the world of the undead. He was the poker to my coals, stirring the fire, putting deep breaths into my otherwise useless lungs. Laith burnt bright with my nymph, so we balanced one another out, but that wasn't the part of him to which I was connected. You do not need a torch in the blazing light of day; Laith was my guiding light in the darkness, the sun behind the moon illuminating the safe path. We were not drawn to one another as nymph and lion, but as vampire and therian.

I'd been hanging on to the part of him feeding that which was already alive within me, instead of opening myself to our true potential. I pulled down the barriers between us, letting the cold touch of death that was my reality run through that invisible tie between us. Scalding energy plummeted to the keen bite of midnight winds, blowing out the fire that gave us warmth and light.

Laith froze from behind me, breath catching in his throat; I felt it vaguely there in my own, inert and unyielding as the cool touch of death rode him. I reached down that line to the part of him that was lion. The last few minutes had sped by in a confusing blur of magick, heat, and shared sensations, so now I tried to draw on the calm that seemed to come with being a vampire and share it with both Laith and Onca. I raised my hand to where his rested on my shoulder, squeezing his fingers lightly. Everything felt calmer, clearer, with my heart slowing to that lazy, occasional beat to which I had grown so accustomed, each breath as unnecessary as the last. The world was a picture of crystalline colour, all of it down to the finest detail noticeable; life moved at a pace just a fraction slower than my own as if I were one beat ahead of everyone and everything else.

Onca's power was rushing through me into Laith; I was the link between them both, as well as the catalyst that left them both breathless and weak in my wake. Neither of them had expected this, but I should have known better, as my power wasn't new to me. It was my responsibility to be more in control of myself. With that thought, I sent the calming void of a vampire's touch down the line between Laith and me, as well as to Onca, where she touched me. Her fingers jerked away from my face as if I had burnt her, though I knew it was not fire she felt but ice. Onca sat up from her slump, eyes wide and fearful.

I turned to Laith, using that same cooling 'touch' to reach the beast he was desperately fighting to keep contained. All the whites in his eyes had vanished behind a veil of golden brown. His face was different; at first, I couldn't put my finger on what had changed, it was so subtle, and then it hit me. His eyes had rounded just enough to be less almond-shaped and wider, his nose had shifted from out and pointed to one of flatter definition and a broader bridge, and his jaw had widened to more square and wide than long and pointed. It was startling, so much so that for a second, I forgot what I was doing, staring into those eyes, losing their endearing diffidence.

I caught my concentration slipping just in time to pull the reins back. Onca had also regained herself enough to withdraw the call she had put out on the lion. I sensed the withdrawal in a similar way to letting a human go from being allured; it was off-putting being on the other side of it this time. She released Laith's beast from her call, sending him flopping back onto the floor and into the lap of one of Onca's people who had come closer to the show. His eyes blinked rapidly up and down, up and down, before finally closing with his whole body going limp.

Bones merged in his face slowly, the flesh of his cheeks contorting with the change of structure until his regular face was slack and handsome once again.

CHAPTER 27

'*Madre!*' Otorongo II called out, rushing to his mother's side from outside the room.

He knelt in front of Onca, taking her hand in his, kissing it lightly with that tenderness reserved for mothers and their sons. Onca stroked her son's hair, his forehead going down to rest against her knees.

'*Está bien, mi querido, estoy bien,*' she soothed, hands still gently working down his dark hair.

Kai rushed to my side, picking Laith's taller body up with an ease I'd never have been able to manage—I was strong enough, but trying to princess-carry someone who is at least five inches taller than you isn't easy.

I stood with him, both of us turning to look at his Queen.

'Reina Onca, I beg pardon to take this 'ere lion to the bedroom with Lettie'—he looked out the window to the rapidly lightening sky—'before the sunrise.'

'I think it best we all retire to our respective places of sleep,' she agreed, fingers slowing their pattern over Otorongo's hair, her eyes looking droopy and tired in a way I hadn't noticed amidst the chaos.

'I'm sorry,' I said, under my breath, exhaustion smashing into me. I leant my head on Kai's shoulder by Laith's face, his breath blew steadily against my cheek, which was reassuring. 'I don't know what happened, but it was an accident.'

223

Onca's face softened as she held her other hand out to me before thinking better of it and letting it drop back to her side. 'Rest, *pequeña vampira*, tonight has taken something out of all of us.'

I opened my mouth to say something else, anything to make right what happened this evening, not that I really understood any of it, but Kai's bald head brushed against my own. I rolled my eyes up to him, and he shook his head. Best let it go, let it all rest until tomorrow. We'd wasted another night. Another night that could have been spent searching for Gwydion, Kai's husband and the love of his life, another night of working on protecting so many people who had come to Sylvie for their aid. I never meant to be selfish, yet it seemed to happen far more frequently than I was comfortable with, and not meaning to isn't an excuse. Metaphysics had a vicious habit of derailing everything, nothing was ever simple where magick was concerned, but I especially seemed to invite chaos. When Gwydion was with us, he took on a mentor's role, offering the answers and solutions to all the things I didn't know—which was a lot. Now we had to work without him, not just for ourselves, but to find him from what we presumed was an ill fate at the hands of the Syndicate. What if tonight was what cost him his life, cost Kai his husband?

Tears brimmed in my eyes. I kept my eyes wide, refusing to cry over this. Woe is often justified; this was not one of those times. At least in part, this was my fault, and that meant standing up straight, facing the issue head on, and working on it without letting it crush me. I had to be strong for Gwydion, for Kai, for Sylvie, and for myself. At least Nikolaos was safe with

Amphitrite. Despite my eternal love for Nikolaos, I could also admit that it might be easier with him out of the way for the time being. If last year had taught me anything, it was that he was an act-first-ask-questions-later sort of person, who thought the ends always justifies the means, no matter the cost to others.

Kai and I took our pardon in silence, walking through the maze of bodies, all of whom were now awake and alert, watching me too closely for comfort. There was an intensity to a therians' gaze more so than any humans' as if they were looking at you as not just another person but something different, something they could not relate to in the same way. Once, I wouldn't have questioned it; since finding out about the tensions between them and vampires, I found myself wondering if it were only us they looked at in such a way.

Ethan and Tanya curled under the covers at an angle that didn't look particularly comfortable. Ethan's head stuck out from halfway down the side of the mattress, the tips of his orange hair poking out from the duvet. His knees also made an appearance below his hair, so he was in a near-perfect foetal position. If I hadn't known she was there, I might not have noticed Tanya, who had pressed herself so tightly against Ethan's body, their vague figure looked like one under the cover. They'd both stolen the duvet, cocooning themselves in like butterflies not wanting to be disturbed. Kai lay the still-unconscious Laith down beside the cuddling duo, gently lowering him on top of the coverless mattress. Someone had left the bedroom window open, and the keen winter wind blew through the room with a bitter crispness. The air smelt like predawn, with the dewy chill of winter promising a perfectly turquoise sky under the bright rays of sun. We didn't have long at all until morning would conquer my sentience.

Even in his torpid state, Laith found his way to the bundle of sleeping people, wrapping himself around Tanya's hidden form. Tanya groaned as Laith flung his arm over both of them, nestling further into the huddle.

'I thought he'd passed out, but now I think he's just sleeping,' I whispered to Kai, who had come to stand behind me.

'It happens to us when we first shift,' Kai surprised me by saying.

I turned to look at him, noticing the dark bags under his eyes, which had never been there before, accompanying a slightly red tint to his eyes.

'What do you mean?'

Kai rubbed his eyes with his thumb and index finger.

'I've told ya about the two different types of therians, right, darlin'?'

'The two different levels and their forms?'

Kai nodded. He had told me before; when we'd first become closer, and I'd asked about Kai's cat-like eyes and the points of his canines. I'd wondered how so many people were walking around with such inhuman features, and no one was questioning it. The answer had been that there aren't. Most therians have only two forms: human and beast. There's no in-between, nor do any of their animal features translate to both forms. Basically, you're either human, or you're not. More powerful therians have three forms, the third being a midway point between human and animal, which is closer to what we see in movies and literature about werewolves. Their full animal forms are also generally slightly larger than normal. Like all magick, power comes with a price, and that midway point also means you are always at least partly trapped in animal form. It seemed that most commonly, teeth and eyes were affected, although Luís was proof that wasn't always true. Kai hid his eyes with contacts when out around humans, and his teeth weren't too jarring as even humans can have pointy teeth. He'd told me that there was a particular brand of contact lenses brought out by therians that were specifically catered to eye shapes and colours differing from the norm.

'Onca's call only affects therian's with one form, who ain't strong enough to reject her call.'

'I felt it, Kai. It was like how Gwydion's magick feels to vampires.' I shuddered at the thought of it.

'Yeah, we can still feel it, too, but it's more like a sailor's song than a siren's call. The point is, it's irresistible.'

'Yet Laith resisted.'

Kai nodded again.

'That he did.'

'I still don't know what you mean about him shifting for the first time.'

He turned heavy-lidded eyes to me, blinking slowly, lids drooping lower down his eyes. Kai always seemed sleepy; this morning he was exhausted.

'Sorry, darlin', I got sidetracked. Laith has one form, but tonight his face only partially shifted 'n' he resisted Onca's call.'

My mouth gaped. 'Can that happen? Can a therian suddenly level up in power?'

Kai chuckled. 'Level up; I like that. But no, Lettie, they can't. Or at least, not that I know of, and I grew up around enough of 'em to have some idea.'

I didn't really know anything about Kai's past before he'd come to England, or after, come to think of it. Even Gwydion volunteered information about his younger self more freely than Kai. In fact, this might have been the first time that he'd ever volunteered any snippet of his pre-Gwydion life. Laith only partially shifting was weird, but I didn't know enough about therians to be able to say just how strange it was. I'd ask him about it tomorrow when he was awake, and I wasn't being weighed down by the blanket of pale sky outside the window.

'What are ya thinkin' about so intensely?' he asked, knocking me lightly under the chin with his finger.

'Just that I don't really know anything about you. Of all the men in my life, I always think of you as the most relaxed and open, but I actually think I know less about you than either of them.'

'I don't talk about my past much, to anyone. All we have is the future; why dwell on what's already happened?'

'I guess that makes sense. If there's one thing I've learned from Niko and Rune, it's not to push people when they aren't ready to talk.'

'I told you before, I ain't never seen my husband open up to someone the way he does to you. I know he has a funny way of showin' it, but he loves you.' Kai whispered the last words, turning his face away from me. I placed my hand on his arm just as he took in a deep, shuddering breath.

'Kai...' He turned to me, stealing the words from my lips before they'd had time to form fully. What could I say to take the pain from my friend's eyes? What could I do to make this better?

Kai sniffed, wiping the tears from his cheeks.

'We'll find him, Kai. We have to be strong and cunning the way he is for us.'

'For once, I'm bringin' the guile to this relationship. I'm out of my depth, Scarlet. I... I just don't know what to do.' He sounded so helpless, the shadow of a scared boy overwhelmed by the dangers of the world and not the kind-hearted, head-strong man I knew so well.

Kai was academically intelligent and had a pearl of wide-eyed wisdom to him, but he was neither sly nor cunning. Right now, what we needed was a plot, a scheme, to outwit the evil threatening us boldly and without fear. They say good conquers evil, but who really knows evil better than the morally ambiguous?

Kai had been sleeping on a blowup bed in Sylvie and Angelika's bedroom since he'd arrived in Edinburgh. I'd suggested he brought it in with us tonight; even though I'd be asleep for the daylight hours soon, he'd agreed it would be more comforting. Sometimes comfort isn't about logic—it's about familiarity and safety, even in the wake of despair.

Whilst he was off collecting his bedding, I went back to the bed to check on the sleeping Laith. The sleeping therians had reshuffled so that Laith was the little spoon of the trio, not that either of them had shared any covers with him. The blanket he'd given me last night was now shielding him from the chilly wind blowing through the room. Exhaustion crumpled my knees, sending me down on the edge of the bed. I managed to catch myself on the faux-leather headboard in time, shaking arms lowering myself down to the mattress. Laith responded to my movement, shuffling himself along the bed, his head finding its home on my lap. I froze for a moment, arms midair, not sure how to react.

Once again, I was battling with the urge to touch Laith, to stroke all of that soft, sandy hair back from his face and feel the warmth of his skin beneath my fingertips, or to put the boundaries in place more socially acceptable to strangers. Because we were strangers; so, why did I feel like I'd known him forever, since before I even existed as Scarlet Cherie?

Master vampires make their vassals feel at ease; it's why only some vampires can become masters and keep their vassals from killing the town; if they aren't strong enough, vampires become wild revenants with only blood on the mind. I'd been lucky with Nikolaos, who was old and experienced enough to take a lot of the craving away from me. He had absorbed a lot of the insatiable yearning for blood, taking on the burden to give me some peace. Even now, when I touched him, I felt more at ease. Being around Laith felt similar to that in some ways. Where Nikolaos took away some of the edginess, Laith's presence was empowering. I think if I hadn't had a similar experience with Nikolaos, I would find this connection unnerving, but I'd learnt to accept the pleasantness of the arcane with open arms. None of it may make any sense to me, but as long as it felt good, there was no reason to fight it because it could feel ten times worse just as easily. You take whatever hand you're dealt with the capricious nature of magick, and then try to work with that hand. Protesting or fighting it doesn't work, only controlling it, working with it as one, can really tame the wildness.

Tactile gesture outwon reserve, my fingers going down to stroke the deceptively coarse hair back from his face. My mind wandered to thoughts of a lion's mane... is this what it would feel like to stroke the king of the jungle?

I missed Nikolaos. However pleasant it was to run my fingers over Laith's feverish forehead, there was only one man who truly had my affections. I'd been angry with him since the opening of Atlas, but now, amidst the chaos with the Syndicate, all I wanted was to feel his cold, pale flesh pressed against mine. At least he was safe with the Empress; that really was the saving grace through all of this. On my way to Edinburgh, I'd wanted to alert him to what had happened, but now I thought it was probably best that he didn't know. If Nikolaos knew that they were after us, he'd only fret and try to involve himself, which probably wouldn't be any help. For as long as I knew the Empress and her many guards protected him, a part of my heart could be at ease.

Kai walked through the door, swarmed by a duvet and two pillows thrown over his shoulder, the blow-up mattress trailing behind him. Laith let out a slight noise of protest as I let his head back down onto the mattress, shuffling over to Kai to ease him of the feather-stuffed burden.

We set up the mattress on the floor by my coffin; Kai had changed into pyjama trousers, he was pulling off his t-shirt whilst I made the bed. Whilst fluffing the second pillow, I looked out the window. We were pushing it dangerously close to sunrise, my leaden eyelids were indication enough without the trembling of sun on the horizon. Topless, he plodded over to the curtains, drawing them shut.

Kai slid himself into the freshly made bed, snuggling up under the cover pulled halfway up his face. I tried to get comfortable in the coffin. The pyjamas I'd packed had been wasted so far.

'Goodnight, Kai,' I whispered into the newfound darkness.

My only response was his soft, sleepy breathing. I pulled the coffin lid closed just in time to collapse into slumber.

CHAPTER 28

Raised voices echoed through the walls, too many talking over themselves at one time until it blurred to a united angry noise. I sat up, my forehead slamming against the coffin lid. A low chuckle came from closer to me. The coffin lid opened, flooding in the glaring light from above my head, blinding me for a moment more than any darkness could. Ethan's grinning face faded into clarity.

'Good morning,' he said.

'Morning, or evening, I guess. Who's arguing?'

Ethan rolled his eyes, doing a lip-trill. 'The panthers.'

'Where're Laith and Kai?'

'You ask a lot of questions,' he said, standing back from the coffin lid so I could stand up.

I heaved myself up from the coffin, stretching my legs and arms out after being trapped in a small space for so long. 'You're not the first person to say that.'

'I bet. Your pet cats are fine. Laith is showering, and Kai is part of the debate. Everyone non-panther have been kicked from the room.'

Readjusting my top from last night, I frowned at Ethan. 'They aren't my pets.'

'I heard about what happened last night, bloody chaos if you ask me.'

'Luckily, no one did ask you, then.' What was meant to come out as lighthearted and teasing was snappier than

233

intended, but, to be honest, Ethan calling Laith and Kai my pet cats had annoyed me. Nothing hits quite the same as a quip too close to the bone.

'Oh, bite me,' he joked back, though the bitterness in the tone wasn't lost on me.

'*Woof.*'

Ethan and I stared at each other long enough for the bedroom door to open and a dripping Laith to walk in, towel tied around his waist and a bundle of clothes in his arms. He raised his eyebrows at both of us, hair slicked back from his face with the water. It made his hair look dark brown, almost black, with the slick ends trailing down his neck, which meant there was more wave to his straight-looking hair than I'd thought.

'What's with the tension?' he asked.

I began to say something when Ethan grinned at the lion. 'No tension here, unless you count between you two.' I opened my mouth to protest when he added, 'Anyway, I'll leave you both to it. No interruptions this time. Scouts honour.' And he finished it off with an infuriating salute.

'You weren't interrupting anything,' I mumbled, and it sounded indignant even to me.

Ethan walked away from me, patting Laith on the shoulder as he walked past the man. 'Make it a quickie, alright, mate? We might need a hand breaking up the fight.' Then he closed the door behind him, leaving Laith and me in tense silence.

'What was that about?' I asked.

'Shouldn't I be asking you that?'

Laith walked towards the bed, dropping his earth-toned garments onto the rumpled sheets.

'I thought we were just joking around, but it felt like I said or did something wrong. Maybe it was because I woofed at him.'

Laith raised his eyebrows, lips cocking into a smile.

'Tensions are running high tonight,' he said, readjusting the towel at his waist. A bead of water dripped from his hair down his neck, drawing my attention to the beating vein beneath all that silken skin of gold, following it down to it's journey along the hair on his chest and the soft flesh of his belly. I forced myself to look back at Laith's face. My little display of waning self control was not lost to him from the look on his face.

'Ethan is here because the panthers have been let in without prior permission from the Reynard. He's been tasked with keeping an eye on the situation and being a mediator between the local Reynard and Vixen and the panthers' Reina. It's not an easy job, especially when the panthers keep arguing.'

Laith walked to the other side of the bed, bending down to go through his suitcase.

'Why do they keep arguing?' I asked his back.

'Because they've lost their Rey, their king, and they're scared, but no one's admitting it. Onca came here admitting weakness, asking for solidarity between the species, but some of her soldiers don't like that. Fear breeds anger and tension more than any other emotion.'

'I didn't know they'd lost their Rain,' I said softly.

Laith looked at me over his shoulder, a pair of grey boxers caught in his fingers.

'Rey, not rain. Has no one told you why they're here?' I shook my head. 'I'm sure the Reina will explain it to you herself. She's asked to see you, but some of the guards are saying they don't think it's safe after last night, and have even recommended that the rest of the untrained, weaker Shadow members leave.'

'Oh god, are they arguing about me? How do you feel after last night?'

Laith collected the rest of his clothes and came back towards the bed, closer to me. The movement flashed the wound on the bend of his arm, still not healed from my feeding on him. I took a step towards him, my hands going for his arm automatically, turning it to the light. Two not-so-neat puncture wounds looked red and bloody, the edges of them raw and misshapen where I had become over-excited with the feeding. 'Oh, Laith, I'm so sorry.'

I looked up from his arm. Our faces were only inches away, my eyelashes close enough to brush against his chin. His towel brushed against my jean-clad legs, damp through the material.

'It's all good,' he said, pulling his arm free from me.

I wasn't convinced.

'Laith—'

'Really, Scarlet, I'm okay. I need some time to process last night; I don't want to talk about it until then, okay?'

'Okay, but I'm still sorry.'

Laith forced a smile. 'You might want to go talk to Kai whilst I get dressed. He's backing his Queen on this one. Go prove you're not a menace to us all.' With that, he grinned.

I stepped back, covering my face with my hands. 'Oh, god, everyone already seems to think I've slept with you, and now I'm a danger as well! This was *not* the first impression I wanted to make.'

Laith gently moved my hands from my face, holding them between his own with a light grasp. He took a step closer towards me, pressing our entwined hands to his chest where the water droplet had distracted me only moments before. There was no jolt or spark between us this time, just that uneasy sense of peace as if we belonged together. I pulled free of him.

'I'm sorry, did I hurt you again?' he asked, sounding genuinely concerned.

'I, uh, no. It feels right, and that's the problem.'

'That doesn't make sense to me, but if it does to you, then I'll accept it.'

I was going to mention my guilt towards Nikolaos when I realised I hadn't told Laith about my master and lover. No, not just lover, but the man with whom I was in love. It felt horribly like lying by omission; why hadn't I told Laith about Nikolaos? And why did I still not want to? Damned if you do, damned if you don't. It would have felt more of a betrayal to Nikolaos if I hadn't seen him with his male companion days ago. I hadn't done anything with Laith, nor was I going to—I didn't even *want* to—and yet still, just him holding my wrists like that had felt like we were doing something far more intimate.

It wasn't that I was attracted to Laith, though I could admit he was a good looking man, or that he was touching me in a platonic way, it was the betrayal of power. The only other person who held my metaphysical heart and soul in this way was Nikolaos. He was the only one who had ever touched me in places unable to be touched by human hands, and I associated that feeling only with him. We'd never defined ourselves, but we'd sworn more than just our bodies to one another, and now someone else had come along with a shadow of that same feeling. I'd never meant to do it. Whatever had happened between Laith and me still made no sense. All I could do, until I had Nikolaos and Gwydion back to discuss it with, was not further indulge all that felt so wrong in all of the right ways.

I fled from the lion and the storm of conflict he brewed within me to face the conflict amongst the panthers; this time, I was the cause of debate. On the days that being the catalyst in discord amongst the panthers outweighs the burden of facing internal conflict, you know you're trapped in too much dissension.

The raised voices only got louder as I closed the door behind me, leaving Laith to get dressed. I wanted to change my clothes as well. I wanted out of the room more.

Dressed all in black, Tanya stood in the hallway, silently listening to what was being discussed in the front room. Angelika leant her back against the wall beside her, cold eyes staring out over the steam of her coffee. Sylvie twirled one of the dark curls over their shoulder, slender fingers winding round and round the silken hair.

'You're awake,' Angelika spat.

'I am.'

'Good, maybe you can put an end to this.'

'I don't know what I've done, but I feel like I should apologise.'

'Not to us, but to them,' this from Tanya.

'I didn't mean to make anyone angry.'

Angelika rolled her eyes; we all ignored her.

'They're not angry. They're scared. We're all scared. From what I've heard, quite the commotion was caused. After losing their Rey, any threat, no matter how small, posed to their Reina, is going to be even more perturbing,' Sylvie said. 'I'm an empath, and trust me, these people are not angry. But their fear is almost too much for me to block out.' They shuddered as if the point needed furthering, though I don't think it was just for theatrics.

'Will someone catch me up on what's happened before we go in there?'

'Ye fucked the doctor, then ye mind fucked their Queen, and almost made her lose control ae her call. Wit did ye think wis gonnae happen?'

Both Sylvie and Tanya looked shocked.

'Angie!' Sylvie exclaimed at the same time Tanya let out a low whistle and turned her face away to hide her somewhat amused expression.

'Wit? She cannae come intae our hoose and cause sae much fuss.'

'Just go, Angie, just go somewhere else. I cannot deal with this right now. We can discuss it later.'

'But—'

'Now!' Sylvie snapped, sending Angie walking off with her tail between her legs, though not after she spared me another villainous look.

'No one has done anything wrong, Scarlet. We just need to go in and sort this out.' They took a deep breath in, holding it for a beat, and then let it out. 'The Guild mediates; it's part of our charm.' They grinned, flashing their smiley piercing. 'We can resolve this.' Sylvie's sheer conviction of the statement was fierce, and I got a strong inclination as to why Gwydion was so fond of this particular witch. He valued passion and drive in people; even if it was about something he disagreed with, he could respect it. There was something motivating about knowing you are close to someone who values your fervour, and though he may never outwardly commend it, Gwydion would nurture it like a soft breeze nurtures a flame.

That same resolve had helped Sylvie build the Guild up from nothing so that we now had a house filled with different creatures united against one cause. Maybe it wasn't all smooth sailing, but it was unprecedented; that counted for something.

Otorongo II spearheaded the dissidence within the Shadow, which was giving it more power. Panthers, whilst not usually pack animals in nature, are patriarchal. After the death of their Rey, Otorongo II was due to take the throne from his mother. Their monarchy was already in disarray, and now the Shadow was being dragged into a familial dispute turned political. Otorongo II did not trust me; he thought they best brave the Syndicate's wrath alone without involving anyone else. Onca knew that their Shadow needed help, and an allegiance between us all was not only safer, but a bold move politically within the supernatural community. The enemy of my enemy is my friend. We may not be enemies of the panthers, but the Syndicate were, which made us associates at worst, allies at best.

Onca was so willing to act as equals with us because she knew it would not be long until her own son dethroned her due to a system that favoured men. Onca was using her last dregs of power to unite her Shadow with a common ally, whose relationship could extend past this battle. That's a key difference between a leader born to rule and a leader just born with their claim to the throne; a true Queen knows when admitting defeat is a strength and pride their downfall.

Onca was on course to lose everything: first, her husband; soon, her throne; and potentially her son and their people if they did not defeat the Syndicate. Onca wore her woe with poise and reserve, still fighting to thrive despite all her despair.

Most of Onca's people had been sent off with a handful of guards to explore Edinburgh's nightlife before covertly making their way to the country. By nightlife, I mean hunting grounds. Edinburgh is a huge city, or at least compared to Britchelstone, built around mountains and woodland, giving them plenty of open space to explore. Some of the panthers were getting antsy. They'd made last-minute travel plans to come from Peru to the United Kingdom with no pre-warning or planning in order to escape. The unexpected change in environment was unsettling, especially after the sudden loss of their Rey. Being this close to the full moon didn't help to ease anyone's unrest.

By this point, there was a very high chance that the Syndicate knew the panthers were here with us. There was no way that something so unparalleled could happen right under their noses without any inkling. That was part of the reason why so many of Sylvie and Onca's people had been sent farther away from the danger. Only those who had volunteered their skills and potentially their lives were asked to stay closer to the city centre, with almost all of the Guild's board being sent away. Personally, I didn't remember volunteering myself. The board, which made up the Guild, had joined exclusively for safety and companionship—most of them being creatures close to extinction—and not battle. Some of them had come after the rise in power of the Syndicate, but again, they had come asking for asylum without wanting to offer up their lives to the cause. Sylvie passed no judgement on those people; they invited any and all no matter what they needed, as long as they didn't practice dark occultism.

Despite the Guild not being a new concept, it was small in numbers. Sylvie had nurtured a good relationship with most of the local therian groups, they often acted as a mediator or offered a safe space for conflict resolution, but none of the groups had been active members of the Guild. Until now.

Sylvie also understood if anything happened to them, having the other board members safe away from the danger gave the Guild the best chance of survival. They were willing to sacrifice themself for the greater good.

Some of this I knew from Sylvie, who was briefing me on what to expect when we joined Ethan and the panthers in the front room. Some, I could make out from the shouting. Onca did not raise her voice the way her son did. She didn't need to. Her command carried itself without faltering. It made me sad to know that she would have to step down from the control over people she so clearly cared for as a mother and a Queen. Though I had no qualms with Otorongo II, it didn't take a political aficionado to notice the naivety that one does not expect from a leader. Crown does not a king make. But, hey, no judgement from me. I'd be no better at ruling a Shadow of panthers, especially not if the throne was forced upon me after the abrupt death of my father.

Kai looked relieved to see Sylvie and me. Otorongo and the two guards I instantly knew were backing his corner did not. Onca and the others in the room remained impartial, including Dario, who surprised me by bowing his head at me when we entered the room. Onca sat on the sofa with Dario and Luís at her back. Kai and Ethan had positioned chairs to the side of her, enabling their view of the pacing prince and the guards trying to follow his movements. Luís's body remained totally still, only his eyes sliding to the sides of the room to keep an eye out for danger. I vaguely recognised the two guards who had been following the pacing panther from last night. One of them was a woman whose dark eyes kept flickering nervously to her Queen as if she were unsure whose side to be on. The other guard, a man with skin almost as dark as Kai's and ulotrichous locks in that awkward stage of growing out from shaven, looked far more certain of his decision to stand by the soon-to-be king.

Otorongo whipped around to look at us, pointing a long, tanned finger in my direction. Tension sang through his arm, all the way into that aggressive, shaking point. I really didn't know what I'd done to cause this much rage aimed at me. Laith and

Sylvie had both said that the panthers were scared, not angry. You could have fooled me.

'You!' he hissed at me, the words shaking with uncertain malice.

Legs stiff with tension forced their way towards me, painfully slow and strained. I backed away from the towering man with his two guards at his back, sending a pleading glance to an exhausted-looking Reina.

My back hit the wall, shoulder brushing the silver frame, lightly rattling it. Otorongo didn't stop his harsh movements towards me, finger pointing as if he were trying to smite me down through sheer force of will. Rage is a powerful force, and the look he gave me did not lack will.

I caught the gaze of the female guard, her uncertain eyes too wide, flicking side to side to each person in the room. None of the panthers came to my aid as the man neared me, not even Kai, even when Otorongo used all of his strength to slam his fist into the wall above my head, sending plaster raining down into my eyes and the zebra print poster crashing to the floor. Glass shattered into the carpet, spikes of near invisible crystals catching the light where they lay. Otorongo may have been a therian and a prince, but I was a vampire, and we were strong. I blinked the white dust from my eyes and put my full force into a push to his chest, sending him flying down to the floor.

Everyone went still, breathless in stunned silence, until finally Luís, Kai, and Dario all rushed over, leaving the two guards who had trailed their would-be-king looking uncertain and shocked. I don't think anyone had expected Otorongo to act on his violence, nor for me to respond to it, which had surprised even me. Becoming a vampire hadn't changed my dislike for wonton violence, but I would not be anyone's victim again. Too many men had stolen my power from me. This time, I had all my strength to fight back. I stood over Otorongo's hunched figure on the floor, his breath coming in pants, a trail of blood leaking onto Sylvie's white carpet where his palm had broken the fall right into the glass. I would have felt bad if that glass hadn't been broken from his lack of control.

I remained standing over him even whilst the two guards helped their ill-tempered prince to his feet, an arm under his on either side. Kai and Dario came to stand by my side, Kai's hand reaching for my shoulder. I brushed him off. His aid had come too late as far as I was concerned. Luís stayed in the middle of his Queen and me, not making any attempt to help Otorongo rise from where he had fallen.

Turning angry eyes to me, Otorongo brushed off the two guards much the same way I had with Kai, though his movement was more jerky. It seemed I was no longer the focus of all that hatred as he changed his gaze to Dario.

'Help me up,' he demanded, holding his bleeding hand up towards the mountain of a man. The female guard responded by taking his wrist in between her hands, but Otorongo snatched it back from her. 'Not you! Him! I am your king, and I demand you help me up.'

Dario did not respond, his face shifting into a look of blankness.

Otorongo made a disgusted sound. 'You then! Luís!' he spat, shifting his body backwards to the furred guard.

By this point, he could have been on his feet and back to intimidating me, if he weren't so hell-bent on the theatrics. Luís actually took a step back, putting him closer towards the Reina.

'I am your king!' he whinged, and by now, it was just pathetic to watch.

Kai seemed to think so, too, as he gripped the man's wrist and pulled him to his feet so hard he stumbled.

Otorongo II gave each of us a death glare in turn. It was Luís who spoke first, cutting through the tense silence Otorongo's grousing had left. 'You may wear *la corona*, but that does not make you my *Rey*.'

Onca finally decided to rise from her seated position, coming closer to her son with no expression. Luís and Dario both parted out of the way instinctively, letting her glide through the space. She was so much shorter than her son, yet her presence filled the room with a regality imposing reverence. She stood in front of him, neck craning up to make direct eye contact with Otorongo II.

Onca placed her hands on either side of her son's cheeks, having to go on tiptoes just to reach, and somehow managing to make even that seem poised and controlled. Otorongo II let his eyes flutter close, the fists at his sides unwinding.

'*Mi hijo*,' she whispered, 'what has come over you tonight?'

Otorongo II dropped his head, hands reaching up to close over his mother's, pressing them tightly against his cheeks.

'We are not safe here, *mami*. If I am to be *Rey*, I must keep our people safe.'

'You cannot lead without a crowd; *Rey* is nothing but a word if you have no court. These are our people, to demand of them when you offer nothing in return is not how to rule.'

Otorongo II's eyes flared open, glaring at the smaller woman, who did not look phased in the slightest. She'd had around thirty years to deal with his tantrums; I doubted it was new to her.

'I have something to offer!'

'Of course, you do, *hijo*, you have the coffin in which my crown will be cast, and with it my power.' I turned to look at Kai, whose eyes had widened much like mine at such a scathing comment delivered so softly. 'You may bury me, but I will not let you bury the harmony that your father spent a lifetime building.'

All the tension that had been disappearing came back tenfold, choking us. The female guard shifted from one foot to another uncomfortably. Onca squeezed Otorongo's cheeks, squishing his face up in an affectionate gesture, and drew his head down so he could either relent to her touch or pull free. He relented, pressing his forehead down to her's, back bowing.

'*Reys* do not show weakness,' he whispered, almost silently.

'Your *padre* was killed trying to unite our Shadow with the Clouded Leap. Do you think his arrangement of matrimony between you and Neofilis's daughter was weakness?' Otorongo II tried to pull away, but she clasped her hands tighter, hard enough that it had to hurt, and Otorongo II let out a small pained sound deep in his throat. 'Do you?' she demanded.

'Of course not!'

'Then why do you think us uniting with these people is any different? As Rey, you will learn that your enemies are always stronger than you, that is why they are enemies and not prey to hunt. When you join arms with those of a different kind, you are not only defeating your enemy, but strengthening your hand. Your crown is only as strong as your resolve, and your word is only as strong as your actions. To let your people die is weakness, Otorongo.' With that, she let go of her grasp on his face, sending him stumbling backwards.

'We will pay for these damages, and my son will clean up this mess,' Onca said to Sylvie, gesturing to the shattered glass on the floor and blood-stained carpet. Before Sylvie had time to reply, Onca turned to address me. 'You have faced a lot of disrespect at the hands of my people, and for that, I am truly sorry.'

I looked at Kai for reassurance, who nodded his head. 'It's okay, I understand these are turbulent times. We're all on edge.'

Onca smiled a sad smile at me. 'On edge, yes, I think you are right, Scarlet. Where is your lion tonight?' I tried to fight the frown, pulling my eyebrows together, and failed. 'I have offended you.'

Sylvie whispered something to Tanya, which was a futile effort as we all had superhuman hearing. I made out enough to know she had asked her to show Otorongo II where the dustpan and brush was. Sylvie's whisper betrayed no emotion; the same could not be said for Tanya, who looked positively smug.

I turned back to the waiting Reina as Tanya trailed off with the prince. 'No, uh, no you haven't. He's not my lion, though, we don't know each other really.'

248

All of the guards had gone back to standing to attention, even the nervous-looking woman with the big brown eyes. Ethan, blending in eerily well with his surroundings, had not stood from his front-row seat of all the drama. I'd almost forgotten he was there.

Luís's ears pricked up a moment before the other panthers in the room, Dario's head whipping in the direction of the window. And then I heard it, too. The pounding thrum of a frantic heartbeat, the deep breath, and, distantly, the taste of fear and adrenaline like something sweet and salty on the tip of my tongue. Seconds later, the banging came. A beat as loud and pounding as the knocker's heart on the wooden door, threatening to shatter it.

CHAPTER 29

Luís and the female guard both made their way over to the window to look outside whilst Dario and the remaining guard journeyed to the door, moving between their prince and potential danger. It would have looked smooth and perfectly rehearsed if it weren't for the skittish woman going for the same window Luís did, despite there being two unguarded and one closer to her than the one she chose, subsequently crashing into him. Luís grabbed her around her upper arms, looking at her very seriously out of his wide, chocolate-coloured eyes. The woman was actually taller than Luís, though her timorous air made her seem smaller than even I. What Luís lacked in height he made up for with a constant strum of energy and, on a non-metaphysical level, an air of confidence and reserve. That confidence was *really* not shared.

'Dayana, think before you react,' Luís said, his tone softer than I'd heard from him before.

'*Lo siento, Luís,*' Dayana replied with a tremulous voice, matching the rest of her.

I remembered enough of GCSE Spanish to know she'd apologised. Never did I think that GCSE would come in handy four years later when I was surrounded by Peruvian therianthropes. If I'd known, I might have pursued it further at college.

'It is one of our own; I can sense them,' Onca said, her vibrant eyes sharpening.

'I can taste their fear,' I added, not necessarily intending for it to be said aloud.

Sylvie gave me a look, one I couldn't decipher, which seemed to be a common theme between them and me.

'It is Cyrus,' Luís said, glancing past the vibrant pink curtains.

'Cye,' Onca whispered, her eyes wide and sounding a little breathless.

Before I had a chance to question the obvious significance of the name, the buzzer rang through the flat, making both Ethan and me jump from our respective spots in the room. It echoed in the silence like static noise morphing into thunder—one long buzz, and then a rapid procession of presses.

'I'll get it,' Luís growled after what felt like hours of the chaotic noise.

I was feeding off the room's abrupt tension, which felt like it was stealing some of the oxygen.

'Who's Cye?' I asked Sylvie.

They turned to look at me, pupils wide, energy pulsing against me; I knew that they were putting invisible barriers up to protect themself from the influx of emotions. Barrier magick has a certain feel to it, not hostile as such, but not exactly friendly either. It's more like someone putting a *Do Not Disturb* sign above their aura. If magick and energy are doorways between the physical and impossible, barriers are the lock on that door, or curtains closed over the windows to the soul.

'Cye is one of Onca's guards sent to keep tabs on the Syndicate base.'

'Oh,' I said, and then realised what they'd just said. 'Oh, shit.'

'Shit about covers it,' Ethan finally said, drawing my attention to him and subsequently the perturbation I could taste coming from him. Vampires' main meal may be blood, but fear is the garnish turning the dish into fine dining. Usually, my control was better than this. Even when I hadn't fed. Ethan's eyes flickered from side to side, his teeth gnawing on the skin by his thumb.

'What's with that buzzing?' Laith asked, walking through the door with his hair all but dried and now fully clothed. The moment I saw him, I beamed, as the air came back to the room, and everything felt just that tad less overwhelming. And then I caught myself doing it, feeling it, and forced my upturned lips down. What the hell? Laith, who had also been smiling at me, saw the change in my reaction, eyebrows furrowing as he tried to work out what he'd done to upset me. If only I knew the answer to that, too.

Luís walked past Sylvie and me towards the door, his presence remaining urgent though unhurried, with none of the fear or unrest coming from him like it did the others. In fact, he was totally tranquil, from the gentle flow of blood through his veins to the alert yet calm demeanour. His presence was enough to pull me from my fixation on Ethan's syrupy fear and, as he walked between us, he brushed against Sylvie's arm, which also seemed to bring a sense of that same calm to them. It was as if they'd been holding in a breath, making their body rigid and hunched, but the second Luís shared physical contact with them, Sylvie unwound, even their eyes going back to dynamic hazel as opposed to solid black. I very much doubted that it had been unintentional. Therians aren't the sort of people to accidentally bump into things, especially not Luís. He'd known how to calm the empath down. Interesting, I thought, and something to take note of for later.

Laith came to stand beside me, giving both of us a questioning look. He spared a glance at the broken glass and forgotten picture on the floor; at Tanya, still hovering by the prince with a certain eagerness to her not appropriate to the situation; and to Ethan, who looked tired. Finally, his gaze landed on me, and it felt like if molten citrine had eyes, they would be placed with that same earnest intensity into the face of my lion. I avoided eye contact with him. Cowardly, maybe, but I still didn't like the way he made me feel.

'Cye is out there,' Tanya said, though out of all of us, she sounded the least concerned. Bored, maybe.

'Cye. Oh, shit.'

'That's what your vampire said,' Ethan teased, earning a flat look from both of us. I guess some people just feel better when goading others.

Buzz, buzz, buzz.

All the noise was beginning to put me on edge. Fists pounding on the wooden door shattered through the sound, and then came a male voice from outside the window, 'Let me in, damn it!' Surprisingly, the man shouting didn't sound Spanish like the rest of the panthers I'd met so far, except, of course, for Kai, but a combination of Middle Eastern and American as if he'd been born somewhere exotic before migrating to America.

'Luís is coming down now, Cye,' Dayana called down from the window, though her voice was so soft it barely carried.

My surprise must have shown, because Ethan said, 'The Panthers are the only group with one Queen for multiple species globally. Reina Onca is the Queen of melanistic pantheras worldwide.'

I turned wide-eyed to Onca, who had pulled herself together enough to address me.

'Our main Shadow resides in South America, with many migrating to Peru to be close to our throne, but my people live around the world. Strains of Pardus are native to many countries; if they happen to be born as panthers, then they are a part of our Shadow, especially as they are often rejected by those of their kind with no colour variant.'

Kai nodding caught my eye.

'You nodding from experience?' Ethan asked, also curious.

'I ain't never had a Pard.' Pard is the term for a pack of leopards.

'You have always had a Shadow,' the male guard, of whom I still didn't know the name, piped up, sounding not so friendly.

He had that proud tone of someone who thought his view was superior, that their Shadow was the one and only needed for survival, and for anyone to question that they needed or wanted anything else was an insult. Zealots so often cannot empathise.

Kai hung his head slightly and nodded in a display of diffidence that sent a shock of sadness through me. 'My mama and daddy tried to integrate me into their Pard as well as the

Shadow, but I was just too different to them. In 'n' out of leopard form.'

The buzzing had stopped, turning the newfound silence heavy and deafening; I could hear the quiet in my head as my mind and ears readjusted to being free. I glared at the guard as I went over to my friend, leaning my head on his shoulder and sliding my arm around his back. Kai had never let on before that he'd experienced any types of prejudice in child and teenhood. I knew he'd been born in Louisiana, and so I had presumed being a Black and gay man growing up hadn't been easy from what I knew about that area, but it'd never been confirmed. There is a special type of rage you feel knowing someone you love has been cast out for things they cannot change, that they'd suffered at the hands of ignorance and prejudice. Who knows how many people had kicked him to the curb because of his race and sexuality, losing their opportunity to get to know one of the sweetest, kindest, most sincere people I'd ever met.

I may not have been able to erase Kai's past, but I could try my best to validate what he meant to me. Seeing this new insecure and sensitive side of him had thrown me, but who could really blame him? Kai had lost his lover to the arms of the Syndicate, all of whom were out for blood.

'We love you, Kai,' I whispered.

Kai turned his face at an awkward angle to plant a kiss on my head. He was trying so hard to control his response to the current situation, but I could feel his pulse beating too fast and the strain in his body. Cye returning to the Guild could have more significance for Kai than us. It might mean news on his stolen husband, an update on his whereabouts, which was still unknown to us all.

We heard the front door fly open, banging against the wall, and then slam shut hard enough it rattled the walls. Probably a good thing that the zebra print had already fallen or it certainly would have been knocked to the floor from the impact.

Tanya and Otorongo II moved from the doorway in time for Luís and Cye to burst into the room, Cye panting with droplets of sweat brewing above his brow and hairline, and Luís unaffected by the admittedly short run up the stairs. Really I'd expect one of Onca's guards, and a wereanimal at that, to be in better shape. I guess that explained why Cye had been put on lookout duty, which required a sharp gaze over physical prowess. Onca seemed like the sort of Queen to utilise her people by playing to their strengths instead of passing up on aid by judging their stamina.

Cye was older than everyone else in the room, except maybe for Onca, though she was so spry and firm-skinned, it really was hard to tell her exact age. Only her son being about thirty made me put Onca's age at the better part of fifty. I didn't actually know how therians aged compared to humans, all I did know was that all the ones I had met so far seemed very well preserved. I'd ask Kai about it when all this was over. Assuming that Cye hadn't come to shower acidic rain down on our current parade.

Cye's hair was almost entirely grey with patches of deep brown close to black peeking through some of that grey, trying hard to hang onto the shreds of youth. Most of his face had been covered by a bushy beard growing down long enough to brush his chest. He'd tied a silver bead into the end in the shape of a jaguar head—I doubted it was real silver, unless Cye was a secret masochist. Like the rest of the guards, he was wearing a black t-shirt tucked into black jeans; it did nothing to complement his bulky frame, which may have once been muscled and now was more soft flesh than hardened bulk. His doughy stomach hung over the belt around his waist, the buckle on the loosest hole still straining against his mass. Tattoos lined his arms, most of them faded into blotches of dark green, blue, and red on his arm, but I could make out most of them were shapes of animals set in amongst figures of women. I wondered if vampires could get tattoos, I'd always assumed that something about our healing meant we couldn't, but then I would have thought the same about therians, too.

Combined, the beard, tattoos, and all-black outfit gave him a biker feel, as if all he were missing was a leather jacket and Harley. It was also about the way he held himself, confidence befitting all that six-foot-plus, bulky frame.

Cye's eyes, a reddish tone just enough lighter than Kai's to be paler brown rather than true orange, though he had whites unlike Kai, settled on Ethan where he stood behind me, a look passing over his face which I couldn't quite read. The energy level in the room inexplicably raised, with some strange and uncertain energy between the two men. I shuddered, which drew his attention to me. Cye made a show of sniffing loudly.

'Vampire,' he said, taking another sniff.

'Panther,' I said back.

'Damn straight I am,' he said, raising his fist to the air, sort of shaking it in a gesture I could only describe as pumped and proud instead of aggressive. 'And proud of it, too!'

I actually grinned at him because he had that sort of passion that managed to be contagious without being overzealous.

'As you should be,' I said, smiling up at him.

Cye seemed to really take me in then, his expression slipping into one of sadness, which confused me and sent a thrill up my chest. That look could only mean bad news.

'Cyrus, however much I appreciate your fervour for our kind, may I enquire the reason you almost beat down Sylvie's front door and woke the whole street up with your buzzing? I'd expect there to be a reason for such a display of panic.'

Cyrus—Cye—fell to his knees in front of the Queen, all of that meaty weight slamming into the floor, making the walls rattle all over again. Sylvie's poor flat, would it survive another week of antsy therians?

Cye bowed his head down, calves tucked under his body, palms flat on the ground. Onca gave him her hand, which he nuzzled accordingly.

'Reina Onca, the Syndicate's base has fallen to ruin,' Cye said into her hand.

I saw her whole body tense, eyes widening just a touch.

'What on Earth do you mean, Cyrus?'

Cye raised his head and shoulders, all of his height pulling upwards until his face was level with her sternum, though his eye contact didn't waver for even a second.

Cye was all business as he announced, 'Insurgence, my Queen. Civil war has broken out amongst the Syndicate.'

CHAPTER 30

Fourteen of us were gathered around Sylvie and Angelika's six-seater dining room table. Of the four guards, only Cye took a seat. Dario and Luís stood one apiece behind Otorongo II and Onca, who, of course, were seated at one head of the table, with Sylvie at the opposite. Really, Onca was at the head, with her son by her side, the same way Sylvie had Angelika and Ethan on either side of them. Dayana and Xavier, the fourth guard whose name I'd only just learnt, scanned the night sky for any potential danger. Dario was such a broad mountain of a man that he needed to stand more to Onca's side as his frame wouldn't fit between their backs and the wall.

There was an unspoken yet obvious divide between the panthers and Sylvie's people, though Cye's eyes kept flickering to where Ethan sat. Tanya had taken a seat beside Ethan, taking the last chair left, which put Laith and I standing behind Sylvie. Kai was hovering between the table and the wall just that bit closer to his Reina. His head fit perfectly in the bridge of the alcove shelf containing a range of spirits.

All of our collective attention was on Cye, who looked positively out of place against the vibrant pink tablecloth with its retro placemats done in bright fuchsia-and-orange psychedelic patterns prevalent in the 1960s, and monochrome coasters of naked women. Actually, the coasters seemed fairly in place with the rest of him.

We'd all heard Cye's chilling retelling of what he'd witnessed at the Syndicate base, though not through his eyes. He'd recounted seeing two men, dressed from head to toe in black robes, go towards the graveyard in the heart of Glasgow, the one in which they had made their base, and how he'd felt the thrum of power in the air, like a live wire leaking energy into the night, enkindling sinister power.

'I could feel them,' he'd said, shuddering. 'They have no power over the living, or so I'd thought, but my fucking god, it was like nothing I've ever felt before. They smelt wrong as if their power were tainted with something dark, something... evil. It's the only word I have for it.' Then he'd turned to me, and added, 'Vampire, they smelt like vampire. I didn't recognise it before, but the moment I smelt you, I knew.'

'That's not possible,' I'd said. 'Vampires aren't allowed to consort with necromancers. It's like a mortal sin of our kind.'

'I know what I smelt. If insanity was made into perfume, that's what it'd be. And they tainted the necromantic scent of the base with their deadly cologne.'

Onca had asked if Cye thought more vampires were in the base, but he'd said: no. Our smell was, apparently, distinguishable, and he'd have smelt it before then. The scent had trailed the two Syndicate members like a malodorous cape which they wore with pride. I felt I should have been offended by that but let it go, as the terror in his eyes was not one with which I wished to argue.

'Then the screaming started. Some of them sounded like fucking children as they howled their last breath into the night. I swear it was enough to wake the dead from their slumber, just scream after scream after fucking scream. It was pitiful. I had a half mind to rush in there just to make it stop.' We'd unanimously agreed that it was lucky Cye hadn't decided to act as a Lone Ranger. 'Then the blood, so much blood.'

'How did you see blood if you didn't go inside?' I'd asked, which I thought had been a valid question. The looks every therian in the room had given me seemed to disagree.

'Humans' reliance on sight is a hindrance. What a small world it must be to only see with your eyes,' had been Luís's response.

Cye had seen the two original necromancers leave the base with another man in tow. Kai had eagerly asked if it had been Gwydion, to which Cye had replied he didn't know what Gwydion looked like, but after we'd described him, he had confirmed it had not been our missing demon. He wasn't exactly hard to spot standing at around seven foot tall and as wiry as a decaying tree. Cye had waited around for a while longer to see if anyone else would emerge from the base, but, apparently, it had been as if an energy he didn't realise had been there exhausted at the death of the necromancers; there had been nothing left for him there besides a depleted energy colder than any dead.

All we really knew was that two of the necromancers, who Cye was certain were far more powerful than the others, had slaughtered their hoard, and, as far as Cye could tell, only three remained. We still didn't know why the hell they'd kill their own, or where Gwydion was, but even lacking so much information, it was more than we had before.

'We must act now whilst they are still weak,' Otorongo II commanded, for what felt like the hundredth time since Cye had finished bringing us all to speed.

'Yes, Otorongo,' Onca agreed, with a sigh, 'we all concede this, but we must agree on what it means to "act".'

I was beginning to get déjà vu; this conversation had been going around and around with no one finding any solution. So far, all we'd established was that Otorongo wanted to act first and think later, and no one else thought that was the best course of action.

'Advantage is a better soldier than rashness,' Kai added.

'What?' Otorongo snapped, turning sullen eyes to Kai, face twisted into lines of almost disgust.

'Shakespeare, Henry the Fifth.'

'What are you talking about?'

'I think he's trying to say that the better part of valour is discretion,' Laith said from beside me, grinning at Kai, who returned his smile. Laith and Kai were the calmness in the storm, lightening a mood that was so dark, even they were struggling.

Otorongo looked furious at the grinning men, and I couldn't help but feel they were taunting him a bit. Now really wasn't the time for games.

'Paraphrased, and the wrong play, but it works,' Kai said, rolling his lips into his mouth to try and stifle the smile.

Laith shrugged.

'Still a Henry.'

'That it is.'

I gave Kai a warning look and nudged Laith with my elbow. Laith turned smiling eyes to me, his lips twitching with a smile. The way he lit up was enough to make me smile back, and I realised that, although bad timing, this was the first time I'd seen Kai genuinely smile since I arrived in Edinburgh. Laith had been a better friend to Kai than I had, distracting him during this time of adversity. Otorongo II chose that moment to slam his fist onto the tabletop hard enough to send the coasters flying into the air, some coming down to land with their cork bottoms facing upwards. The one closest to Onca and Otorongo II went up the highest; Luís's furred arm was a blur of speed as his fist shot outwards and grabbed the coaster mid-air. Even to me, a vampire, with my superhuman vision, it was a blur, which meant he was bloody fast. Xavier and Dayana, both of whom had been doing an excellent job of ignoring the back and forth until now, whipped around to look at us all.

Otorongo II leant across the table, sending his chair backwards into the wall from the force, this time deciding to slam his palms onto it as he gave both the lion and leopard a death stare.

'How dare you laugh at me!' he hissed, voice gone low with rage.

Laith pursed his lips, eyes widening and rolling over to me. Like a stubborn student being told off by the principal, he was not taking Otorongo II seriously. Though, really, it's hard to respect someone's cavilling when they go from zero to one hundred so quickly. I shrugged, because I didn't have a good reason to explain Otorongo's rage.

Onca stood up, placing her hand on her son's shoulder and pulling him back to his seat.

'Ease down, Otorongo. We will leave Scotland both beaten and poor if we keep having to replace Sylvie's furniture. I know you're upset, but—'

'I'm not upset! *Estoy asado*! They are making jokes, *mami*, when Father is dead!' Otorongo shrugged free of his mother, bringing his fist down onto the wood over and over again until I could hear it crack and protest. Coasters and placemats went flying into the air, cluttering to the floor. 'These *bastardos* have killed my fucking *papi*!' He screamed the last, a lament to all that the syndicate had stolen from him and the panthers, from Kai, and even from me to some extent.

We had all been trying to make the best of a bad situation by distracting ourselves from the horrible truth: we were all here because there was a target on our backs, and none of us thought we were strong enough to shield the arrow alone.

Even Onca had said before that she'd leave here broken and beaten, and it was the first indication that even now she had no faith in us against them. Otorongo let one final scream of frustration, of rage, of pain, of loss into the air, bringing his fist down the hardest time yet, and this time the table gave way, cracking down the middle and collapsing. The wood shattered, crumbling in all directions. The cloth slid with one of the large pieces, sticking like a discarded gown atop the spier.

I'd half expected Otorongo to cry, but no tears fell. He stayed hunched over, panting into the suddenly thick silence, everyone else holding their breaths whilst his came out violently. No one said anything to the grieving prince. We let him have his moment of grief, because it was grief shared by all. We'd all lost something to be in this room, whether that be a king, a father, a husband, a home, safety, or hope. We were united not just by a common enemy but by shared affliction at the hands of the Syndicate. Otorongo's requiem to the melody of shattered wood and jagged breath was a song in all of our hearts, one sung loud enough to be a release for everyone in the room. His outburst was a fragment of the release we all needed, a splinter of our shared anger and pain.

We were still silent when Otorongo pulled himself up from his hunched figure like a snake uncoiling itself from slumber, and already a tension in his shoulders seemed less. It was Kai who sliced the cape of silence settled over us all. With ease, he pushed the bit of wood holding him to the wall, sending it clattering down to land on the rest of the dead wood. Thirteen pairs of eyes watched him walk towards the panther Prince as one, following his movements until Kai settled beside him, as the broken table ruined the path to face him head-on.

'I lost my daddy and brother when I was sixteen. It was hunters. Twen'y-two years later, and I still wear the scars. I wasn't bein' facetious about caution and valour, Otorongo. The Syndicate has my husband, and I will be damned before I let them take him from me, too.' Kai's voice cracked on the last few words, his voice showing the strain of acknowledgement.

Otorongo turned, so he was facing Kai, all six-foot-plus of him towering above Kai's shorter frame, and then he gripped his hands around Kai's upper arms hard enough I could see the indents straining Kai's skin.

I was tense watching the same man who just moments before had smashed a solid wood table—which I imagined weighed more than anyone in this room—like it was kindling, wrapping those same hands around my close friend. I shared my anxiety through a look with Laith, who surprised me by already looking in my direction when I turned to him. He gave a small smile as reassurance, wrapping one arm around my shoulders and squeezing me to his body in a gesture far too familiar to strangers. Which we were. Before I had time to sink into his arm, which was more tempting than I cared to admit to myself, I pulled away, shrugging his hold on me. The problem was, I did feel calmer just from Laith putting his arm around me as if he'd soothed the anxiety I'd had only a second before he touched me. Too many little things between Laith and I had mounted up, taking it from coincidence to unavoidable fact. Problem was, I still didn't know what that fact was. Ethan had turned his head back to look at us, our little display of affection not lost on him. I was beginning to think that Ethan missed very little. His eyes and ears on constant guard, astuteness hidden behind a facade.

Otorongo had tensed back up, his nails looking close to breaking into Kai's skin. Kai didn't try to move away or stop looking up at his prince with his earnest and unreadable mask. I'd never seen Kai around this many strangers before, it was a new experience witnessing his own version of a blank face. I'd always just assumed Kai was perpetually open, but I was beginning to realise just how much about my favourite panther I didn't know.

I'd been prepared for many reactions from Otorongo, mainly anticipating the brandishing of his wrath, but for him to grab Kai by the bruising grasp on his arms was far from any expectations.

Otorongo pulled Kai into his chest and just held him there, taut and unyielding, until, finally, he rested his chin atop Kai's hairless scalp and his body began to shake with the tears he'd held in for too long. Surprised, Kai tensed up in his arms before relaxing into the softly-crying man's embrace, wrapping his muscular arms around his waist. I'd been on the receiving end of that particular hug on many occasions, and let me tell you, it is one of the most comforting hugs I've ever experienced.

Kai's closed lips vibrated with a sound coming from low in his throat, which sounded close to a purr, but not quite. Still weeping, Otorongo responded to the sound by brushing his chin along Kai's head, the rest of his body swaying gently against Kai's, so they were rubbing against one another. Dayana joined in next; she came from her post at the window to grip on to Otorongo II from behind, sending the plank of broken table to the floor and extending her arms around both men. Beside Otorongo, she looked taller, as if being pressed against his body brought out a confidence in her, which meant she extended all her long spine up, and we got to see all five-foot-ten of her frame. Next, Cye, who had scooted his chair back from the splitting table to stay seated, joined the pile, consuming the three far more slender panthers in his meaty arms. His face rested on Otorongo II's shoulder, cheek rubbing up and down the other man's neck. One by one, all the guards left their respective positions to join in the allorubbing, each of them fitting together so perfectly it was as if their bodies were jigsaw pieces made for each other. Their eyes closed collectively, all but

Cye's, who looked over the other's heads behind me to where Sylvie, Ethan, and Tanya sat.

For the first time, I understood that being a pack, or a Shadow, or Pride, was more than just a title. It wasn't just a subculture in human society offering them an outlet to their animal selves, it was a family made to be together. Maybe they didn't always get on at times, but isn't that the same with all families? I could certainly attest to that with my sister, Anna. How wonderful it must feel to know so wholeheartedly that you belong, that something magickal in your genes, which gave you insight to a whole new way of life and being, also gave you an unbreakable unit. Kai had never met most of these people before and yet still, in this moment, they shared the familiarity of comradery spanning decades and not mere days. The Syndicate had tried to break this. They had attempted to shatter the box which held the pieces of the jigsaw together, keeping it safe when the pieces were apart. Looking at the panthers, there was no doubt in my mind that they completed each other, and, my god, was it beautiful. To look in the face of such unabashed belonging and want to destroy it made someone either pure evil or so consumed by rejection, their mercy had decayed.

Onca was the last to join the huddle, slotting herself into the purring nest of bodies. I couldn't tell you what drew my attention away from the captivating display of affection, but something did, and I turned in time to see Laith wipe a tear from his eyes. Instinctively, I reached out to touch Laith, not letting myself finish the movement before beginning to withdraw my hand from him. No one else left me feeling this confused, especially no one I'd known for under a week. Every time he was beside me, I was overwhelmed with the yearning to touch him, to feel his skin against my own as if we were made to be as united as the nuzzling panthers. Laith didn't have to vocalise his pain for me to understand; it was hard to stand in the face of perfect unity and not feel the crippling weight of loneliness.

I gave in to the urge to comfort Laith, my hand finding his, giving it a squeeze. He returned the gesture with a surprised smile, and that was enough to have made giving in worth it, as Laith had a smile bright enough to warm a hundred winter nights. There is something very beautiful about a smile after crying, the crinkling of their lips disheveling the trail of tears, the return of happiness in their eyes vanquishing the woe.

'You are all my children, my friends, my brothers, sisters, mothers, fathers,' Onca said, her voice clear and cutting even in the embrace of purring bodies. 'We are family by more than blood, we are a Shadow, and magick has bound us to one another. I will fight unto death not to let anyone else steal a stone from our monument or extinguish our individual lights that ignite the darkness.' Onca shuffled free of the cocoon enough that she could direct her gaze at the rest of us, her face peeking out. 'You are all included in my sentiments. We have spent too long as individual species in the name of naive ventures of strength, when it is solidarity which gives us vigour.' Onca rested her green eyes on Laith, asking, 'What is wrong, my boy?'

Laith sniffled and shook his head, but I squeezed his hand, encouraging him to speak.

'I've never felt lonely until this moment.' He sniffed again. 'Watching you all like this, it's like thinking you've been happy your whole life and then someone showing you what ecstasy feels like, and you realise your happiness has been mediocrity.'

'You have your vampire,' Cye's growling voice said from the huddle, which meant he'd noticed something after only a few hours of being back.

'We don—' I began to protest, until Laith clutching my hand faltered the words.

'However pleasant this is,' Kai said, changing the subject, 'Otorongo is right, we need to strike whilst the proverbial iron's still hot. We need to save my husband.'

Kai pulled himself free from the huddle, and as he was in the centre, it broke the circle of bodies. Even in the newfound silence, the air vibrated with the dissipating rumbles.

'What do you propose?' Onca asked.

'I ain't thought that far ahead. All I know is that'—Kai's voice cracked—'that Laith was right, 'n' I found my ecstasy in the form of a seven-foot demon. I ain't gonna wait any longer 'n' risk losin' him.'

'If the Syndicate has fallen into discord, they will either be humbled or grow desperate. If the former, your husband will be safer whilst they nurse their wounds, but if the latter, then they will be careless in their sadism,' Xavier said, surprising me.

I'd only heard him utter a few antagonistic sentences before. This calmer, rational side of him had been unanticipated.

'What do you want to do, then? So far, we still don't have a plan other than goin' in guns a blazing,' Ethan added.

'You have guns?' Dayana asked, voice a pitch too high.

271

'Uh, no, it's a saying. It means... like, going in on the attack with no plan, I suppose,' Ethan said.

'What are we waiting for?' Dario asked, looking around the room at each of us in turn. 'All this talk of guns and flaming irons, we don't need weapons.' *Note to self: use English idioms sparingly when in a room with people who have English as a second language.* At least when it comes to discussing going into battle. 'We outnumber them, we outpower them, and'—he glanced at Cye—'we outweigh them.'

'You bastard,' Cye muttered under his breath, though through his beard, I could see the slight smile that came with the words.

'What about all your talk of valour and caution?' Otorongo asked, with an indignant undertone.

'We don't have a plan, we ain't gonna establish one tonight. There ain't a thang we can do except use their friction to our advantage.'

'What do you think, Sylvie?' Onca asked, drawing our collective focus to them.

'A think that if ye gonnae break anymoor furniture, it best be theirs a no ours,' Angelika said, and though I don't think she intended to be funny, both Tanya and I choked back a laugh. Angelika glared at us both. Oh, I guess she wasn't trying to be funny.

Sylvie took in a breath deep enough to rock their shoulders, letting it out heavily through their nose. 'I think that our only eyes on the Syndicate's base is in the room with us, and anything could have happened between then and now. I think we still have some of your people wandering the night with no idea that we may be about to leave for battle. I think we are being rash. But Xavier raised a valid point, if the Syndicate is weakened, they might be growing desperate. If they know about us, and I am quite certain they will by now, we are not only their biggest threat, but their closest.'

'If we give them time to recuperate, they may come on the offensive when we aren't prepared. If we leave tonight, we could take them in the midst of their unrest,' Ethan said.

Sylvie nodded. 'Exactly.'

'Do we know why they have broken into civil war?' Dayana asked from her post on the window to which she had returned.

We all shook our heads.

'This sounds like a set up to me,' Tanya said.

'I heard the screams, trust me, that wasn't no set up,' Cye said, shuddering slightly. 'You can't fake screams like that.'

'We still need to be prepared that Dayana is right. This could be a setup and we could be falling into their trap,' Sylvie proposed.

'Better that than sitting ducks,' Ethan said.

'We've wasted enough time,' Dario added.

'You are proposing what I suggested an hour ago!' Otorongo protested. 'If you'd all listened to me earlier, we'd already be in Glasgow.' And I had to admit, he had a point.

'Your speech earlier was what led me to change my mind, and your embrace as my leader. You did as a king should, you won my favour through logic and empathy,' Kai soothed.

'Yeah, he's right,' Ethan agreed, and nods began across the room, including from me, until that affronted glower was replaced by a chuffed smile.

'I've always said that none of my people will be forced to do anything they aren't comfortable with,' Sylvie said.

'Nor mine,' Onca agreed.

'And I won't send anyone into a potential trap without them knowing the risks and agreeing to them.'

'Then let us wield the power of democracy and put it to a vote.'

And so they did, and we all agreed to enter the potential dangers of the unknown together. When Onca said she would put the call out to her panthers in Edinburgh town, the ones who still didn't know of our plan, or lack thereof as the case may be, I thought she meant something mystical, and not a literal phone call. She briefed them whilst Sylvie looked into transport for us all to Glasgow, which was just under an hour away. Dario suggested the panthers would be quicker to run to Glasgow than taking a car; she argued that a group of panthers running through the roads of Scotland was absolutely not a way to remain inconspicuous. He relented. In the end, we settled on who was going in whose car, with only Cye getting to ride solo on his motorbike—see, I'd called it on the biker front. The panthers in the town were told to start their journeys further up north immediately—the guards with them were to stay by their sides until safe.

When going into battle with the scourges of the supernatural world, I'd expected armour, weapons, and a solid plan. You never anticipate stepping into the line of fire in the same clothes you woke up in, but in the end, all we had were the clothes on our back as armour, four cars as cavalry, and weapons carved from our sheer determination to end this before more lives were lost.

CHAPTER 31

Onca and Otorongo II rode with Sylvie, Luís, and Dario.

Sylvie had managed to convince Angie that her coming with us wouldn't actually be of any help, as she was human, and we still weren't confident that this wasn't a trap. Angelika had tried to argue semantics, drawing the "I'm a Wiccan" card, but Sylvie had not relented. In the end, it had been Sylvie's tears falling and the pleading in their tone as they begged Angelika not to come, saying that they couldn't lose her. Maybe it was the tears, or maybe it was the realisation that she really was just human and what we potentially faced tonight was more than mere mortal. Either way, Angelika finally gave in with a melancholic goodbye, kissing her partner with a passion reserved for the knowledge you might never see them again. As Sylvie was transporting royalty, they got the most—and strongest—guards.

Kai and I got to sit in the back of Laith's car with Xavier riding shotgun. We'd been driving for twenty minutes, and so far, no one had made any attempt to break the strained silence. I still hadn't fed yet tonight, but I wasn't willing to take the risk of feeding on Laith again quite so soon, and everyone else was an unwilling meal. Not that Laith had offered himself up again. Besides, we all needed our strength, and donating blood can really take it out of you. Surprisingly, I wasn't feeling too hungry as of yet. Come to think of it, since feeding on Laith, I'd generally had more energy and a persistent contentment as if I'd had a meal that not only filled me, but satisfied all urges. I was trying to work out which was more detrimental to our nonexistent plan: potentially facing a sudden crash of hunger when going up against the unknown, or spending more of our limited darkness hunting down suitable food. Oh, hail the glamour of war and all the decisions with which it came.

Ethan, Tanya, and Dayana drove behind us, with Cye taking up the rear on his motorbike. Sylvie knew the way to Glasgow Necropolis better than the rest of us, as they'd lived here their whole life, which meant we were all following their lead. Under other circumstances, I might have been excited to see somewhere new, but the tension in the air of this small confined space was heavy with hypotheticals, most of which did not work in our favour.

The A8 was quiet in the late-night darkness, with the soft mist of rain obscuring our view of the world outside. Occasional beams of light would break through the silence as cars passed us. I wondered who occupied each vehicle; what were they off to do on this night? Were any other of the strangers who passed us, their faces flashing sudden and shocking in all of the Scottish rain and black skies, off to face their fate, equally as unsure as we all were that they'd live to see another day? I hoped not. From the bottom of my heart, I truly hoped that every person with whom we just happened to be crossing paths, even abstractly and distantly, found themselves safe and warm, that the only tears they found themselves shedding were ones of joy, and the only shrieks were of laughter. And then I hoped the same for us. Because we all needed hope right now.

I had no qualms admitting that I was afraid; even though I was trying to focus on anything but the worst-case scenarios, the knot in my stomach would not concede. With every irrelevant thought with which I was trying to distract myself, a little voice, one I could not silence, echoed through my mind, saying, '*You are going to die. This is a trap. Everyone you love is going to die.*'

And each time it did, I would try and counteract it with another thought, but it just came back, louder and louder, faster and faster, until my mind was a merry-go-round of explicitly dancing images depicting us all lying dead and abandoned on the ground, spinning to the melody of that evil little echo.

I wanted to speak to Nikolaos and tell him that I loved him. More than anything, I wanted the opportunity to bid the same passionate farewell to him that Angelika got to give Sylvie. Attempting to open the barriers between us was an energy expenditure that I couldn't afford if I wasn't going to be able to feed before we went to the base. I should have been being sensible, but love is not about common sense. Going on the past few times I had tried to contact him, there was little hope that it would work.

I was just giving up on the idea of trying when something in Laith's side-view mirror caught my eye. Tumbling from Ethan's passenger side window, cigarette smoke curled into the night sky, dancing off through the darkness. Images of Nikolaos exhaling flooded my mind, the way his mouth could frame smoke to look like a work of ghostly art, and the taste of his nicotine-tainted lips against mine. The thought of never feeling his lips against my own, his barely beating heart under my fingertips, or the way his satin hair fell between my fingers like water again, filled me with an inexplicable pain. Pain, and guilt.

For if I were to die now, he'd have no warning of my demise, left only to deal with the aftermath.

The last two times Nikolaos had 'seen' me had been when Amphitrite's Prince was assaulting me, and then with another man between my legs as I feasted on, not just his blood, but his power. Since he'd vanished off to the Empress's side, I'd had no opportunity to tell him that I loved him, or that he was in my thoughts. But that was only because he'd shut me out, making the mental walls between us almost impenetrable. Oh, god, in the chaos of Edinburgh, I'd almost forgotten that Vodan had been Prince to the Empress, the same Empress whose presence Nikolaos still currently revelled in.

One thing at a time, Scarlet. For as long as these two problems were separate, I could compartmentalise them. Right now, I had pushed all the fucking rage and despair I held for what Vodan had done to me, and the potential consequence of my self-defence, to one side. Once we'd dealt with the current problem at hand, I'd let myself experience the inevitable onslaught of emotion. One good thing about becoming a vampire was our innate ability to process and separate issues, as any born-predator can.

Once again, I went to that place in my head that I always go to when trying to connect with someone metaphysically. I lowered my own walls that us magick-wielding creatures had to have in place or risk unwanted entry to the intimacy of our soul. I sent my 'self' out searching for my avoidant lover, only to find a different energy far closer to home answer my call.

Laith's golden tiger glowed in the darkness of my closed eyes, his silhouette blazing like a fire in a time when all the earth had was stone below and the endless stretch of sky above. If it were a time when darkness was something fearful and unexplored, Laith was the torch to light the night until day broke again. Warmth and safety when there were none. Now there was something new to his alight energy as if within the figure of his golden tiger, a humanoid shadow lay dormant and waiting.

The car swerved suddenly, tyres screeching along the wet road as Laith tried to regain control of the vehicle. My eyes flew open in time to see his feet fight with the brakes; Xavier slammed one palm onto the dashboard, the other reaching for the handle above the door.

'*Mierda*!' Xavier called out breathlessly.

I was thrown to the side, my weight colliding into Kai's body, sending him against the door. The car came to a screeching stop, flinging us both forward, my head hitting the headrest of Xavier's seat.

From behind us, Ethan honked, his brakes fighting to match our sudden halt.

'Jesus Christ, Scarlet!' Laith exclaimed, sounding as close to dishevelled as I'd ever heard him.

'I'm sorry! I'm so sorry, I don't know what happened,' I said, intentionally resting my forehead on Xavier's headrest.

Music rang through the speakers, with the digital screen in the car's dashboard flashing up, reading: *Ethan. Incoming call. Accept or Decline.*

Laith slammed his finger onto the little green phone sign, hands still shaking.

'What the hell, Laith? Are you trying to get us killed before we even get there?'

Laith turned the wheel, getting us back onto a straight line, starting us on our way to Glasgow.

'It wasn't me. Scarlet did something to me'—he shuddered—'and it made me lose control of the wheel.'

'That girl is a lot of trouble in a small package. How many times has she tried to kill you now? Twice, in just as many days, is it? Hope that ass is worth it, mate.'

Everyone in the car fell silent, with Kai tensing beside me. Laith peered over his shoulder to give me raised eyebrows, as if asking what he should say. I hid my face in Kai's shoulder, my embarrassment palpable.

'Hi, Ethan,' I said.

Laughter came through the speaker, Tanya's surprisingly deep chuckle dominating the rest of them.

'I, uh, I didn't know I was on loudspeaker.'

'Mhmm,' I mumbled sarcastically.

'Sorry, Scarlet.'

I don't know what possessed me to say the next, it was very out of character for me to be so bold, but something about the weirdly masculine tension in the car made me respond with: 'Uh-huh, I'll try not to get us killed again on the way, but just so you know, this piece of ass is definitely worth dying for. You're just jealous you'll never get a chance trying.'

Laith hung up the call to the sound of raucous laughter with that edge of nerves shared by us all after I'd almost caused a seven-man collision.

CHAPTER 32

The city lights of Glasgow emerged from the motorway, golden in the darkness, old buildings painted black by age stretching high above us. We drove up to George Square, a patch of concrete surrounded by a cage of old, dark stone buildings. I'd never seen so many statues in such a small area other than at a museum, standing above the ground with their regality caught in metal. I counted eleven in total. In the centre, higher than all the rest, was a pillar faded to a sandy stone. Lion's heads stuck out from the plinth upon which it was built.

'Sir Walter Scott,' I said aloud, reading the name chiselled into the stone. 'I wonder how tall that is.'

'Eighty feet,' Laith said.

'Wow.'

Laith slowed the car a fraction so I could take in the sight, my nose pressing into the glass. Behind the Costa was a monster of a building, ugly and rectangular and higher than the rest with huge white lettering on a pink background reading: *People Make Glasgow*. It was such a shocking contrast compared to the vintage buildings and statues. Glasgow City Chambers was the one that really stole the show for me, a Victorian-style structure with turrets pointing to the stars. More statues were built into the balconies as if Medusa herself had cursed those of old to be forever stuck staring out over the evolving cityscape of Glasgow.

'It's beautiful here,' I whispered, watching the light of the Chamber building climbing up the stone, igniting it in the darkness.

'It is. Very different from Peru,' Xavier agreed, breaking his apparent vow of silence he'd taken for the journey here.

Laith's phone buzzed, pulling me out from my Glaswegian trance. Sylvie's name flashed up on the screen.

'What's up, Sylvie?' Laith asked into the car.

'We're five minutes away. There's a car park just down on Duke Street. Meet me there, and we can arrange a course of action.'

'Will do,' Laith said, with Sylvie hanging up before he had time to finish the second word.

'I guess this is it, then,' I said, as Laith turned the corner onto Duke Street with its far less impressive buildings.

A man and a woman walking hand-in-hand stopped outside a cash point, the car lights catching on the shining purple strips on the surface of his jacket. The woman laughed at something he said, turning her head just in time to see us passing. From behind black-rimmed glasses, stunning blue eyes sparkled with a shared joke. And then we were gone, passing the strangers by, their lives falling back into obscurity.

Oh, what I wouldn't do to be mindlessly laughing with my hand in Niko's, off on an adventure of feeding and sensuality instead of facing potential impending doom. My hands took on a mind of their own, picking at the skin around my nail, peeling the skin back until my nail beds were stinging.

Laith flicked the indicator of the car, turning us into the car park. We'd lost Sylvie for a while when Laith had taken us on a slower detour through George Square, but now we were back to tailing them with his front almost touching the bumper of Sylvie's car. I looked in Laith's rearview mirror to see Ethan creeping up behind us. Everyone in their car looked positively sullen, their mouths set into downturned, unmoving lines. Ethan flashed his lights at us.

'It'll be okay, Scarlet,' Laith said quietly, pushing the button on the ticket machine to trigger the barriers.

'I didn't say anything.'

'You didn't need to, darlin',' this from Kai.

'Your anxiety is blatant,' Xavier said.

'None of you are nervous?' I asked, settling back into my seat with my anxious hands fidgeting in my lap.

Kai reached over, his fingers finding mine, hand squeezing my own.

'I'm shitting it,' Laith said, squeezing into the space beside Sylvie.

'Me, too, but I'd give up my life in a heartbeat if it would save Gwydion.'

'I would, too, Kai,' I said, choking on the words as the first tear began to slide down my cheek.

'He'd never sacrifice you for himself, Scarlet. You know that, don'tcha?'

I put my spare hand on top of Kai's, pulling our clenched hands to my chest, holding them against my breast. I reached my lips down and planted the softest of kisses on his dark skin. My lips caught a taste of the iron and salt from my tears, massaging the moisture into his hands.

'He'll be okay, Kai, and so will you. No one's sacrificing themself for anyone. Cye's adamant we have the upper hand. We have to believe him.' And yet, as I said it, that formidable nagging voice in my head refused to listen to my words of wisdom.

'What about you, Xavier? How're you feeling?' Laith asked, slotting us into a free space in the surprisingly busy car park.

'I'd die for my Reina and *Príncipe*,' he said with no inflection.

'I know.' Laith turned off the engine, the car suddenly silent in that intimate way that cars seem to always have in darkness, though the glaring luminescent lights of the car park ruined some of the illusion. 'But that doesn't mean you have to like it.'

'Reina Onca and this Shadow are my only family. I have no wife, no brothers, sisters, or children to leave behind.'

'I do.'

'Oh, my God, Laith, your son. Why are you here when you have a son?' I asked.

I'd completely forgotten that Laith had a young child. He had so much more to lose, and the loss of his life would be more selfish than any of ours. He should have stayed home with Angelika.

Kai gave me wide eyes and mouthed, '*a son?*'. I nodded.

Laith's fingers wrapped around the steering wheel, his hands rubbing up and down it in his version of an anxious gesture. 'I don't know, Scarlet.' He turned his head back, golden-brown eyes settling on me with an intensity that made me want to squirm. 'I don't want to be here, and under any other circumstance, I'd have stayed back at the base. Damn, I'd have driven all the way back to London, scooped my boy up, and never let him go.'

'What made you come here tonight?' I asked, afraid I already knew the answer.

Everyone else in the car seemed to disappear; for that extended second, all I could see was the honey of Laith's eyes staring at me with a look I couldn't read and wouldn't even know where to begin to try. Just below the surface of his tangible form was the shimmering shadow of his beast self. I had such an overwhelming urge to reach out and touch his glistening aura that I clenched Kai's fists tighter into my chest, reminding myself that we were not alone.

'You, Scarlet Cherie, something about you means I can't leave your side knowing you are in potential danger. I just can't.'

'I'm sorry,' I whispered, so quietly even I wasn't sure the words were real.

'Me, too.'

Laith opened the door without another word, not so much slamming it behind him but close enough.

'Everyone is very dramatic here,' Xavier said, his hand on the car door handle.

'Wait 'til you meet Niko,' I said.

'And Rune,' Kai added.

'Yeah, they take the cake on the drama front.'

As if to prove how dramatic we could be, Kai and I left the car in a flourishing unison, both slamming the door closed so they shut at the same time. Maybe Nikolaos's dramatic flare had rubbed off on me—and Kai.

Ethan leaned against the back of his black Ford S-MAX, with Tanya beside him smoking a cigarette. Dayana was a little behind them as if she were trying to blend into the background instead of being a part of the group. We approached them with Sylvie and their passengers in tow.

'I rolled you a cigarette,' Tanya said to me, lighting the second smoke off the one between her lips and holding it out to me. I walked past Laith's disapproving look to breathe in the reassuring sensation of tar down my throat. I spared a dirty glance at Ethan, who was doing a good job of looking anywhere but me.

The thunderous roar of a motorbike echoed through the concrete car park, announcing the late arrival of Cye. He did a theatrical turn low on the ground, semi-skidding round the corner and zooming into a free space. With driving like that, it was shocking he'd come so much later than the rest of us.

Cye came bumbling towards us with his thick legs taking inelegant steps. He reminded me more of a bear walking on two feet than any graceful feline. The glass on his helmet was pushed upwards, revealing sweat dripping into the bush of his beard.

'You took your time, mate,' Ethan mocked, and honestly, I was growing tired of his attitude. It had been endearing at first, but the subtle jabs were becoming more like thorns in the side.

'I got lost.' Cye pulled the helmet off his head, shaking out his greying beard and the waves of his wiry hair.

'You were literally here earlier tonight.'

Cye shrugged. 'I ain't the best with directions.'

'Weren't you a biker?'

Tanya threw her cigarette onto the ground, stomping it out with the heel of her boot, Cye frowned at him but it was Tanya who spoke. 'Shut up, Ethan,' she said.

'What did I d—'

'Seriously, mate, stop talking,' Laith warned, though he tried to make it into more of a joke than Tanya had.

'Just because I insulted your girlfriend.'

I peered around Tanya's body.

A flare of irritation shot through my body, up from my tense stomach into my chest, where I seemed to feel most intense emotions. 'What is your problem, Ethan?'

My fire stirred with the awakening of my frustration, feeding on the negativity of irate tension and acute anxiety at what we were procrastinating through arguing. With that thought, I realised I was letting myself be wound up more than I usually would because I'd rather argue with Ethan in this car park until sunrise than go to the Syndicate's base and see what death and destruction awaited us.

My fire worked in many ways as a protective barrier between the world and me, so my comforting flames were also more inclined to let me feel rage at the werefox and fight it out with him than potentially step foot into danger. Laith reacted to their flareup, his body shuddering before taking a step towards me.

'This is my problem, Scarlet.' Ethan pointed a finger at the lion, his head also peering around Tanya so we were both caging in her torso. 'You've come in here with your uncontrolled magick and done some weird shit to Laith and Onca. We're here because your friend was taken, that same friend who set up this fucking Syndicate in the first place. You reek of death and danger, and I don't trust you.'

Tanya sucked her stomach in, pushing her body against the car boot as if she wished to melt away into the metal and not be in the middle of our argument. Couldn't blame her, really; Ethan's anger had caught me off guard. I'd previously underestimated his threat level; maybe it was him being a werefox, which, compared to the panthers and lion, seemed pretty low on the scary-animal scale, or maybe it was that he had done a masterful job at hiding the potential of his power. Whatever the reason, I was beginning to regret it.

The heat of Ethan's power slashed through the space between us, making Tanya twitch and bend over so that she took the brunt of his second attack of burning energy. It was so unexpected, so startling, that I jumped backwards. My mouth hung open, breath caught in my throat, and despite all of the surprise, there was something strangely familiar about Ethan's magick.

I'd never met a wereanimal who could inflict damage from energy alone, especially one who I had assumed only had one form from his lack of animal features. I'd also never met a wereanimal whose power felt like a genuine slash through the air as if it could cause physical damage. Ethan was the spokesman for the largest weregroup in the United Kingdom, trusted enough by their Reynard to come and be in the front line of negotiations and potential battle, to have thought anything less of his potential was a garnish of arrogance over bitter ignorance.

Tanya let out a piercing wail, her body shuddering, doubling over, and finally collapsing onto the ground. The crunch of bone on concrete as her knees made impact was shocking. She'd managed to catch herself on the floor, head hanging down, and blood pooling on the grey stone below her.

'Ethan, Ethan,' she whimpered, head still down as the blood streamed out down from her face. 'Ethan, I can't see.'

Tanya turned her face up to us all, and everyone took a collective step backwards, with a gasp coming from here and there. Claw marks ran along her face; they were small, more like a cat than a dog, but deep enough to have sliced through her right eyebrow, over the upper bridge of her nose, and through the left eyelid. Tanya's right eye was cloaked by blood falling from her eyebrow wound, chunks of dark-hair-covered flesh stuck out from the gaping wound with its seemingly endless supply of blood. The left was worse, with the eyelid entirely shredded and thicker substances leaking from the claw marks. The slice in Tanya's eyeball tore through the solid colour of her once pretty eye, shredding it into a wound, leaking a watery jelly within all the blood. It looked disturbingly similar to a grape which had been butchered with a bread knife and all the green flesh inside was squeezing out, except this substance was not green, sweet, or fruity, and was being washed away by all the blood pouring from the tear in her eyebrow and upper nose.

I looked up at the sound of footsteps to see Laith running to his car, clicking the button on his keys to open the boot. I spared barely a glance in his direction; my focus lay on something else, something sanguine and enchanting. The hunger, which I'd managed to avoid up until that moment, hit me like a ten-tonne truck and all I could see was the way the thick, warm blood shone under the light like a red pearl glimmers under the rays of the sun. I staggered, arm reaching out to thin air. I'd not felt hunger like this before, even when I'd first become a vampire. It was as if Laith's blood had indulged me in fullness and ecstasy to such an extent, that now it'd worn off the touch of him had left a gaping wound needing to be refilled. The sight of Tanya's jellified eyeball should have been enough to put me off my appetite, but it felt as though nothing could deter me from needing to fill this insatiable emptiness.

This was not starvation but famine, and I felt as though every hunger we have as sentient beings, whether it be food, blood, love, comfort, companionship, happiness, had been ripped from my very core.

If I'd been just a vampire, I don't know what I would have done, and I don't even want to think about it. I was more than this hunger. I was a nymph, a creature that took the essence of the elements and gave it life. To succumb to the bloodlust would be a failure of will.

'Kai,' I said breathlessly, and for the first time, I realised that since feeding on Laith, each breath I'd taken had been clean countryside air after a lifetime of city living, and now it was gone, I was choking. 'Kai, get me out of here. Now!'

Kai didn't need telling twice. He half-led/half-dragged me away from Tanya and her wounds, out of the car park.

'What happened, darlin'?' Kai asked, once we had crossed the road, his hand touching my shoulder from behind me.

My head was pressed into the cold plastic of the bus stop walls; besides me, someone had burned marks into the timetable border, giving my thumb something to roll over anxiously. My breath fogged up the plastic walls. Was that right? I was focusing on the minutiae of our current situation, but I honestly could not remember if my breath had fogged anything up since becoming the undead.

I didn't have an answer for him, not one that could justify the absolute chaos of what had just happened between Ethan, Tanya, and me. Luckily, a shudder up my spine signalled a distraction was heading my way.

'Laith's coming,' I said, turning around to watch him running across the road to join us.

'What happened back there?' he asked, the moment his foot touched the curb.

'You were both there for it, you know as much as I do!' I snapped, and then quietly added, 'Is Tanya going to be okay?'

Although Laith's face may not have changed, his eyes flickering to the side was not lost on me. He reached his hand out to me, and I laced my fingers through it, using the other to reach for Kai.

'Ethan is driving her to the hospital now. Therians don't usually bother going, but as a shifter, she might not heal this. She needs medical care I can't offer.'

'Is this my fault?' I asked, the first tear falling.

I had been so hungry up until the moment Laith had touched me, and now I could really focus on the horror of what we had witnessed. I'd seen some stomach-churning things since becoming a vampire, mainly the murder of a girl named Sophie, another victim of Maglark's, and then his decapitation and the reanimation of his broken, bloated corpse, but this had to top the scale. Something about seeing eyeball jelly leaking and the perfect shred of Tanya's eyebrow, so the flesh was white and displaced from her face, was truly horrifying. The fact that my bloodlust had won over the disgust of what had happened concerned me; no one should be able to look at a scene like that and feel hunger. Just thinking about it now made my throat clench, my tongue feeling like it was gagging me. I let go of both men's hands to cover my mouth, hoping it would chase back the nausea.

Such a split-second reaction was a mistake, as the moment I let go of Laith, the visceral, penetrating hunger, which felt like it would tear me apart, drew me to my knees. Kai reached for me, but I swatted his hand away, instead holding it out to Laith. He accepted my offering of flesh, in return giving me the strength I so suddenly needed. Oh, something was wrong. I didn't know what, but none of this was 'normal', even by my standards. And really my bar for normal was set seriously low.

'Don't let go of me,' I said, wide-eyed and breathless.

I half-expected Laith to argue with me or ask questions I didn't have the answer to, but instead, he just nodded his head and squeezed my hand harder, drawing me up from the ground.

'The night's wasting away, we should go back to the Reina and see what the plan is. If there is one,' said Kai, sounding tired.

Hand-in-hand, Laith and I turned to the road with Kai. We were ready to take our first step off the curb when a movement out of the corner of my eye caught my attention. Against the block of flats to the left of me, between the walls of a strange, misshapen alcove, a shadow moved. I tugged on Laith's arm, pulling him back towards me.

'There's someone there,' I whispered, tilting my head slightly in the direction of the shadow.

Laith froze, his whole body going almost as still as I'd seen any vampire go. Therianthropes seemed able to match that same calm stillness of the undead, the type of stillness that only predators know how to master. Kai responded to us, matching Laith and my motionlessness, so we were just suddenly unreal in the street, unmoving like dimensional silhouettes frozen in place. Our shared tension was palpable, all of us in that particular state of stillness before pouncing. I licked my newly dry lips, with a predatorial anticipation that the next liquid to touch them might be the blood of our stalker. That thought was so out of character for me I startled, tensing my hand harder around Laith's, using his heat to ground me the way only fire and passion and burning flesh could.

The shadow moved again, and Cye emerged from the patch of darkness into the glow of the streetlamp as if he could manipulate light around him. I'd never have expected such smoothness from him. As therians went, Cye was the least smooth I'd met, or at least so I'd thought. This was my second time underestimating one of the weres in a lone night. Was I growing arrogant? I'd never thought of myself as an arrogant person before, but this didn't bode well for my sense of humbleness.

'Ease down,' Cye said, holding his arms out in front of him in a gesture of surrender.

We let out a collective sigh of relief, our wound-up positions easing to one of calm, or as calm as we could be under the circumstances—which really wasn't that much.

'Why are you lurking in the shadows?' Laith asked with a nervous chuckle.

Cye shrugged his big shoulders, beard scratching along the pure black of his t-shirt.

'Reina has asked us to split up. She wants us to go up from the front and the others to come round the back.'

I widened my eyes. 'So, we have a plan.'

'And you waited to tell us,' Kai said, not sounding particularly happy.

'Reina and her lot will be draggin' behind, they're going the long way to avoid potential detection. Xavier is coming in from the west and Luís from the East, this way we're all covering an angle. We're closest to the entrance.' Cye's eyes darted to the side, his lip rolling under his teeth where he nibbled the flesh.

'You're procrastinating,' I said gently, as we'd all done our share of avoiding the inevitable this evening.

Cye had the grace to look embarrassed, coy even, which is no easy feat for a man built like a small mountain and looking like he'd just stepped out of an uninventive biker bar.

'But you promised us it's safe, so why are you nervous?' Kai asked, sounding uncharacteristically suspicious.

'We're all nervous, Kai,' I said, turning back to look at him.

'I ain't nervous about walking up to that graveyard. I know it's going to be empty.'

'Then what is it?' I asked, turning back to Cye, confused.

295

'What comes next.' Cye gave me a dead-on look with eyes that were wide and haunted. 'I'll never get the sound of those screams out of my head. I'd be lying to say I want to see what caused them.'

'I'm sorry,' said Kai. 'It's selfish to put my loss ahead of yours.'

I turned and held my spare hand out to my dear friend.

'Gwydion's not lost, Kai, not yet. Not ever.'

Kai laced his fingers through mine, and the comfort which came from that touch had nothing to do with metaphysics and everything to do with love and friendship, which was far less complicated than whatever was happening between Laith and me.

Armed with each other's hands, we started the short journey along Duke Street up until we reached Tennents Brewery. From there, all we had left was to walk up the road and we'd be at Glasgow Necropolis, where our fate lay dormant and waiting. Cye was so sure our enemies had come pre-defeated, with their bodies lying crumbled amongst crypts of the long-dead.

Having half your enemies murdered for you by the other half sounded like it might have made our lives easier if it weren't so damn confusing. No, the slaughter of the Syndicate only tempted further demise, and I did not trust it one bit. From the tension running up Laith and Kai's arms, I'd say with confidence they shared my trepidation. But we were out of options, and more to the point, out of time. When you're left backed into a corner, what else is there to do but run head first into the danger?

CHAPTER 33

Sometimes even the shortest roads we walk feel far longer when you know all that's waiting is a dead end. In this case, we were all hoping the dead part wasn't literal, at least not for us. From what Cye had said, death was inescapable, as what awaited us was the scene of a massacre. Maybe we were all taking deliberately slow steps, or maybe the road was taunting us, but either way, that half a mile walk seemed to both stretch on forever and be over far too quickly.

Glasgow Necropolis is guarded by a black wrought-iron fence, tipped with white-painted fleur de lis spikes. The entrance was instantly striking, with long, winding pathways slicing through the beds of decaying leaves, which had succumbed to the wiles of winter, and its old gravestones weathered and grey standing amongst the spindly limbs of leafless trees.

Silver moonlight trailed over the damp ground, illuminating the mist of rain that had started only moments before, subtle yet drenching. Within seconds, my hair was plastered to my face. A drop of rain ran down Laith's hand onto mine, dripping onto the ground below. The last time I'd stepped foot in a graveyard, it had been to raise the dead with Gwydion. I shuddered at the memory.

'Are you cold?' Laith asked quietly, whispering as if he could disturb the dead lying six feet below us.

I gave him a smile reserved for sweet but misguided sentiment and shook my head, finding myself equally as reluctant to speak and unsettle those who rested. I envied them; it felt like far too long since I'd known the comfort of rest. There was an energy to this graveyard, one that called to me like only a dogmatic power over the dead could, and even without knowing what awaited us, I would have known instantly that necromancers once resided here. It was unmistakable, that call like a sensual whisper promising love and affection and safety after so long of being afraid, being the giver of light in a world of darkness. All I had to do was follow the trail of duplicitous whispers, then I'd be free from the anguish of death.

I'd distanced myself from the others without thinking about it, my feet finding their own way up the path, following the trail of magick and lies. I'd felt Gwydion's necromancy before, the touch of his energy and the temptation to cross over from death to life. I knew firsthand from him the deceit of his magickal promise, and from me, he knew what it felt like to hear his siren call. I'd asked him once if his power dealt in light or darkness, whether he worked in the shadows of death or the blue-skies of life, and he'd had no answer for me. Until this moment, I'd accepted that Gwydion toed the line of good and evil like a tightrope walker barely balancing, preparing to take the plunge into the waters below filled with nefarious shadows and a void in which to become trapped.

The touch of this power was tainted by death, with confused vows of life cloaked in the shadows of crypts and graves, where the undead walk and the lines between life and immortality were blurred. I shuddered at the mismatch of energies and knew instantly that it was wrong, that whoever had brought this magick was drunk on poison.

I continued up the path with the world around me blurring to irrelevance. My therian companions and their heavy breathing faded to nothing, though in the back of my mind, I could hear the soft beat of their hearts like distant drums, which played in unison to each of my steps. I was vaguely aware of the path I continued up and the railing of graves sliding down the grassland, lost to the mist and darkness at the slope's cusp. Caught in a dreamlike state, following the pull of the strangely familiar energy, I distanced myself from the sound of boots hitting against concrete as three men struggled to keep up with what, to me, felt like an average pace.

'Wait up,' Cye hissed from closer behind me than I'd expected.

I turned around to the panting man; what was visible of his face had gone bright red, the rain dripping down his nose, getting caught in his beard. I'd been so distracted that I'd barely noticed the mist of rain become a pounding force, soaking me through to the bone. Laith and Kai came bounding up the hill behind Cye; neither of them had broken a sweat. Somewhere in the haze of power, I'd let go of Laith's hand, abandoning his strength to fight the force of the call alone.

'Where are you going, Scarlet?' Laith asked, coming to stand beside me. I was too busy looking out over the necropolis to focus on him.

We'd reached almost the highest point of the steeped graveyard, stepping to the side of the path in a half-circle of grass with a short, crumbling wall built into the slope upwards, gravestones lining it, one of which had half-collapsed into the ground and half into the wall. Behind me, the script on a square grave had been long lost to age, leaving it smooth and grey. It might have looked depressing and unadorned if it weren't for the vase carved into the head of the grave, stone cloth trailing down the mouth of the vase, as if whoever had carved the statue had managed to catch all of the dynamism of falling silk into the unforgiving movement of stone. In the near distance, the black spires of Glasgow cathedral wound through the night sky, with its striking green roof, which had once been shining copper and was now dull and mismatched against the beautiful, gothic building.

Taking a second to clear my head and ground myself, I could think clearly, and from up here, I suffered the formidable necromantic summoning with a previously lacked force. The voiceless whispers and their near palpable caresses were intensified, their power rubbing over my skin like poison-tainted satin. It all felt so familiar, though I simply could not place how. I looked around, searching for the guards who should have been in position by now. I couldn't see them anywhere, but I hadn't really expected to, as I trusted their ability to blend in with the surroundings like any good predator can.

'We're close,' I whispered, turning my focus to Cye, who was the only one of us who knew where we were going.

'How d'you know?' he asked, head tilted to the side.

'Because they're louder up here.'

'Who is?' Laith asked, just as my eyes went unfocused again, and I fell into the embrace of the peculiar, familiar power. 'Scarlet?'

Laith came to stand beside me, reaching out to me, and the moment he did, I jolted out of the weird trance I'd fallen into far too willingly. The night was instantly clearer, each shape crystalline, each colour vibrant in the shadow of the winter night, without any of the soft haze with which I'd been seeing since entering the necropolis. I stared up into his face, feeling the force of his rapid heartbeat through the tips of his fingers where they rested on my arm. So hard, so fast, as if just the strength of his restless heart could drum some life back into my own and make it beat in a way it hadn't for months. Laith was the life I needed to balance out the enamouring stench of death this power blew through the stone graves like a mist of evil. That was part of what was so different: Gywdion's magick had never felt so solidly dead.

'Wrong, this is all wrong,' I said breathlessly, eyes flicking around, taking in everything as if I had mystically appeared in this spot and didn't know where or how I'd got here.

'What's wrong, Lettie?' Kai asked, concerned.

'Can't you feel it?' I asked, looking at Kai but my hand going desperately to find Laith's.

'Feel what?' Cye asked, as Kai and Laith both shook their heads.

I shuddered; how anyone was immune to the immense calling was beyond me. I had to try and remember that therians had no affiliation with the dead, so their sensitivities lay elsewhere.

'She's right, we are close. The base is just down there.' Cye nodded his head in the direction of the path we'd been following, or I'd be following.

'We should be waitin' for the Reina 'n' back up,' Kai said.

Cye nodded his head. 'She's coming up from the other side, but I don't think we should have split up.'

'Are you going to be okay, Scarlet?' Laith asked.

I wrapped my hand around his arm, hugging him to me. He responded by stretching his arm over the front of his body, around to my shoulder, pulling me further into him until we were a united figure. I'd begun to shiver, though whether that was a recent development or been happening since we arrived, I couldn't tell you.

'I'll be fine, just please don't let go of me. I just want to rejoin the group as quickly as possible. I don't like it here.'

'I wonder if slaughtering the necromancers released some of their hocus pocus,' Cye said, and it was so astute it actually knocked me for a second.

'That would make sense. It feels like necromancy but... different. More dead. That's as good an explanation as any.'

'How much do you know about necromancy?' Kai asked, giving the larger man a thoughtful look.

'Fuck all; I'm just thinkin' out loud. Let's go meet our Queen. This place is creepin' me the hell out.'

'Seconded,' Laith said.

'Thirded,' I managed between chattering teeth.

'Let's go then,' Cye affirmed, taking the lead down the pathway.

It was fine with me if he wanted to go first; I'd had quite enough of leading the group. Besides, I don't think I'd been a very good person to follow, letting myself fall into the arms of a nefarious lover. No, definitely time for someone else to take the lead or the only place they'd be following me was into the grips of the devil.

CHAPTER 34

The further down the path we travelled, the higher the intensity of the necromancers' call, which I was now imagining as their ghost's final cry for help, and I just happened to be the only medium with whom they could connect. If it weren't for Laith letting me clutch onto him like a drowning man holding a lifeline, it would have been too overwhelming. We were lagging behind the other two men, with me taking slow, deliberate steps, as the ground below felt uneven and wobbly. I couldn't wait to meet up with the others—safety in numbers.

Cye guided us down the slightly winding path, past some particularly stunning crypts with pillars built up into the stone and ornate gates painted a vibrant red. The next crypt was blue-gated and had more of the stone vases overflowing with cloth, and the last was more traditional with marble pillars separate from the monolithic house of the dead and a black gate.

Down we all walked, with me choking on the despair of departed necromancers, each step I took feeling harder to manoeuvre. My body was too heavy and the world around me too soft; it was like I was a stone statue walking along marshland, waiting for the ground to give way underneath me at any moment and drown me in the dirt.

Stone walls overflowing with shrubbery and the morose stems of petalless flowers guided our way on one side, the other a wall of graves of all different shapes and sizes. I'd had no qualms with the embrace of death since becoming a vampire, but tonight every grave loomed like a shadow, and I felt the unease of the corpses below us. No corpse had been laid to rest in this cemetery, not tonight. Even when I avoided looking to the right of me, the sad stems of wilted flowers lamented the decay of their florets. There was nowhere to look, nowhere to hide, to escape from the impending sense of demise.

We were almost at the curve of the pathway when I stumbled, my hands catching on the crumbling wall, dust from it falling onto the ground below. Laith tightened his grip around me, pulling me into his side. I took a moment to let his warmth and the steady thrum of his very-alive heart remind me that part of this was in my head, and I only gave it more power by letting the thoughts run away with me.

'Are you okay to continue?' Laith asked me.

'You all still can't feel this?'

The other two men, who had stopped just in front of us when they'd realised I'd stumbled, both shook their heads.

'We're close, Scarlet. Really close,' Cye said, pointing his finger in the direction of a concrete slab in the wall tucked just out of sight behind a fourth and final crypt. 'Luís and Xavier will have their eyes on us. We can go in before the others get here.'

'They're taking their sweet time,' Laith said.

Cye shrugged. 'It's a longer route. And Scarlet gave us one hell of a head start when we came in.'

'Sorry,' I said.

'Don't be,' Laith said gently, hugging me to him, chin resting on my head.

Short, square pillars built into the wall we were following marked the entryway to a random door. A weirdly tall step led into a slight dip in the ground, then two smaller steps went up to the stone door, which, to the untrained eye, would appear to serve no purpose. It might have once been a unique grave from the faded, illegible text carved into it, or it could have been anything. One thing was clear: it had not been of use to anyone for a very long time—at least no one human.

Energy pulsated from behind the doorway with a force that should have made the doorway shake, shattering it, collapsing us all into the ground below. Even with my fingers nearly drawing blood from my grip on Laith, nothing could shield me from such force. If whispers could scream, this is what it would sound like; if laughter wept, these were the tears that would fall. So much confliction, so much woe, and underneath it all, the sickly sweet flavour of betrayal. All I wanted was to tear the stone doorway from its position and free all the dying souls of their pain, even at my own detriment. If my death could silence the necromancers' requiem, then it was a worthwhile sacrifice.

'We're here,' Cye said, stepping up to the door, Kai following his lead.

'I gathered,' I managed to cough out, my voice a shadow of the silent screams bellowing through my head. 'You still can't feel it?'

Kai shook his head.

'Not a thang.'

'I couldn't until you started touching me,' Laith said.

'And now?' I asked.

'It's like the scent of death is overpowering, but there's nothing to smell.'

'It's not a smell; it's a feeling,' I protested.

'There's less of a difference to us, Scarlet.'

'Are y'all ready?' Cye asked, though his hand shook on the stone.

Kai, Laith, and I exchanged a collective look of uncertainty. It was too late to back out now. The longer we waited for Onca and the others, the more night we wasted. I needed to find shelter before sunlight; we were quickly running out of time.

'As ready as we'll ever be,' Laith said.

Cye took him at his word, shoving one of his big fingers in a gap in the stone I'd not noticed before, pulling it to the side with a force no human would ever have been able to match without the aid of machinery.

CHAPTER 35

Nothing could have prepared me for the horror waiting for us inside. I forced my way through an invisible barrier between the outside world of mortality and the deceptively large entryway, the base of our enemies. The smell hit us all first. The moment we broke through the barrier, the overpowering scent of raw meat hit the back of my throat. Blood, bone, and freshly sliced flesh choked my senses until my eyes burnt with the stench of so much meat.

Slaughter didn't do the atrocity into which we had stepped justice. At first, my eyes couldn't make sense of what I saw; it was like a human-sized jigsaw had been left scattered over the ground. But once it all clicked into place, I wished I could go back to when it was obscured.

'My god,' Kai managed to say before his hands found one of the walls, and the sound of his retching echoed nonstop within the walls.

Cye went next, rushing past Laith and me to the exit of the door, his foot tripping on the step, sending him collapsing onto the ground outside. As long as whatever barrier had been put up wasn't impacted by us entering, he'd be free of the smell. Oh, I so wanted to run away from it, too. The vigour of him rushing past us had forced Laith and me further into the chamber. We both stared out across the space at the pure desolation left behind, neither of us able to move against the shock and horror of it all.

Shredded cloth lay in tatters across the floor, some of it thankfully hiding the bodies it had once clothed. It could not conceal all of the horrors. Only blindness could save us from such a ghastly scene.

Bits of bodies scattered around us. Legs, arms, torsos, heads, feet, hands, bits I didn't even want to think about being detached from the body had been thrown and discarded haphazardly. In front of Laith and me, two parts of a leg lay bent with no hint of the body to which it had once been attached. Technically, the lower leg was still attached at the knee, but the bone was all that kept the body part together, glistening pure and white in the dim light from the almost-dead candles lining the walls. Pink, red, and yellow flesh and muscle glinted like some sort of macabre satin catching the light. At the top of the thigh, the hip joint stuck out from all the muscle, with bits of tissue and flesh hanging off.

The only head I could see not concealed by the cloaks the necromancers had worn in life had been smashed in at the back, hard enough for the skin and hair to have broken free. I stared at the back of the broken skull, unable to let myself see it as anything more than a bleeding shape. It was not something human. It could never have been something human.

Bodies of all shapes, sizes, and colours had been reduced to bits of bloody meat. Bloody... it should have been bloody. So why was there almost no blood? Some of it had splattered across the walls and seeped into the cracks in the floor, but I'd seen more blood when I'd first become a vampire and accidentally bitten too hard into a human's main artery.

Even the smell of blood compared to flesh, bone, and death was almost nonexistent. It looked as though someone had torn these people limb from limb with their bare hands, and yet they'd managed to do it all without spilling a drop of blood. Impossible.

'Where's all the blood?' Laith asked.

If he hadn't been standing beside me, I'd never have known it was him talking. His voice had dropped to a faint whisper, throat sounding scratchy and strained.

'I was wondering the same thing,' I said over the sound of violent retching coming from behind me where Cye had fallen.

I wanted to look away from the carnage so badly, but something wasn't letting me; I hadn't even blinked since we'd entered the room. Of all the deformed cloth-covered shapes, only one remained intact. The whole figure was entirely covered by the thin cloth worn by all the necromancers pre-slaughter.

The body was closest to one of the carved archways leading down a tunnel. No light flickered down the haunting tunnels; either they'd been carved at a certain angle or the candles in the entryway placed in a particular way for no light to escape from this space and light them, so they looked like toothless mouths gaping black and endless.

Pointing at the body lying furthest away from us, I said, 'Should we take a closer look?'

Kai followed the line of my finger with his red, bloodshot eyes.

'I don't think I want to,' Laith said.

'There has to be a reason this one is whole.'

'We should wait for Onca,' Kai managed to say.

'We're wasting nighttime, Kai. The longer we leave it, the longer we go with no idea where Gwydion is. This'—I waved my hand in the direction of the body—'might be a clue.'

Although Kai didn't respond, I took him pushing himself away from the wall to come over to us as an unwilling agreement. None of us wanted to see what lay crumpled under the cloth, yet we'd come too far to withdraw from bravery now.

We left Cye to remain in his ball of nausea. It wouldn't be long until Onca arrived with her guards to back us up; until then, Cye could nurse his emotional wounds. Still hand-in-hand, Laith and I edged to one side of the fallen necromancer, Kai on the other. We exchanged a long glance over the body, procrastinating. Surely whatever lay underneath the cloak couldn't be any worse than the scattered collection of limbs. We could all only hope that would be the case as we each knelt down beside the corpse, none of us wanting to be too close to the edge of the body. I was very, *very* grateful that none of the body parts had extended to this part of the room. It looked like whoever had massacred the necromancers had killed this one first and then, once the others tried to escape, had taken them out far more violently towards the exit. It begged the question: why? What had the others done differently to deserve such a horrific fate?

Laith pulled a pair of doctor's gloves from his back pocket, sliding them onto his fingers with practised ease.

'I don't have spare, but I'll volunteer to move the fabric,' he suggested.

'Seems fair,' I said, though it didn't really, as Laith was drawing the short straw—even if he drew it voluntarily.

'I'm fine with that,' Kai agreed, face tinted green.

'I thought you might be,' Laith said without any malice; he'd just accepted the fact that he was going to have to do the dirty job without complaint. A refreshing change.

Kai and I watched Laith peel back the thick black cloth with bated breath. He was going too slowly, not that I particularly wanted him to go any quicker, but the anticipation was even worse than not knowing.

'Just do it like a plaster,' I said.

Laith looked to Kai, who nodded. 'Do it.'

'Okay.' And so he did.

I gasped; Kai's hands flew to his mouth as he fell backwards, legs scrambling wildly away from what remained of the man, until he slammed back against the stone wall.

Closed-eyed and slack-faced, the man looked like he'd fallen into peaceful slumber, soft pink lips slightly parted as if at any moment he'd release a gentle breath of air. If he had lungs, that is. Facially, he was perfect, with a halo of golden curls around his boyish youth, but from the neck down, there was no mistaking him for anything but dead.

The angelic corpse had been mauled viciously, turning his lower body into something spectacularly devilish. It looked like a beast had clawed him from the sternum outwards, with a precision I wouldn't have expected from an animal. Perforated intestines moved with the cloth's movement, leaking fluids thick and dark down the bloody remains of his torso. No words could do justice to the eye-watering stench coming from what remained of the necromancer, but the miasma was so bad, it felt as though I should be able to see the fumes leaking from him. I tried to cover my nose; alas, nothing could stop the foul odour, especially not my hands. Enough of his intestine had stayed intact to hang and curl out of his body, dripping along the floor, some of the fluid leaking out towards me. I moved backwards, hiding just a little bit behind Laith.

What might have been the worst of all was the bloody stump left at the front of his body. The soft flesh of his slender, pale thighs coated in a splash of yellow hair contained a scene of true horror. Where the claw marks had come down, had also taken with it his male appendage, tearing it clean off. The small, squidgy stump of pink flesh oozed red fluid, dripping down to make a pool in the crease of his pressed-together thighs.

'His heart is missing,' Laith whispered, using a gloved finger to point to the mess that was his upper chest.

I couldn't make sense of the bloody ruin, nor did I particularly want to. To me, it looked as though his whole insides had been shredded with razor-sharp claws, leaving nothing recognisable.

'I ain't sure what I'm lookin' at,' Kai squeezed out, crawling back to join us.

'Me, neither.'

Laith pointed to the lower part of the torso, where decimated body parts that should never see the light of day slithered like limp, static serpents out from his body.

'Look, all of this lower area is the small and large intestine,' Laith said, readjusting the cloth enough to hide where his penis had once been. He moved his hand up to the mid-area just below the still intact ribcage. 'Here are his kidneys, and the stomach which has been ripped downwards. And these'—Laith's

313

fingers slid inside the ribcage, poking at the huge, red slab of sliced meat—'are his lungs.'

'Jesus H. Christ,' Kai said with a sense of wonderment I also shared.

Yes, it was horrific to see and a scary reminder that, at the end of the day, all we are is flesh, bone, and tissue powering an insignificant creature in the grand scheme of the universe, but, boy, was it fascinating. There's nothing like being reminded of your own fragile mortality as a wake-up call. Even as a vampire, without my lungs, I could not take the few breaths needed to save me from being just dead instead of the undead. With no heart, I could not feast on humans' life source and use their energy to pump through my veins. I might not be mortal, but I was now beginning to see that the veil between human and vampire was not as wide as I'd thought.

'There's something magick happening here, but I think that whoever did *this* was a therianthrope,' Laith said.

'Why?' I asked.

'This room should absolutely stink, but there was no smell until we removed the cover. These are claw marks.' Laith grimaced. 'Although it looks as though someone reached into his chest and ripped his heart out. It's too deliberate.'

Kai braved a closer look at the body, holding one of his hands out in front of the motley of organs.

'Damn, I think you're right.'

'It's too big for a fox,' Laith mused. 'And too small for a lion.'

The chamber had fallen into a sudden silence, as if something in the air had changed course, cloaking us in thunderous nothing. I could tell it was different, but what was different, I didn't know.

'No therian should be in the country without the Reynard knowin'.' Kai flexed his hand in front of the body, face contorting into a mix of pure disgust and horror. 'Oh, my...'

Stone sliding over stone slashed through the newfound quietness, making both Laith and I jump, but Kai was already staring at Cye, who appeared to have recovered from the shock.

'You bastard,' Kai hissed under his breath, the rage-filled weight of the whisper directed at Cye, who stood like a wall of six-foot-plus meat in front of the doorway, blocking our entrance, and exit.

I was confused, still in a semi-state of delirium after taking in the imagery of so much gore. Kai, for whatever reason, was rattled in a way I'd never seen him. Kai forced himself upwards, his movements, which were so often sinuous, gone rigid and clumsy.

One moment, Kai was in a half-crouched position staring at Cye's minutely smiling face, and the next, Kai bounded through the air, arms outstretched.

The first time I'd seen Kai shift had been when I'd first become a vampire, under the light of the full moon in the forests Nikolaos owned and where we all felt safe. It had not been swift, nor did it look painless. Since then, I'd seen him shift into his full-animal form on many occasions, and each time it had been much the same. I knew Kai had three forms, but knowing in the back of your mind and seeing them firsthand are two very different things.

As Kai flew through the air, the sound of bone popping from the sockets and cracking as they elongated rang like a macabre melody around us. Within an instant, the five-foot-six man flying through the air became a six-foot-plus beast slamming into Cye, sending him smashing backwards into the now-closed stone door. Kai's arm, now almost double the length of his usual and covered in a mass of silken black fur, extended outwards to Cye's neck. He wrapped a huge, warped hand around the man's throat, taloned fingernails curling into the delicate meat.

Kai had moved so fast even I couldn't catch up with it all, leaving me no time to react or even really take in what had just happened. By the time they'd stopped being a blur of chaotic movement, Kai was no longer the man I knew and loved, nor the beautiful feline I'd hunted with on many occasions.

All of his short, stocky frame had grown into a long, wide body covered in a mask of black fur. His belly and front were human-looking but too long, with only a strip of flesh down his front not lined by hair. Kai's legs had grown out, bending in a way no human's ever should. Kai's legs seemed to have changed the most, or at least from what I could see from the back of him. His knee was set higher into his long thighs, bending backwards and leading down into the curve of his calcaneus and hindfoot. It looked as though he had begun to form the shape of his leopard-form's leg, but, although the figure had changed, he was still all human anatomy, so that his heel and ankle looked human but highly deformed. His feet still had human toes, with sharp, white claws curling from them.

A voice I didn't recognise snarled from their direction, 'How could you do this?'

Cye's eyes bulged where Kai cut off his breath, face under all that beard turning crimson. Kai had managed to trap one of Cye's hands underneath his other arm, but the one that he'd left free rose into the air, fingers extended and curled.

I barely had time to scream, 'Kai!' when Cye's clawed hand came slicing through the air, talons carving in Kai's back. Kai let out a shrill cry, body bucking backwards, careening off Cye's frame.

That was it; I had to recover from my state of shock and join in fighting alongside my wounded friend. Laith was one step ahead of me, ripping off his clothes, letting them fall to the carnage-strewn floor in preparation for the change. There was no denying his animal-form would be a stronger ally against our surprising enemy. Still, it took him out of action temporarily as his body bucked and bowed, leaving only me to face the panther alone.

I'd finally worked it out. Cye had betrayed not only the three of us but his Queen and his kingdom. All this time, we'd been trying to end the slaughter of our people and potential damnation to all of paranormal kind, and this cat had fed us all to the wolves. Kai'd called him a bastard, but I could think of many words far more suited to Cye.

Cye stood up, his legs set wide apart in a defensive crouch, clawed hands loose at his side. Just that stance alone alerted me to the fact that Cye knew how to fight. I may have the strength and speed to outmatch any human, but wereanimals were not far behind in either of those departments.

At times like these, all it really comes down to is expertise and knowing how to use your strength to your advantage, something I'd never learnt. At only five-foot-three, with no training in fighting or self-defence, I had no chance against Cye. I also didn't know that therians could partially shift until I'd seen Cye's beastly hand, which had further thrown my focus.

And then I felt it. I had one of those crystalline moments where everything fell into place, quickly overshadowed by the crash of power flooding the room. I caught glimpses of movement to my left, then right, then from every angle.

Dismembered limbs began to crawl across the floor, black-edged fingers dragging bodiless arms from the corners of the chamber. If that wasn't distracting enough, the rapid influx of energy that swarmed through the room left me gasping for breath I didn't need. Heat from a thousand suns and the chill of blizzards that wiped out species combined, rippling over my flesh in a painful mix, bringing a sweat to my brow and sending a shiver down my spine.

I knew the power of the necromancers that I'd felt earlier, the one for which Cye had deceived us with his explanations. Once again, it was tainted with something unnatural, as if two opposing powers had united to create something confused and mercurial; as the power drove me to my knees, I couldn't shake the feeling of familiarity.

It didn't have quite the same effect on my therian friends as it did me, as this power lay with the dead, yet even they couldn't fight off the horror of seeing bits of limbs crawling towards them. Laith, who up until this moment had remained so calm in the wake of so much butchery and death, slammed himself back against the wall, his torso bare from where he'd shredded his clothes. Kai, in his huge half-man-half-leopard form, swatted at the pieces of crawling body, his giant, furred hands coated in their blood, which had suddenly started spurting from nowhere. His cat face and muzzle on an otherwise human face drew back into a snarl, revealing globs of saliva hanging from deadly canines.

Within seconds, we were all coated in blood as if the heavens had opened and with it brought red rain. Each limb acted like a sprinkler, soaking us all in the liquid. I screamed, watching as Laith's body began to crack and dislocate, the fur spreading over him coated in molasses-textured plasma. Neither of them reacted to the downpour. I just wanted it off me. I screamed and tore at my face, arms, hair, everything, clawing at my skin to get it off me. Although I may be a vampire, this blood was impure, the plasma of the devil trying to bathe me in his sin.

I tore my flesh open, trying desperately to make it stop, all the while bits of bodies crawled around me towards the other two men, ignoring me completely. I screamed again as the sensation of bone and bloody tissue touched the side of my shin, the top of a black-haired thigh inching past me by its toes. My throat was red and raw from the endless wails, my face a mask of tears and shredded flesh.

Cye began to rush for me, using my moment of weakness to attack, when a black blur flew in front of my vision. Kai bounded across the room, giving up on the body pieces to go back to his original target. His gait had been replaced by a limp, and when he turned his back to me, I could see why. The wound

Cye had inflicted ran from mid-spine all the way down his backside and thigh, the cuts deeper towards the end, so white flesh peaked out from under all the dark fur. Cye crumpled to the floor with Kai on top of him, and then both men were flying backwards into the walls.

Laith, who had been at the beginning of the shifting process, had stopped to come rushing to my side. His usually handsome face was contorted into a shape I no longer recognised; a once well-proportioned nose and full lips morphed into one huge and black-tinged mouth stretched outwards into a muzzle. He had both more and less human in his face than Kai did. His muzzle was smaller, less developed, but his nose had become more animal-like. He dropped beside me, pulling me into his chest, heart pounding like a wild beast trying to break from its cage. Pale gold eyes stared out at me, with thick gobbets of blood dripping down from the thin trail of fur between his hairline and nose. It was infuriating me to watch him being pelted in liquid and him not responding at all, not even to blink it from his eyes, all the while I was flaying myself alive trying to make it stop.

'Get it off me! Please, please, get it off me!' I bemoaned.

In the distance, the sound of music began to echo around me, a song I'd begged the powers that be never to expose me to again. My prayers had been shunned.

Hands larger than they'd been before stroked down the back of my hair. I tried to fight against him, still doing anything to get the sensation of blood crawling over my skin like bugs off me. Laith grabbed my hands, pinning them to his chest, using his other hand to force my face into his shoulder, so my screams were lost to his skin.

'Calm down, Scarlet! Calm down!'

My hands tried to fight against his hold on them, but he squeezed them hard enough the bones began to crack, and the sharp pain drew me back to myself enough to open my eyes. With Laith holding me in all his warmth and glory, both the music and the sensation of necromancy which had driven me to my knees had stopped. I blinked up at Laith, his weird, furred face dry and perfect in its obscurity, without a trace of blood. I looked down at my hands; the only blood on them was my own where I'd shredded the skin to pieces, though it was already beginning to heal.

'What the...' A *whoosh* of air came from behind me; I had time to see Laith's eyes widen when the full force of a six-foot man smacked into my back, and Laith and I were sent down. Cye's knee pinned my back; I resisted the urge to cry out in pain. Laith snarled from underneath me, trying to free himself of our combined body weights pressing into him. He finally managed to wiggle out from below me, clawed fingers scratching into the floor.

We'd descended into chaos, with the bits of body parts now refocusing on us. It seemed that whatever target Cye had was also the aim for the violated arms, legs, and even torsos, though they couldn't make much progress moving.

I was so disorientated. Everything around me was moving too fast, whilst I was too slow. Or, maybe it was the other way round. Cye's full bodyweight cracked my lower spine, the pressure on that one spot beginning to give in. Soon, he'd break me in half completely. I'd had a fleeting moment of relief when Laith had held me; now he was away, I was back to having the line between reality and morbid fantasy blurred. It shone a whole new light on the current situation, making the obscurity of it almost funny instead of stomach-turning and horrific.

Someone laughed. At first, I thought it might have been me until the sound continued to rattle through the room like a melodious serpent's hiss—sickly sweet; chiming and grating all at once. Even Cye seemed taken aback by the strident melody. The shadows around us contorted, the endless darkness of the tunnels shifting into silhouettes, revealing that the corridors did, in fact, lead to doorways, and we were not as alone as we'd been led to believe. Power which had been a whisper of breath before now held the weight of a storm as, from the sable void, emerged three figures.

CHAPTER 36

From the darkness was born a man, who, though not tall, had the presence of regality. Arcane knowledge burned within his dark eyes—wise in things no man should know. Two figures dressed from head to toe in black robes concealing their bodies and faces emerged from the other two passageways. I didn't need anyone to tell me that the unhooded man was the leader of the other two; the air of authority spoke volumes. From the laughter, I'd expected one of the spooky figures to be a woman, but from what I could see of the shapes of the other two, none of them were.

The man I could see looked strangely normal, the sort of person you could pass in the street without noticing. He was neither too tall nor short, hair somewhere between blond and brown, eyes a pale brown. When faced with power like this, you expect someone fearsome, or at least impressive, whilst he was so plain it was startling. Maybe that's why they'd gone with the theatrics of the head-to-floor robes to seem more imposing. Then again, with power like this and the skill he'd demonstrated, he didn't need to look impressive. The magick he'd conjured spoke louder than any physical attribute could. He held himself in a way not synonymous with anyone unimportant or bland, but confident and arrogant.

'Cye,' he said, in a voice surprisingly soft and distant, 'I see you have brought our guests.'

'I've done all that was asked of me, Khemeia,' Cye said, and he actually had the audacity to sound indignant with his weight holding me captive.

Khemeia smiled, his burning, pale brown eyes never focusing on anything in the room for long, his smile lazy.

'Indeed you have, Cye.'

'Then I can go.'

Khemeia seemed to refocus, giving Cye a look somewhere between friendly and sinister.

'Escort our guests to the Great Hall, and then you may go.' His teeth bared in a cruel smile. 'If your master permits it.'

I felt Cye tense, his knee digging me further into the ground. This time, I couldn't be silent. I let out a small whimper as the bone of my spine began to snap, the pain so sudden and shocking I was breathless, everything around me going still in that moment of pain. Cye seemed to notice what he was doing and alleviated some of the pressure; it still hurt, but the physical sensation of my bone snapping had stopped at least. Laith noticed my pain, going to rush Cye.

The two black-clad figures moved before he had the chance. They flashed across the room, a blur of dark fabric flying quicker than anything I'd ever seen, using that speed to catch my two men off guard. Laith growled, trying to break free of the hold, but the presumed man in black squeezed his arms around Laith, sending the sound of cracking bones throughout the room. Laith went limp in his arms, head drooping. If I'd had the breath to call, I'd have cried out to Laith. Alas, Cye winded me under his immense weight.

Khemeia finally focused on me, his lips still twitching into a lazy smile, distant eyes struggling to remain on my face, almost as if he were high.

'My apologies,' he said, bowing his head down to the ground, almost toppling over. Khemeia rose with a sway, head back as he laughed at his own gauche manner. 'I have not greeted our guest of honour. How very uncouth.' And then he giggled, of all things.

I might have quipped something back if I could talk; however, that was still impossible with Cye on top of me. Khemeia seemed to realise what the problem was, signalling for Cye to release some of the pressure. I coughed and sputtered into the stone floor, throat raw and chest burning from the prolonged constriction.

'I'm getting so tired of people expecting me when I don't have a clue who they are,' I managed to spit onto the floor.

Khemeia frowned, his head tilting to the side, and then a high-pitched chuckle rang out from between curling lips. With that came a hiccup, choking on his inappropriate glee.

'Come, let us escort our distinguished visitants to the Queen,' he said, seemingly to everyone and no one, lips tugging back into a strange, sluggish smile. 'We do not wish to tire you any further, Scarlet.'

Something twitched in the corner of my eye, one of the hands that had been lying dormant convulsed its fingers. A horrified shudder ran up my body. I was so grateful that they'd stopped attacking us. Fighting off a mountainous werepanther was one thing, but crawling carcass pieces were something for which none of us had been prepared. Not that we'd expected any of this.

Cye raised from his knees, letting me free, but the second I tried to wriggle from the ground, he reached down, lifting me into the air by the waist. Cye held me to his chest in a princess carry, pinning my arms and legs in a way that it was nearly impossible to move. I'd always thought that vampires were stronger than therians, but tonight was proving I'd been wrong about a lot of things. My long hair caught in Cye's arm, pulling my head back at a painful angle.

I didn't have much movement in my head, so searching for my two companions over Cye's massive chest as he started to follow Khemeia down the middle tunnel proved difficult. I managed to move my head just enough to see Laith being carried loosely in the arms of his capturer. With his beastly face hanging downwards, the rest of his semi-shifted, nude body was limp in their arms, feet dragging along the floor. Kai took up the rear. Though he'd tried struggling at first, Kai had realised that he couldn't outmatch the hooded-figure, and we all needed to conserve our energies. Especially now we were a man down.

Each step Khemeia took brought with it a surge of light in the dark tunnel as if he himself were the torch in the shadows. Down spiral stairs, we journeyed, me constricted by Cye, my body bobbing up and down with each of his heavy steps. Behind us, the sound of Laith's feet bumping into the steps resonated. The further down we went, the more I could feel the beat of capricious energies. They danced and swirled through the air, toxic lovers entwining. They pushed and pulled at one another; I was but superfluous collateral damage to the fight for dominance.

Grand double doors waited at the bottom of the stairwell. I could see them pounding back and forth, the thud of silent music banging against the metal bars and wood. Khemeia, with a dramatic push of his hand, opened the doors, baring with it the Great Hall in all of its extravagant glory.

Built into the underground of Glasgow's gothic necropolis was an ostentatious hall. Warped walls of stone draped in golden and white cloth lead up and up to high, vast ceilings. From the marble pillars around the room grew statues in poses of desire. Some flowed from the marble salacious and tempting, others curved and curled stuck in scenes of death and destruction. In all of them, eyes gleamed with a vicious yearning for bodies.

Tall candelabras in gold and silver stood around the hall's edges, blue candles flickering just enough light to manipulate shadow. As we entered further into the room, my eyes were distracted by the artwork painted along the ceiling, works looking suspiciously similar to the likes of Michelangelo depicted scenes of great beauty and woe.

I couldn't see much over Khemeia's shoulders, but it was hard to focus on anything other than the glitter of silver, gold, and blue, and the corrupting song of power lost to evil. For one glorious second, I was transported to a realm of decadence and magick, where art and debauchery prevailed. It was as if my vampire senses were used to their full advantage for the first time, every slender vein in the marble looking as though it pulsed under the stone; the shine of polished metal radiant, a thousand suns and moons blazing through the room; every shimmer of cloth rich and enchanting. It was breathtaking, glorious...

...And then reality came with me being thrown to the marble floor at the foot of a slender staircase. My head barely missed the edge of the first step, leading up to a white stage. Velvet curtains in silver, graced with lining of shimmering blues like pearls in the ocean, hung low over the stage, concealing whatever lay behind it.

From behind me, another drop came. I turned my face to see Laith's body crumpled at the foot of the caped figure. Kai was still held to the chest of the largest of the hostile hosts, his orange eyes burning with a rage I'd never encountered in him before. We locked eyes, the scathing power of his anger almost enough to bite back some of the ethereal energy into which I had willingly thrown myself. To resist such beautiful degeneracy took a force of will beyond my abilities. Maybe I'd be ashamed of that if it didn't feel so right. I was finally home, bathing in a thermae of sin. My cheek pressed harder against the cold, opulent stone, bringing me back into myself enough to focus on the fallen lion.

I expected Cye or one of the others to try and stop me as I crawled towards him, but none of them did. Khemeia didn't even look at me; he was too busy, lost in a distant haze. I crawled on hands and knees towards the injured Laith. No matter how much I tried to remain focused on him, my gaze kept averting to the covered stage. Soundless music played a haunting number, the phantom of a sound that looped through my mind. If it had been real, maybe I would have known what instrument sang its song through the room, but, as I'd experienced upstairs, this was a too-real fantasy in my head. At least this time, I could tell it wasn't real, not that it made it any less distracting. By the time I'd reached Laith's side, the melancholy melody had sent a trail of tears down my cheeks.

'Once again, I must apologise, Scarlet. What bad hosts we are to harm one of our guests.' Khemiea looked at the robed figure who had crushed Laith as he said it, and with it came a flare of his anger, melting the angelic facade into one of the Devil. The rush of his annoyance sent a spark down my back, his necromancy beating against me.

I scooped Laith into my arms, clutching his head to my chest, fingers trailing down the half-formed mane around his beastly face. He was breathing, thank God, but each breath that came was shallow and forced. I noticed the lopsided slant to his chest where they'd crushed the bones of his ribcage.

'Let the leopard go,' Khemeia instructed. Cye opened his mouth in protest but closed it quickly at the look from the other man. 'Do it.' The robed being holding Kai let him go so abruptly, Kai almost fell over.

He came bounding towards us, all black fur and bare skin, his manhood hanging between his legs. I'd been avoiding looking at that part of the men, but it was hard to avoid when it came running at you. Fingers focused on the soft curl of Laith's golden hair; my distracted eyes wandered off around the room. Kai grabbed my wrist painfully, forcing me to focus on him.

'Look at me, Scarlet,' he growled in that strange, sonorous voice so far from that to which I was accustomed. 'Focus.'

I did as he requested, settling my eyes on his contorted face, but it was so hard to think of anything except the melody flowing like silk over my bare flesh. I shuddered, legs tightening.

'You are a fool,' Cye hissed at Khemeia; I was just glad to have his frustration taken out on someone other than me.

Kai and I both looked up at the tense therian. The other two figures had joined behind Khemeia, all of them standing nonchalantly to the side. Khemeia ignored the panther, instead settling his unfocused scrutiny on me. He wafted his hand in the direction of Laith.

'Heal him, Scarlet. As I said, you are our guests, and we mean you no harm.'

It would have been foolish to believe him; none of the buildup that got us to this point would indicate his honesty, so why did I? Because his voice carried such truth, so tender that it brought tears to my eyes.

I was enough myself to do what he suggested; with encouragement from Kai, I raised my wrist to my lips and pierced the flesh. I'd shared my blood with humans to heal them before, an offer of peace after feasting on them. Whilst I'd not shared it with any supernatural creatures, I'd assumed it would be similar in its mundanity.

It seemed that every small event which had led to Laith consuming my blood met at one climactic point. Mundane it was not. With witnesses of disdain, amusement, and concern, cause married consequence. I'd never given much thought to destiny, but before us she stood, an officiant to the matrimony of all that has been, and all that will. My blood touched Laith's lips, and the world erupted in a flow of golden light and raging fires. Nothing had ever been as sure as the two of us being fated to unite as one. Even me becoming a vampire, meeting Nikolaos, the Syndicate coming after Gwydion and me, all of it had needed to happen for Laith and me to meet. My blood flowed through his veins, the way his did mine, and with it the power of my fire and the Earth, and the curse of night skies and immortality bled into him, through him.

After feeding on him, Laith had given me life and beast, and now I touched him with all that I could offer. His eyes flew open, pure black in all the mass of hair and black nose in his face. In their reflection, I saw myself, knew that my eyes also mirrored a dark void. A halo grew from around both of our bodies, red flames tainted by the touch of shadow curled over his figure as he shared with me the golden aura of lion and the green breath of Sahara trees. Nothing in the world existed except for our two beings suspended in colour and light.

Laith wrapped his hands further around my wrist, rough tongue lapping over the wound. I threw my head back, eyes fluttering with the rush. In the distance, melodies of power still sang, and the brush of necromancy filled the room like water. With Laith attached to me, a new sensation came with it, the feeling of therianthrope. He was not connected to Cye or Kai by beast; yet still, they shared the curse of the full moon. How lonely it was to be surrounded by your people whilst none of them being really *your* people.

Laith rose from the ground to encase me in his arms, letting his bloody mouth free of my flesh. He clutched me to his chest, with the pounding of drums thudding in the noisy quiet. His heartbeat thudded wildly, so forceful I felt it in my own chest. Glorious, how glorious it was to feel a heartbeat after six months of demise.

And then, in the midst of the drumbeat, another came, and he powered my heart to echo his own. We were separate, but one, two insignificant beings in time and space bound to each other by something so important it was ineffable.

I collapsed on top of Laith, my chest pressing against his bare body, the feel of my heartbeat pounding against his smooth, furry flesh. Absently, my fingers ran through the silken hair of his body. My fingers had never touched anything as comforting as Laith's fur, my nose pressed further into his chest, breathing in the scent of lion and, underneath it all, him.

A precision of slow and derisive claps echoing throughout the room pulled Laith and me from our trances of heavy breaths and wildly beating hearts. It started as one pair of hands, and then the others joined in the chorus.

Still blurry-eyed, I barely registered that the veil over the stage had lifted, revealing what had been waiting all along. I didn't need eyes to know what sat upon the stage, bathed in a stream of blinding firelight.

Vampire.

More than just any old vampire, the energy was one I knew so very well, one to which I had been bound through more than species, but a promise of eternity.

I had one of those seconds of clarity, where the puzzle pieces finally fell into place, and with it, the world came crashing down around me. All of this time, I had sensed the air of necromancy tainted by a bitterness beyond their touch of death. Power that was not meant to collide had fallen into the arms of one another, bringing with it a sense of sadomasochistic distraction. Lovers tied together by the ropes of discordance. Oh, Nikolaos, my darling, what had you got yourself into?

What had I?

CHAPTER 37

Sitting on a throne of silver, leisured a woman whose formidable beauty shone pale and bright in the shadows, as if an ethereal glow illuminated her. Blonde hair hung in waves of gold down her front, perfect ringlets framing an angled, emaciated face that made me think of times long gone when peasants starved to put food on the tables of royals.

A gossamer gown in turquoise chiffon fabric floated down around her legs, brushing against the floor. From underneath the fabric, poked a pale, dainty foot, taping against the leg of the throne. The gown and hair were elegant but understated, plain to let her natural beauty speak for itself. Disdainful, glacial blue eyes watched me, glistening with humour to a joke I didn't get, or didn't want to get, where she left me feeling like the punchline. The only other element to her look was a small silver crown atop the halo of white-gold curls, with small sapphire and topaz stones placed in the spires of the tiara. On some, it might have looked gaudy, but the tiara was just small, and the outfit just regal enough, that it worked spectacularly well. I'd never seen a vampire with cheeks as flushed as hers, a spark of pink in all the iciness. Two figures dressed head to toe in white robes stood with the stillness of death behind her and the smaller throne beside her starved, fidgeting figure. Vampires. All three of them were.

The fourth vampire needed no introduction. Seeing his face sent a surge of emotion through me: relief, at first; anger, that he could be involved in something so nefarious; disgust, at his association with the necromancers and whatever the fuck was happening with him; and then, finally, my heart sank into the corpse-filled ground below.

All this time, the terror at what we had faced was eased with the knowledge that Nikolaos was safe. I'd never wanted him involved in it, and, despite my trying to contact him on multiple occasions, I'd always known that he was shielded in his ignorance. To find out that, all this time, he had been playing far closer to the proverbial fire than any of us was harrowing. Now all that was left was the inevitable burn. I had a powerful feeling it would come from the clapping woman in blue and white.

Still wrapped in Laith's arms, held to his chest, both of us riding the weight of a metaphysical high, I reached my hand out to the seated Nikolaos with his unreadable face. It was the first time I'd ever seen him in anything other than dark colours. Someone had dressed him from head to toe in white cloth with golden and cyan threading. In all the time I'd known Nikolaos, he'd had an air of untouchable grace, but seeing him like this, he seemed humbled. The arrogant, sorrowful glint in his green eyes was lost to misery and horror, those full lips I hadn't kissed in days set into a tight line. In all of the white, he looked too pale, too deathly, his stark cheekbones gaunt. Nikolaos's lush, sable hair was flat and too-dark against his marble features. He was still the most beautiful man I'd ever laid my eyes upon, yet this beauty was tainted with the malady of woe.

A fifth man approached from behind the shadows of the stage, he too dressed in black robes, but like Khemeia, his face was visible. Also like Khemeia, this necromancer's—there was no denying what he was—hood had been removed to reveal a dark complexion and mass of black hair. He joined in the clapping, slowly, sarcastically. The look in his eyes was almost as scathing as Nikolaos's, though I imagine for different reasons. Maybe to anyone else, Nikolaos would be a picture of stoicism, but not to me. We were bound by love, magick, death, and soul; his days of being solitary and unreadable were behind him. Whether he liked it or not.

This new necromancer oozed the same arrogance as the throned woman, who I could only assume was Amphitrite, vampire Empress of Europe. My Empress only in title; she'd done nothing to deserve my respect. In fact, I was particularly unhappy with her right now. At least I had the sense not to say that out loud with her sneering smile and sardonic clapping.

Nikolaos was the only one of her bunch not to have joined in with the clapping, instead fixing me with a look even I was struggling to read. From underneath her long sleeve, Amphitrite withdrew a small vial of red fluid, flipping the cap off. The second the metal cap was released, a smell I recognised all too well filled the hall. Blood, befouled by magick, filled my senses, the scent of something so delectable, I knew that with one drop, I'd be hooked. I couldn't help but try to pull free from Laith's arms, but he held onto me, pulling me back into an embrace intensified by the beating of his heart. Our fingers entwined; with his hands in mine, I felt the strength of a titanium shield, giving me the resistance needed not to fall at the feet of Amphitrite and beg her for a taste. It wasn't the first time his touch had helped calm me since we'd met, not that I had any explanation for why. I wasn't about to look a gift horse in the mouth—or gift lion, as the case may be. Amphitrite poured a droplet of the blood onto the tip of her dainty tongue.

Amphitrite arose from her seat, bare feet jumping up and down on the stage lightly, hands fluttering together wildly. Her expression had instantly changed from distant mocking to pure rapture, eyes blinking rapidly, grinning at us all. Khemeia joined the side of the other necromancer, his two fledglings taking position to the side of the stairway. I was still too distracted by Nikolaos to give the others much focus. I didn't know whether to run into his arms or shout in his face. What trouble were we in?

'Bravo! Bravo! What a wonderful performance,' the presumed Amphitrite sang, still bouncing on the balls of tiny feet. She turned to look at the two necromancers. 'Wasn't that wonderful, Khemeia, Orcus?'

Khemeia flashed her that inappropriately beatific smile, though Orcus didn't change much in his response. In fact, he looked positively disgusted at the Empress and her altered state. Whether she'd seen the fleeting hatred in his eyes and ignored it, or failed to notice, Amphitrite turned to Cye without a second glance at the scornful Orcus.

'Cye?'

'Yes, my Queen?' he asked, looking sombre. I had no sympathy to spare after his betrayal.

'Did you like the show?'

Cye didn't respond, instead trying to hide the rage in his face by looking down at the ground. Amphitrite dismissed him with a waft of her dainty hand, hanging sleeve waving through the air like an unsettled ocean.

337

'No matter. I enjoyed it. I enjoyed it greatly. Such passion, lust'—she shuddered—'power. It must make our darling Nikolaos's tender heart bleed to see his lover in the arms of a beast.'

I didn't so much see as feel Nikolaos flinch, his shoulders tensing minutely. I didn't think it would be noticeable to anyone else, but the shrill laugh Amphitrite released indicated otherwise.

'Oh, oh, it did indeed!' She laughed, a grating sound that I recognised from the tunnel, and then she pouted, her whole demeanour changing to one of great, sardonic sorrow. It was such a change that I physically flinched, feeling as though I'd missed something of great significance to warrant such a shift.

Laith tightened his arms around me, which really didn't help.

'I am quite torn,' Amphitrite said wistfully, small mouth pouting. 'For you, Scarlet, are a guest in my home, but so is Niko. And I, as your hostess, am required to keep you both happy for as long as you are my guests. But it seems as though you've upset him.' And she made a little *hmph* sound, arms crossing over her chest. 'What on earth do I do?' Each syllable was delivered slowly as if she were a Wiseman and I nothing more than an imbecile unable to grasp the wisdom of her words, despite their shallow, simple nature.

Nikolaos appeared to catch on quicker than I did, his own facade changing to as amiable as I'd ever seen him, though I knew it was fake. He took on a persona I'd never before seen from him, one so out of character it was disconcerting.

Standing from the chair, Nikolaos went to Amphitrite's jittering side, plastering a smile to his pallid face. I could count on one hand the number of times I'd seen Nikolaos smile and still have fingers left over. His fangs glinted in the firelight, but that shimmer never met his cold eyes.

'My Queen,' he began, and his voice was silk over my skin; I hadn't realised how much I missed him until I heard him speak, 'I am not irked by my vassal's actions.'

She stopped bouncing up and down to turn huge, pale blue eyes to my lover in a way that resembled a child. 'You're not?'

He shook his head, fingers going to trace a lock of hair behind her ear. I felt my body tense at the sight, the way his long, slender fingers worked so gently through her white-gold locks.

'Scarlet and I do not have that sort of relationship; you know this. She is free to lay with whomever'—he turned to look at me—'or whatever she wishes.'

'You bastard,' I muttered very quietly under my breath, so quietly that, if it weren't for the side-eye from Kai, I'd have been sure it was silent.

Kai stood from the ground, offering me his hand, which I took. He pulled the two of us up, but I made sure not to let go of Laith's hand. I wasn't so foolish as to ignore the help his touch gave me, even if I didn't understand it.

'So, everything is okay, then?'

'*Oui.*'

She clapped rapidly, grinning at the taller man.

'That's good then!'

Orcus interjected the two vampire's intimate moment. 'May I suggest we get our guests some clothing. We weren't expecting them to be quite so nude.'

I felt myself try to blush; in all of the fickle happenings, I'd forgotten that both men were naked, their bits only made larger in their semi-state of beast. Amphitrite turned to the three of us, pale eyes darkening. She seemed to forget about Nikolaos, stepping away from him to come towards us, thin lips curling into a nefarious smile. It gave me the opportunity to glare at Nikolaos whilst she focused on my naked friends. We locked eyes, and the apathy was scathing.

'Hmm, it seems a shame to cover up such strange beauty.' Her gaze lingered too long on Laith, long enough for him to feel the need to pull his legs together, using his spare hand to cover his crotch. Amphitrite found this quite amusing, giggling. She brushed her hand through the air, wafting us all away. 'Ah, fine, fine. Orcus, send someone to fetch them some clothes. And some chairs, whilst you're at it.'

'Cye—' Orcus began, but Amphitrite interrupted him.

'No, not your pet. I want him here.'

With a sigh, Orcus relented, sending off one of the necromancers in black with a white-robed vampire.

Cye did not look happy at being left to enjoy the party, in fact, he looked positively miserable.

'You said I could go once I had delivered them to you,' he bemoaned.

Amphitrite turned away from us and started the short journey towards the waiting panther with his shadow of betrayal.

Amphitrite patted her chin with her too-skinny finger. 'I did, didn't I?'

'Then let me leave.'

She placed her hand on her chest, smiling up at the beefy man with his hunched shoulders and angry eyes. 'I have no qualms with you leaving, Cye. But then, it's not down to me.'

'Orcus, please, I ain't got nothing else to offer you.'

'On the contrary, I think your uses have only been brushed upon.'

'Orcus, please...'

Orcus, with his mass of dark hair and wide, scary eyes, held his hand out to Cye, and I felt the jolt of magick like lightning in the room. It was enough to startle both Kai and Laith, too, who both rocked with it.

'Oh, Cye,' Kai whispered under his breath, more to himself than anyone else in the room.

Cye's body shook with the force of power, his back straightening and legs beginning to make the journey up the stairs. At first, he battled the influence, his knees refusing to bend with each step. By the time he'd reached Orcus's side, it was a different story, with his whole body relaxing next to Orcus.

Orcus fished into his pocket, pulling out another small vial of blood, almost identical to the one that Amphitrite had used earlier. I tightened my grip on Laith's hand, preparing myself for the addictive smell to hit me, but, as Orcus popped the lid off, all that came was mediocrity. Vampires can consume their ilk's blood, though it serves no purpose and has a certain stale smell that makes it borderline unappealing.

Orcus let a droplet slip onto his finger, pressing it to Cye's face. Cye bent down, one finger over his left nostril, and sniffed the blood off Orcus's finger. Orcus repeated the ritual for Khemeia, who gave his nose up readily. Now, this was a new one. I'd seen some peculiar things in my time as a vampire, but never someone snorting our blood.

Orcus did the same thing for himself, raising an entirely clean finger to his nose, sniffing the air as if it had something on it. Neither of his companions, nor Amphitrite, noticed his deceit. The other two men were too busy riding the wave of their come up. I watched with my stomach knotted in intrigue and disgust as Cye's iris went from a terrified pin-prick to saucers in his face. Khemeia's barely changed, which was hardly surprising considering how big they already were. Whilst I'd never much experimented with anything, Anna, my older sister, had lived the student lifestyle, and this was not my first rodeo of seeing someone off their face.

Amphitrite was just making her way up the stairs towards the throne when the two who'd been sent off for the chairs returned. One of the two figures plonked the chairs down at the foot of the stairs, giving us front row seats to Amphitrite's one-woman show. She was playing every role, from woebegone host to wild Queen, and I was already beginning to get whiplash from it. The other handed a set of white robes to Kai and Laith.

Laith had to let go of my hand to put them on; the change was instant. Once again, I was floating in space, and Amphitrite was Venus, from which dawn and light radiated. Each of the four necromancers were the stars around her, flickering bright and tempting in the heavens, their grace a beam in perpetual darkness. We may have been suspended in a room of white marble and pale cloth, but it was all shadow compared to their brilliance.

And, amongst all of their dazzling magnificence, Nikolaos was Saturn, a black star, shining brighter than all the rest. Tears filled my eyes at his debased beauty; all of that perfection tinged with sorrowful starvation. I don't remember taking a step closer, but I must have, because within a blink, I was at the top of the stairs.

Nikolaos held his hand out to me; my fingers found his, and we were one again. I practically fell into his arms—okay, my foot tripped on the top step, and I *did* fall into his arms.

A familiar sensation of an exasperated exhale and soft chuckle tickled the top of my head. When we'd first met, the laughter had never accompanied his rasping, and now, it seemed the other way round. I wrapped my arms around his body tight enough we should have melded into one, hard enough he let out a little sound of protest.

My damp cheeks rubbed against the soft cloth of his white garments, soaking up some of the crimson tears. Around us, the sensation of necromantic energy and blood was a tornado, we the log cabin soon to be taken away in the storm. The urge to turn from him and give my mind, body, and soul to Amphitrite and her merry band of evil was almost too much, but my being had been promised to another, and he was currently wrapped in my arms. Laith had offered me a strength that sang the melodies of life; Nikolaos was the Grim Reaper, my master in death, my husband in immortality.

Consumed by his beautiful brush of death, with it came a weakness to the wiles of necromancy. I was the fortified shield against their power with my nymph blood, Nikolaos could not strengthen that aspect of me, and my shield was currently weak.

'I've missed you,' I whispered into his shirt.

'Release me.' Nikolaos let go of me, pushing me backwards so that I slammed into the floor at his feet, my palms striking against the cold stone.

I turned to look at him, surprised, my hands stinging almost as much as my heart. Even Amphitrite looked momentarily taken aback, and then she giggled, radiating arrogance as her hands found Nikolaos's. From the floor, I watched their hands entwine, her ring-adorned fingers settling over his.

'Go back to your flock of beasts, Scarlet.'

I started to pick myself up from the floor, more confused than anything. I could not stop staring at Amphitrite's hands, as if they were the most mesmerising thing on earth, with their slight blushed hue and blue veins under lily-white skin. Laith, now-robed, had made it halfway up the stairs towards me, picking me up the rest of the way.

Once again, we shared that spark, but I noticed it more after touching Nikolaos. His life-tinged power was less of a smooth transition into reality and more a jarring jolt. Combined with the touch of my, however much I may hate to say it, master, Laith was the puzzle piece I'd not known was missing.

Life and death united, one a ball of blinding electricity, the other a dying star of light, and I was an outlet for them both to meet. The sensation of Nikolaos's cold, etiolated figure was palpable despite his distance, so much so that my free hand flew to my chest as if I could still hold him to me. Pushing through Nikolaos's phantom impression was the distinct pulse of a beating heart and scent of sun-blushed fur.

Yin and Yang, both men were the entrées to a banquet held in my soul; a feast, providing nourishment from harvests reaped, dished with debauchery and precious fluids. If this was how it felt to touch them separately, I could only imagine the experience of simultaneous stimulation.

Amphitrite would give me no leeway to find out, though, as she was wrapping herself around my master. Her tall body slid around him from the back, fingers trailing down his chest, playing with the gilded buttons on their bright thread.

Laith led my reluctant frame down to where Kai waited for us. He sat on one of the cushioned chairs, watching the show cautiously. Kai had always been bulky, if not short, but now his body was a mountain; I was surprised the chair could hold his weight.

We took our seats in perfect view of my Empress pawing my master. Amphitrite had taken another droplet from the vial, waving it under Nikolaos's nose, causing him to look physically pained. I tightened my hand on Laith's, curling my fingers over the fur on his knuckles, grounding myself in the sensation of a lion's tuft on human flesh.

'Thank you for joining us tonight, Scarlet and companions. I believe you must be Kai. But you'—she cocked her head to one side, a shaking hand playing with the fabric on the arm of the throne—'were quite unexpected.'

345

'This is the lion we told you about,' Cye mumbled from her side, standing between the two necromancers. He was by no means a small man, but Orcus and Khemeia made him look shrunk beside them, hunched in on himself. He looked so weak it made me sick; he wouldn't even be worth bleeding.

'The doctor?' asked Amphitrite.

Cye gave a curt nod, avoiding looking at us like the coward he was.

'Ahh, the doctor. In which case, Laith, is it Laith?' Laith nodded. 'Laith, you were indeed expected.'

Kai picked up on something that I'd missed in my state of rage and magickal overpower.

'We?' he growled.

Cye startled, realising the error of his slippery tongue.

'Oh, Orcus, your pet has no delicacy with his speech. Maybe you should get him a muzzle to compliment the metaphysical leash.' She glowered at him. 'Or he'll spoil all the surprises.'

'It seems I am not the only one with a newfound pet,' Orcus said, looking at Laith and me, drawing everyone's attention back to us, including Nikolaos.

I was just plain confused now; this seemed like a weird insult to be throwing our way. Of all the things to insult us for, Laith and or Kai being animals wasn't exactly on the top of the list.

'Do you mean us?' I asked. 'I don't get it.'

Surprisingly, Kai was the first to seem exasperated, followed quickly by amusement from the rest, all except for Nikolaos, who remained quite disdainful.

'Is she joking?' Amphitrite asked Nikolaos, who shook his head.

'I forewarned you of Scarlet's folly.'

'Is it folly, Niko, or is it that I'm only twenty and known about the arcane for six months whilst you've been a part of it for two millennia?' I raised Laith's hand, using the spare to point at Kai. 'And these two have always known the preternatural world. If you hold me to your standards, I will never measure up. But that doesn't make me foolish.'

Amphitrite looked taken aback.

'I've never heard a subordinate talk to their master this way. You have a particularly impudent manner.'

'I did not fail to mention her certain tenacity, either, my Queen,' Niko said, and he sounded something close to smug.

'I thought you meant it to be a positive trait; I now see that is not the case.'

Niko gave that graceful shrug he'd spent a lifetime perfecting, managing to make it both nonchalant and suggestive.

'Not always.'

'Tenacity, when wielded correctly, is a powerful tool, my Queen,' added Khemeia.

Amphitrite mulled over this, cocking her head to the side.

'Yes, Khemeia, you raise a good point.'

'Amphitrite,' Kai interjected, 'may I enquire as to why you've brought us here.'

'You, kitten, are here as leverage.'

I felt movement behind me, turning my head just in time to see the two hooded figures flash from the wall towards us. They took up a place at Kai and Laith's back. Then, once again, they were still. Technically, they'd done nothing offensive, their stillness non-threatening. But the Queen had moved her pawns; it was only a matter of turns until checkmate. Kai visibly tensed beside me, more noticeable in his enlarged, furred state.

'Leverage for what?' I demanded, growing increasingly weary at the erratic Empress and her games.

'For the past few months, I've adjured Nikolaos to bring you to my side with him. Alas, much like you, he is insubordinate and has dismissed my command.'

'Why do you want me? Why would you want both of us? We're nothing special.'

'Oh, on the contrary, Scarlet, you are quite extraordinary. The Syndicate were made aware of what you did last year, the power you summoned, the true heritage that runs through your veins. I know an awful lot about you, but there is something you may not know about me.'

Amphitrite seemed to want me to enquire further, so I humoured her. 'Which is?'

'As a human, I was nothing more than a peasant; as a vampire, I became something beyond even immortal. My magick finds affiliation with the elements much the same as yours, water, in my case.'

'I'm still confused.'

Amphitrite rose from her throne in a blur of speed, her agitation palpable.

'Think of what we could achieve together! Nikolaos is older than even any of the monarchy. He has been in the frontline of major history, playing his role in the evolution of vampires. Together, he and I could be powerful. But the three of us together, that would be mighty. I have plans, Scarlet, plans for the three of us that would douse us in riches and power beyond your wildest dreams.' She spoke with such ardent enthusiasm that I couldn't help but be caught up in the energy of her words.

'Niko never told me any of this.'

Amphitrite dismissed my statement with a shake of her skinny hand. 'Eh, he is a fool! He cannot see beyond what he knows.' She started coming down the stairs towards me, skipping jollily. 'But I am quite certain that, if I can convince you, then you can show him the error of his ways.'

Amphitrite's gown brushed my knees, her hand outstretched to me. A part of me wanted to take it, the part of me that, as a vampire, acknowledged her position as my Empress and wanted to fall into the throes of deathly power. My hand was halfway up to hers when Laith squeezed my fingers, pulling me back into myself.

'Let her go, runt,' Amphitrite spat at Laith.

'I'll be fine,' I lied, letting go of his hand.

Laith reluctantly let go, giving me the freedom to take her invitation. Her fingers wrapped around mine and, without Laith there as a buffer, her extraordinary and confused power was immense. The vampire side of me drank down her throbbing energy, feeling the warmth of her tainted magick like carcinogenic rays of the sun.

Both Laith and Kai reached out to me as she pulled me from the chair, but the vampire and necromancer behind them were put to their task, reaching over to grab their shoulders and pulling them back into the chairs. Being led up the stairway by Amphitrite, I was too distracted to watch them struggle against the weight of their almighty strength. I should have cared more that hostile creatures were detaining my friends, but the song of necromancers harmonised with Amphitrite's queenly melody, and it was all too beautiful to worry. My fire had all but been forgotten, the nymph blood in me replaced by the blood of a hundred strangers giving me life as a vampire.

Nikolaos rose from his seat; I instinctively reached out to him. He was the rationale I needed, both exacerbating the vampire power and clearing my head.

'What *is* your plan?' I asked as he pulled me closer to him, immediately dropping my hand as if he suddenly thought better of touching me.

I thought I was asking a fair question—a good question even—but the exasperation from Amphitrite made it clear I'd said something wrong. I turned to Nikolaos to ask what I'd done, but Amphitrite grabbed my wrist, squeezing down.

'You don't understand what it's like!' she cried out so unexpectedly I started. The abrupt anger from her was shocking, causing me to stumble as she pulled me. Amphitrite's fury was lightning, and I the tree, a beam of emotion that sliced through me, splitting me from root to head. 'The women today act as if they know hardships, but you know nothing of true inequality. I grew up when women were burned, tortured, raped, imprisoned under the guise of witchcraft when our only crimes were deigning to be born female.' Her disgust was palpable, a beautiful face contorted into one of hatred. Her fingers tightened around me as she continued, 'I was born into true poverty, with the riches of the elements on my side. From childhood, I was brought up battling the force of Canon law and male eye. Grown men beat me, starved me, threatened me with death for being unnatural, a woman of the devil, all the while still using me to satiate their many needs. On good nights, I was their favourite pet, their toy who could manipulate the water in their chalices, the little peasant monkey who would dance for them. And on the worst...'

Amphitrite let go of me abruptly, and I fell backwards into Niko's chest. I was so enthralled with the horrified Empress before me he was insignificant. Bloodied tears ran thick and dark from her eyes; blood turned black with impure magick and a deathly host.

Amphitrite didn't finish her sentence; no one asked her to. I think we had all had quite enough horror for the night without needing to know the abuse she'd faced in mortal life.

As arbitrarily as they'd begun, her tears ceased. Amphitrite wiped them away with a pale sleeve, smearing black blood over the fabric. She sniffed, pulling the small vial from its hiding place once more, letting another droplet fall on her tongue. Nikolaos preemptively squeezed me to him, letting us share the commencing burden of the flavourful blood.

Before, Amphitrite's indulgence has been borderline mocking, antagonising us with her vial of temping sin; this time, she lapped the fluid desperately, caring for nothing but the blood. None of us mattered to her; we were superfluous to her sedated craving.

Popping the lid back on, she shuddered, turning wide, wild eyes back to Nikolaos and me.

'What was I saying?' she asked, and then grinned, blood catching in the subtle lines around her thin mouth, making them look deep and painful. 'Of course, I was detailing the mundane woes of mortality.'

Amphitrite fell back into her throne, one leg throwing itself over the other as she slumped further down.

'I've always had a magickal affiliation with water; scrying was my divination of choice. Unfortunately, I was born in a time when elemental magick was particularly sacrilegious in the eyes of pious Catholic men. Of seven sinful divinations, hydromancy was amongst the worst, a tie to that which is truly natural, beautiful: water. Necromancy was passed off as black magick when it was convenient; pyromancy, what you hold, Scarlet, was another.'

Amphitrite rolled her lip into her mouth, sucking on it as she thought, face fierce with memories of a troubled mortal life.

'By the time I was turned, I was close to death and content with acceptance. Death was the key to my imprisonment. Do you know how I became Empress? Has Nikolaos told you?'

I shook my head, re-feeling Nikolaos's arms loosely around me. Amphitrite may have been wild in her manor, but she was also intriguing and a great storyteller, the sort which had her audience hanging onto every inflection in her tone, each change of facial expression. I was quickly beginning to understand how our erratic Empress had been given a crown, back in a day when she was not hooked on dirty power.

'No? Well, I can't say I'm surprised; Nikolaos is not one to waste words.'

I shrugged, hardly in a position to disagree.

'I got this throne through wily moves on the monarch board game which Osker and Erik have set up, the one on which they sit above on their thrones of ancient stone, watching their pitiful players ousted from their positions of power. I uncrowned the king before me, but how much longer must I wait before a measly joker topples my Queen.' She sighed then, a deep, woeful sigh. 'I am sick of the games that we have been sentenced to play, where winning crowns you with paranoia and losing brings demise.'

'Your plan is—is what, revenge?' I asked.

Amphitrite mulled this over, tilting her head to the skies, thoughts whirring behind eyes the colour of frozen oceans.

Amphitrite pouted. 'That makes it sound so callous.'

I spared a glance at those surrounding us, all of whom had blended into the background of her stories. Khemeia swayed to a tune no one else heard; Orcus remained intense and aggressive with his glare. The two vampires still stood behind Kai and Laith, pinning my companions to their chairs like vines of steel. I had to navigate this carefully, find the words to keep Amphitrite content with our presence until one of us knew what to do to save us. Easier said than done with a woman whose mood changed like the seas of a storm, the imposing air of vampire magick married to necromantic wiles, and Nikolaos's cold distance behind me. Surrounded by all these people, I felt entirely alone. Nikolaos had abandoned me to blindly face the Empress; the burden of knowing I'd endangered my friends was isolating.

Amphitrite sighed theatrically, forcing my attention back on her.

'I suppose you're right, Scarlet. I do want my revenge. I want to thrive with my magick, and the magick of those who were also oppressed by a system based on faith in divinity but not the divine of God's creatures. I yearn for the vengeance against my master, the one who forced me into a vampiric rat race instead of letting me finally find peace.'

Amphitrite stood in a flash, going towards Cye and the necromancers. She ran a hand down Cye's cheek, stretching up on tiptoes to reach, making him shudder in a conflicted state of repulsion and awe. Amphitrite stalked behind the delirious Khemeia, leaning over his back, running her hands down his chest.

Over his shoulder, she watched me, continuing, 'It is more than revenge, Scarlet. I seek power. Together, we could have *immense* power.'

Though she did not address either of the necromancers directly, Amphitrite must have signalled them to respond as the influx of power that came with her words was colossal. Their energies were the hands to quell the fear of solitude; their essence the liquid to quench all thirsts, bodies borne of bread to satiate all which was insatiable. The necromancers were the twin bodies of God himself, with Amphitrite the crown of thorn and gold upon their skulls.

Transcending the confines of human mortality and vampire permanence, their power lay within the welcoming arms of elemental divination. Water, cold and capricious, the source of all which lived, danced around Amphitrite in spectral shades of blue. Worth its weight in gold with altruistic potential, all the while remaining deadly and formidable. She had the power to take life as easy as she could birth it. My power lay somewhat more with destruction; it was the fiery passion toying a line of pain and pleasure, of comforting warmth and scalding pain.

I fell to my knees and wept at the ethereal glow that Amphitrite had become, abreast with her dark steeds. I understood it all; all the fears of mortal man and their insidious faith. Dark angels walked amongst them, dethroning God from the heavens, belittling him to an angel fallen further than all others. All of us with elemental power played with death and life, our hands the paintbrushes on an easel of our own decadent desires, playing with colour like God played with monochrome. I'd never before realised how Gwydion's power was so in tune with my own. Necromancy was the top point on the pentagram, the spirit, bringing together earth, water, fire, and air.

I'd never cared much for power, magickal or otherwise. It was a concept so far from my expectations that it was a word I'd never thought to utter. Even when I'd found out my true heritage, it had never occurred to me to use it to my advantage.

With Amphirite towering above me, her vampire heart pumping necromancer blood through veins as blue as sun-lit seas, I fell into the grasps of temptation. And so did my fire. For the first time since entering the necropolis, Amphitrite and her

355

companions let me breathe, and each breath brought with it the lick of suppressed flames.

A vial dripping with liquid so pure and dark appeared in the hand of Amphitrite, the other she held out to me. I let her raise me from the ground, my eyes torn between the burning intensity of her icy eyes and the vial of black-tinted crimson.

Amphitrite led me to the throne, urging me to sit, with Khemeia and Orcus beside her. Nikolaos edged slowly closer to us, his face a blank mask. Amphitrite's thumb played with the lid, a teasing caress filling me with anticipation. Down the stairs, I got a vague sense of movement. It took me a second to remember that I'd come with Kai and Laith to fight the very people into whose magickal embrace I was falling.

'Join us, Scarlet, and we will rule over the mortal and immortal realms. Man and God alike will kneel before our wrath.'

I had just enough wit left to ask, 'What of my friends?'

And then the lid came off, and blood like no other was released from the vial, a droplet falling onto the tip of Amphitrite's boney finger. So beautiful against her skin, vibrant ink on paper flesh. Oh, the smell! Of roses on the brink of decay, soil clinging to roots and thorns; degenerate and indulgent. Everything mortally sinful and eternally good compressed into that small, crimson droplet.

I was the Maiden bride, Amphitrite the Mother as she married me off to the powers of twin Crones. Blood had become more than our life source, it was the band around our ring fingers binding us to one another forever. All I had to do to be their bride, daughter, sister, Queen was drink down the blood, let the ring bind my innards.

Time had all but stopped as Amphitrite's bloodied finger neared my lips, the world around us becoming insignificant. Her finger was so close I could feel the heat from the blood coming off her as if the pumping of a heart still heated it. The closer it got, the more of a sense of familiarity I gained from the blood, but nothing could penetrate the walls I'd built around the four of us and the rest of the world. Of all the parts of me screaming to inhale the blood from her finger, it was the fire within my soul that was timorous in our surety.

CHAPTER 38

Nikolaos struck just as Amphitrite was about to touch me, his hand gripping hers, flesh slapping on flesh. Amphitrite stared daggers at his hand before turning eyes of burning ice up to him. Nikolaos guided her hand away from me, running his fingers down her palm in a gentle way, once again his demeanour shifting into one of amiable tenderness quite out of character.

His ploy seemed to work; Amphitrite took his hand, swinging it back and forth playfully.

'I cannot let you be deceived as I was, *ma reine froide.*'

Nikolaos let go of her hand, barely sparing a glance at the bloodstain on his fingers before rubbing it into his skin, disappearing it.

Amphitrite pouted. 'What on earth do you mean?'

Nikolaos led Amphitrite away from me, but not enough that I could see over their bodies to Kai and Laith, both of whom had remained silent throughout our theatrics.

Nikolaos spared me a look of disgust with his hand stroking up Amphitrite's arm, playing with her until she shuddered.

'I, too, believed Scarlet to be of great power. I am certain you had heard my name long before embarking on a quest for the crown, as I am also sure you questioned why I did not make a flurry of vassals.'

'It has crossed my mind, as I'm sure it has crossed many others.'

Nikolaos flashed her a coy smile, though his arrogance was not so well concealed.

'I thought I had finally found the one to whom I would bestow my legacy. A nymph, of all things, would make a fine child of my bloodline.'

This was the first time Nikolaos had ever referred to me as his child, and, for obvious reasons, I absolutely hated it.

'But this is exactly my point, Nikolaos! She will be the Princess to our Queen and Kingdom.' Amphitrite went to pull away, but Nikolaos gripped her harder.

'*Non*, I was a fool. At first, I thought she was but a waste of great potential whom I could school; alas, I was sorely mistaken.' Nikolaos curled his lips at me, eyes burning pits of emerald disdain. '*Oui*, when she is around others of great power, her own rears a piteous head—this I cannot deny. But she is merely a barely spitting fire.' Nikolaos deigned to look me in the eyes as he struck the killing blow. 'If I could reverse time, I would discard her back to the mercy of the Redcap.'

If I could protest, I might have, but the pain of a thousand heartbreaks shattered me into nothing. I had never felt rejection so forceful it tore me from head to toe, an intensity that made me feel as though I had been smashed to dust and blown away from the mortal planes. Even tears did not fall; they too had turned to dust to accompany my heart.

Orcus was the one who piped up from where he had distanced himself. 'You told us she brought back your lost ability. That she was of use to you. To us,' he accused.

Amphitrite nodded her little neck up and down. 'Orcus raises a valid point. We went to a lot of trouble to get her here. Orcus even suggested that you were intentionally stunting her arrival. I didn't believe him, but now, I simply don't know what to believe!' She thumped her arms against her side, foot stomping on the floor.

Nikolaos fixed Orcus with one of his infamously holier-than-thou glares.

'So, what is it, Nikolaos, did she return your long-lost powers?' she asked.

A flash of uncertainty fleeted over his face. '*Oui*. Though it could have been any vassal I made who sewed the final threads of my fraying strength.'

I knew for a fact that was a lie, and wondered what game Nikolaos was playing. A dangerous one, it seemed, as well as one to which I was clueless of the rules. He'd gained strength the first time we'd made love when I'd shared my energy with him in the midst of sharing bodies. And then again, when we'd caught Maglark, and I'd protected him from the killing blow of baleful magick upon which Gwydion and Adalia had called. Like hell just any vampire could do the same.

I was just about to protest that final statement when Nikolaos shook his head at me; I settled back into the throne, arms crossing under my broken chest.

'We heard of the darkness she called when defeating the Redcap, that could not be done by just anyone,' Orcus said.

'That wasn't me,' I blurted without thinking, making them all turn to me, Nikolaos looking particularly enraged. He was silently telling me to keep my mouth shut, and for once, I listened.

Nikolaos began to edge slowly towards me. At the same time, the others were also crowding us. I had quickly become the bunny being hunted by a pack of feral hyenas. Nikolaos was a lone wolf, and I wasn't so sure whether he was here to rescue me or throw me to the rest of the enemy pack.

'We know you were helped by Rune,' Orcus spat, sounding disgusted by the name. 'We know about everything! We watched you consort with the cats and their weeping Queen, of your foxes and false treaties. Do you think you could just call such insidious energy into this realm and not have the word spread? You are dangerous!'

'Danger is a powerful weapon when wielded by the right knight,' added Khemeia.

I felt Nikolaos's stress like a blowback of emotions we should have shared more solidly.

'So, what is it, Scarlet, are you another weapon in our growing armoury or a threat to my throne?'

'Nikolaos makes it sound as if she is neither, my Queen. Neither of them is of any use to us.'

Both Nikolaos and I went to open our mouths, though really I had no idea how to work our way out of this one.

For once, he was rendered speechless, mouth opening before closing again and pursing into a tight, unhappy line.

'I told you, he could not be trusted,' Orcus said, looking far too smug.

'He has denied all offerings of our blood,' Khemeia sang, hands swaying with the out-of-tune hum.

'You've starved the man, and he has still been disobedient. I say, put the dog down before he learns to bite back,' once again Orcus added, quite unhelpfully.

The sinister glint in his eye reflected a bloodlust borne not from necessity for survival, but inherent evil.

Both of us realising the depth of the hole into which Nikolaos had dug us, Nikolaos reached his hand out to me. I let him pull me away from the crowding trio. Without them in front of me, I got to see why Kai and Laith had been so quiet. Suddenly, the hole was looking even deeper.

They'd positioned themselves intentionally to hide the two vampires who had silently bound the half-men in chains of silver. Now I had noticed, and with Niko's hand in my own, the distant muffle of Kai and Laith's protests through the leather gags were obvious. Sizzling flesh and burning fur filled the room with a sickening miasma.

Nikolaos continued to lead me backwards, down the steps. Amphitrite let out a shrill laugh, one that struck fear through me.

'Oh, Nikolaos, you know there is nowhere to run.' She laughed again, clapping her hands as she called out in glee, 'How I've always wished to say this: guards, seize them!'

From behind the curtain emerged an army of white-hooded figures, each of them with the thunderous energy of a vampire combined with necromancer blood. Within the crowd, there was another energy, too, one which I recognised as wereanimal, but diluted amongst the rest, I couldn't tell theirs from Laith, Kai, and the approaching vampires.

The room had become a beam of chaos as over ten creatures stalked towards us, some with the grace of a village drunk, others with intoxicated fury. Nikolaos tried to lead us farther away from them, but it was hopeless. We were well and truly trapped, outnumbered. I took the incentive to lead him towards where our other men were chained. Maybe we'd be able to get to them before the others; maybe we could fight off their captures and release them in time. They were all slim chances, especially considering Amphitrite had starved Nikolaos and I was coming down from Laith's energy high, but I'd been at the mercy of others' whims for too long.

Down we fled, using what little we had of our vampire energy to spare. Our feet hit the last step, Kai and Laith were an arm stretch away. Hand-in-hand, there was a brief moment where it looked as though we would make it…

Alas, it was too late. Within seconds, chaos unleashed over us. We were drowning in the arms of our captures.

CHAPTER 39

Cloth and flesh slapped against me, the claws that vampires grew if left unmanaged tearing into my skin. They tore Nikolaos's hand from mine, bending my fingers to get to his, others pulling my arms behind my back. One of the taller vampires came behind me, lifting me up from behind, using my pinned arms as leverage.

Of the ten, four were on me and six on the taller vampire at my side. Despite his state of starvation, Nikolaos was putting up a fair fight, crouched down on the ground, snarling up at the crowd around him. Through gaps in their legs, I could see his fangs bared, eyes furious as he fought off the horde.

I had my own flurry of aggressors to worry about. In front of me, from inside the hood, I got a flash of red hair as a gloved hand pulled from inside his robes chains of silver. I'd experienced this pain before and knew I never wanted to do it again. Using all the fury I could muster, I kicked back at the vampire who held me, aiming for the knees. I missed, but the force was still hard enough for the vampire to stumble, his grip on my arms loosening.

Using my advantage, I pulled free from his arms, falling to the floor. From beside me, I caught a glance at silver flashing in multiple hands where they tried to contain Nikolaos. Niko, who was over two thousand years old, born in Ancient Greece, and proficient in survival, used his years of knowledge and skill against the vampires. He might be starved, but they were intoxicated and babies compared to him.

I had mere seconds to make the next move. Did I continue to fight the four vampires crowding me, make my escape towards Laith and Kai, who were still helpless, or join Niko's fight? Time had both slowed and was fleeting faster than I could keep up. I had all the time in the world and less than a fragment of a second to know what to do. Yet, I simply didn't. This was so far out of my comfort zone that I was temporarily inert against my own wallowing.

In kicked the survival mechanism of a creature made to walk the nights until the sun had exploded and all that was left was ash. I was more than just a vampire, I was a nymph, and their vampire and necromantic powers held no weight against that part of me. Nikolaos could handle himself, Laith and Kai couldn't. I used the advantage of my lack of height to slip between the legs of the vampire in front of me. He reached down, grabbing my ankles, but I kicked him, and he had no choice but to let me go. Using vampire speed, I shot across the floor to the two vampires where they crowded the animals.

Amphitrite watched the entertainment from upon her stage, looking as though all she was missing was a bag of popcorn. Orcus and Khemeia were at her side, with Cye nowhere to be seen. I flew towards Laith first, using the momentum of all my body weight to knock into the vampire behind him. Our bodies collided, sending us both to the ground. Before the other vampire even had time to react, my lips were around his throat, tearing through the fabric of his hood. My teeth sunk deep enough to hit bone, and then, with a mouthful of his beating throat, I ripped backwards.

No doubt the vampire was wounded, but it was not a mortal blow. Not yet. Blood poured from the wound instantly; I spat gobbets of meat onto the marble, nearly choking on the thick bit of neck I'd torn out. I was almost lost to the horror of what I'd done, but survival is a powerful thing; survival, when combined with protecting those you love, is a magic unto itself.

His blood was sweet in ways a human's wasn't. Underneath it all, was the garnish of a necromancer. If I'd been in my right mind, I might have spat it out. I needed all the strength I could get; we all did if we were to make it out alive. I buried my head into the gaping hole of his throat, my nose touching bone, drinking down gulps of the liquid. Near-feral, it was as if some primal instinct I'd always been conditioned to ignore ignited within me.

As I drank down the liquid of life and death, my hand found the soft flesh of his belly. It takes a lot of force to dig onto someone's stomach; luckily, I was a vampire, and strength was nothing new to me. I forced my hand into his underbelly, fingers meeting the warm, slippery sensation of organs half-decayed to vampirism. Up my hand went, farther and farther until his heart beat in my palm.

My tongue continued to work at his throat, lapping up the spurting blood. In my hand, his heart beat harder than any vampire's ever should. I marvelled at its glorious sensation, the way it felt so warm and round, silken and squidgy all at once. It beat like a hummingbird in my palm, and I felt the godlike power of knowing that I held the fragile image of life and death between my fingers.

Stroking it one last time, I gripped the heart, tearing it out down the hole I'd made in his core. Bone and innards brushed past my arm, scraping my skin. Fresh air was cold compared to the blanket of blood covering my arm from wrist to shoulder.

I'd wasted too much time playing with my food; the necromancer who had been at Kai's back pounced on me. He had a headstart as the blood rush was beginning to kick in like nothing I'd ever felt before. I was stunned at the intensity of it as life and death pulsed through my veins. Blood that was both so dirty to a vampire and so fucking good coursed through my being. Sensation inflamed me. Colour burgeoned with a depth I'd never experienced, every shadow a piercing black, the bare threads of fraying cloth as clear as heavy rope. Florets of light bloomed in my vision, fireworks exploding in vibrant pinks and blues and reds. My eyes rolled into the back of my head, lips parting, a moan escaping my throat. Each flash of colour matched the newfound thrum of my heartbeat, a display of passionate iridescence celebrating the return of life in my body. My veins burned with so much sensation I waited for it to tear me apart.

The necromancer gripped me around the throat, pulling me off of the body. I let the heart roll from my fingers onto the floor, where it flopped sadly. He yanked me backwards hard enough that we both cascaded into the chair where Laith was chained, knocking it onto its side with a furious bang. Laith let out a pained cry, echoing in the hall. Over his legs, I caught a glimpse of Nikolaos. Bodies were strewn on the ground around him, bits of flesh and limb in tatters by his side. Pure white garments were stained red, torn over his chest where claws shredded his body. Niko's mouth was a mask of blood, eyes burning pure black in his face, demonic and sinister in all the eldritch beauty.

Only half the horde remained; the ones that did were too focused on him to pay much heed to my more minor fight. All but one even spared me a look. His hood had fallen to reveal a wealth of flaming hair and feral eyes.

Ethan snarled at me, going on all fours to pounce at us. The necromancer at my back had me pinned around my stomach. I raised my elbow above my head, bringing it down to smash into his face, bone cracking. Ethan chose then to make the final leap, his clawed hands outstretched in front of him. Claws hooked into the front of my body, forcing a cry from my mouth. Wereanimals are fast; vampires are faster. I shot up from the floor with his claws still locked into me with a speed neither men could foresee. Vampire and necromancer blood had given me such a boost it threw even me, making the world spin. Ethan used that to his advantage, flexing his hand inside me, tearing me further.

Pain crippled me, doubling my body over. Fire was a sure way to kill any vampire or therianthrope. All I had to do was pull out the fire inside of me, set them alight. Whether it was accidental or planned, Ethan had manoeuvred us to right beside Laith's chair, so close his legs brushed against my own. Any damage I inflicted on them had a high chance of getting Laith as well, a chance I wasn't willing to take. I'd have moved away if

Ethan's claws weren't still puncturing my insides with a nauseating pain. I could feel the sharp edges of his weapon digging into organs deep within my belly, organs that should never be touched.

My whole body spasmed with the shock of it, collapsing me down, forcing Ethan to release me. Laith's morphed feet brushed the tip of my scalp. I rolled my eyes up, looking through the tufts of fur towards Amphitrite. Her aura of arrogant victory had bled to nervousness. She sucked her lip under, chewing. Ethan kicked me onto my stomach, making me groan with my weight pressing down on my leaking insides. Somewhere along the way, I'd begun to shiver. Noticing it now, I couldn't seem to stop.

To my right, Nikolaos still fought the remaining three vampires. They'd pulled out silver chains, metal flying through the air. I looked just in time to see the first blow hit him on top of the head, the second whipping into his legs. I felt it as if it had hit me, too, the force of solid, burning metal crashing into our fragile skulls. Stunned, Niko dropped to his knees, eyes rolling, blinking too fast and too hard. Blood spilt from between locks of thick, black hair. The three vampires wasted no time taking their opportunity to overpower him. Within minutes, because at our speed, this really was only minutes, we'd gone from winning to wounded.

Ethan knelt on my back, allowing the other necromancer to tie my arms behind my back in silver. Overcome with pain, I had nothing left with which to fight them. My focus was concentrated on trying to remain conscious. Deep inside, I was still buzzing with energy, the thrumming high of consuming

369

necromancer and vampire plasma. It forced itself through me, sending jerks through my body, legs tapping manically against the floor. My mouth refused to be still, teeth grinding into each other—so much energy; nothing to do with it.

Unfortunately, this wasn't just about me anymore. With Nikolaos regaining strength from his own consumption of necromancer blood, the line between us was more confused than ever before. Every hit he took was a blow to me and vice versa. Physically, he was stronger than me; I'd taken as much damage for two people as I could whilst still remaining semi-functional. Anymore, and I would be indisposed.

My head ached, legs burned, stomach screamed. Fluid leaked out from my underbelly, pooling around Ethan's legs. Ethan used the chains on my wrists to jerk me up, leaning me against the turned over chair where Laith was. My head fell onto the side of his thigh, staining the pure white fabric deep red. Everything in front of me strobed where my eyes were struggling to stay open. Inside, my fire spluttered and wept, dying embers defeated.

'That was quite a fight you put up—both of you.' Amphitrite sighed. 'Orcus was right. Nikolaos, you are a man of betrayal, and your vassal is mediocre at best.'

'What do you wish to do with them all, my Queen?' Orcus asked, bowing down with a shit-eating grin.

Amphitrite looked weary, rubbing her eyes. 'I don't care anymore. String him up with your toy, punish him befitting a traitor.'

'We should wait on killing them,' Khemeia said. 'We had such a show planned; it seems a shame to waste it. And now the cast has grown.'

Amphitrite waved her hand at him. 'Fine, fine. Get Cye to seat the girl; the rest of you string him up.' Their voices were flowing in and out of silence; the world had become a haze around me. I peered up to Kai, whose body smoked in the chains. As if he felt me watching, Kai turned to me where I leant pitifully against Laith.

'I'm sorry,' I wept.

Kai cast down his eyes, and I could see all the fight in him had gone, all the vibrant orange lost to the murk of tears and defeat. If Laith were awake, I wondered if I'd have seen in him the same sorrow of someone who had given up. It was hard to argue with such conviction, especially as all the evidence pointed to our failure.

We'd lost, but we'd also fought furiously. At the end of the day, if we were going to die, at least we could face the grave with the comfort of our own valour.

CHAPTER 40

Cye, as requested, sat me down between Laith and Kai whilst the vampires dragged Nikolaos behind the curtain. Amphitrite ordered the remaining standing guards to escort the plenty of limp bodies off somewhere out of sight, lest their suffering spoil the performance. Nikolaos had really done a number on them; those who had survived the force of his wrath were hanging onto life by thin threads.

Amphitrite was taking no more risks with us; she instructed Cye to stay at our backs at all times whilst two other vampires flanked behind him. Ethan had asked to stay with his master, Khemeia, as it turned out, but Amphitrite had said, as he was the highest rank after everyone on the stage, he was to go with the remaining militants. Begrudgingly, he'd agreed, though I'd still earned a positively evil look as if this was all *my* fault. I didn't remember asking to be kidnapped and held hostage by a scarily powerful, blood-drunk Empress.

In the chaos of the bustling, Cye tapped my shoulder. I was barely conscious enough to register what he was doing until the prodding became a consistent annoyance that I realised I wasn't just imagining.

I turned my face upwards, neck flopping against the back of the chair. Cye's singular form looked like three in my vision, his multiple shadows floating and distorted. I could barely make out the solid lines of his figure. I was still riding the wave of the necromancer blood, trapped in a trance of flowery distortion and eldritch uncertainty. If it hadn't been another preternatural that hurt me, then I'd have been untouched, but vampires aren't invincible—especially not when it comes to other unlikely creatures. Healing a wound inflicted by a therian is no easy feat.

Cye gripped a handful of my hair, wrapping it around his first like crimson rope. My lips parted, neck strained against the pull of his grasp. He lowered his bearded lips to my ear, the rough hairs scratching over my lobe.

In a voice so silent it was barely even a breath, Cye whispered, 'The lion. Touch him.'

Amphitrite's voice echoed out through the hall, 'What are you whispering to our little vampire? Please, share with the group.'

I felt Cye stiffen at my back, the tension in his body flowing through his hand, into my head, my scalp, like a palpable cord of unease. He inhaled deeply at my neck, beard scraping along my skin, his hand tightening its grip on me.

'I was just tellin' her how she smells like lion.' He sniffed again, deeper, with the theatrics Amphtrite craved.

'We'll soon fix that,' came a voice I knew all too well.

Ethan had returned, his snarling fox-like face ignited with distaste at the sight of me. Ethan returning meant the show must be starting soon. I didn't share the same eagerness as Amphitrite and her people.

I felt Cye turn at my back to face the approaching fox. *Touch the lion.* Laith and Kai were both sitting a foot away from me on either side. Kai was seated straight-backed in his chair, lines around his eyes and mouth deeply creased where his features contorted in pain. Whoever had tied them up made sure to tear the robes, so the silver chains had access to their flesh—a nice sadistic addition from the Empress and her cruel army.

Black smoke curled from the wounds, bringing with it the scent of charring flesh. Kai looked straight past me to Ethan. Cye and Ethan had committed far heftier a betrayal against Kai than me, and maybe even Laith. Cye was his own kind, Ethan a companion in their shared beast blood. Cye had sworn fealty to their Reina, he was one of her people, and he'd lured us all to danger, helping those who had assassinated his own Rey.

Yet, still, knowing all of this, I held some sympathy for Cye. His reluctance to abide by their command was continuous, but a forced tie to Orcus bound him. Ethan was not remorseful, nor reluctant; in fact, he seemed quite happy, looking down on his high, skeletal horse. His fox face twisted into an arrogant snarl, proud to watch us suffer. My stomach knotted in rage at seeing him look at us like that, a rush of adrenaline jolting through my body. I had the very vivid image of serving him the same dish of fate as the neckless necromancer.

A small whimper brought me back to the horrors of reality, over to Laith, where he curled in on himself in the chair. Whole body limp, only the weaponised constraints kept him upright. Laith's body shook, jolting from time to time. The white robes he wore were stained black and red, more so on his right side, where patches of blood from the fall leaked through.

Laith was still too far away for me to reach without stretching my entire body outwards. Not only would that make my antics obvious, but I also wasn't sure just how much stretching my pained body could take. Besides, Ethan was close enough to touch me; I had the strong inclination he would take up the post behind me.

Unsurprisingly, I was right. Ethan came to my back, invading Cye's personal space.

'Move over, Cye,' Ethan growled through his muzzle.

Cye gave him a dry look back, fingers curling tighter around the chair back, the metal creaking.

'Just take the Lion, Cye, the girl's mine.'

From behind the curtain, a symphony started whispering. Their instruments were low, a hint of the horror yet to come. It was time for us all to take our seats. Upon the stage, Amphitrite lit up, little hands clapping. Orcus and Khemeia sat beside her, a guard on either end of them, both of whom also watched the curtain.

Golden candlelight danced up the shimmering fabric, each movement reserved as if they too were fearful of what was behind the curtain. Mesmerised, I watched it flicker and jolt and felt the heat of the fire in the room like a pressing weight on my heart. If only I could reach down to it, alas, I'd fought between my vampire and nymph self. So far, the vampire had won. Through all the pain, I got the lightest sense of comfort from knowing my flames were still with me; they were there to be my logical compass in a time of hardship and confusion.

Cye relented, reluctance stiffening his body as he moved from behind me. His thick fingers brushed against my ear, reminding me once again of his words: *touch the lion.* I looked behind me, bracing the pain to lock eyes with the disgruntled Cye. Fixing me with an intense raise of the brows, Cye fleetingly flicked his eyes to the right where Laith was still barely conscious. Cye's jaw clenched, teeth grinding under his beard, eyes almost popping out the socket. He was so desperately trying to tell me something silently. I was still half-delusional from agony, fear, and the necromancer high, but I thought I knew what he was hinting.

I gave Cye the curtest of nods, hoping that this wasn't a case of crossed wires. Cye turned his back to the chair, blocking me from the sight of Ethan over his broad shoulders. I spared a glance at the stage where Amphitrite and her crew rested, bored of our little trio on the floor below. Ethan's exasperated confusion came in the form of a sigh rasping from between a fanged face. We had only seconds. There was no time to question Cye, only place blind faith in the hands of someone who'd done nothing to deserve it. Sometimes, all you have is hope, even when it's irrational, foolish.

This was one of those times.

Cye leant his back against the chair, bodyweight pushing it forward just enough to add the momentum I needed. I chose that moment to lift myself from the seat, every inch of my body screaming in protest. The relief of my body weight gave Cye the leeway to lean the left side of his body heavier on the chair, pushing it to the side, me with it. I collapsed with the metal onto the stone floor with a loud crash, drawing everyone's attention to me. My cheek cracked against the stone, echoing. Multiple pairs of eyes stared daggers into me, but instinct had kicked in. Collapsing onto the more pained of my arms, the right, I rolled over in shock. It might have carried the swiftness expected of a vampire, something I'd yet to perfect, if it weren't for the deep wound of my belly.

My cry rocketed through the room, the flesh tearing further open from where I'd stretched outwards. Pain, so excruciating it winded me, forced a strained gasp from my shuddering lips. Blood spilt out of me as if a dam had broken from my insides, thick and warm as spots sparkled in my vision, the light of dying stars amidst the horrifying reality in which we'd found ourselves.

'What the fuck!' Ethan exclaimed, his head poking from behind Cye's figure.

'She tried to escape,' Cye spat, laughing silently at my failure.

Ethan cocked his head to the side, musing over Cye's humour, and then relented to the same joy.

'Pitiful.'

'What on earth is going on down there?' Amphitrite sang from her throne.

Cye came towards me, huge, muscled legs like the trunks of trees moving towards the hunt.

'Nothing, my Queen, just a flailing vampire.'

'Get her seated. The show is soon to begin.' She frowned at me on the floor. 'And no more interruptions. From any of you.'

Cye was upon me, the energy he had radiating against my spine, tingling the small cracks in the bone caused by his weight on my back. Effortlessly, he scooped me into his arms, cradling me to his chest like a child. The movement was enough to make me groan, the room spinning, stomach churning. Soft grey clouded my vision where flecks of light danced. It was almost beautiful. Almost.

I was so conflicted by Cye's intentions that I didn't know whether best to fight off his grasp on me or sink further into the deep, comforting warmth at which all therians run.

With his other hand, Cye bent down to grip the head of the chair, dragging it upwards. Metal screeched on stone, and then I was being placed gently in the chair. My knees brushed against someone's warm legs. I must have closed my eyes because, when I opened them, I was leaning against the cloth over Laith's shoulder.

'You take the lion and girl,' Cye said to Ethan, and then nodded his head towards Kai. 'I'll get the panther.' It looked as though Ethan was about to say something, maybe even question his methods, but Cye quickly added, 'I want to keep 'im separate. He's one of my own'—Cye's lips curled into an evil smile—'which means his treatment gets to be extra special.'

Ethan, coming beside Cye to take his desired position behind us, smiled and slapped the other man on the back.

'Go get 'em, tiger—or, would that be panther?'

Cye chuckled along, chest rumbling with forced humour, but, as he turned away, I caught the way his eyes turned cold, lips dropping into a pressed line of discontent.

Music started playing, the deep, tangible melodies of horsetail on gut ringing bright and steadfast through the room. Harmonising to the specks in my vision, for one beautiful moment, all I could see were stars twinkling to the sombre flow of music.

And then, my eyes opened as the curtain rose, and the fantasy in which I thought I'd fallen became a daunting reality.

CHAPTER 41

Pins and needles ran up my shoulder and arm where I leant against Laith's shaking body, each inhalation a stertorous, gurgling breath. I shook with my body's discomfort reacting to his, a thousand tiny pinpricks like lightning in a storm of agony.

Shining, black-shoed feet glinted in the low light as the stage curtain rose, revealing the legs of the orchestra and their haunting symphony. The curtain peeled itself higher up with each deeper strum of string until fully baring the first row to us.

In a semicircle, the strings were first, playing their violins, violas, and cellos. The ensemble of corpses forced my breath to catch in my throat. Arms worn thin by decay clumsily pulled bows back and forth, managing to bring beautiful noise to the vision of terror. On the women, evening gloves of black satin fell loose down their wrists, stark and black against the glint of bone and dried, pink muscle.

Gowns draped over boney shoulders slipped to the side, exposing the hardened flesh of putrescent nipples. Pearls shone pure and pinkish around their throats, so bright they seemed alive. Opaque eyeballs stared lifelessly out at everything and nothing, eyelids dry and tight around the bulging eyes. The men were in no better shape, but at least their tuxedos covered most of their bodies, leaving more to the imagination. I felt myself groan, wrapping my arms around Laith's arm, holding him to me. I had the urge, the need, to run over to all the women whose dresses had fallen down and lift them up, cover their bare bodies, protect them from the watchful gazes of a sadistic Empress and her people.

Laith shuddered beside me; from the deep, strained noise his throat made, I knew he was looking, too. Across the room started a thudding, drumming loud and fast, out of tune to the soft, deathly strings of the orchestra. It rattled through my body, my bones, sending the stolen blood in my veins dancing. I had a confusing second of straining to concentrate on the new band member, when I realised it was nothing to do with the musical corpses. Through Laith's shoulder, his heart pounded, rocking my body until we both itched with the sensation. Like a bird brought back from the dead, my chest fluttered and faltered, trying to match up to the crazed beating.

The curtain rising further uncovered a backdrop of painted clouds hanging from thread, their edges swirling and silver, reflecting light as if the first drops of a storm's rain were suspended in the paint. A second-row showed a grand piano that had yet to play a note, as well as oboes and flutes. With Laith's heart pumping throughout my body, I watched aghast as blue, cracking lips rasped over the woodwind instruments, collapsed lungs trying to force dirtied air through the slender mouthpieces.

Higher and higher, the curtain crept, inching up at an agonising pace, suspending us in anticipation. It was all just another part of the show; the theatrics a contrivance to leave us on the edge of our seat, forcing us to drink in the gore of the symphony, wondering what further horror awaited us. Mesmerised by how the glimmer of silver curtain gave way to such ghastly scenes, I had fallen into their ploy like the perfect hostage. I was a passenger on a quickly sinking ship, enchanted by the glittering waves, too caught up in the moment to fight against the watery grave which awaited me, us.

More clouds appeared, white and silver like jewelled ghosts breaking free from their cover. Other tiers were coming into light, platforms for clarinets and bassoons, then horns and trumpets. Some of the zombies were in better condition than others, almost human-looking, playing their instruments with the strained skin of the semi-sentient; others were too lost to decay to really put on a show. It should have made it better that not all of them were rotting corpses, but it didn't. If anything, it made it even worse, a stark reminder of the fragility of mortality, how delicate flesh and bone are.

As the curtain cleared, it revealed a new stage, one that hung suspended from the ceiling, wide and circular. From the surface fell an arm, palm flopping downwards from the circle. Percussions and pianos, the last of the musical instruments, were uncovered. Now all that remained was to see whose arm had fallen free of the stage, with that limpness that only comes from fresh death. His hand reached down to the audience below, begging even in death for one of us to rescue him. There was no saviour to answer his prayers.

Bare, muscled shoulders crept close to the edge of the ledge, brunette hair brushing along his tanned body, the owner of the desperate arm. He was not the last of the bodies.

Contorted cadaverous piled upon each other, each male, each perfectly nude. Like art, they were deliberately placed in positions of fear and recoil, flesh statues forced to forever cower from what was above. Some knelt, their heads pressed to their knees, arms covering their heads. Others stared wide eyes to the sky, arms cast outwards, warding off the Gods in heaven. Eyes cloudy with death had been forced open, refusing them, even in their departure, to dare look away. I didn't know what kept their arms so perfectly in place at first until I saw the subtle glint of thread holding them in place. The clear plastic had broken free from the first corpse, defiance of his forced placement letting him partially break free, hand reaching to the depths of hell to pull him away. Even the Devil did not answer.

Some of their heads were shaved, with bits of bone sharpened and stuck onto the smooth surfaces to fashion what appeared to be sorts of morbid horns. At least ten bodies, which I could see, piled on top of each other—all of them utterly still. All except one, the curtain revealed, atop the mound.

Devilish wings fastened to his bareback, arms shackled in silver held high in the sky, ankles chained down. The fastening for the makeshift wings was also silver, the flesh on his back burning and raw. They'd even attached a pole between the clasp on the back of the wings down through the bodies to keep his body rigid and straight, higher above the rest, letting us all see the wings.

Nikolaos's neck was limp, tresses of black hair collapsing downwards, so long that it brushed the lips of the man below him. Smoke pirouetted from his body, where silver defiled the flesh, almost as if it had been planned all along. The barriers between us were down as far as they'd ever been, I knew that much from the agony of his wounds burning through my body when we'd been initially bested. All that gave away his affliction now was the tightness around his eyes, and their harrowing rage at being chained in such a way. I knew, logically, how much this must hurt, yet I felt none of it.

In fact, even my own wounds felt calmer, a deep, dull ache as opposed to the soul-eating depth of trauma it had been earlier. Nikolaos peeled his enraged gaze from the Empress to me, the dark, drowning viridian of his eyes as green as I'd ever seen them in his anger. I was lost in hopelessness and fury, my indignance suffocated by the overwhelming sense that we'd lost. No pain could match that of my heart in that moment, watching the man I loved at the mercy of the merciless, tortured and humiliated to the soundtrack of the symphony for the departed.

Nikolaos tried to drop the barrier between us—I could feel the press of his power like a weak tap at my metaphysical door—but, the moment he did, the first press of silver burning started over my wrist, ankles, and back. It was what I imagined a hot poker stabbing into the centre of the spine would feel like. Just the barest touch of his energy was enough to send me forward, mouth wide in a silent gasp stealing the scream from my lips.

Nikolaos was taking the full force of the torture in his stride, refusing to display anything more than anger to his Empress, and I could not handle but a teasing of the sensation. It might have been his pride or millennia to build a dangerous threshold to pain; either way, he composed himself in a way I'd never have been able to match. Instantly, he shut down the line between us, cutting me off from the shared feeling. The combination of the underground palace being necromancer galore, and Nikolaos's starved state, left him little control over our tie as master and vassal.

Hands gripped me from behind, clawed, shapeless fingers pulling me upwards, slamming my back into the chair back.

'The Empress doesn't want you to miss the show, Scarlet,' Ethan sneered in my ear. 'It's getting to the best bit.'

My pulse sped up, for the grand finale could only be worse than what we had already seen. The pounding of my heart echoed in my chest, stomach, throat; fear so thick I could taste it. Except it wasn't my fear. Beside me, Laith had raised his head, conscious enough to turn like a moth to the theatre light's stark brightness.

The curtain continued to rise above Nikolaos, showing a leather-sandaled foot pressed against his shoulder. The ankle was so skinny it was mere flesh barely stretched over bone. I didn't think you could recognise someone from shin alone; my heart catching in my throat would beg to differ.

I prayed it not to be true, but the curtain ascended higher and higher, growing impatient as if matching the racing of my heart—of Laith's heart. Blue silk wraps wound up his shins, armour of depraved sensuality. I wanted to look at Kai, to see his face at what I knew would come next, but my eyes were stuck on the terrifying inevitable.

A dirty blue tunic brushed along knees as knobbly as I'd ever seen. Red cloth danced behind him, thread capturing it in dynamism. Green and gold strips of fabric stuck out from beneath the cobalt blue muscle cuirass, too wide on his sickly chest and short on the long torso.

Gwydion's wings were like those of an albino bat, huge and thin and grotesque in their beauty. Amphitrite's people had glued perfect white feathers along the thinly-stretched, see-through wing membrane.

The curtain was almost up, and now I could see legs and arms hanging down from higher than I'd expected the stage to be set, vines of limbs dangling limply. It was almost too much gore to take in; the trauma had bled to such harrowing levels the pinned limbs blended into insignificance. Thin, white hair curled over his shoulder—his, not Gwydion's, this could not be Gwydion—the perfect ringlets falling loose. One of his arms extended backwards, poised and placed, the other raised upwards above his head.

I could see the chin of a face I'd seen a hundred times before, a jaw so sharp it could slice through metal. The luminous lights shone down on the paleness of his skin, highlighting just how opaque it really was. Even from that high up, I noticed the veins under his flesh like serpents slithering with blood.

I felt my fingers reach for the bloodied robe on Laith's body, emotions I'd never experienced before forcing them to shred through the fabric, breaking through to his skin. Some of the pain evaporated to burning fucking rage, coursing through my undead veins. Without thinking, I forced my nails into Laith's skin, curling with anger that cast my body in a rigid line.

Wan turquoise eyes shone through a halo of curls, white-blue lightened with defeat, so they were almost colourless as he stared down at us. A black helmet hung over his head, tip brushing the lines of his white eyebrows. Blue, black, and gold feathers curled from the metal, paling in comparison to the silver shine of his faux-angel wings.

The curtain raised to the top of the ceiling, and my stomach churned. Gwydion held a mighty sword in his right hand, the golden hilt gleaming in the dimming lights. The slender tip pointed towards the makeshift stars of flashing lights, near the face of a struggling Onca.

Onca and her people hung from metallic ropes, fish hooks digging into their arms, legs, and backs. Cherub-painted faces stared down at the crowd below, some of them with petite white wings, others bare. Onca was one of the few winged, body stark and nude for all the world to see. A little further away, hung her son, head drooping down, unconscious. She had no eyes for anyone but her boy, his body limp and death-like. Tears dropped like pearls down her pallid cheeks, one of them catching on the metal of Gwydion's sword, slithering to his palm.

Tanya's bare body hung in the distance, only her face concealed by layers of silver silk cloth. Of them all, only Sylvie and Dayana remained clothed, white tunics hanging from their suspended bodies. Blood from the hook-induced wounds soaked through, their flesh slowly tearing.

I didn't know where to look. Nowhere. Everywhere. It was all too much to see at once, my brain barely making sense of them, as if their faces were blurred and inhuman.

I took in each of the detainees, leaders and followers alike, each of them facing the same fate. Until, finally, I settled on the one I'd been ignoring most of all. Gwydion had eyes for no one but Kai, a lone tear trying best to escape from his eyes. I followed his line of sight like it was a rope entwined of woe and adoration striking into Kai's heart.

Kai's face turned upwards, the light from above illuminating a golden glow over his features, casting him the light of a dark, angry angel. I didn't need to see his countenance to understand the look shared between them. It was one too intimate for words, one not made to be seen by any others. I turned to my lover, determined to share in that experience. With Nikolaos shielding as hard as he ever had, all that remained between us were two pairs of eyes filled with the knowledge of our demise.

Was this our goodbye? After only six months of what should have been a lifetime together, was this how it was to end? With Nikolaos a theatrical footstool for his oldest friend, for the strongest people I'd ever known reduced to props in a sinister production. I knew what it felt to be at the mercy of evil, but Amphitrite had twisted even that into something darker. We'd collapsed into her malevolence head first, our dignities falling with us.

Nikolaos's rage had succumbed to apathy so cold it was a blade of ice through my soul, painful enough I began to turn my head away. And then, in the light, I saw the first red-tinted tear fall from his eyes, down his cheek, and a new pain hit me. One which crippled me, so furious it might have killed me if I'd not already been dead. My fingers curled further into Laith's side, scratching his skin.

I'm not sure at which point in all of this I'd given up, but the moment I saw the tear from Nikolaos's eye fall down to the orchestra below, a new fight drove into me. Despite Laith's protests, I forced my fingers further into robes, palm stretching over the soft flesh of his belly. The movement pulled the wound in my stomach, my teeth grinding into each other, but, by now, that physical pain I felt was but a pinprick in a gash of deeper hardships.

Laith's flesh was warm beneath my touch, fur soft and silken and comforting in the midst of so much discomfort. I stroked along his body, and again, a tingling sensation ran up my arms, through my body, into areas that both did not exist and were all too real. He was so solid it brought me back into myself.

When I'd been nothing more than a stranger to Gwydion, he had risked what remained of his moral compass to help me. Kai had offered his home up to Nikolaos and me. Nikolaos had found me on the side of the road, dying, and wedded me with immortality. Sylvie had opened their home to all of us, Onca her heart, and Laith a vein. Every single one of our allies in this room had, at some point in our short stint of allegiance, bared their hearts, souls, and skills to me and my own. To lie down and let us all die without a fight now would be the final brick in the mausoleum of injury to which we had already added enough insult.

If we were to die anyway, what harm would fighting to the bitter end really be? There was only so much evil Amphitrite and her people could inflict on us, and I did not doubt for one moment that she would do it whether we acquiesced or not.

CHAPTER 42

'He lied,' I said, chair feet scraping on the stone floor as I stood. The slice in my belly violently protested, forcing me forward. I caught myself with a hand on Laith's knee; even through cloth, the reaction between us was electric and instant. It hurt. This time, I did not fight the pain. Instead, I reached my hand out to Laith, his fingers entwining with my own. 'Nikolaos lied.'

I felt multiple pairs of eyes settle on me, but I only returned those of Amphitrite. Ethan moved at my back, ready to take me down, until Amphitrite shook her head at the fox. We were so significantly outnumbered that she had nothing to fear from my rising.

I knew the cool touch of Nikolaos and Gwydion's focus on me; it was not a sensation so easily ignored. There had been a hundred times where I turned to them both—more Gwydion than Nikolaos—and met their faces with the eyes of a child thrown into the lion's den, scared and lost. I was still scared, more so than I'd ever felt before, the residue of Laith's heartbeat making my chest tight and my stomach knotted. I was still lost, my body broken and brain overcome with the power of necromancer blood. But I was no child, and I would face the fear of death with the reserve of someone who had life for which they would fight. Because, at the end of the day, I may be dead in body, but the people hanging from fraying threads above me made sure my soul was very much alive.

From her throne, Amphitrite raised a pale eyebrow, not bothering to stand.

'Yes, we've established this.'

I shook my head. 'No, he lied about me not being powerful. About how any vampire could have given him his powers back.' I stood up taller, forcing myself to ignore the burning in my belly. 'I can prove it to you.'

'I don't believe you,' Amphitrite responded, though she was looking less confident now.

I looked around to the candles surrounding the room, all of them dimming with the press of the hours, dampening their flames. I finally did what I should have done all along, opening myself up to their heat, letting the distant warmth of their dying glow fill me.

The hall ignited in gold and orange, vibrant light catching on every shimmer of cloth, every polished metal. Amphitrite's white hair shone as red as my own, the pale robes of her vampires caught in crimson shadows. From above, the darkly angelic scene was a hellish inferno; Gwydion's Archangel Michael morphed from ghostly to devilish. Under his foot, Nikolaos's pallid face gleamed red, green eyes reflecting the colours of roaring flames.

Warmth fed into me, opening my chest and third eye up to a flash of heat and comfort. Laith's hand burned in my own, the pins and needles of his touch soaring up my right side like the wings of a butterfly brushing through my veins. Laith's figure shone bright and golden at my back, the shadow of his inner beast magnificent in its sunlike beauty. He was the torch from behind, a guiding light, and Nikolaos, from where he draped like a swiftly falling angel, was my moon. The moon when the sun had exploded, filling the sky with one final touch of deadly crimson.

I let the fire fill me, consume me, bring me back to a place of strength in which arbitrary vampire laws did not confine me, only the power of the Earth as she sang through my soul.

Other of her natural energies glowed in the shadows cast by my fire, the aura of myriad slaves to her Queendom. Amphitrite a silhouette of ethereal blue like the clear fabric of her dress, her veins burning black with the touch of necromantic death. At her side, Khemeia was an obsidian orb, his own shadow marred by the blood of a vampire. From the ground, Orcus stole the show, his aura true black, untouched by the impurity of the dead he controlled.

It was Gwydion who truly drew my attention; he shone both the brightest and the darkest, the glow around him as if a black hole could radiate the colour of space when all the stars had stopped burning, and even heaven itself were cursed by eternal darkness. Through Amphitrite's pumping veins, I saw the pure black of Gwydion's blood streaking with the reddish tint of Orcus's energy, and I knew that she'd been feeding on them both. All of those who remained on the ground gleamed with some caress of death, all but Kai, who was as pure as any creature could be.

'Parlor tricks,' spat Orcus, the evil of his being a dull, ugly thread in the weaves of magick. Even Amphitrite beamed with once good intentions lost to darkness.

Still caught in the arms of my own magick, I took a step towards the stage, my hands pulling my lion with me. Through our bodies, metaphysical silk spun, connecting two hearts as one. I could see it, though not with my eyes. That line of loving silk cast outwards, upwards, towards the man who had given me the key to immortality, but between us lay a locked gate, and the fabric frayed. I sensed the connection between us was broken, blocked by something that did not want us to unite as one, that feared us. It was the same block I'd felt last night in the shower, though the distant sensation of it was now tangible.

I was connected to everyone dead in this room one way or another—whether it be from something obscure and metaphysical or something personal and deeply loving. Through Laith, I was also distantly tied to the animals, their therian energy soft and purring in the background of my mind. I felt the flood of my fire extend through the room, touching on all of the hearts of the people with whom I had acquainted myself. They responded in turn, a shudder, a gasp. All of them but Ethan and Cye, whose ties to the necromancers had made them impenetrable. And Nikolaos, though I still didn't know why.

They missed out on the purity of my affections, the deep yearning to save those whom I loved and respected, extended like a hand offering companionship to the love-starved. With each step I took towards the stage, it flowed further. Gwydion hooked his own hands around the threads, throwing it outwards to the zombies whose instruments faltered, to the breachable necromancers, and, distantly, back to me and the vampires. Laith extended the hand to Onca, her own fierce magick distributing the sensation to all of her many people. I felt

Otorongo II open his eyes, struggle against the pain in his back, and then he was gone again, lost to the others and their many thoughts and feelings.

I was almost at the top now, the silken scarfs of allyship and shared want for unity wrapping over nearly all of us—even Amphitrite, who had welcomed the warmth after so long of being cast to the cold hands of men who'd never respected her, who had defiled her. Orcus looked around the room, confused, his eyes narrowing at the tears falling down Amphitrite's starved face. The tie between them darkened, his blood in her veins shining the red of toxic mud. We were losing her as Orcus tore her between the two sides. One promising the power she'd always craved through shared cause without bloodshed. The other an outlet to the depravity she so desired, the debauchery to which we all yearn to succumb. One of these, she knew well and trusted the atrocity of it. Friendship and alliance were not only foreign concepts to our Empress, but ones that could never be trusted. She was the tie to the necromancers, zombies, and vampires in the room. Her openness to us was the thin rope on which we balanced, precarious, ready to tip either way. The moment she fell in favour of Orcus, we would all fall, outnumbered once again.

My body was growing full on the feast of their many combined powers, all offering me a hand in the final fight, doing what they could to set us all free. I drank it down, satiating parts of my body that had never before felt full.

My feet walked on stone, on grass, on burnt sand. Above us, the full moon burned in the Savannah sky, and stars twinkled in formations not seen for centuries. The therians did all they could to aid in the battle, but it was the vampire Empress before me whose power really cooed the loudest.

She'd been right; there was so much potential if we joined our forces, endless possibilities of what we could create together. With the elements combined, we could bring about bountiful art painted in colour and unity; not a torn canvas washed with blood. I was drunk on sensation, high on endless histories merging to one present. Blinded by what we were creating, I opened my eyes to find Amphitrite on her knees, black tears thick down her flushed face.

In a flurry of hands holding, bodies falling to one, Orcus was the broken link. Overcome by adrenaline, both blind and seeing more than I'd ever seen before, I craved to force the lock open, letting his captives free.

As if knowing that very thought, Orcus responded, flexing his hold over Amphitrite. Within seconds, the line had tipped, and down we all fell to the darkness of Orcus's control.

CHAPTER 43

Metaphysical rope slipped through my fingers, burning my palms as it collapsed into a serpent by my feet. The chain was broken, shattered into shrapnel. I tightened my grasp on Laith, desperately trying to hold onto what ties remained.

Orcus gripped Amphitrite by the arm, pulling her to her feet. He strangled his arm around her throat, locking her to his chest. Orcus took his other wrist and forced it into Amphitrite's mouth.

'Bite!' he shouted, face furious.

Amphitrite struggled against his grasp, trying to break free of the hold.

'No!' I cried, voice cracking, making a run for the struggling vampire, pulling Laith with me. Wide-eyed, Amphitrite reached one hand out to me, but the other was already curling around Orcus's arm, pressing his flesh into her pouting mouth. White eyelashes fluttered over eyes lost to pupil, nostrils flaring with a deep, yearning breath.

Amphitrite's jaw tensed before we reached her, fangs sinking into Orcus's wrist. The scent of blood filled the room, sanguine wine spilling out, tempting us all. It smelt so good, so very, very good. Perfection in liquid form, true love dashing from the vein. I might not have noticed taking a step further towards the duo if Laith hadn't pulled me to his chest. I gripped onto his body, fingers snaking under the robe to find the fur over his chest. He was the anchor to the ship on which I might have quickly sunk. Together, we ignited the element of me that was very much alive. My fire sparked, the room once again casting the darkest of shadows and brightest lights. The part of me that Laith coaxed called out to a piece of Amphitrite, the side of her that, much like me, death could never touch. We couldn't help but connect to her and, subsequently, the spirit of the necromancers.

However, we needed to reach more than that. Orcus could pull those sides of our damned Empress as much as we could, and his enticement was more potent than anything we had to offer. If we could get to Nikolaos, hold him, unite the trio as one, then maybe we stood a chance, but our unity was still severed; I didn't know why.

Amphitrite had succumbed to the temptation of drugged blood, her body limp on Orcus's arms as she slipped into his magickal embrace. I felt the side of her that was water falling to the wiles of vampirism, the press of Orcus's necromancy a sinister reminder of our weakness to him. The more she sipped, the more she became his fledgeling, and her power over me as my Empress was a growing weight on my shoulders.

Orcus locked eyes with me over her bobbing head, his eyes wicked with triumph. His necromancy filled the room the way water fills up a sinking ship, damning us all. If it weren't for my hand on Laith's beating heart, I know I might have fallen willing victim to his call. I knew when he'd connected to Amphitrite's many henchmen and their zombies. I felt it like an electric shock, his darkness consuming Amphitrite, taking control of all that was hers. Soon, we would be outnumbered. We already were.

I fought against the increasing urge to fall at his feet, seeing the damnation that faced us. Orcus was a centre of the universe, above which the heavens were imploding. We had to free her. From up here, I could see behind the curtain to the mechanisms of the stage above. Ropes and leavers held up our army, keeping them pinned to the ghastly clouds. If we could get them down, we might stand a chance, but we also needed to get rid of Orcus. I'd felt a whisper of what a trio between Nikolaos, Laith, and I could do earlier; we needed to hear our power scream.

I dared to look away from Orcus, staring down at the struggling Kai where he was pinned to the chair by Cye and Ethan. I had to trust in his strength, that he could fight his own battle. For as long we let Orcus consume Amphitrite, we stood no chance. There was no way to communicate with Kai metaphysically. All I had was my voice; I used it.

'Kai!' I screamed, startling the three men. 'The ropes! Get the ropes!'

If I thought he was struggling before, I'd been wrong. With instructions to fight, Kai harnessed what was left of his hope, using a clawed hand to stab at his humanoid restraints. At the same time, I rushed at Orcus.

He may have been strong, but no necromancer could match the strength and speed of a vampire. Pulling Laith with me, we collided with the duo, smacking full force in Amphitrite's body. Though I'd healed most of the damage, the impact winded me, alerting me to the fact I wasn't as healed as I thought. The four of us went down. Orcus's head slammed into the concrete, echoing.

Amphitrite was limp underneath me, her intoxicated body in my way. Orcus used her as a shield, pulling her body up to cover himself, so all I could get was his arms.

'Get Amphitrite!' I shouted at Laith.

'But—'

'Do it!'

I put the command in my voice, flexing the link between us, so he had no choice but to obey. I don't know how I knew what to do, but something had kicked in, and I wasn't going to argue.

From my back, Laith released his grasp on me, pulling Amphitrite by the ankles from sandwiched between Orcus and me. The moment we were apart, the tidal wave of Orcus's necromancy smashed into me. Orcus bared his teeth in what was meant to be a grin, his mouth bloody from the head wound. He let Amphitrite go so suddenly, Laith fell backwards, and I was instantly pressed against Orcus's body.

Orcus gripped me by the hair, extending my head to the side. My fangs felt the chill of the room, head reared back to strike, but between his grip and necromancy, I was weak. Logically, I knew I could outmatch him if I wanted to.

I didn't want to.

Everything in my body was lost to the sensation of his magickal ability, seducing me to subjugation. My mind was ignited with colour, vision lost to the sensation of life. Orcus's right wrist still bled, the one with which he held me. All I could smell was his blood; all I could hear was the melody of its seductive chanting, begging me to taste all that impure goodness.

My head moved further to the blood; soon, I would be his, and he mine. We would join as one, our blood bond no match for any other connection I'd formed as a vampire. All it would take was one sip, and life would be mine again. Orcus was all I needed to live again. I'd licked the skin of the necromantic apple with the vampire whose throat I'd torn, but Orcus was the whole fruit. Like Eve, I lowered my lips to the serpent's vein.

Oh, so soon I could feel the sun on my cheeks once more. Just one drop and I'd be free from the prison of death. I was so close, so very close. Under my jeans, I felt a furred hand grip my ankle. I physically recoiled, spitting on Orcus's face as if I'd already taken a sip. It was a lie! It was all a lie. I was dead; he could not save me from my own demise. Being dead didn't mean I didn't get to live. I had so much to live for. So much to fight for.

Nikolaos, above me, was one of those things. I thought of him; it all fell into place. The connection between us had been damaged, a rat chewing at the wires of our soul. I held that rat in my hand. I opened myself up to Orcus in a way he'd not expected, letting him inside of me as much as I could go inside him. Not with the part of me that was vampire, with the part that was fire.

I ignited him from within, forced my fires through his very being, and felt every line he'd put up torch with it. Orcus was trying to control so many strings, his shields were almost non-existent. From Cye, to Khemeia, to Nikolaos, Amphitrite, the zombies, even Gwydion, he had his fingers in every single one of our paranormal pies.

It was unnatural. No necromancer should be able to have this level of control over us all. All that was truly his were Cye and the zombies. I could do nothing for the zombies, but Cye, maybe I could help.

We burnt through all those flammable threads, freeing all that we could of his hold over them. I felt my connection to Nikolaos return like my soul returning to my body. I was whole once again. We both were. In the corner of my eye, I saw a black figure scramble across the stage towards the controls. Kai had fought off Ethan and Cye.

I'd empowered myself by freeing Nikolaos from Orcus's hold, but it also meant he had more hands with which to play, and those hands were in the puppet of Amphitrite's mind. She was too lost to death, consumed by sinister blood, for me to be able to sever his hold over her. Laith whimpered from behind me. I couldn't help but turn my head to see Amphitrite riding his body, fangs tearing into his throat.

Orcus used the leverage. With his grip in my hair, he forced me backwards onto the concrete, riding me. I let out a scream, pushing him with all of my might off my body. Backwards down the stairs, we tumbled, bodies entwined as we crashed to the floor. He let me go in time for my body to collide into one of the statues, sending it smashing onto the floor.

Orcus crouched on his knees, mouth bloody, face twisted in pain. From above us, metal creaked, the wires lowering our many allies to the ground. Kai had pulled the lever! I felt a sense of relief, then Orcus shouted at Cye to join him. The battle was back on. I was still open enough to Orcus to know that Cye was resisting the best he could, body a rigid line, each movement jerky and forced as he struggled against a more intimate fight.

We all had our individual battles happening concurrently. Whilst we waited for the rest of our fallen soldiers to join us, Orcus was calling in his unwilling henchman. It wouldn't be long until our people were with us, even if they were injured. Kai and Laith could fight the other three. They could hold out until the floating stage was on the ground.

We could do it. We were winning. We would all live to see another day. I was so sure Orcus had lost, so wrapped up in my serenity from freeing Nikolaos, that I didn't even think of the army he had on standby.

The music stopped—I hadn't even realised it was still playing.

A new militia was embattled, one who felt no pain—an army of cannon fodder powered by magick. The sound of instruments falling to the floor shattered the air. And then came the zombies.

CHAPTER 44

The stage was getting lower and lower, inching ever closer to the hoard of zombies under Orcus's control. All of our people were still bound by chains and hooks of silver, sitting ducks waiting to be ripped apart by zombies.

In a split-second decision, I turned my back on Orcus and the slowly approaching Cye to go help the others. Using all the speed I could muster, I nearly flew up the stairs towards the stage where Laith and Kai still fought. It was the first time I'd had the opportunity to see what was happening with them. It wasn't going well.

Laith and Kai stood back to back, both of them crouched on their inhuman hind legs. Laith held his right hand, his fighting hand, in the left, blood pouring from a wound down his shoulder and neck. His whole demeanour drooped; each second the injury was left to flow leaving him weaker. I recognised the shape of fang marks, the damage they could do as they tore flesh from the skeleton. Kai was in a better way, though not by much.

Both he and Ethan were covered in claw marks, some so deep that he'd need stitches if he were human. Ethan's face was a mask of blood, red hair spiking from the gel of it. Khemeia remained unscathed, hiding behind the werefox's figure. The zombies were slow and shaking in their movement, most of them dead to the point of decay, but they'd feel no pain nor guilt. They were the perfect predators, controlled by the ultimate sadist.

Too wrapped up in the fighting, neither men had noticed the climbing zombies. Some fell from the steps of the stages, clambering along towards us. It was mainly the more decayed of the lot, easy cannon fodder. Those in better shape were climbing upwards, faster than I'd expected, towards their target, coming straight towards them. The floating stage was an arms-length away from the top of the musical area. Zombies reached upwards, fingers almost brushing against it.

I hated to leave Laith and Kai alone to fight, especially now that there would be two new enemies on their backs, but I had to go for the others. I had to. Amphitrite noticed me on the edge of the platform, looking up to where the zombies climbed and fell. Her dress was in bloody tatters, ripped to reveal the slashes in her skinny legs from Laith's claws. I sensed her notice me like a target had just appeared on my forehead. She crouched, let out the wail of an enraged banshee, and lunged for me.

To humans, it would have been a blur. To me, I'd gone to a vampire place of pristine practicality, a survival instinct that I'd never experienced before kicking in. I saw her coming for me, flying outstretched in my direction. She'd have gone full force into me if I didn't dodge. I slapped my hands onto the ground, using the momentum to roll me closer towards Laith and Kai. It was not elegant, but it did the job.

I scrambled up, hands slipping over the stone, using whatever momentum I was still on to gather pace and run towards the zombies. The pitiful ones that were coming towards us could be left. It was the zombies above that I needed to focus on. Behind me, I heard Amphitrite's screech and a wounded

403

lion's roar; it was almost enough to make me turn around. I had one focus; that was all that mattered.

With speed unlike anything I'd ever felt, I ran up the stairs to where the majority of the zombies were. The stage was low enough now that they were trying to make their way onto it, some of them dragging their corpses half up. Bodies forced into artful poses contorted in front of me, the ankles of some of the pile on which Nikolaos and Gwydion stood by my hand.

Hands clutched at me, the army of the dead focusing on their moving target, gripping onto my arms and legs. One of them was on my back, their body far taller than mine and stronger than I'd expected. They locked their arms around my neck, dragging me backwards. I reared my head back, striking fangs into the arm, tearing away gobbets of flesh soured by death. Putrid, their blood and skin made me gag, almost throwing off my attention. I thought it would deter them, but they truly were impenetrable to pain.

More of them were climbing me, their bodies suffocating mine. The platform was low enough now that I could edge my body onto it, but they were using me as a plank, climbing onto the ship. I tried to throw my body back to get them off of me, yet my foot was too close to the edge of the musical stage, and I would have slipped. I was trapped under the crushing weight of ten humans, some clawing me from my feet, others climbing up my body. One stood up on the stage, using my neck as leverage. I gripped her ankle, feeling the skin of it soft and pussy under my fingers like a juicy plum. I dug my fingers in, flesh giving way, juices flowing as I yanked my arm backwards. I was strong enough—it was just the angle that was wrong. Instead of flying backwards as I had intended, the zombie crumpled and fell, taking with her two others.

Continuing to scramble up the slowly ascending platform, I was almost halfway up, only my tiptoes still resting on the largest of the musical stages. At that moment, something crashed into my thighs and pelvis, claws ripping through my jeans. I screamed, hand losing grip as I was torn from the stage. My legs slipped off the edge, sending me down back first onto the lower stage, narrowly avoiding being skewered by one of the abandoned clarinets.

Cye's huge looming figure scrambled up on top of me, black fur over his body like tufts of silk. He'd been big as a human; in this form, he was an ancient tree and I a sapling. With all of my might, I pushed Cye's form off me, howling with the effort. Though my limbs protested, the sockets in my elbow and shoulder screaming to give in, I managed to force him off of me. I rolled on top, pinning my forearm into his throat, pressing down in the fur to cut off the circulation.

Cye's panther eyes widened, muzzle parting, showing off rows of both human and animal teeth. From the corner of my eye, I saw the clawed limb rise above me, readying to slash down, end it all.

I braced for the impact, awaiting the pain of what might finally be the death of me, but Cye's eyes rolled back with the struggle of his breathing. He fixated on something above, hard enough that his whole body went limp, and I looked behind me, past the raised arm. Onca stared at the two of us, horror and rage painted over her face, but more than that, there was woe. Unlike Amphitrite, Onca ruled with a tender fist, one with which she nursed and fed her followers. The failure at her queenhood, the loss of one of her own, was so evident it was like we could see through her naked chest to where her heart crumbled.

Cye tensed below me; I thought he was about to strike the hesitant blow. Instead, the tension ran through his whole body, writhing with the internal fight.

Through gritted, deadly teeth, Cye squeezed out, 'Go! Now, go!'

He didn't need to tell me twice. I pulled myself up to where Cye had forced me to leave the zombies, their mission of reaching my lover and our people accomplished. Ten of them clambered up the pile of bodies towards Nikolaos, the first target. No. I would not let them have him. The platform shivered under their combined weight. Was it even strong enough to hold this many people on such a thin thread? I was about to add more kilos to it.

Propelling myself up, I grabbed the first zombie in front of me, gripping him by the hair at the nape of his neck. The hair came off in my palm, pulling with it a section of his scalp, making him look at me. Lifeless eyes turned to me, startled and confused, mouth open to reveal decaying, toothless gums in a hiss. His attention refocused, hands reaching to grab my throat. Swatting him away, I gripped his wrist, propelling him into the air.

Pushing the zombies onto the ground below should have been a good tactic—in fact, it was the only one of which I could think up at the moment. The second I looked down, I saw the flaw in my plan. Laith and Kai were barely fighting off

Amphitrite, Orcus, and Ethan. With the additional necromancer and his flock, they were well and truly outnumbered. The two men had managed to flee to the other end of the room, drawing them away from me, but the hounds of hell were quickly descending, and soon my men would be consumed.

Laith looked up at me, his golden face ethereal in the lights of the candelabra. I let him see my conflict, the pleading of a plan that would work, after so many failures. The moment cost me, Cye finally losing the battle with himself, the headstart I'd been given falling to fiasco.

Within seconds, I was on my front, pressed to the ground, staring down as my two friends were encroached upon. I knew above me the zombies advanced on the helpless. So, this was it. This was the end.

Would there have been a more dignified end? At any point tonight, could I have changed a course of action, saved us all? I wondered if vampires have an afterlife, or even if humans do. What awaited me?

Pinned down under Cye's body, arms trapped by his grasp, I knew I was about to find out.

CHAPTER 45

One final time, I opened my connection to Nikolaos. Strung up in silver, his vampire power was all but lost. Tears flowed from my eyes, not because I was dying, but because I would not get to hold the only man I'd ever loved one last time.

Opening all my vampire powers up to him, silence befell me.

'I love you,' I whispered through the tears, knowing he'd hear it. 'I'm sorry.'

I was about to close the connection between us, to succumb to death, when I sensed it. What *it* was, I did not know. But it was something formidable, a great force of deathly energy, riding on steeds of its own vigour towards us. Amphitrite must have summoned her remaining hoard, waiting out for the final blow. We were already doomed, so why not make it even more theatrical, further the humiliation of our defeat?

Footsteps violently rang through the hall, the sound of approaching defeat. Nearer it came, from both behind and in front of us, some coming through the corridor down which Amphitrite's wounded vampires had disappeared.

On the ground, Amphitrite and Orcus both froze, frowning faces looking around. Orcus's control over the zombies and Cye faltered, a loose connection in the field of electricity he was generating. Enough so that Cye lessened the pressure on my back, giving me the opportunity to struggle underneath him, pulling my hands free of his clawed grip.

Laith and Kai were forced to move out of the way of the double doors, closer to the ring of undead patiently waiting for them. Such patience, accompanying the knowledge that they have eternity to hunt down their prey. Zombies, it seemed, shared that arrogant calm with vampires. It was the dangerous composition of immortality, was arrogance.

Laith and Kai were more urgent in their demeanour, breath so heavy I could see the rise and fall of their beastly chests from across the room. Wide eyes flicked to each individual face, taking in the decaying features of their would-be murderers, along with that of Amphitrite and her pet necromancers.

The double doors flew open, smashing into the wall, narrowly avoiding grazing Kai and the already injured Laith. Simultaneously came the sound of footsteps breaking into the Great Hall, chains crashing onto stone accompanying them. I assumed that Amphitrite had sent her vampires to fetch the silver chains, until the darkness behind the new vampires dissipated, three faces suddenly illuminated by candlelight. Halfway between a display of obeisance and enervated defeat, Amphitrite collapsed to her knees between the hoard of the undead, dropping dead-weight to the ground.

Of the three vampires, only one was a woman. Tiny in every way, her dainty frame practically shone with her own will, tilted eyes severe, but lips curled into a slight smile. One of the men towered above the other two vampires, his straight hair long and sunbleached to pale gold, despite not seeing sunlight in centuries. His face was angled and handsome, perfect with its broad nose and slender, high cheeks. The third new arrival was short, stocky, and wide, shirt tucked into jeans failing to hide the tightly wound muscles beneath the cloth. Dark brown hair spun with copper shot out wiry and untamed around his face, leading to a bristly beard more ginger than brunette. Small hazel eyes glared out from beneath a deep brow, squinting as though he might need glasses, though that was impossible.

The three vampires barely acknowledged our presence above, but somehow I knew they'd noticed us. Khemeia turned to look behind him towards the sound of chains and people approaching. His face dropped, already wide eyes widening to the point of looking like they might bulge free of his skull.

We'd been lowered to stage level now, the stand we were on brushing against the lowest steps of the abandoned orchestra setup. I turned my head to the left to see the first hint of white, hooded robes, feet shuffling over the stone. My heart dropped to my stomach, watching them approach, until I noticed that they were not alone.

Beside them, a parade of vampires and lone human walked, holding the chains. One face I was stunned to recognise, black fur around dark eyes scanning the room. A tall, dark vampire with a sword as long as my body took up the rear, her piercing blue eyes otherworldly in features so dark. Sparkling in the low light, the tip of the blade pressed into the nape of the last vampire's hooded neck.

Everyone had a moment of stunned silence, taking in the new arrivals, weighing up the consequences of what this meant. Prone, I lay tense in my confusion, unsure whether or not this boded well for us. Cye seemed uncertain too, a tension in his body pressing into me, shaking involuntarily against my back.

The room shook with a collectively held breath, fear and damnation stealing all of our heartbeats. Utter silence chimed through the Great Hall, anticipatory and tense, and then the bell dropped, and in kicked fight or flight.

Kai leapt on the undead closest to him, muzzle tearing through his throat, sending gobbets of flesh and torn shirt to the ground. The zombie collapsed into a heap, crumbling in on himself. Though he was down, he was not out, body writhing on the floor, clawing at the exposed bone in his throat. Laith mirrored Kai, attacking the two approaching him. He was slower, limping, blood crisp in his fur.

Orcus retreated from the doors, edging further into the room away from the approaching vampires, leaving Amphitrite to lament her lost victory alone and vulnerable. The new vampires held themselves with less urgency, though no less fight.

The taller of the two bore long fangs in a malicious grin, charging headfirst into the zombies, large palms tearing through heads and throats, pulling them clean off. Still, the headless zombies crawled, bits of arm and leg slithering towards them. The other man crouched, fighting stance ready, waiting for them to come to him—which they were.

It was the woman who shocked me. One moment, she was standing poised and unphased by the hoard; the next, she had vanished. I blinked my eyes slowly, unsure if this was another hallucination caused by Orcus and Khemeia. When I opened them, she'd appeared behind Orcus with such a speed it went beyond preternatural into the impossible. An unexpecting

Orcus was totally oblivious to his new shadow until this teeny-tiny woman knelt down, sweeping his legs out from beneath him.

Orcus toppled over, with the vampire riding his back, small fists curling between dark hair, smashing his face into the ground as he went down. Commotion from beside me drew my attention back to Amphitrite's captured vampires. Luís bound towards us, a shadow of sable fur blurred from his speed. I just had time to notice a human woman following at his back, the flowy fabric of her pale dress streaming behind her, when Luís's figure struck Cye on top of me, knocking the gigantic panther clean off my body. I stayed pressed to the ground, breaths ragged and sore, body rigid with fear and relief.

Growls and shrieks reverberated around me, each collective group in a battle of their own. There was too much noise, movement, panic around me to take it all in, the world becoming a combat nebulous. So caught up in the chaos, I didn't notice the human approaching, not until she touched my shoulder, enticing a yelp.

Lined with age, gold and blue-stone rings embellished soft fingers; I turned my head to see her withdraw a tanned hand from my shoulder.

'Are you okay?' she asked in a voice so tender it brought tears to my eyes.

I looked up at her softly smiling face, hazel eyes too kind, and knew I looked pitiful. I sucked my bottom lip under, eyes widening, all the fight in me lost to the hopelessness of a child. Something about this woman, this tanned, aged angel, reminded me of the touch of a mother as if she would hold me to her breast and lull my fears.

With the help of her hand, I sat up, body shivering to the rhythm of bodies hitting the floor.

'I'm the only one who can touch the silver,' she said, and I only just now realised she had an American accent.

I looked up to where our people were still caught in webs of silver, watching as the smoke drifted from their bodies, bringing with it the stench of burning flesh. She saw my eyes flicker to the side, where a glimpse of the fighting distracted me.

'I should go help them,' I murmured through the tears caught in my lips.

'It's okay, sweetheart, you stay with me. Help me bring them down. They have the floor covered.'

I nodded vehemently, seemingly unable to stop once I'd started. I didn't at any point think to question who *they* were; my head was empty and echoing. Saskia, I came to find out, helped me up, the claw wounds in my legs protesting. Saskia and I climbed up the dead bodies towards Nikolaos, where he lay supine and helpless atop the cadavers. I nearly fell racing up to him, tripping over loose arms and flesh gone soft with the threat of decay. His head hung back, eyes limp and lifeless.

I grabbed his cheeks between my hands, lowering myself down to his face, planting kisses over each of his eyelids. Tears crept onto his face where I kissed every inch of it, red fluid caught between my lips and the overly cold skin of his face. When I pulled back, his eyes had opened, the vibrant green listless. It took me a second to realise some of the tears did not belong to me, his a deeper, darker red burning across his face like wounds.

'I love you. I love you. I love you. I love you...' I repeated over and over until the words tripped over themself.

Saskia pulled a screwdriver from a pocket in her dress, which surprised me for some reason. It was so very human in all of the madness of magick, such a mundane but valuable tool. With it, she reached up to undo the first of the shackles on his wrist, falling limply to his side.

'*Ma chérie*,' he croaked, voice dry and cracked. 'Rune is tied by lead; release him before me, lest he fall.'

I looked up to the limp man, only Nikolaos's body stopping him from hanging from the wires deadweight. I didn't want to leave him. Since touching his face, feeling his tears make love to my own, I never wanted to let him go. All of the fear that I had kept contained, the visceral terror of losing him, was only intensified by the relief of Saskia and the vampires.

'I'm going to have to tread on you to reach him,' I said, measuring the distance between Nikolaos's torso and the necromancer. 'I'm too short.'

Nikolaos managed a weak smile. 'Hasten.'

With Nikolaos's consent, I stood on his exposed stomach, reaching up as far as I could to the lead chains holding up Gwydion's arms. Gwydion, at the best of times, was almost two foot taller than me; dangling upright, the length of his body stretched longer than I'd expected. There was no way I could reach.

'Climb, *ma chérie*,' Nikolaos coughed weakly, almost lost to the sound of Saskia undoing his other wrist.

Grimacing, I jumped up, wrapping my arms around Gwydion's body so I could shuffle up him. The unconscious necromancer stirred, blue eyes fluttering feebly, closing again. I apologised to Rune under my breath, shimmying up his body like he was an elongated twig. Blood from my leg smeared over the cloth of his front, dark over the silken fabric.

Gwydion nodded his head, trying to shake himself free of grim repose.

'I'm going to get you free,' I said, clutching onto his shoulders, reaching up with the screwdriver angled in the nailhead.

'Hurry,' Rune croaked, then, fixing me with a stronger look, added, 'thus I can rid myself of your weight.'

I might have frowned at the choice of phrase, but the peevish quip instead brought a smile to my face. Oh, this was the Rune I knew and loved. Mean in his wit, kind in his apathy. Gwydion looked out across the room to where his beloved husband fought alongside our mysterious vampire saviours.

In a more assertive voice, he urged me to hurry again, which I did. Unscrewing the screw, it dropped with a metallic ring to the ground below. Gwydion's arm fell loose with me hanging onto it. Balancing on Nikolaos's shoulder, Gwydion managed to regain his footing whilst also keeping me from falling off him.

'Take the sword,' Gwydion instructed through gritted teeth as if in pain.

Obliging, I reached up to take the considerable iron weapon from between his still-chained hand.

'Pass me the screwdriver and climb down. I will release myself.' Both the sword and screwdriver stayed in my left hand, the right clinging to Gwydion with all my strength, his free arm wrapping around my body. Gwydion opened his mouth at me; I reached over to place the screwdriver between rows of dagger teeth and serpentine tongue. Gwydion's eyes widened as I brought the blade nearer his face, both of us knowing my disposition for clumsiness.

With the handle caught between his teeth, Gwydion managed to squeeze out, 'Careful on your journey down.'

I nodded, being as cautious as I could slipping down a seven-foot-tall skeleton with a sword almost as long as my body in my hand. If I'd been human, the weight of it alone might have collapsed me. Nikolaos's free arm reached up to steady my legs, guiding me down to the floor.

Gwydion undid his last shackle, knees buckling beneath him. His body fell to the ground with a loud bang, metal helmet rolling off onto the floor. I startled, rushing down to help the heavily panting man up, but he hit my hand away.

'I am fine!' he growled, low and angry, back heaving with the words.

Gwydion rose, knees shaking, pupils small and distant in the ice of his eyes. Saskia helped Nikolaos up, undoing the silver back of his wings. She peeled them from his body, bringing with it strips of raw, sticky flesh and the stench of burnt meat. Nikolaos did not once protest; only the slight pinch around his eyes alluded to any pain.

Both men instantly turned their frail attention to the fighting. The chained vampires knelt, heads down to the ground, surrounded by two of the new vampires, both of whom watched them with painful disdain.

Across the room, the other new men had Khemeia caught between their arms, playing with him like a cat with a mouse. The sword-wielding woman was joined by a new, dark-haired vampire, fighting the tenacious zombies. Her blade rose, slicing clean, ghastly lines through their bodies. Abdomens slid off torsos, falling to the ground but not stopping them. Each time the other vampire pulled a body part off, the limbs would creep towards them, sending a shudder down my spine.

All the while, Amphitrite stayed collapsed on the ground, her back shuddering with silent, ragged sobs. I recognised the look of defeat all too personally; that particular set of shoulders, hunched and distraught. She knew it was over, even as the others still fought.

Kai and Laith both had Ethan pinned to the ground, knees pressed into his lower spine. Blood flowed from the man, pooling around them both, soaking into Kai's fur.

The two Asian vampires still circled Orcus, crouched down, in a fighting pose. Yet neither of them made a move to get him.

'Why aren't they killing any of them?' I asked, surprised.

Nikolaos's mouth twisted into a bitter smile, but it was not he who answered. From across the room, the stouter of the male vampires looked up to us and grinned.

'This is your fight, Nikolaos. Finish it.'

The tall, blond one added, 'Justice is yours!'

Nikolaos and Gwydion shared a look over my head, some of the ailment bleeding to primal instinct. Still shaky and injured, the two men lept into battle, though not before Gwydion picked up his sword.

Nikolaos went straight for the men, joining their fight against the zombies. Gwydion ran for Orcus, a trail of feathers dancing through the air in his wake. With an approving nod from Saskia, I left her side to join Nikolaos, leaving Gwydion to fight his own battle supported by our newfound allies.

CHAPTER 46

The stouter vampire slapped Nikolaos on the arm in an affectionate gesture reserved for old friends.

'Good to see you, brother,' he said with a smile, effortlessly holding the struggling Khemeia in his other hand.

The blond vampire looked at them with an expression I couldn't quite read; his face had contorted into an attempted blankness, but pathos shone in his eyes. His cornflower-blue eyes lingered moments too long on Nikolaos's bare chest, following the curve of his jaw, the swirl of his lips. Curious, I watched him drink in the sight of my lover like he was art at which he would weep.

Noticing me watching, his eyes fell to me, darkening to a shade of stormy blue, angry and disappointed. I felt as if I had unimpressed him somehow. I touched Nikolaos's arm, tentatively, feeling the blond's focus on my hand as if he could burn it from gaze alone.

Nikolaos turned to look down at me, the dim green of his eyes reignited with some lost passion. For a moment, we stood in silence, my touch on him awkward and disconnected.

Just as I was about to draw back, Nikolaos did something he'd never done in the entire time I'd known him. Collapsing to his knees in front of me, he gripped me around the waist, pressing his face into the softness of my belly. His arms were steel around me, locking me into an embrace rigid with desperation and loss. My fingers wound through the thick silk of his hair, holding him to me. My body was stiff with the residue of fear, still feeling vaguely uncertain in his arms, as if it were too good to be true that we had found each other once more.

Nikolaos turned his head up to me, red liquid staining the dark circles under his eyes, leaking down to the gaunt hollows of his cheeks. With shaking fingers, I wiped the bloodied tears from the shadows of his face. I lowered my face down to his, lips brushing softly against the thick hair of his eyebrow, over the upper part of his nose where the bone slightly crooked. He threw his head back as far as it would go, enabling my lips to touch his.

We kissed, kissed with a passion we'd never shared—a passion I never wished to share again. Tainted by sorrow and a thousand possibilities of what might have been, we kissed the way lovers do who are saying their last goodbyes.

When we finally drew back, I was breathless as well as sorrowful and tight-chested. The blond vampire cleared his throat loud enough that we both turned to look at him.

'Finish this, Nikolaos,' he purred, accent peculiar and blended. 'This one is yours. Let the girl help the beasts.'

'Amphitrite is ours,' said the shorter man.

Nikolaos nodded, pulling himself up from the ground.

'Go, *ma chérie*, let us end this now.'

I let him slip from my arms, turning to where my feline companions held down the weakened Ethan. His fur was soaked through with blood, though not all of it was his. Laith wore a mask of red, fur mangled with blackened crimson. I went to him first, hand reaching for his.

The moment we touched, my heart roared to life. My body jarred with the shock of his energy racing through me so soon after touching Nikolaos. Crimson hair fell down my back as I threw my head backwards, seeing the world through vision skewed by cat irises. I was transported to a mindset I'd had previously in the night when I'd seen the potential for what could be when the trio was forged into one.

Still gripping Laith's hand, I jerked him away from Kai and Ethan, so caught up in my own fragility that I barely had to register what I was doing. I reached over to Nikolaos, brushing the end of his long fingers. He just had time to begin to turn around when I latched on for good, and time shattered to insignificance.

CHAPTER 47

Golden light broke through the room, the last sunset before the world burned, shattering through the darkness. With the blinding radiance came shadow, dark and seductive, dancing through the gloom of the room, slithering through cracks in the stone.

To my right, Laith was the day, warmth, safety; to my left, Nikolaos was nighttime and all the sin that it promised. And I, in the centre of the two men, was the sun, promising either to rise and shatter the tempting tenebrosity or relinquish myself to gloaming.

The three of us burned, taking a collective breath, a shared paused heartbeat. The warmth, the golden glow, built within me. Within us. Whether it started at my feet, my head, my heart, or somewhere that had nothing to do with me at all, I did not know. All I could tell was that it was growing like a pressure about to erupt, and when it did, I did not know if that would be pain or pleasure.

Fires burned behind my eyelids. I realised my eyes were open. The world was aglow with flames—my fire, our fire, leaked into the men beside me. Nikolaos shared with us the cold embrace of thousands of nights, of uncountable hours spent as the moon's lover. Laith gave us both the touch of transience lost to the darkness of vampirism. The fear of death; the hope of achieving something, anything, on his short stint on earth.

The grandiose shadow of a tawny lion stretched high above us, climbing up the walls, the light of my fire elongating and misshaping him. That same shadow reached into me, through me, until his Herculian paw encompassed both Nikolaos and me. We'd achieved something similar earlier in the night, but now we had the missing piece to this peculiar puzzle.

Nikolaos's own shadow started small, a foetus in my fiery womb, evolving with each millisecond. Stretching tall and wide, the uncertain infant grew into a cold, poised man, a trick of light making what appeared to be a wreath around his head. In the back of my mind, I saw it, the wilted petals of crimson roses, thorns bleeding him.

With him, I grew, too, though I was no shadow. I had no beast nor human figure. Erratic as waves, burning like the sun, the black silhouette of wild flames emerged over the hall. The light ceased suddenly, casting everyone in true darkness in the wake of our figures.

Our heart sped up with the sensation of tension building. We were pressure cookers about to explode. My knees went weak beneath me; both men caught me in a perfectly mirrored action, pinning me between them. I couldn't breathe over the passion of our power. It would not stop until it tore us apart and shattered us into shards of meaningless glass. How could anything so right come with such pain? Because pain, I realised, was always the consequence of pleasure. It was human folly to sin with consequence, be bound to mortal reigns leaving room for only good or bad. For us, the line was a perpetual tightrope, morality and immorality entwined to form a thread on which we balanced.

My scream echoed the sensation of being torn apart from the inside out. I was being burnt alive and frozen to death, my organs ballooning with the need to break free from the confines of flesh. Distantly, I recognised that thought as Laith's, then the next bout of tension crippled me over.

'Niko! Gwydion! Help me. Please, help me!' I cried out, blind. All I could see was darkness burning endlessly before the pits of Hell. Life had met its end; death had no ramification. Everything had fallen into disbalance, meaningless and insignificant.

'*Ma chérie,*' came Nikolaos's voice, seeming to thunder through the room as it whispered through my head.

The breath of his words caught in my throat, my teeth cold from the words he had spoken through me. I watched the lips of the shadows move, the jaw of the lion, my own dry mouth whispering, shouting, screaming the words over and over and over through my head.

'Scarlet!' he barked, voice strained. 'You are the charioteer of this carriage, the queen, and we your cortège. You alone must control the reins.'

'How?' I whimpered, turning to try and see him through the blindness of shadow and fire.

Nikolaos's physical form was paltry compared to the new beast of life, death, and everything in between that we had created. Pure black eyes burned in a pale face illuminated by darkness. Full lips moved out of time with his words as if those human lips could not produce the godly voice I heard in my head.

'Tame the beast. The fire. Our bond. You are what unites us all.'

I did all that I knew how to do. As Gwydion had taught me, I visualised. Closing my eyes, I looked deep within me to where the pressure built. A vine connected us by heart, soul, each chakra point on our bodies. Black, gold, and vermillion, it was a vein throbbing through each of us. The power pumped between us all with nowhere to go, searching for a release in parts of our bodies not made to be touched by such intense magick. If I'd had a better understanding of what was happening, maybe I would have been able to control it better from the beginning. There was no use thinking of what might have been. All we had was the current situation.

Screaming in pure desperation, I directed the flow of our combined energy outwards from our bodies, flinging the full force of it into the open space of the hall, seeking anything that it could find other than us.

In my head, it worked as a physical thing that we could toss away from our expanding limbs. The reality was not so simple. This was magick; it had no physical form, really, or not in the way I was picturing it. I had sent it on an impossible journey, so it had responded accordingly.

Volcanic and magnificent, the lava of my soul engulfed the room. I forced the energy out of me in a breath of fiery air that smashed into everyone in the room. Instantly, I knew who the two vampire men were. Osker and Erik, the Wulf Cyning Brothers, and founding kings of the vampire monarchy were hit first. I had a moment of shocking clarity, images of barren English lands overrun with werewolves fighting against the vampires. Nikolaos and Erik, the tall blonde, seducing the noble men and women of the lands together, torturing the wolves with whom they battled. All the while, Osker planned their next move, his vampiric power lying in ingenuity and strategy. Osker was a man born to rule as king; Erik was the perfect companion, his charm enough to beguile even the most stubborn oppositions.

Through Nikolaos, we hooked our claws into them, moving on to the next victim to drown in our dark glory. The vines of our ignited rose grew through them, slithering across the white stone to each person. Our thorns hooked in the hearts of the stunned crowd, flaming petals caressing tender flesh. Some, it burned; most, it soothed. Some we could not bind ourselves to. Nikolaos nor I had any ties to the rest of the vampire monarchy, or not enough to do little more than acknowledge them. Other than Gwydion, the necromancers were not ours to touch. Even Ethan was too distant. Our enemies could not be drawn upon, weakened, but our allies could be aided.

I used the building pressure of what we were creating to force strength through the wounds in the panthers' backs to Gwydion, where he still hunched, weak and skeletal. Three figures with one shared purpose, we cast the raft of our aid out, and even when it had been drunk down by our people, the pressure did not stop.

My body was filling with too much, and soon I thought we would explode, implode, vanish to nothing. In one final attempt to dispel what we had created, I wailed into the air, pushing the fire, the beast, the dead within me to be free.

Beams of light erupted, the Great Hall drenched in the backwash of heat. I did my best to contain my flames, those I knew well, but the rest was not so easy. The forcefield of what we had created shattered through the room, blowing everyone backwards, including us.

Gwydion, Orcus, and the two petite monarchs catapulted against the far wall, Gwydion dropping the sword as he did so. The zombies flew dead weight and limp through the air, crashing down like obscene bags of flour. The world was a blur as we were carried backwards until my head, slamming into the stone steps of the entrance, knocked me back into consciousness. The sound of shattering glass and stone erupted in my eyes, the largest chandelier from above smashing into broken shards of crystal, stone statues collapsing to the marble below.

Two hands worked to pull me up. My eyes were open, but shadow had fallen over the Hall, and I was blind. I sent out a touch of my flame to each in-tact chandelier, to the candelabras, basking the room in light once more. Beside me, Laith and Nikolaos's eyes blazed black, their hair blowing around them carried by some invisible force.

Fighting lazy with disorientation had broken out once more, everyone working to regain their upper hand. But now, we had more soldiers. Saskia had managed to unhook each of the panthers. Initially, they had been out of action, wounded beyond this evening's repair. Oh, how that had changed.

Naked and glorious, Onca stood poised and proud with her eyes crisp and bright. Beside her, her cherub-winged and nude hoard gathered. All but Tanya had recovered. We couldn't help her the same way as the panthers. Maybe it was because she and Ethan weren't feline, or perhaps we just felt less connected to her. Whatever it was, her face was still a bloody mass of oozing silk bandages.

Black fire eyes fixed on her, then looked at me. I nodded in approval, watching as Laith darted with a newfound speed across the room towards Saskia and Tanya. Onca let loose the potential of her call, releasing the beasts of her people from their fleshy prisons. No one fought it. Each panther cracked and dislocated until from their human bodies was born a magnificent, dark creature. They went straight for the chained vampires, huge, wide jaws tearing into hooded necks, claws slicing through hearts like animalistic stakes.

Nikolaos flashed past me to where Erik struggled with Khemeia. A vial of red fluid had fallen to the floor by his feet, glass smashed, blood messy around his thin lips. The necromancer was giving it all he could.

Osker was across the other side of the Hall, grappling with Amphitrite, though the fight was pitiful. With hearing like nothing I'd ever heard before, I made out the words, 'Capitulate with dignity, Amphitrite.'

Amphitrite fell loose in his arms. 'I yield, Ethelwulf. I yield.'

Finally, I settled on Gwydion, who had regained control of his blade all the while Orcus had regained control of his zombies. What little good they did him now. What little good any of it did.

Unsure where else to go, and disoriented with shock, I hobbled to Rune's side, staring down in disgust at the snivelling man bowing unwillingly before us. As if I were the weak link of empathy, Orcus tried one final attempt to save himself, reaching out to me with an arm barely covered by the tattered fabric. I had almost moved away when his fingers caught me at the last minute. With the hall surrounded by candlelight and me still riding the high of the explosive energy of whatever the fuck the three of us had created, something all too familiar and just as unwelcome happened. My entire being was transported to an unfamiliar history, watching dark tales and foggy follies unfold before me. Months of machinations that lead up to this moment sparked through my memory, seeing the ploys of this man.

I'd had enough practice with this to know what to do. I slammed the boundaries between us down, collapsing headfirst back into the here and now. Orcus jerked away from me, looking at me as if I were the evil one who had done something truly heinous. It startled me, but there was no time to think over the morality of this unhappy accident. Either way, Orcus would die.

On his knees, with blood streaming down his face, Orcus's dark eyes widened as he watched the thick wedge of brandished steel rise into the air. The candlelight above caught in the silver, giving it the illusion of catching fire.

Gwydion executed Khemeia with the skill of someone who had done it before. Bone, blood, and thick fluid collapsed with the curly-haired head. A flurry of white feathers tumbled from Gwydion's wings, floating down to land in the river of blood. As soon as he wilted, so did the zombies. Limbs, torsos, even some fleshless bones faltered in their spot, never to move again.

A wail of protest drew my attention back to Nikolaos and Erik. The blond vampire grinned at Nikolaos over the necromancer's head. I could not see Nikolaos's expression and was grateful for that. Each man held an arm and a leg, pulling slowly as if recreating some ancient torture method. Too synchronised for comfort, Niko and Erik each pulled their separate ways, tearing Khemeia clean in half. Well, maybe not clean. Khemeia's offal fell to the stone with a wet slap, parts of the human anatomy I'd never expected to see revealed far too starkly for comfort.

Nikolaos and Erik let the halves fall, Erik dusting off his hands. I took a step back to take in the scene of the room. All around us, bodies lay strewn and bloody, bits of flesh and blood and bone and meat discarded like a pillaged butchers. The room stank of execution, of rotting meat, and bodily functions given way to death. The miasma burned my eyes, the back of my throat, falling over my skin as if the stench could mar my flesh.

All that remained of Amphitrite's people was herself. The fallen Queen upon her wilted throne.

CHAPTER 48

Dawn trembling on the edge of Glasgow forced our stay in the palace for the night. There were enough chambers to sleep each vampire comfortably, as well as Onca and her Shadow, who understandably wished to stay together. Nikolaos showed the way to the sleeping chambers, down dark stone halls draped in dim silk.

He also showed us where the prison room was, in which Gwydion had been kept, and where we would be storing Amphitrite for the daylight hours. Placed in a coffin bound with silver, the monarchs swore she would not escape until they permitted it; however, Luís and Dario did not relent on wishing to stay guard. It took some convincing for the poor, frightened Dayana to leave her brother's side. Eventually, soon-to-be-king Otorongo picked her up gently, carrying her silently sobbing body to their bedroom for the night.

Saskia, the saint she was, agreed to drive Tanya to an actual hospital for treatment. Laith wanted to go with her; Sylvie and I said, no. When Sylvie had argued, he'd tried to fight back. When I'd stepped in, the fight had quickly ended. Sylvie disappeared swiftly after, saying they needed to call Angie and tell her they were okay. Not once did I see a tear fall from their hazel eyes, nor a change in their calm expression, but the moment the door closed, no wood or metal could silence the screams.

We lent them the dignity of lamenting in private. The monarchy sauntered off with little regard for us, all except for Osker, who gave Nikolaos a hearty hug. Oh, and Erik, who planted a blood-stained kiss on Nikolaos's lips, then walked off with a sway in his hips no man his height and build should be able to pull off. But he so did.

In the hush of the predawn silence, air too heavy with sorrow and death to breathe, Laith, Kai, Gwydion, Niko, and I all sat. Nikolaos lay back against the headboard of the bed, bare-torsoed, his eyes still burning with pure fire as black as starless skies. Some vigour had returned to his being, causing a gleam in his dark hair and fullness to the swell of his pink lips. Still, the ghost of red tears stained his cheeks, haunting Nikolaos with sorrow. At the foot of the bed curled Laith, still in half-lion form, his head resting on the contorted shape of his pawed hand. Black blood clothed all the golden fur in garments of pain. Heavy breaths raised his furred back and the curve of his bare arse. Now we were alone in this room, I realised that Kai and Laith were fully nude. No one else had a problem with it except for me, and even I was too tired to care.

I sat in the middle of the bed, between my two men, hugging my knees to my chest. At some point, I'd started shuddering; I had yet to be still. Nikolaos's feet brushed against my leg, causing me to jerk away from him. Laith watched the two of us interact curiously, his pure black eyes glowing. None of our eyes had returned to normal yet; I found it disconcerting to see black pits burning with our combined power etched in each of our faces. I let myself be between their figures, Niko cold at my back, Laith warm in front of me, whilst adamantly not wanting either to touch me. The comedown of consequence sent a chill through me that could not be warmed.

Tonight, I'd seen horrors beyond anything I'd ever thought conceivable, drank the drops of blood of those upon whom we should never feast, and brought about shocking power. The physical, mental, and emotional toll of the evening merged with the exhaustion of near-sunrise, causing me to sit distressed and uncomfortable.

Across the room, Gwydion leant against the doorframe, a blanket of feathers scattered around him. Of all the times I had seen Kai and Gwydion together, Kai had been docile, subdued in Gwydion's arms as he petted our favourite feline. Kai sat up higher above Gwydion, though the other man was far taller, letting him slump into his chest. Kai's body hummed with tension, the muscles in his arms flexing as he clenched a pawed hand, the other stroking along Gwdyion's side. With eyes on high alert, orange irises scanned the room back and forth, refusing to ease. The flicking back and forth made me anxious as if I should also be checking for the next potential danger.

'We have mere minutes remaining,' said Gwydion, breaking the uneasy silence.

My heavy eyelids blinked slowly; the evaporating night had become a waiting game of sentience slipping to sleep.

'Take the daylight hours to beat a hasty retreat, Rune,' Nikolaos suggested with a tone of command. 'The monarch's clemency for necromancers will have perished after tonight.'

'Surely they won't hurt, Rune!' I cried out. 'He helped us. He was as much of a victim as we were.'

Both Nikolaos and Rune protested my use of victim, but I waved off their petty disputes.

'The wings would have been a diversion, but it will not take them long to decipher your affinities.'

Gwydion mused over this, bony fingers reaching for one of the fallen feathers, fiddling with it.

'I had met Osker and Erik before, long ago, when the Syndicate bargained a sort of armistice with the newly established monarchy. I am surprised they did not recognise me.' Gwydion let the feather fall, all of us watching as it fluttered slowly to the cold stone.

Nikolaos shrugged a bare shoulder.

'That must have been long past my time with the Wulf Brothers.'

Gwydion nodded. 'Yes. Once I had moved to England, before the unfortunate departure of your golden-haired friend to Australia.'

Nikolaos nodded as if that vague timeline made perfect sense to him, though I had no idea what they were talking about. This might have been the longest conversation I'd seen the two men have without any backhanded comments or quips. I think all of us were too tired of fighting to continue it in private. Or at least I was. Nikolaos was actually quite fond of battle—a trait carried over from his human life.

'In which case, take that as leniency. I doubt the others will be so forthcoming.'

Gwydion rose from his seated position, Kai following him upwards like a shadow. I was so used to Kai being barely taller than me that it was startling to see him almost the same height as Gwydion in this form.

Still curled up, Laith managed to growl, 'My jeans are shredded upstairs; somewhere in the tatters should be my keys to Sylvie's. Take 'em.'

'Thank you, Lion. I shall be sorrowful to miss tomorrow's colloquy.'

'If you shift back to human, you can take my car, mate,' added Laith to Kai.

Kai tipped his head in the direction of the lion. 'Thanks, Laith.'

Gwydion shook his head. 'Kai, you must stay with your Reina and people. They will need you more than I.'

Kai gripped a pawed hand on Gwydion's arm. 'No, I'm comin' with you.' Softly, intimately, he added, 'I need you.'

That was the thing about Kai that made him so easy to love; he wore his heart on his sleeve with a refreshing, and sometimes scathing, honesty. It's hard to say no to someone who is so unapologetically earnest. Still, Gwydion tried to argue. The couple eventually compromised, with Kai promising to return to our side tomorrow evening, in time for the vampires to rise. He also said he'd bring a change of clothes for Laith, which I think I was more grateful for than the lion.

We bid our farewells to them. I hugged Kai with a strength that probably would have broken any human, eventually pulling Gwydion into it, forcing him to be a part of the affections. Once I held them, I never wanted to let them go. Laith shook Gwydion's hand and gave Kai a slightly awkward hug. Nikolaos said nothing, but he did rise from the bed and acknowledge their departure with a nod of the head, which Gwydion returned. For them, that was monumental.

Then came the problem of sleeping. The logical part of my brain said that I wanted to be alone with Nikolaos; the part of me that was illogical and inhuman couldn't stand the thought of letting my lion go. I wanted to be wrapped in the comfort of my two men, though I was also terrified of what it would mean to touch them both again.

Laith volunteered to go and stay in a spare room without any press of guilt, but I still saw the flash of something close to fear in his eyes at the thought of being alone. If he'd been clothed, it might have been different, but there were too many elements that made this seem like a bad idea.

'You are both witless. This is no time to be alone,' Nikolaos surprised us both by saying. 'It is very human of you to be so modest, *ma chérie*.' It usually would have been a rebuke, but tonight Nikolaos smiled. 'Ah, how I have missed your human foibles.'

'Are you sure that's okay with you?' asked Laith.

'Yes, are you?' I added suspiciously, remembering Nikolaos seeing through my eyes a vision of deep intimacy between us.

Nikolaos just barely wasted a glance on us, his eyes shining with the humour of an adult watching silly children. Oh, that was my Nikolaos. How I'd yearned to see that look in his eyes again.

Laith bundled up covers and rested them on the floor, making a little bed for himself. Once he'd shifted back to human, I refused to look at him until he was safely under the covers. I don't know why it felt less intrusive seeing his manhood in animal form, but it did. I guess it was easier to depersonalise the nudity when you're thinking of him like an animal.

Nikolaos pressed the line of his body against my back, holding me to him with some element of unfamiliar urgency. I huddled into him as if trying to merge us into one being. In some ways, I was. His lips found the nape of my neck, resting over the fine line of hairs as he inhaled a deep breath, hand flexing over my stomach. I raised his hand to my mouth, our fingers entwined, kissing each knuckle over and over.

A drop of something wet touched my neck, and I realised that Nikolaos's body softly shook. I turned in his arms, lips brushing the tears away. Nikolaos tried to turn away from me, but I caught his face before he could.

'I'm so sorry they hurt you, Niko. I'm so sorry that we couldn't have been here sooner,' I whispered, voice cracking with my share of sorrow.

Nikolaos smiled through the tears. '*Ma chérie*, I have never wept for pain, starvation, or bloodshed. But in all my years as the undead, I have never felt agony like thinking I might lose you.'

Silent, I gripped him to me as hard as I could. There were no words that could do justice to his fear, only action.

We settled back into spooning just as the sun rose. My hand flopped off the edge of the bed, finding Laith's hand waiting for me. As our fingers met, I had a moment of fear that something awful would happen, that we'd lose control again.

But in the end, it was the comfort I needed to fall happily into repose.

CHAPTER 49

I awoke to hushed voices outside the bedroom door. I snuggled further into the covers with still-closed eyes, feeling the comfort of heavy blankets over my body. I revelled waking up in a bed and not a coffin, giving the illusion of momentary homely comfort. It was rare for Nikolaos to wake before me, but tonight, it seemed everyone had woken up long before me.

'She's awake,' I heard Laith say, shuddering at the sound of his voice as if it had alerted something else within me.

At that thought, my fires stirred, empowered with newfound confidence after what we had done last night. Not that I knew what exactly that was. I just knew that Nikolaos was out there also. I could 'see'—though maybe see is the wrong word—their two golden and black shadows lingering outside the door, waiting for me to awaken. I didn't have to wonder who else they were with for long, as the door crept open at that moment to reveal Kai with them. Three pairs of eyes fell on me still in bed, red hair wild around my face, eyes yet to fully open.

As promised, Kai'd brought a change of clothes for Laith. Nikolaos had also changed into his usual dark attire, snubbing the all-white and then demonic-angel outfits into which Amphitrite had forced him. Standing side by side in their human forms, dressed in their usual style, Laith and Nikolaos looked entirely opposite. The golden-brown and black of Laith's hair curled around his angled face, dark green of the cotton shirt illuminating the yellow tones of his brown eyes, with the rest of the outfit all tan and brown. Beside him, Nikolaos was a dark shadow, wearing all black, turning his face into a ghostly slash of white appearing between the curtain of his hair.

'Mornin' darlin',' Kai said with a smile I'd not seen on his face since arriving in Scotland. I promised never to take that smile for granted again, treasuring his happiness.

Kai reached down to the bag I'd packed, waving it in front of him. 'A change of clothes.'

I looked down at my tattered clothes crisp with dried blood, feeling dirty.

I already suspected the answer, but still asked, 'Is there time to shower?'

All of them shook their heads. Resisting the urge to grumble, I got up out of bed, taking the bag from Kai's hand.

Nikolaos grabbed my hand, pulling me into his chest. I let the bag fall to the floor, wrapping both arms around his body, collapsing into the beautifully familiar sensation of cinnamon and rose-scented silk against my skin. When we'd first met, I had thought it was cologne. It wasn't; it was just him. Perfect and tempting, it was a scent that now meant home and safety to me.

'Get dressed, *ma chérie*. Let us end this ordeal hastily.'

'I want to go home,' I sighed into his chest, feeling his fingers get caught in a knot in my hair.

'*Moi aussi.*'

I pulled out an all-black outfit, grateful to have a clean pair of knickers and unbloodied clothes. Once dressed, I met the trio outside the bedroom.

'How's Gwydion?' I asked Kai, stroking his arm.

He offered me a listless smile and shrug. 'He made me promise not to let you worry about him.'

I frowned, then shook my head with a smile. 'Easier said than done.'

'Don't I know it, darlin', don't I know it.'

'What were you guys talking about whilst I was asleep? What time even is it?' I looked at Niko, trying to steady my heart as it sped, slicing with love, gratitude, and residue fear. My hand went to it as if to say, be still my beating heart. It did not yield to my instruction, as hearts so often don't. 'I'm not used to waking up later than you. We should introduce you to Onca and her people.'

Kai and Laith exchanged a look that I didn't like.

'We have been summoned to appear in front of the monarchy.'

'I was expecting as much,' I said suspiciously, narrowing my eyes at Niko. 'Are the others already in there then?'

'We have been summoned on vampire business. The therians are exiled from any further discussions.'

Kai and Laith both looked angry. 'Not just from the discussion,' added Laith, 'but from the palace, too.'

Kai said, 'As soon as night fell, we were banished. I was only allowed back to drop you off clothes.'

'Seriously? Why?'

Nikolaos shrugged. 'Osker does not want to further share the fiasco brought about by Amphitrite. It is degrading to all he has built.'

I opened my mouth, closed it, and felt my shoulders slump. This was very on-brand for vampires; what else did I expect? They'd accept the aid of the therians when it was convenient, then discard them just as quickly.

'Why are you here, then?' I asked Laith, by no means unhappy he was.

'Your pet lion is allowed to stay,' Nikolaos replied.

'How come?'

'Jesus, Scarlet, I'm beginning to think you want me gone,' Laith semi-joked, running his hands through his short hair.

I tutted. 'Don't be silly. But I am suspicious why.'

'There was a vote, four against two in favour of your pet.'

I frowned again. 'Six? Were there six monarchs yesterday? I thought only five, not including Amphitrite. Oh, my god, is she released? Did she get a vote?'

Nikolaos reached for me in response to my wide eyes and clumsy, too-fast words, pulling me into the circle of his arms. 'I will explain on the way, *ma chérie*, but we cannot keep them waiting any longer.'

Kai gave a curt nod. 'I'm gonna take that as my cue to leave.'

'Sorry, mate,' said Laith, slapping him affectionately on the arm.

Kai's face lit up with a wide beam. 'Don't be. I'm goin' home to my husband and Queen. You I don't envy, though.'

Oh, to go home sounded so wonderful. Alas, vampire duty called.

The three of us walked towards the Banquet Hall, through winding corridors with low, flickering lanterns and the occasional step. On the way, Nikolaos tried to explain to us the different names of the monarchy.

'So, there are six monarchs?' I asked.

'*Non*, seven. I did not see Yule yesterday. Though the most elusive of the unit, he is here tonight.'

'This Yule was the fourth vote in favour of Laith.'

Nikolaos nodded, guiding us around a dark corner to a hall decorated with old paintings depicting scenes of elfin women luxuriating in waterfalls.

'And the human who helped me yesterday, Saskia, she is married to Osker, as well as being his Princess,' I reiterated.

Nikolaos nodded once. '*Oui*. Their son, Osker's Prince, is Edmond.'

'They had a baby? I didn't think that was possible,' asked Laith, who had taken such a keen interest in all Nikolaos had to say that I'd almost asked him if he wanted to take notes.

'Do you know much of our kind?'

'Well, no.' Laith smiled. 'But I'd love to know more. Scarlet's already taught me so much.'

Had I? I didn't think I had. I remembered Laith saying how he loved the arcane history of the preternatural world, so didn't interrupt any of his eager questions. After the night we'd had, he deserved a chance to unwind with his passion.

'It's amazing how your blood can heal. The medical world would go wild for it. I'm a doctor, I don't know if I mentioned that. If we could examine what about it made it a cure-all, then it could lead to some revolutionary breakthroughs,' Laith continued to babble in his nervous-excited tone.

Though he could learn a lot from Nikolaos, from his clumsy speech and the way he kept running his hands through his hair, sticking it on end, I got the impression Laith might be intimidated by him. Naturally, my vampire did nothing to soothe his unease, delivering each verse with his usual stoicism.

'We have laws; one of those is never to alert humans to our existence, lest we can put forth an argument as to why it should be allowed.'

'Surely solving all maladies would be reason enough?' an earnest Laith asked.

Nikolaos gave him the look the question deserved, and for the first time, Laith got to see how disparate in character they indeed were. In fairness to Nikolaos, I did have to give him some credit for even bothering to answer Laith's persistent questions. He was not fond of enquiry; in fact, he rarely even bothered to answer any of mine. Less so now, but when we first met, getting anything out of Nikolaos was like trying to get blood from a stone.

We were nearly at the door leading to the Hall. I touched Laith's arm gently, soothing some of the agitated confusion in his eyes. Nikolaos really could be so callous; I'd adjusted to it, the same could not be said for those meeting him for the first time.

'Vampires don't really think the same way you do about humans, Laith,' I tried to reason, knowing it was a weak excuse.

'So you agree with him?' he asked, the question in his eyes holding more weight than it should, as if his judgment on my character would shift dramatically based on how I replied.

Uncomfortable, I shifted the weight of my feet, trying to ignore the building tension in the hallway.

Nikolaos's hand locked around the door handle, saving me from having to think too deeply on this moral conundrum.

Opening to reveal a hall of satin-draped walls and pale marble statues, Nikolaos let the door hit against the wall, alerting everyone to our arrival. A grand banquet table, breathtaking and big enough to sit fifty, sat in the middle of the Banquet Hall. The room managed to be both modest and decadent, with silver and cyan fabric draping across the walls and over the table. Silver candelabras twisted up from the tabletop, holding unlit golden candles matching the throw along the top of the blue tablecloth, the underneath layer revealing silver tassels. In vast glass bowls of water floated white comet orchids and pink-tipped Victoria water lilies.

At the back of the room, a statue of a woman draped in stone fabric poured water from a jug painted the soft blue of spring skies. The gentle trickle of water mixed with the floral perfume in the air, giving the illusion of late spring when the air is ripe with sweetness and sun-kissed stone. It would have been tranquil if it weren't for the coffin resting on the floor beside the marble basin, silver chains winding around the white-metal casket. Pearl handlebars acted as hoops for the threaded chains, crisscrossing over the decals on the smooth corners and above the handles. Delicate paintings of ivory water lilies floating on water glistened behind the decals' glass case, their frames ornate and silver. I never thought I'd say this, but I had coffin envy. I never wanted to sleep in a coffin again, but if I were going to have to, then I'd rather it looked something like this.

Osker sat at the centre of the table with his wife and son on the left and Erik to his right. Nikolaos had made sure I was aware that Ezra, Erik's companion and partner, was the only exception to the Prince and Princess rule. Ezra was Erik's

Princette. Their green eyes watched me curiously through a cape of straight silk hair spun to copper. Slender shoulders contained within a soft-coloured dress flexed as they moved their hand across the table, reaching for Erik's. Ezra flexed their fingers over Erik's hand as their vision trailed to Nikolaos, and some of that curiosity was lost to insecurity.

Erik's ringed-fingers reacted to Ezra, turning his palm up to engulf their long, thin hand. Nikolaos, for whom the show was intended, I presumed, did not react, which seemed to irritate the blond vampire judging from the darkening of his eyes. Circling them were the rest of the vampire monarchy. Habibah, Empress of Africa, and Lapis, her sword-wielding Princess with the striking blue eyes, sat looking unhappy. Inacio, South American Emperor, was alone in his seat. Nikolaos had warned me that, other than Saskia, non-vampire Princes and Princesses would not be in attendance. Inacio's Prince was Bo, Ajaw, or king, of the South American weresnakes, and lover of Inacio. Bo, apparently, rarely left the country with his husband, taking on the responsibility of ruler of vampires and snakes in his absence. Inacio's soft brown hair had been cut short, red and copper highlights glistening in his tight, corkscrew curls, dark stubble trailing along the sharp cut of his diamond-shaped jawline. His suit was perfectly tailored, the rings on his fingers real gold. There was something very preened about Inacio.

Sora, Empress of Asia, sat beside her identical twin brother, Natsu. Both vampires were tiny and delicate, built of smooth, dark china. Black hair hung straight and satiny to their shoulders, fringes cut neatly above black almond eyes. Sora observed us with a seemingly eternal patience, face set into content lines. With her height and kind eyes, she'd be far too easy to underestimate. I saw beneath the layers to the catlike tilt of her head and slow flicker of eyes. She was a predator in its most dangerous form, a smiling assassin, the agile cat camouflaged amongst a society of mice.

Lastly was Yule, Emperor of Antarctica, who'd not been here last night. If I'd not known he was a vampire, I wouldn't have guessed. There was something otherworldly about him beyond vampirism. Yule's body was long and slender, his face covered entirely by a bushy white beard. Opal hair fell in long tresses down his back, tumbling to brush the stone floor. From underneath white eyebrows, the most peculiar pale-purple eyes looked at me, through me, behind me. His lilac gaze flitted like the wings of a butterfly through the room, never settling on one thing. I was almost uncertain if he'd registered our entrance when a smile curled the corners of slender pink lips, lazily flashing fangs. In spite of myself, I smiled back, almost unable to resist it.

The monarchs had laid out three chairs on the other side of the table for us. I waited for Nikolaos to go first; he'd understand any vampire protocol to greet the Emperors and Empresses more than I did. With that in mind, and the entire focus of the monarchy on the three of us, I anxiously followed him further into the Banquet Hall.

CHAPTER 50

Up close, I could see that Osker and Erik wore matching necklaces. A large canine encased in delicate silver metal hung from a chain on Erik's neck; Osker just had a piece of leather threaded through the tooth's root.

'We have a lot to discuss,' said Osker, fingers tapping on the table.

Nikolaos gave a curt nod in response, which made Osker smile. 'Still a man of many words, I see, Niko.'

My vampire gave that equivocal shrug, the corners of his mouth twitching into the slightest of smiles.

Habibah was quick to bring down the friendly tone.

'I do not like the lion being here,' she said, accent thick and dripping like molasses.

I observed the little lines around Osker's eyes deepening, shoulders pulling forward just a touch. For a vampire as old and powerful as I knew he was, he was surprisingly open with his emotions.

'This is vampire business,' she added.

Yule smiled gently, purple eyes drifting over each of our faces, though I got the impression he was never focusing on any of us.

'The lion is connected to the girl. He is a part of vampire business.'

My eyes widened.

'Wait, what do you mean?' I asked urgently, hands pressing onto the tabletop.

Yule got no chance to reply as Osker took back control of the conversation.

'For someone who likes being in the shadows, you do seem to seek trouble, Niko.'

Nikolaos shrugged and smiled, hands held out in front of him. 'Trouble seeks me.'

'I can see that,' jibed Erik, looking at me.

Ezra's painted fingernails brushed a strand of copper hair behind their ear uncomfortably, looking at neither Niko nor me. Erik sat back in his chair, arms crossed over his chest with an arrogant smirk playing over his lips. How quickly beauty could crumble in the face of envy.

'I wouldn't look so happy; you have broken one of the cardinal laws of the vampires,' said Habibah, looking indignant.

I reached for Nikolaos's hand, suddenly anxious. I hadn't thought we'd done anything illegal. Nikolaos gave my fingers a reassuring squeeze.

'A bold accusation. May I be granted a platform to protest my innocence?' asked Nikolaos, withdrawing from my tense grip.

Laith shifted beside me, so I reached for him instead; his palm was clammy against mine. Osker's smile faltered with the shift in mood.

'If you have drunk from the vein of a necromancer,' he said listlessly, 'that warrants instant death.'

A spike of fear shocked me to my core. In the madness of last night, I'd forgotten that both Nikolaos and I had accidentally bled and feasted on necromancer's blood. I was by no means as mastered in the art of facial control as Nikolaos, terrified that my guilt was evident in the lines around my brow and eyes or the way I sucked my lips.

Laith seemed to share some of my fear, his hand clenching around mine, palm hot and sweaty. I felt like we were school children in front of the head faculty, trying to protest our innocence, knowing full well we'd broken the rules. All we had to do was leave Nikolaos to argue our defence. Unfortunately, if he couldn't wangle his way out of this, our fate was a doom far greater than expulsion—death. True, final death.

Erik slammed his hand onto the table, making both Laith and me jump. 'This is asinine.'

'Be calm, Erik,' Nikolaos said, rising from his chair, seemingly unphased by any of this. 'I have lived for millennia as a vampire and centuries under vampire decree. To you, my word as a man will mean nothing, and as a vampire little. But, as an upholder of our laws, one who gave muscle to the trepid knees of the monarchy's infancy, I ask you to trust me.'

Sora cocked her head to the side. 'Your plea is only that we trust you? You seem confident in this request.'

Again, Nikolaos shrugged. 'Other than my word, I have no proof. Besides my honour, I have nothing at all.'

'He was the one who alerted us to Amphitrite's atrocities,' cried Erik. 'Nikolaos would be a fool to do any such thing if he himself were a part of the crime. And this man is no fool.'

Nikolaos's lips quirked at the sides.

'Ah, Erik, a premature introduction to my second point. Both Erik and Osker can act as character witness to my loyalties.'

Habibah waved her hand in front of her angrily.

'Oh, an expected ploy. We all know of your *relations*'—she made it sound like something dirty—'with the Wulf Kings and their peculiar sentiments towards you. But what of the girl?'

At some point, when hanging around with people who had lived lives spanning hundreds, if not thousands, of years, I had given up on protesting being referred to as *girl*. Twenty years seemed pretty measly compared to their vast lifetimes, and so often, their extensive knowledge and experience made me feel like a child.

Nikolaos narrowed sparkling green eyes, glowing brighter, it appeared, since our forged connection the night before. 'What of her?'

'Where is her character witness? For what reason did Amphitrite yearn for her company? You are hiding things from us.'

For a moment, I forgot how to blink, breathe, and talk. I had no argument for myself.

'Scarlet is more a victim in this than I. I was called to Amphitrite's side out of duty; Scarlet was forced here upon necessity. Without her rescue, Amphitrite would have gone mad with the drug of power. I watched her unravel,' Nikolaos continued, sounding truly horrified now. 'I watched madness and addiction quickly consume her. I was starved for the days prior to Scarlet's arrival lest I let her force that tainted blood down my unwilling throat. Amphitrite exercised her power as my Empress over me like a madman holds insanity over their sense of guilt.'

'You waited a long time to tell us, Nikolaos,' this from Inacio.

Nikolaos sat back in his chair with the overt air of hauteur I knew was his way of coping with the pressure of failure. This particular failure held the burden of our lives as the undead.

'As I said, I am loyal. And Amphitrite had necromancers watching my every move. Through the power of the necromancers, I could not contact my vassal and lover nor seek safety and refuge. She made me a prisoner within these very walls,' and he gestured around the room. 'I can assure you I knew little of her plots and even less of her intentions. For weeks, the Empress threatened me with bringing Scarlet to her side, which I refused. You yourselves all know that one must protect themselves utmost and their vassals even more. Surely the greatest sin of vampire-kind is not seeking survival.'

Under the table, Nikolaos reached for me, and I gave him my hand willingly. Through his arm, I could feel the song of tension, the vein on his wrist taught against my palm. Still, from the shoulders up, his demeanour was one of pleasant apathy. I knew some of what he said was a lie, though not really how much, but each line was delivered with the earnestness of a man who'd never had a lie taint his lips.

'You speak dangerously of sin and laws as if you have any say in what these are. You didn't take the throne centuries ago, and you get no voice in what laws we make. Your death would be no such crime as the ones committed under your eye,' said Inacio, who I was struggling to work out.

Habibah, it was clear, was adamantly against us. I was certain, if she had her way, we would be sentenced to death without hesitation. Yule was barely present, and I wasn't convinced he knew why we were all here. Sora seemed on the side of Osker and Erik, though she also had questions regarding our part in the ordeal. Inacio, however, I wasn't sure if he liked us or not.

'I was rendered powerless. To alert Osker of the Empress's activities was a great risk.'

Erik grimaced, saying with crestfallen eyes, 'That is your true crime, in all of this, Nikolaos. After centuries of running from us, you seek his voice before mine. I am, to say the least, offended.'

Osker sighed as if this particular heartbreak of Erik's was not a new affliction and one of which he grew weary.

'I'm tired of this,' Osker said, rubbing his eyes. 'Without Nikolaos, we would not know of Amphitrite's plans. I fear what would have become of all of us if she'd been left to her own devices any longer.'

'We are arguing minutiae,' added Sora, 'when this evening is one shadowed by sorrow and loss. We will be losing one of our own, a vampire we trusted and held as an ally; to keep fighting the sufferers of Amphitrite's wrath seems a petty prerequisite to a violent climax.'

A heaviness fell upon the monarchy, all except Yule, who I didn't think had been listening to any of the discussion.

As if he noticed me watching him, those violet eyes settled on me with the precariousness of a butterfly's wings.

'So, we are just to ignore what these three did last night?' protested Habibah with a wave of her hand. 'You do not expect me to believe they did this without the aid of a necromancer.'

Even Nikolaos tensed, which meant he knew as little of what had happened as I did.

With a smirk, she scoffed, 'No explanation for this, I see.'

Yule's bearded lips curled into a wistful smile as he announced his knowledge of last night's events, much to the surprise, and relief, of our trio. Yule followed through with a singsong voice explaining the Animus, though, along the way, there were many detours before finally getting to the point. By the time Yule concluded, he'd melodically fallen down so many holes of irrelevant speech, I barely understood the point.

It was something along the lines of Laith being my *Animus*. Vampires born of non-human blood, such as nymph in my case, on infrequent occasions had the power to bind themselves to a particular wereanimal. According to Yule, Animus, or Anima, if the vampire is male, cannot be chosen by anyone but the delicate hand of destiny herself. The bond between us is unbreakable and unyielding, instant and spectacular and passionate, forged on endless histories all aligning to the magick moment of meeting. Until sharing blood, the relationship is a familiar comfort, where each other's presence is a pleasure, such as smelling a rose is pleasant on the senses. Once blood is shared, however, it becomes a necessity.

From this point forth, Laith would lend my heart a distant beat, my lungs a bated breath, and my soul a companion. Yule assured me it was so rare that, in his lifetime, he'd only ever seen it happen once before—to him and his wife, with whom he resided in the Antarctic as she was Queen of the orcas. When I'd asked how long that lifetime had been, Yule had simply smiled and fallen back into his chair with a finger raised to upturned lips, purple eyes glittering with joy.

It might have been, if Yule had a master still 'alive', he could have forged the power of three quite like we did, though of that he was not sure. It offered some explanation as to what we'd done, how I'd pulled all the parts of my two sides together, all the while raising a hundred more questions.

Opportunity to ask any of these would not be granted. Habibah was quick to remind me they had more important things to worry about than my silly questions, as if she herself had not listened with intrigue and surprise at all Yule had to say. Nikolaos eased me from my chair quickly, accepting the victory without my shared need for further knowledge.

'Nikolaos,' Erik said, standing with us, 'I expect to hear from you again, I am quite sure you have spent too long in solitude.' With a glance at me, he continued, 'I think it is time your horizons are broadened.'

With a timid smile, Nikolaos retorted, 'I do not seek the sorrow of nostalgia.'

'I am certain I can show you the pleasures of it.'

With a bow of the head, Nikolaos yielded, which put a sour expression on both Ezra and my faces.

'I would be humbled to hear your voice, brother, though your name, not so much. If I am to be brought back into your life, let it be through invitation and not force of entry,' said Osker. 'I do not wish to hear whispers of your dark endeavours again, and even less to have to involve myself in them.'

To that, we all much more readily agreed. Just as Nikolaos had his hand on the door handle and my lungs were beginning to catch back the breath that fear had stolen, Sora called Nikolaos's name.

'Oh, Nikolaos and Scarlet, we have searched the palace from floor to ceiling and can find no sight of Amphitrite's Prince, Vodan, was it?'

If I'd had a steadily beating heart, it would have faltered and brought demise to me right then and there. My entire body clenched, retracting in on itself. Laith, who recognised the name, and now knew the importance of it, also responded, his face such a performance of emotion he was forced to turn away.

Composed, Nikolaos turned back around. 'Yes, Vodan. On the opening night of Atlas, my newest business, he summoned me to Amphitrite's side. We travelled up together, but from thenceforth I do not recall his presence. I believe him to have grown quite jealous of Amphitrite's relationship with Orcus, which was deeper than I care to admit, and had got in the way of the Empress's desires,' Nikolaos lied. I knew from Vodan himself that it was not Orcus of whom he'd grown jealous, but Nikolaos.

Sora nodded as if that all made perfect sense.

'Keep an eye out nonetheless,' Inacio said. 'Just in case.'

On a final note of feigned geniality, Nikolaos added, 'If you ever find yourself sojourning in Britchelstone, do make sure to pay a visit to Atlas.'

With one final glance at Osker's shaking head and humble smile, Erik's overly eager beam beside his lover's sorrow, and the twisted range of expressions over the other's faces, I was whisked from the room by Nikolaos.

The three of us ran up the steps into the early-morning darkness of Glasgow. Above, stars glittered in the sky, the moon a slice of silver in the deep blue, the wind cool and refreshing over my cheeks.

Collapsing to the ground, I gulped down the sweetness of the grave-kissed air, appreciating it more than I'd ever appreciated anything. For a long while, I had thought we'd never see moonlight again or feel the embrace of rain on our faces.

Cold moss, wet beneath my knees, felt soft, the stone comforting. Nikolaos rose me from the ground, clutching me to his chest with an unmatched ferocity. In the arms of my lover, with my lion, my Animus, at my back, I felt a sense of safety and relief that tore a wail from between my lips and joyful tears to my eyes.

CHAPTER 51

Britchelstone had never felt as much as home as it did upon our arrival. We'd stayed three more nights in Edinburgh before finally journeying home with Kai. On our first night awaking together in Sylvie's flat, Nikolaos met Onca and her people formally.

After greeting us, Onca had held out her hand to Nikolaos, giving him the option to either respond as her equal or acknowledge her dominance.

Nikolaos had taken her much smaller hand in his, skin stark against the rich tones of Onca's flesh.

'We have not been formally acquainted,' she'd said, hand resting in Niko's.

'Your reputation precedes you, Reina Onca.'

She smiled. 'Ah, you flatter me.'

'I am Nikolaos Midas,' Niko'd said, lowering his head to her hand. With his fingers resting over her ring, he'd rolled sensual eyes up to her face. 'I do not recognise your dominance over me, but as an uncrowned man I bow to your Queendom, and what that has meant for me and mine.'

Nikolaos had glided soft pink lips over the warm metal. As Niko rose, Onca had said, 'Tell me why, *Señor* Midas, I have not heard your name but feel as if I should.'

Nikolaos had returned her smile, and it'd seemed genuine. 'I prefer the privacy of solitude.'

With introductions over, we'd had the opportunity to sit as a collective and discuss the events from our respective perspectives. Kai and Gwydion did not attend, instead locking themselves in Sylvie's bedroom to sleep the night away together. The panthers relayed their tale of loss and woe; the murder of the king by the Syndicate, out of fear of the power marrying the panthers to the Chinese Clouded Leopards would bring about.

Nikolaos shared with us the horrors of his time with the now-dead Empress—how the necromancers had disabled his ability to contact me and vice versa. Amphitrite had been starving him on and off, some days letting him feast on the blood of humans, other days forcing him to go without, unless he gave in to drinking the necromancer's blood. It was on the night Niko'd seen what happened between Vodan and me that he'd clandestinely alerted the monarchy of her behaviour, risking his life in the process. On that same night, Gwydion was brought in, with Orcus taking particular pleasure in his torment.

If Amphitrite had noticed Vodan's disappearance, she hadn't shown it. But Amphitrite had been too preoccupied with a strange dream where she made me her Princess and Nikolaos her Prince, and, with the necromancers, we took control of all the dead. Nikolaos had never really been able to work out an actual plan of hers, he wasn't even sure she had a set goal, but he'd mastered feigning delight in her confused dreams.

Putting two and two together, Laith had been thoroughly excited to realise the fantastical tales of a third Wulf Brother were more than hearsay. Now, he comes down to visit us on the weekends he doesn't have his son, which gives him lots of opportunities to pester Nikolaos and even more for Niko to grow weary of him. This new arrangement hadn't been preplanned. After a week of being apart, both Laith and I had grown quite uncomfortable, with him experiencing levels of anxiety very new to him. At first, we'd both thought it was just to do with the trauma of what we'd seen. However, once we'd finally found each other again, it was as if I could breathe for the first time in a week. So, Laith gets to keep Nikolaos and me, and sometimes Kai, company. It's nice to have him around so often, especially now that Nikolaos is busy with Atlas, which is doing exceptionally well.

As for the Mystics' Guild, they are now expanding not only on a global scale, but preternatural scale, too. As the only nymph Sylvie has met, I was offered a place on the board, which I accepted readily. Sylvie hopes this might mean we can attract more creatures, and maybe I'll even get to meet more of my kind. For the first time since becoming the undead, I feel I have a purpose beyond just being a vampire. Being in the Guild is my way of connecting to the part of me that is still very much alive.

Gwydion was also offered a place, one that Sylvie was adamant he deserved, if he promised to stop practising dark occultism. Gwydion, of course, refused, but he is staying in Edinburgh for the foreseeable future to help them on the sidelines.

The Reynard of the United Kingdom personally paid for Tanya to attend a private hospital of the highest quality, where he knew one of the head doctors. It turns out that a lot of wereanimals become doctors of some sort.

None of the original monarchs have yet to visit Britchelstone or Atlas—which I am by no means complaining about. However, the new Emperor of Europe, Konrad, spent a day here to meet us after hearing of all that had happened. Laith was also there on the day, and he put forward the suggestion of Konrad meeting Sylvie to see all the work they'd been doing. Much to all of our surprises, Konrad had seemed not only willing but excited to meet Sylvie and the Guild. They're now in conversation about finding a way to incorporate some of the vampire politics with that of the therians and other creatures of Europe. He is, I suppose, what you might call a forward-thinking vampire. I really like him, and it seems that Nikolaos does, too. In fact, even Laith left his company feeling heard and acknowledged, which is rare when you spend time with a vampire. I have high hopes for him as an Emperor.

Konrad had known of Nikolaos long before the fiasco with Amphitrite, his reputation preceding him. Technically, Magnates are meant to be elected democratically. Still, Konrad hinted that he could make sure Nikolaos became Magnante of Britchelstone if it meant becoming a hub for more vampires. Okay, so maybe he's still a bit corrupt. The two vampires are now in discussion about how to make Britchelstone a haven for more vampires, whilst also not overcrowding it. Nikolaos is thinking that the thriving Atlas can only employ vampires as an incentive.

Nikolaos sought solitude for centuries, so this is a big change of tune for him, but I love seeing the side of him slowly creeping out from the woebegone shadows. Whether it was what Erik had said to him or something about almost losing his life,

Nikolaos is finally beginning to shed that very hard-won shell of his. Baby steps, but steps nonetheless.

All of us got an invite to Otorongo II's wedding to Nebulosa, future Queen of the Chinese Clouded Leopards and now of the panthers, too. We decided, due to the sudden busyness of our lives here at home, it was too far to travel. Nonetheless, I'm genuinely really happy for them, and we sent them a wedding gift. What do you get a King and Queen as gifts? I had no idea, but one night, when Laith and I had been walking along the beach, I'd spotted a painting of panthers dressed in sixteenth-century clothing sitting at a theatre show. It had been so perfect, there'd been no hesitation buying it—and it was hand-drawn, too, so nice to support local business.

Nikolaos hated the painting, and thought it was wildly inappropriate as a wedding gift, *especially* for a Prince and his bride. We'd compromised on him getting to choose the frame—which he did, and massively overcompensated. I refused to know how much money he'd spent on the jewel-encrusted frame. We got a handwritten note thanking us for both, and it seemed as genuine as any note can.

Nikolaos resolved the problem of Vodan's abandoned corpse. I don't know what he did with it, nor do I want to know. He also found the necklace Vodan had stolen from me along with my clothing, bringing it back to me. For a little while, I'd been reluctant to wear it, thinking it tainted by Vodan's cruel, evil touch. Nikolaos understood my reasoning, but after a while, I began to resent Vodan taking another precious memory from me. Now, I wear it every single day without fail. It's not a reminder of Vodan, but of Nikolaos's tenderness. No one can steal the beauty of the gift, or taint the love with which it was delivered. Like so much of my relationship with Nikolaos, the necklace signified more firsts—my first Valentine's Day, my first gift from a partner. No, I won't ever let something so sweet become bitter.

There is a whole day unaccounted for under Vodan's seize. I don't know what happened to me during that time—hell, I don't *want* to know. I am certain there will soon reach a point where I break from the thought, but for now, I'm thriving on us surviving near-certain death, whilst Vodan and Amphitrite's corpses rot somewhere. They deserve to rot, and I refuse to feel guilty for what I did, even if my moral compass cannot so easily be vindicated.

Vodan is a horrible chapter I wish very much to not only close but tear from the book altogether.

The last month and a half have been a myriad of emotions, most of which, at the time, had broken my soul to a level I feared irreparable. Now, I'm not so sure that's the case. From all of the horror was born friendship; from the heartache and pain, we were met with the hope of advancement and positive change.

There was an old saying my dad used to tell me: out of the shit blooms the flower. Well, we've faced some truly horrendous shit, but I already see the seedling blooming. Oh, what a beautiful flower I'm sure it will be.

Printed in Great Britain
by Amazon

63157726R00281